THE ORIGIN PROPHECY

GrayReign

GrayReign

THE ORIGIN PROPHECY

Cover and Interior design by We Got You Covered Book Design
WWW.WEGOTYOUCOVEREDBOOKDESIGN.COM

SHIRE-HILL PUBLICATIONS
UNITED KINGDOM

ISBN: 978-1-914483-16-5

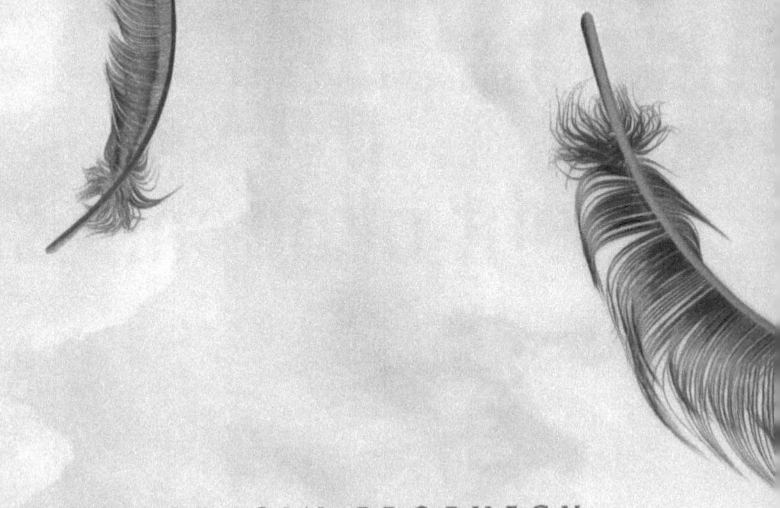

GrayReign

M.A. PHIPPS
REBECCA JAYCOX

light academies

The Serapeum
EGYPT
Gabriel

Mount Nebo
JORDAN
Remiel

Petra
JORDAN
Serathiel

Mount Sinai
EGYPT
Raphael

Sidon
LEBANON
Amenadiel

Mount Zion
ISRAEL
Uriel

Qumran
ISRAEL
Azrael

dark academies

Megiddo
ISRAEL
Lucifer

The Tower of Babel
IRAQ
Asmodeus

Sodom
ISRAEL
Leviathan

Gomorrah
ISRAEL
Belphegor

Ashkelon
ISRAEL
Beelzebub

Tyre
LEBANON
Mammon

Machaerus
JORDAN
Abaddon

prologue

GABRIEL SITS ON A stone step outside Virupaksha Temple, in the ancient city of Hampi, elbows resting on her knees, hands dangling between her legs. Her head droops, as if all the ice that normally resides in her body keeping her rigid and upright is melting. Even her bones feel pliant. Her daughter began the thaw, and her time with Lucifer has completed it. All the love she has for both of them, lying frozen inside her in a deep icy well, is boiling up, burning her insides. The onslaught of feeling so much is a sweet pain. A terrible pain. She can no longer deny she loves something more than the Creator.

The guilt that usually comes with such blasphemous thoughts doesn't suffocate her this time. Gabriel sighs, weary to her marrow. She doesn't need sleep but she craves rest. The rising sun warms her face, and light invades her closed lids. A single treacherous tear slides down her cheek. A gentle, familiar touch wipes it away, making her ache, and she opens her eyes, blinking at the stunning beauty standing before her that rivals the sunrise. The budding illumination haloes the Morningstar's golden hair, marking him as a celestial being, despite his Fall. His bottomless blue eyes rove over her face, a much-missed tenderness blossoming in their depths.

"He's still guarding the gates?" Lucifer says before taking a seat beside her, long legs stretching out and pressing against her own. Gabriel's body heats further at the contact.

Frowning, she nods. She's being kept from her daughter by a cocky, young Dark Nephilim. One who has the audacity to stand between her and her only child. The same boy bold enough to stab her to save his teacher. The phantom ache in her gut deepens her frown, but she can't quite hold a grudge against Caleb. He succeeded where she failed. He took Luna from the Council and kept her safe. Safe enough until she and Lucifer could come for them, that is.

That doesn't mean she likes him. Or isn't hurt by how Luna turns to Caleb for comfort instead of her mother. Luna clung to the boy after they escaped Alexander, never even acknowledging her parents' presence. She only wanted Caleb. Gabriel knows she's responsible for the crater of distrust between them, but still, she'd like the little Dark Nephilim to kindly get out of her way so she can at least beg her daughter's forgiveness.

It's a shame she can't just cut him down, but Luna would never forgive her. The look in her eyes when she gazed at Caleb reminds Gabriel all too well of how she looked at Lucifer. How she still looks at him when he's not watching. She wants to warn Luna of the pain there but that is a fruitless endeavor. Besides, Luna is not a Light but a Gray. Her path will always be different.

"You're not thinking of smiting the poor boy?" Lucifer asks when the silence goes on too long.

Gabriel glances up, surprised to see amusement reflected in his eyes and a hint of violence. She gives a delicate snort. "No more than you are. I know you're ready to storm the proverbial gates as well, and you would be on your way if your daughter wouldn't hate you for all eternity for it."

His frown matches hers. "She does love him, doesn't she?"

"Quite desperately, I fear."

A long sigh escapes him. "I believe you're right. And though I'm loath to admit it, he's not wrong keeping us away. We'll… smother her with our love."

"And guilt," Gabriel adds, voice morose. Lucifer's hand clasps hers, and shock jolts through her at the contact. Her fingers curl reflexively around his. That's three times he's touched her today. Deliberate touches.

"Would it make you feel better to know I harbor guilt as well?" the Morningstar says, eyes fixed on the rising sun.

"Why in the Creator's name would you harbor guilt? I'm the one who kept you from Luna. I'm certain she won't bear you any ill will. I'll be the monster she despises." That last confession slips unaided past her lips, never meant to be spoken aloud.

Although he doesn't look at her, his hand tightens around

hers. "You're not a monster."

Her laughter is brittle, mocking. "Seventeen years she's been gone and I didn't know. *Seventeen* years! I never felt my wards being breached, and I…the truth is I stopped going inside to see her." Her throat feels like a python has wrapped around her neck, coils squeezing. "It was too painful. And too tempting. I know I kept her from you, and I know you hate me for it, but you must understand I never really had her, either. The prophecy stole her from me, from us both."

Silence stretches like taffy between them, sticky with all the things unsaid and the wounds of the past.

Lucifer's chest heaves, another large puff of air escaping his lips. "I find I cannot hate you, much to my regret at times. It would've been much easier to hate you. And when I found out about Luna, there was a moment when I believed I could—a betrayal that would finally sever these ties that bind us." Fissures splinter across her heart at his words. His blue eyes trap hers, forcing her to hold his gaze. "But…I do understand. The divide was in place, and you were alone and fearful of the prophecy. And though you'll never admit it, fearful of the Creator and his retribution. While I'd like to believe I wouldn't have been petty enough to demand you fall to your knees and beg me for my help, I might have been. You destroyed me."

Pain lances her chest. "I destroyed me, too. You think it was my pride that kept me from you. Falling on my knees and begging wasn't beneath me to save our child. No, it was the certainty that even if you were to take her, the Council would've found her. The prophecy would find a way. Just as it has. Just as the Creator ordained. I was a fool to think I could stop it." She can't hold back the hot splash of tears scalding her skin. "Perhaps I should've given her to you. For however long you were able to shield her, she could've thrived. Instead, all she's known is abandonment and horror. Her pain is my eternal burden to bear."

His arms wrap around her, unexpected and undeserved, but the strong bands of iron surrounding her offer immeasurable comfort. Gabriel sobs against him, thousands of years of pain pouring from her into him. She knows he can withstand it. He can withstand anything. He's the mountain that will never break.

"The blame doesn't solely lay at your feet," Lucifer says against her hair. "Whoever released her into the world knew what she was and allowed her to go out unprepared, a danger to herself and others, uncaring of the damage she'd cause. They must shoulder some of the burden of her pain."

His kindness thaws the remaining frosty edges she uses to shield herself, and they fall away like bits of glacier breaking off into the sea. Gabriel sags against him, boneless, the love she still has for him dissolving all the jagged pieces she's been carrying around inside. Being steel is exhausting, and now she feels like she can bend for the first time in millennia. She twines her arms around him, and he allows it, hand sliding down her back in a caress that sends a delicious shiver through her.

"They remind me of us," he remarks, amusement and nostalgia coloring his voice.

She snorts again. "We were never that young."

Lucifer draws back to look at her. "Yes, we were," he chides. "We were that young when we discovered love, when we discovered passion. In that, we were completely new." His eyes heat as they travel over her face, and desire floods her at his expression.

And she, the Messenger, an Archangel and warrior of Heaven, blushes under his lustful perusal. His grin turns wicked as he observes her pink cheeks. She remembers their journey into pleasure all too well.

"Your memory hasn't failed you after all," Lucifer teases, blue eyes alight with mischief and desire.

"I remember everything," Gabriel admits, taking a precious moment from her consuming guilt to savor her former lover like this. Seductive and kind. Gentle. Then worry for her broken daughter wrenches her back to reality. "Let us hope they have a kinder ending than we did."

Lucifer sobers, his bright light guttered, and she feels the loss like a physical blow. "They *are* young, so perhaps they will outgrow their attachment."

Her brow arches in patent disbelief. "Have you seen the way she looks at him?"

His smile is grim. "Yes, she looks at him the way I looked at you. But he's...mortal. Not in the normal sense obviously, but eventually winter will come for him, and he'll wither on the vine."

Her fingers dig into his sides. "I don't want him to break her all over again."

"That won't happen for a thousand years at least."

"I want to protect her from heartbreak, the way I haven't before."

Censure fills his eyes. "That is not the battle to choose, Gabriel. She will neither welcome your intrusion, nor will she stand for it."

Her mouth tightens at his disapproval, and she glances away, though she knows he's right. Another weary sigh escapes her. "I know."

He tips her chin up to meet her eyes. "But I will have a talk with the boy. Not to separate them. I am not entitled to suppress their free will, but he needs to understand his situation, and I don't think he's quite grasped it." Lucifer runs a finger over her bottom lip, pressing lightly into the center. A faint gasp escapes her at the intimacy. "And Gabriel, we haven't had our ending yet."

one

LUNA

A FLASH OF GOLDEN light burns across my vision, and suddenly, Alaric stands before me, shielding my body from Alexander's wrath with his own. His arms spread out to the sides like great wings—as if, in this moment, he has finally Ascended—protecting me.

Always protecting me.

His name is a breath on my lips that's instantly stifled by silence as the disbelief and shock of what I'm seeing consume me. This can't be happening. This isn't real. I'm imagining this.

Please... Please, let this not be real.

Time seems to slow as Alaric glances over his shoulder and meets my gaze, the handle of Alexander's dagger protruding from his chest, a blossom of red blooming across his white shirt where the blade pierces his flesh, the gleaming steel buried to the hilt.

There's so much blood, and when he falls to the stone floor, the crimson seems to form a sea around him, engulfing his limp figure, much like the familiar tide of grief rises to swallow me. As it drags me, body and soul, down into its depths, I feel the water in my lungs, choking my breaths, filling me to the brim until I am only heartache and nothing else. And when I finally scream—the pain slamming against the dams of self-preservation that surround the fragments remaining of my sanity—something inside me cracks, letting the water burst through, flooding me completely.

I thought I knew what it felt like to be broken. I thought I had experienced the full extent of anguish.

But I was wrong. Only now, do I understand it.

Only now, do I feel its true and unrelenting hold.

I startle awake, my eyes bleary as the images of my nightmare linger for a moment before fading, granting me a much-needed reprieve. In their place, I struggle to make out my surroundings, and at first, all I can see is a hazy painting of blue, green, and purple tones smeared together and mixed with faint traces of gold. As I sit up, noting the shift of a soft mattress beneath me, the colors sharpen into definable shapes. A plush blanket. Pillows. A grand bed in the middle of an even more elegant bedroom.

My brow furrows as I scan the lavish space, taking in the exquisitely carved wooden furniture, ornate decor on the walls, and elaborately woven rugs, trying to figure out where I am. I don't recognize this place, which under normal circumstances would scare me. Beautiful or not, this could be just another cage someone has erected to confine me. And yet, where I should feel uncertainty or fear, I feel nothing.

Only a hollow ache in my chest that I'm not sure even time will be able to heal.

As the images of my dream return to haunt me and the familiar burn of tears creeps in, I fall back against the bedspread and bury my face in the nearest silken pillow, wishing I could claw the picture of Alaric in those final moments out of my head. The way he looked back at me with acceptance in his eyes, the subtle smile that turned up his lips knowing he had saved my life—that he hadn't failed me the way he told me he had failed Alexander…

The price for that sacrifice was too great. How many millennia had he walked this earth? How many years of his nearly immortal life were erased in the space of a heartbeat when that dagger tore through his flesh? He didn't owe me that.

No one owes me that.

I grip the pillow tighter. Who else will suffer because of what I am? Who else will I lose because of Alexander's mad lust for power?

Another face fills my thoughts, and I bolt upright again, shivering against the prickle of apprehension creeping over my skin.

"Caleb," I gasp.

What happened to him? What happened to my parents? I try to remember the events that brought me here, but there's a frustrating hole in my memory situated between our fight with Alexander and my waking up in this bed, as if the moments following Alaric's death have been completely erased from my mind. I remember watching as Gabriel and Lucifer faced off with Alexander and his cohort of faithful Nephilim. I remember the throne room erupting into chaos and fire. I remember watching as the Gray nearly killed Caleb in front of me, and I stood by, helpless to intervene or stop him—a victim to my own paralyzing terror. But I can't recall what became of them after…or if anyone else made it out of the fray alive.

Ironically, *cruelly*, the last thing I remember is the one thing I wish I could forget.

Panic courses through my veins like adrenaline. Whipping the blanket aside, I jump out of the bed, barely registering the golden gown from Alexander still hugging my body or that my wings are out and on full display, my feathertips brushing the lush rugs underfoot. I'm aware of nothing else except the resurfacing anxiety that Caleb and I have been separated again, and that my parents are gone from my life so soon after finding them, our reunion cut short. Perhaps for good this time.

That fear of never seeing them again pushes me across the room toward the door, and without a thought as to where I am or what danger might lurk on the other side, I throw it open, nearly tearing the wood off its hinges. The brass knob crumples beneath the strength of my grip, but I let it go almost at once, my hand snapping back as if the metal has burned me. I stop short just as quickly, pausing within inches of colliding with the familiar face blinking at me from across the threshold.

"Luna?" Caleb gapes at me, frozen in the doorway, seemingly as surprised to see me as I am to see him. An ornate silver tray laden with breakfast pastries and juice is held tight in his hands.

My heart jumps into my throat at the sight of him standing before me, every fear, every anxiety I've had since waking up forgotten at the tender caress of his eyes on my face. I can practically feel the tension leaving my muscles as I drink in his presence, and yet, there's a part of me that wonders if this is real—that remembers my time in my prison all too well, the tricks Mammon played to unhinge my mind teasing my every thought with doubt.

My fingers ache with the urge to reach out and touch him, to prove to myself that he's actually here. To take solace in the comfort of his arms, my one certain place in this world.

Sensing my distress, Caleb nods for me to let him into the room and carefully places the tray on the gilded table beside the door—the wood inlaid with what looks like real gemstones— only turning to face me again once his hands are free. For a moment, we stand in awkward silence, and I watch, transfixed, as his tongue darts out to wet his bottom lip, his eyes sweeping up and down the full length of my body. Then, as if some spell between us has broken, he pulls me into his arms, his hands slipping under my wings, his palms pressing flat to the exposed part of my back. I relish the delicious warmth of his fingers where they touch my skin, their heat intense and almost searing—not painful, but if it was, it would be a pain I crave. Addicted to the sensation, I burrow into his embrace and rest my cheek on his chest, listening for each thump of his racing heart, the repeated *ba-bums* a needed balm to my nerves.

As my hands clutch at the back of his T-shirt, my nails pinching the fabric in a talon-like grasp, Caleb presses his lips into my hair, pulling me close and yet, somehow, never close enough. Desire and a barely restrained need for comfort overwhelm me, forcing my hands to clasp tighter.

"Well, good morning to you, too, Sleeping Beauty," he murmurs with a breathy laugh.

My pulse thrums under my skin as he leans away just enough to raise his hand between us and tuck a lock of hair behind my ear. His palm then moves to my cheek, and when I lean into his touch, there's a moment where I almost smile before the pain of reality drives a wedge into my battered heart, reminding me what we've lost. What was *sacrificed* to get us here...

Wherever here even is.

"Where are we?" I lower my voice to a whisper, my eyes shifting between every visible nook and cranny, searching the rare pocket of shadow in the spacious room, nervous Alexander might step out of the darkness to gut me the moment I let my guard down. He already tried to kill me once. I have no doubt he'll try again.

"A safe place," Caleb assures me, squeezing my shoulder.

I blink up at him, frowning. "How long have we been here?"

"Two days." Although he grins down at me, there's an uneasy edge to his voice I don't like.

"Two days?" I blurt out. "I've been asleep that long?"

I search his eyes, but I don't find any trace of the apprehension I thought I heard in his tone. Maybe I imagined it. It wouldn't be the first time I saw or heard something that wasn't actually there.

As if determined to prove as much, he combs a hand through my hair, his smile turning mischievous as he tugs me toward him again. "Yup." He drags the finger of his other hand up my spine, coaxing a shiver over my skin. "I was beginning to worry you really were Sleeping Beauty and I'd have to wake you with a kiss—"

I snort and he pauses, his lips just shy of brushing mine. He immediately pulls away, a look of mock affront on his face.

"What exactly are you implying, Goldilocks? Are my kisses not magical enough for you?"

Another smile tempts my lips, but the ache in my chest obliterates any happiness in this moment, and all I manage instead is a weak grimace. Maybe I'm not even capable of smiling anymore.

With a faltering sigh, I step out of his embrace and rub my hands along my upper arms, my body struck by a sudden chill despite the warmth in the air.

"If it's been two days," I begin, shaking my head, "then my parents—"

"Are wearing holes in the floorboards waiting to speak with you," he finishes. "Kali would obviously never say as much to their faces, but you can tell she's getting aggravated with their constant pacing and lurking. I don't think she's used to having so many people crash here."

"Kali?" I ask, cocking a curious eyebrow. Just like this place, I don't recognize the name.

"Our host," Caleb clarifies.

A soft "Oh" is all I can think to say in response.

"Don't worry," he adds, closing the distance between us again and taking my fidgeting hands in his. "I'll take you to meet her later if you're feeling up to it. She's actually pretty cool. I think you'll like her."

I nod, but meeting yet another new celestial is the last thing I'm concerned about. My mind wanders, and my insides twist at the thought of seeing Gabriel, of meeting her again after everything that's happened. The image of her appearing behind Alexander in a blaze of golden light, her body adorned in her armor from the Great Battle of Heaven, sword held to his throat as she demanded he hand over her daughter is branded into my memory. I haven't had a chance to even process what occurred at the citadel, let alone examine that moment too closely, but one thought does find its way to the surface above all the other noise in my head.

She came for me.

Despite what I've learned about my birth, despite what

she thought about me in regards to the prophecy, despite the danger of going to battle with Alexander—despite all that, Gabriel came. And when I heard her call me her daughter, it was like the entire world had turned upside down, and all the resentment and anger I felt toward her as I watched her fight for me was gone. Or at least, momentarily forgotten.

But now… Now, I remember it again, and I'm not sure how I should feel or if I'm ready to see her. With distrust and lies as the foundation of our relationship, where do we even begin to cross the chasm between us? Do I forgive her for locking me away for thousands of years, even if part of me can understand what drove her to do it?

Does she even want my forgiveness?

Or did she only intervene to lock me away again? To prevent the prophecy from coming to fruition, no matter the cost.

"Are you hungry?" Caleb asks, interrupting my thoughts. When I look up at him, blinking away the haze of my worries, he gestures toward the tray by the door.

"Not really," I mutter. If anything, I feel nauseated just thinking about everything I've been avoiding.

Things I know I can't put off any longer.

"So…" I hesitate, pausing to swallow around the sudden tightness in my throat. "You've seen my mother? How did that go, considering…" I trail off, wincing at the thought of Caleb coming face to face with the Archangel without me there to act as a buffer. The words of warning she spoke to me back at the

Serapeum are still fresh in my head, and I can only imagine what she might have said to him in my absence.

"The divide exists for a reason, Luna."

"Keep your distance from that one."

After seeing her with my father, I can't help wondering if those were really her true feelings or if she was just speaking from a place of pain, irrespective of her responsibility to ensure the divide. After all, I saw how Lucifer reacted when he arrived to find her injured after Alexander escaped. There was an intimacy in their exchange that, even lost in the throes of agony as my wings pierced my skin, I would've been blind not to notice.

Whatever they once shared—the forbidden love that led to my birth—still lingers millennia later, even if they aren't together. I assume that's why she tried to warn me away from Caleb back at the Serapeum and why she'll probably try to do it again, especially now that she knows who I am to her. I wonder if she even cares that Caleb is the only reason I've survived this long. The only reason I didn't break sooner.

Then again, things are different now. Me being a Gray changes everything. And unlike her and my father, I don't fit on either side of the divide.

I straddle the line.

Caleb scoffs, snapping me out of my thoughts. "Oh, you mean considering I helped set a vengeful angel whose cuckoo for Cocoa Puffs free from imprisonment and then stabbed her with a dagger that could've ended her immortal life?" He considers for me a moment then shrugs, his expression unbothered, although his eyes say something else altogether. "Quite well, actually. She only *sometimes* looks like she wants to kill me."

A strangled breath parts my lips. "I should probably talk to her. And to my father."

My father. It still feels weird to say it aloud. After so many years as an orphan, alone in the world, part of me suspects it always will.

Caleb gently knocks me under the chin, tilting my face upward when my eyes drift from his. When I meet his gaze again, there's an intensity in the warm swirl of his irises that wasn't there a moment ago. "Don't let your parents or anyone else rush you if you aren't ready to talk. If you need more time to…process everything, I can tell them all to fuck off."

Everything meaning Alaric.

Tears threaten at the edge of my vision, but I blink them away. As much as the thought of the older Nephilim pains me, the guilt of his death a stain on my conscience, I know I can't stay in here forever. I need to come out at some point.

More than that, I need to face reality, even if it hurts.

"You can talk to me about it, you know," Caleb says softly.

I shake my head. "I don't think I'm ready for that."

"Well, whenever you are"—Caleb cups my face in his hand again, grazing his thumb across my cheekbone—"I'm here."

Forcing a watery smile, I nod. Then I curl into the comforting loop of his arms again, wishing time could stop and freeze us like this, just for a little while. I want to believe we really are safe here, but Alexander doesn't strike me as the patient type when it comes to exacting revenge—not after thousands of years waiting and plotting in his cell. Having witnessed his brutality and seen the madness in his eyes for myself, I can't help wondering how long this peaceful interlude will last. How long before he returns to finish what he nearly accomplished before Alaric stepped in to save us? How long before he tries to kill me again? Or Caleb?

How long before he succeeds?

Shuddering at the thought, I grind out, "We need to come up with a plan. Your grandfather will be out for blood after what happened." *Not to mention, there's still the threat of the Council to consider.*

I can't bring myself to voice that last part. Not when the threat of Alexander alone seems like an insurmountable hurdle.

Caleb exhales a strained breath, and I feel the hum of his words against my hair when he mutters, "I know. And we will. We'll figure something out. We have help, and now that your parents are with us, we have some serious muscle on our side. If anyone will know what to do, it's them."

I hope you're right.

And I wish I shared his confidence in that belief.

I offer a noncommittal "Mm" then reel back just enough to

peek up at him. "First, though, I need to talk to them about what Lilith told me. I want their side of the story." Especially Gabriel's.

As if he was expecting me to say this, Caleb unlatches his arms from around my torso and holds out one hand for me to take before signaling toward the open door with the other. "Oh-kay, then. Let's go hunt them down. Not that we'll have to look very far." He mutters that last part under his breath.

My brow reaches for my hairline in question, but he says nothing else, instead interlacing our fingers when I take his proffered hand. Despite his silence, I can feel the tension radiating off his body like heat, and as he leads me over to the door, his aura whips and laps across his skin, more agitated than I've ever seen it.

Eager to know what's bothering him, I tug on his arm, stopping him just short of the threshold. He looks over his shoulder, his expression half bewildered and half something I can't quite put a name to.

"What's wrong?" I ask, unnerved by the strange apprehensive look flitting across his face.

He flashes me an uneasy smile and laughs once—a stilted, choked sound I've never heard him make before. "Uh, maybe, while you're speaking with your parents, you can slip in a few kind words on my behalf? You know, so they stop prowling around this place like two hungry lions who want to rip my guts out."

I stare at him for a moment, confusion lancing through me when I note the obvious tremor in his voice. It's almost like he's nervous. *No, that isn't quite right,* I realize the longer I look at him. He's not nervous.

He's afraid.

Surely, that can't be possible. Caleb is fearless. I've seen him outnumbered in a fight and still come out on top. I've witnessed him bravely take on Nephilim millennia older than him, not to mention he cut off Mammon's wing and double-crossed his own grandfather—an angel an entire band of ancient celestials together struggled to subdue—just to rescue me. He kept it together when we were at the citadel despite the horrors we both experienced there. Plus, he back-talks to Hammurabi so often I think he has a death wish.

I scan his face, assessing every detail, right down to the almost imperceptible twitch of his lips.

No, I say to myself again. *Caleb isn't frightened of anything.*

Is he?

"Are you…afraid of my parents?" I whisper.

I'm not sure how I would feel if he is. On the one hand, I can understand it. He's a Nephilim and they're full-blooded angels with the power and years to crush him like a grape. But I also don't ever want him to have a reason to feel uncomfortable in my presence. Because if there's anything I've learned from my time in the mortal world, it's that fear pushes people away.

Caleb averts his gaze, and the column of his throat shifts

when he swallows, the sound audible in the abrupt silence between us. Even if his writhing aura wasn't a dead giveaway, I can practically smell how anxious he is. But why?

What happened while I was asleep?

"Caleb?" I hedge. Desperate for him to look at me, I touch a hand to his cheek, but his eyes still refuse to meet mine.

Finally, he says, "I'm not afraid of Gabriel or Lucifer. I've lived almost my whole life around Nephilim way older than me and Archdemons who could fold me into an origami swan with basically zero effort." He swallows again, more loudly this time.

My heart rate quickens. "Then what's wrong? Caleb, you're scaring me."

He lets out a raspy laugh devoid of humor. "Spending the last handful of months with my gramps made me realize that, in some respects, angels and demons are like animals. When it comes to their blood, they're territorial and violent, possessive in a way humans can never understand. They would cut down anything and anyone in their way—without thinking or remorse—to claim something they believe to be theirs." The *or someone* in his comment goes unsaid.

Panic is a bubble in my chest about to burst.

"Is this about Alexander—"

But before I can get the full thought out, he grabs me by the sides of my face and crushes his mouth to mine, kissing me long and deep like he's worried it will be the last time he ever will. My lips part on a shaky inhale, my knees buckling slightly, but despite the pain in my heart that threatens to pin me to the floor, the taste of him dulls the sharp edges of my grief as I sink into his touch. I feel it everywhere. In the smooth slide of his tongue across mine. Where his fingertips dig into my scalp as they wind around the strands of my hair, pulling me closer. In the heat building between us where his body presses against mine.

But, too soon, he lets me go.

"I'm not afraid of your parents," he says again, more fervently this time, his warm breath a kiss of its own against my lips. "But I *am* afraid they'll take you away from me. You haven't seen it—the way they resent that I've kept them from you. They want to stake their claim, and when they do, I'm terrified it will push me out of the picture. Hell"—he rakes a trembling hand through his hair—"I think part of me is waiting for it."

My eyes widen, my thoughts a confused jumble as my mind is violently torn one way then the other. On the one side, I hear those words again—"stake their claim"—and while I can picture my father feeling that way, it's hard to imagine my mother sharing such a sentiment. Of actually wanting me and viewing me as anything other than a burden. A mistake from her past that's finally caught up to her.

But before I can look at that thought too deeply, my mind is jerked in the opposite direction and I'm focused on Caleb again—and on the visceral fear of what he's saying. Of my parents actually trying to tear us apart, even after everything we've been through.

"That won't happen—" I begin to protest, but Caleb cuts me off.

"What if they make you choose?" True, unadulterated fear shines in the wells of his eyes, and my heart breaks at his words. That he could ever think I'd let that happen… That I would ever willingly let him go, especially after I came so close to losing him at the citadel…

"If they do, then they'll be disappointed," I retort. "Because I *will* choose you."

Caleb winces. "Luna—"

"No," I growl. I know what he's thinking. That this is my second chance to have the one thing I've been deprived of my whole life. But what he doesn't understand is that, as much as I crave that connection with my parents, I don't need it.

Not like I need him.

"You don't get to look at me like that and say these things and then act as if there's even a choice. There isn't. I don't care if they're my parents. They haven't been here. They weren't the ones who came for me when I was in that prison—" My voice breaks, and I draw in a ragged breath, shaking my head. "Gabriel gave up any claim to me when she locked me away. She doesn't get to dictate my life any longer or tell me who I can love."

His aura responds to that word—*love*—and I glimpse a flicker of hope in his eyes.

"What about Lucifer?" Caleb presses. "He never locked you away."

"Lucifer *fell* for love," I remind him. "He would never make me choose."

Caleb worries his lower lip between his teeth then whispers so softly I almost don't hear it, "Not even if he thinks I'm not good enough for you?" The confession is sour, tainting the air and plunging my heart into a tumultuous tempest of pain.

After everything he's done for me, how could he think that? No one will ever be right for me the way he is. We fit. And even if this world will never accept us together, I would rather waste a thousand lifetimes in a cage than spend even one without him.

Snaking my hands around the back of his neck, I yank him toward me and kiss him again. It's rough—a clash of teeth and lips—and hungry, with a raw desperation I've never let myself submit to before. When we pull apart, I finally say, my voice hoarse, "If he thinks that, then screw him. I love you, and I will never let anyone keep us apart. I promise."

For as long as we have together…even if it isn't forever.

two

CALEB

LUNA'S FIERCE WORDS ECHO in my mind and her even fiercer kiss has left me in such a state that I'm not fit to be in front of polite company right now. I allow myself a moment to indulge in her wings, running my fingers down the satiny feathers until she jerks against me, and I groan. My forehead sags against hers, and we catch our breath for a moment.

"I love you, too," I tell her, voice raw. "And I trust you to choose me." Like I've chosen her. I know how much I mean to her. It's in every look, every touch she sends my way. "I shouldn't have laid all my shit on you about your parents. You've got enough to deal with." I can't deny I'm terrified they'll try to separate us, but Goldilocks didn't need to know that. She's dealing with Alaric's death. I should have swallowed my insecurities like a big boy.

Her full lips twist into a frown. "That's not how this works, Caleb. You always giving and me taking." Reproach lies heavy in her eyes. "I'm here for you, too, whatever you need. Always."

Guilt flushes through me at her words. "I know… It's just, I'm used to taking care of people. And with everything that's gone down lately, I want to make sure you're taken care of," I confess.

She pulls me close again with that supple angel strength. "Best we take care of each other, don't you think?"

Her earnestness wraps around my heart and squeezes. I kiss her again, pushing her up against the wall and she wraps one long leg around my hip. My tongue slips past her lips, and she tastes like strawberries and Champagne. Even when I thought she was just a Nephilim, she always tasted sweet, and the sweetness has grown richer since the bind on her was lifted. Despite sleeping for two days with nary a toothbrush or shower near, she's like decadent shortcake I want to devour. Little moans escape her, driving me crazy. I wrench myself away from her, holding her at arm's length. I have got to stop doing this.

"My timing is really the worst," I tell her. "At this rate, we're both going to have a permanent set of blue balls."

A surprised laugh escapes her, just like I wanted. And it's a real laugh, not a fake or brittle sound hiding pain. I chuck her under the chin with one finger, my eyes running down her lithe figure.

"As much as I love this dress on you, maybe you want to change into something more comfortable before dealing with your mom and pops?"

"Something to hide my blue balls?" she asks, smirking.

I roll my eyes. "You've been hanging around me too long. The Luna I met would blush at the word balls."

To my utter delight, a flush creeps over her cheekbones, staining her creamy skin. Then her eyes sober, and we're back in the ugly, uncertain present.

"You can put it off a little while longer," I tell her, knowing she's stalling as I hook a hand through hers. "I'll stand guard as long as you want. I don't think they'd outright murder me." Maybe. I do know Hammurabi would try to save me at least. That's something.

Her bottom lip trembles, and she catches it with her teeth. She gazes at me with huge hazel eyes. "No, I should go talk to them. It's better to rip off the Band-Aid and get it over with. Right?"

I shrug. "If that's what you want. But it's okay if you want to hide out. It's been an…intense week." I avoid directly mentioning Alaric. Or the fact that Gramps almost killed me. Or any of the other horrifying things bombarding my brain.

She grips my fingers, and I manage not to wince. She doesn't know her own strength yet.

Her chest heaves, and a huge sigh escapes her. "No, I can't hide anymore." She glances down at the gold gown, scowling. "You're right. I need to change. I don't need to go around looking like Alexander's prized pet anymore."

I nod. "I'll be waiting for you. There are some clean clothes in the chest over there. I'll just step outside."

Luna doesn't release my hand. "You don't have to do that," she says, her voice shy.

I grin. "I don't trust myself to be alone with you half-naked, Goldilocks. Let's not tempt fate."

She blushes again but dips her head, and I head for the door, letting myself out. As I wait for her to change, my anxiety ratchets up again. I meant what I said to Luna. I'm not afraid of her parents. No one is more terrifying than Grandfather. But what if Gabriel wants to hide her away again? Now that the Council and Alexander are hunting Goldilocks, what if Lucifer agrees with the Messenger, and they stash Luna where I can't find her? That's one way they can ensure they have their daughter to themselves. I also know Luna will fight them tooth and claw. She won't be caged again, even by them. *Especially* by them. I take a deep breath. I just have to trust that Luna can handle her parents.

She certainly has millennia of guilt to wield against them. I hope she's ruthless.

The door snicks open and Goldilocks steps out, clad in tight jeans, a fitted white T-shirt, and sneakers, her wings tucked out of sight. She gives me a rueful smile.

"Not exactly what I was expecting," she says with a shrug.

I chuckle. "Kali isn't exactly traditional. Then again, she predates tradition, so…"

She closes her eyes for a moment, her chest heaving. Then she looks at me. "Let's go now before I lose my nerve."

"You got it." I hold my hand out, and she clasps it.

"Um, where are they exactly?"

"Just down the hall. Their bedrooms share a common space," I say and note the way her brows arch.

Yeah, I was a little surprised the Morningstar wanted to be that close to the woman who betrayed him, too. But there's an unresolved tension between the two immortals that makes you very uncomfortable when you're around them for too long, which I try to avoid at all costs. They're either going to fuck or kill each other. I'm betting on them getting naked. Either way, I imagine it will be epic.

Half a corridor later and we arrive. Luna stares at the intricately carved door. She releases my hand, her fingers hovering over the doorknob. I hear her swallow.

"I was hoping it would take us longer to get here," she says, and I notice a fine tremor in her hand.

"We can go outside and come back if that'll help," I offer, mouth twisting into a lopsided smile.

"I don't think that will help," Luna says, then clasps the doorknob.

"Do you want me to stay?" I will if she wants me to. I'll stare down Gabriel the entire time.

"I'll be fine. Besides, I should probably do this alone."

"If that's what you want."

"I'll see you soon?" Her eyes snag mine, and the vulnerability I see there makes me want to wrap her in silk and run away with her. But that's not a way to live.

"I'll be in our room, waiting for you." I bend down and brush my lips over hers. "Don't let them give you any shit," I murmur. "You've faced down Alexander the Great. You can do anything."

She squares her shoulders. "Thank you." Turning from me, she twists the brass knob and the door nudges open.

I watch the room swallow Luna as the door shuts behind her, and I stare at the space she occupied just moments ago. I don't like her going in there alone but I get why she needs to fly solo here. Besides, if I'm with her, it'll just create more tension. As much as I want to be her shield, she has to establish boundaries with her parents herself. They won't respect her otherwise and think I'm the one influencing her decisions. Like I need to give Gabriel another reason to gut me.

My skin feels like it's too tight for my body—and not just because ten minutes ago I was making out with Luna. I'm not used to this restlessness. This uncertainty. This…fear. As a Nephilim, you get used to danger because you're around dangerous creatures who can kill you with their pinky finger. But there are rules, and though I bend them and let my mouth run away with me, I never felt truly unsafe. Sure, I got punished, a beating here and there, but nothing I couldn't handle. And those punishments ensured I understood what the line was and when not to cross it. But things are different now. I've been around angels and Fallen when they don't pump the brakes.

They are terrifying. They are monsters.

Phantom talons rake at my mind and I shudder. I feel like Humpty Dumpty, all the king's horses and all the king's men couldn't put my brain back together again. It's like an egg that's been cracked, and all the pieces are glued back together, but you can still see the fissures. Gramps took two shots at me, and the last nearly killed me. Suddenly, I'm back in the throne room, the smell of smoke burning my nostrils, and Alexander is digging into my mind. Even though I know it's not possible, lancing pain pierces my skull and I bend over, panting. Taking a deep breath, I straighten with effort, blinking myself back into the present.

I turn away from Gabriel's room and amble down the hall, past the room I share with Luna. I need some fresh air, and I doubt her meeting with her parents will be over any time soon. I stumble out of the temple, breathing in lungfuls of humidity. I sink down on a step, the hard stone digging into my ass.

If it weren't for Alaric, Alexander would have killed me and Luna. I see him die in my nightmares. And I know Hammurabi says it's not my fault, that I'm not the reason he's dead, but guilt still haunts me like a ghost I can't shake. I liked Alaric, he was a good guy, and even though we weren't besties, I still miss his presence. He was soothing, even without his Calm. If his absence carves me up with grief, what does Luna feel? She loved him. She's been basically catatonic for two days over him. Other than me, I think he was the first person she connected to in a significant way.

My fingers curl into fists as the image of him bleeding out flickers in my brain. I give a violent shake of my head. The pain in my mind increases, and I grunt. Fuck Grandfather. I can't let him win. I deliberately relax my fingers one by one and stand. I have to keep it together for Luna. She doesn't need to know I wasn't ready to take a seat at the adult table. We're all eating there now.

I turn around and enter the cool dimness of the temple once more, blindly finding my way to our room. Kicking my shoes off at the threshold, I close the door behind me. A few quick steps and I'm at the bed. I flop down and close my eyes. Maybe I can sleep off some of my misery before Luna returns.

three

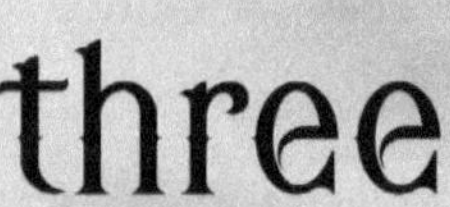

LUNA

WE SIT IN SILENCE for so long, I begin to think the figures on the cream-colored sofa before me are actually statues rather than my mother and father. Now that I take the time to look at them—to take them in and see them in a way I never had the chance to before, with the knowledge of who we are to each other in mind—I can accept how unnervingly beautiful they are, so much so they really could be carved from stone.

Lucifer is pure ethereal light despite being a Dark, earning every syllable of his nickname, and yet, between the two of them, my focus is drawn to the raven-haired angel beside him. Gabriel seems…different. I can still see the cold headmistress of the Serapeum in her dark eyes, but now, I see something else in her gaze as well.

Something almost like fear.

They sit side by side with their hands in their laps, their bodies frozen in anticipation as they stare at me, waiting for this uncomfortable silence to end. Their eyes are fixed on my face with an intensity I struggle not to recoil from, but there's no heat behind their rapt gazes, only curiosity and what my racing heart assures me is affection. Maybe even love.

Love. It's hard to believe I could have parents who love me after so long without family or anyone of consequence who mattered. When I think of love, I think only of Caleb, although I know there's room in my heart, however damaged it may be, for more. There already was room in my heart for another, but Alaric is gone now, snuffed out of existence as quickly and permanently as a flame doused by water. What's left after his loss is a gaping void, making me all the more starved for something to mend it, to take this gnawing pain away. Pain that makes me all the more afraid of losing anyone else close to me—even Hammurabi, who I haven't known for long, but whose loss would be a blow I can't take, shattering what's left of me like a hammer against glass.

Pushing aside these thoughts, I flick my eyes between the Archangel and Archdemon, noting the way their auras twitch with impatience—Gabriel's more so than Lucifer's, the golden tendrils lashing across her skin going rigid and forming a mountain range of stiff peaks, creating a spiky exterior that seems to fit her personality well. As I meet her gaze for the hundredth time since I entered the room, I wonder if this is as difficult for her as it is for me.

Swallowing the lump in my throat, I let out a timid sigh, and my parents shift in response, leaning in toward me, as if that one breath has freed them from the confinement of stillness.

Unable to hold her tongue any longer, Gabriel chokes out, "Luna, I—"

"Wait." I hold up a hand, and although her mouth snaps shut, her eyes flash, their depths simmering like water over heat. "Please," I beg. "I… I just want to say something first."

Lips pursing, Gabriel fists her hands in her lap. Without looking away from me, Lucifer wraps his fingers around hers, as if it's second nature to him to want to ease her distress. It doesn't escape my notice how she instantly relaxes at his touch, and although part of me is overjoyed to see them like this—to see them bridging the divide, even if only for a moment—the rest of me is angered by the inescapable thought of Gabriel's hypocrisy. By the realization that if she had only chosen love from the offset, so much pain and hurt could have been avoided.

But then, you wouldn't have Caleb, a voice says in the back of my head.

I bristle at the thought, unable and unwilling to imagine that scenario—to picture even a heartbeat of my life without him in it. I suppose, looking at it that way, I really should be thanking Gabriel for splitting up with my father and locking me away for thousands of years. If it weren't for her, if it weren't for my father's war against the Creator—hell, if it weren't for the prophecy that led to Alexander's imprisonment—Caleb and I might have never found each other.

Lucifer clears his throat, shaking me free of that grim train of thought. When I glance up at him, he nods for me to continue, a reassuring smile gracing his fair face that shines so bright despite the swath of darkness around him.

Licking my lips, I straighten then murmur, "Thank you, both of you, for coming for me. And for not killing Caleb," I add with a glance at Gabriel.

With a haughty look, she lifts her chin. "He might be a fool but I would never intentionally do anything to hurt you."

Now that you know who I am, you mean.

Although I know she was only doing her part to ensure the preservation of the divide, I can't forget the things she said to me at the Serapeum—the way she tried to deter me from a friendship with Caleb just because he's a Dark. My anger toward her during those months in Alexandria resurfaces at her use of that callous word *fool*, crushing any fleeting gratitude I felt a moment ago.

"Why is he a fool?" I snap, white-knuckling the hem of my T-shirt in my shaking hands. My fingers squeeze tightly around the bunched fabric. "For wanting a family? For being deceived by people he thought he could trust?" My indignation grows when I think of Ishtar. Although he's never outright said she was the teacher who sent him to the Serapeum to find Alexander, the full extent of the goddess's involvement was confirmed by her presence in Kandahār. Wherever she is now, I hope she gets exactly what's coming to her for dragging Caleb into this mess.

My insides curl in on themselves as I envision her whispering manipulative words in his ear, playing his own wants and vulnerabilities against him. Even if he blamed his own need for a father figure for why he ultimately went through with their mission, I know the truth. I know Ishtar was pulling his strings.

A harsh scoff breaches my lips. "I think it's safe to assume we've all experienced that kind of betrayal."

It's an unnecessary dig, but I can't stop myself. Unlike my mother, when faced with the decision between duty and love, Caleb chose me, even if by doing so, he sacrificed a monumental tie to his bloodline. Perhaps the only tie he has left. In that respect, he and Gabriel were faced with the same choice, but unlike when she chose the Creator over my father, Caleb chose me and he *keeps* choosing me, regardless of the danger that choice puts him in. If that isn't loyalty, if that isn't love, then I don't know what is.

Gabriel immediately opens her mouth to respond, but Lucifer shakes his head at her before she can speak. "From what I've heard," he interjects calmly, "Caleb is the one who set you free from the prison realm where the Council was holding you. For that, I'll be eternally grateful to him. As will your mother, I'm sure."

My gaze shifts to the Archangel, who clenches her jaw with such force, I hear the muscles pop. When I raise an eyebrow, she forces a thin smile and nods.

I let out a relieved breath. "Good. Because Caleb isn't going anywhere. I won't let him go, and if you have any intention of being in my life moving forward, you both need to accept that." My eyes narrow, flicking between them again. "Can you?" I ask, the words a low growl.

"Of course," Lucifer answers without hesitation, offering me a tender smile. The comforting undulation of the shadows encompassing his body make me believe him.

The light surrounding Gabriel, on the other hand, is so rigid it almost looks solid.

"Yes," Gabriel grumbles after a moment, her own expression tight-lipped.

The anxiety biting at me eases a little. "Good," I say again, softer this time.

A chuckle interrupts the abrupt swell of silence that follows, dragging my attention to Lucifer, who plants his chin in his hand, his elbow firmly propped on one knee. Cocking his head to the side, he appraises me with curious, cerulean eyes that are otherworldly in their vibrance. I don't think I've ever seen anything so blue before.

As I get lost in their depths, he asks, amusement heavy in his tone, "Do you have any other terms for us, Daughter?"

Heat spreads over my cheeks. Is that how he sees this? As some sort of negotiation? Or is he just teasing me, the way a father might had I actually grown up with that kind of bond in my life?

"Not presently," I mutter a little too stiffly then quickly add, "but I do want answers. I met Lilith, and she filled in some blanks, but there's still so much I don't understand."

I peer at Gabriel, who leans back into the sofa cushions, crossing her arms, her gaze hazy, as if lost to some faraway thought. "Where to start…"

"At the beginning." Her eyes snap to mine, and I stare at her, pleading. "I want to hear it from you."

With an encouraging nod from Lucifer, she sits up straight. Then, sweeping the curtain of her sable hair over her shoulder, she clears her throat. "Your father and I have known each other since we were brought into existence. We were children together, we grew up together, and it was in Heaven where your father and I—"

"Fell in love," Lucifer finishes, his voice a gentle purr.

He turns to look at her for only a second, but in that instant, a deep scarlet flushes the ivory of her cheeks, exposing the unresolved feelings I sense burning between them. The tension is pervasive, and the longing in their gazes makes me feel like I'm intruding on a personal moment. It also reminds me of something I'd rather not think about. Something that has haunted my thoughts since I spoke with Lilith.

What must it be like to love someone that intensely and that deeply even after millennia spent apart? For my mother and father, they have an eternity to reconnect—to make up for the time they lost together—if they choose to rekindle that flame. But for me and Caleb…we don't have that kind of time. One day, mortality will strike and he will die, and I will be left alone to harbor these feelings for him, possibly forever.

That thought is like a lead weight in my stomach. Desperate to change the subject and escape it—to push it away for as long as I possibly can—I rasp, "Was I conceived before or after the Fall?"

Gabriel's complexion returns to its usual color when she answers, though there's a darkness to her gaze that wasn't there before. "Just before." She stiffens, and there's a trace of what I think might be shame in her voice when she says, "Although, I didn't become aware of it until shortly after the Great Battle. In truth, I wasn't even aware angels *could* conceive as much as part of me secretly hoped for it. At the time, I believed it a blessing reserved only for humans."

I nod slowly then go still when another thought occurs to me.

When I was in the Council's prison, I spent a lot of time deliberating over the circumstances of my birth. When I was born. How old I actually am. These same questions, among others, tormented me constantly with no clues to elucidate the answers.

Even before my illuminating conversation with Lilith, I assumed I was born after the Fall. Mainly because Lucifer had no idea I even existed before we met at the Serapeum, and because Lilith had told me my parents weren't on speaking terms when the Creator delivered the prophecy and I was sealed away to prevent my fate as either Destroyer or Savior of this world. With what little I knew about the bloodlines of the Faithful and Fallen, that timeline made sense. After the Fall, my mother was a Light and my father a Dark, the perfect recipe for creating a Gray.

But what I never considered before now was my conception. If I was conceived before the Fall, before the angels' decisions were reflected in their bloodlines…

Before the chaos of war and strife split them into sides…

"Then how am I a Gray?" I whisper. At my parents' bewildered expressions, I add, "Before the Fall, all the angels were the same, right? So, when I was conceived, you weren't a Light and a Dark yet. You were both…something else."

Understanding dawns in Lucifer's gaze.

"If I had to wager a guess, I would say we had both already chosen our sides at the time of your conception. The physical change hadn't yet occurred but the psychological…" He trails off, peering at Gabriel, his brow lifting slightly. "Am I right?" he asks, though his tone holds no malice. Only the fleeting hint of what might be regret. "Did you know then that you would side with our Father?"

A long moment passes before the Archangel dips her head, offering a silent *yes* she can't seem to bring herself to voice.

"You weren't born until after the physical change was complete," she explains, avoiding Lucifer's piercing eyes. "The only logical answer is that the piece of your father inside me would have undergone that transformation as well. I can only assume that's why you are a Gray."

"So, short answer: because magic," I deadpan.

A smile tempts the edges of Gabriel's mouth. "You could say that."

I nod again, appeased with the resolution to that mystery, although there's something else I still don't understand. My brows draw together as I recall my lessons at the Serapeum and what I learned in *History of the Fall*. Gilgamesh said that before the Fall, all the angels were the same.

But *what* were they, exactly?

"Were you all Grays before the Fall, then?" I press. "Is that why you fear them so much? Because we symbolize a return to before?"

"To be a Gray is to be of both the darkness and the light." Lucifer's lilting voice draws my focus away from my mother, and I blink at him, captivated, as he says, "Before the Fall, we were the purest versions of ourselves as the Creator intended for us to be, molded for one purpose and made only of light. We were not Grays because that darkness, that desire for free will that led me to lead the revolt, and which triggered the biological change in our bloodlines, had not yet been born in our hearts." He reaches across the low table between us, brushing a hand across my right cheek. "You are a Gray, my darling daughter, because you have that darkness inside you as well, thriving alongside your light."

Goosebumps pimple my skin at his touch.

"So, before the Fall, you were all Lights."

Retracting his hand, he offers me a barely-there smile, but the only part of it that reaches his eyes is the pain and remorse I sense behind it. "Bound by our duty to the Creator. As the Lights remain to this day."

Gabriel bristles when he utters these words but says nothing, instead lowering her eyes as if conceding to the subtle accusation in Lucifer's voice. It isn't bitter so much as regretful. A sad truth about the wedge that lingers between them. That lingers between all the Lights and Darks.

And in the middle of it, there's me.

By their logic, I understand why I'm a Gray, but if they're right about the mechanics of how this all works...then why isn't Caleb one, too? Alexander is his grandfather by blood and was already unbound long before Caleb was even a twinkle in his father's eye. So, why is Caleb a Dark and not a combination of both factions, like me? Can Grays even pass on their mixed DNA to their children, or is there some magical barrier in the very essence of who we are preventing us from continuing a bloodline so many view to be blasphemous? Maybe that's why we're so rare. Why Alexander and I seem to be the only two of our kind in existence.

Frowning, I peek up at Gabriel, figuring—of the two of them—she's more likely to know the answer to this particular mystery, having dealt with blood binds personally. After all, she put one on me. "At the Serapeum, when Alexander was speaking to me, he showed me some memories of when he was young."

Her eyes flash, her expression wary, as if she's not sure where I'm going with this.

Shifting uncomfortably under her scrutiny, I push on. "I know he was bound, like me, and I'm just wondering…could a blood bind affect what's passed on through the bloodline?"

Alexander seemed so young in those memories, but that means little when angels like my mother, who are hundreds of thousands of years old, remain trapped forever in immortal youth. For all I know, Alexander procreated before his blood bind was lifted. That's the only explanation that makes any sense.

Gabriel's lips pinch together in silent deliberation, and I can see the war raging behind her eyes as she considers what to tell me. "Blood binds are powerful but dangerous magic, and there are different kinds, some of which are more…permanent than others."

"Permanent?" I echo.

She nods. "If done correctly, certain binds are strong enough to completely sever the call between blood…" She places a hand over her heart, and I know she means that sweet song I hear even now, plucking at the strings in my heart, pulling me toward Lucifer, whispering in my ears that he's family. It's a song I don't hear with Gabriel, and now, I'm beginning to understand why. Because while Lilith might have helped her perform the bind to stifle my Dark side, there was another element to the magic they placed on me all those years ago.

A more permanent aspect, as she stated, that would ease the burden of attachment she felt.

To make it easier to leave me entombed in infancy forever.

"Others," she continues, "can fully subdue one side of your essence."

"But it wasn't fully subdued," I counter. "Alexander and I both experienced our powers breaking through the binds on us long before that magic was lifted. Does that mean the spells weren't done correctly?"

Gabriel shakes her head. "Powerful doesn't mean invulnerable, and certain binds, however strong and restrictive, can still be immensely fragile. It can break under the slightest strain, as we have seen with the...complications you and the Conqueror both endured."

Complications like the red fire that instantly marked me as *other* to the Lights. Complications like possessing powers everyone told me I shouldn't. Complications like the madness Alexander and I have both struggled with. That I still struggle with, even being unbound.

"So, given the evidence we have, to answer your earlier question, yes," Gabriel says. "Had Alexander reproduced after the bind had been lifted, Caleb would also be a Gray."

I gape at her, and she offers me the first glimpse of a genuine smile.

"That is what you were wondering, isn't it? Why Caleb isn't a Gray, like you?"

Biting my lip, I bob my head. "Then for Caleb to be a Dark, that means his dad must've been conceived before Alexander was unbound…" My thoughts immediately turn to Alaric. They were together then. In love. Alaric told me as much and the memories Alexander showed me confirmed it.

So, where does Caleb's father factor into that timeline?

Sensing my confusion, Lucifer says, "It was a different time, Daughter. As a prince and then king, it was expected of Alexander that he produce heirs for his throne. Before learning what he really was, his sole duty was to his mortal parents, to ensure the longevity of their family's reign. That included taking a wife and having a child."

I balk, my jaw dropping. "Alexander was *married*?" While I knew he had a child with a woman at some point—hence the existence of Caleb and his father—the thought of him being married to one is a different matter entirely.

Once again, I contemplate how these events fit into the picture Alaric painted for me of his and Alexander's past. Does this mean Alexander was unfaithful to him?

Is that why he helped imprison the Gray?

"Three times," Gabriel answers. "To three mortal women who had no idea what he was."

"Did he have any other children?" I press. "Ones who could be Grays?"

I don't know why it matters so much. Maybe I'm hoping for someone else to shift the burden of the prophecy onto…or maybe I just want to believe a love like the one my mother and father once shared—like Caleb and I share—is more common than everyone in our world seems to think. That we can not only co-exist but co-habitat this planet without a wall built between us. And Grays are proof that such peace is possible. That we no longer need to be split into sides.

To my dismay, Lucifer shakes his head. "No. But that's likely due to Alexander's mindset once he discovered his true lineage. His preoccupations once he was unbound became… singular. By then, he cared for nothing other than his self-righteous campaign to declare himself Lord and Savior to the humans. By that point, he wasn't thinking of a future where he wouldn't be present."

"How can you be so sure?" I ask. "Maybe you just don't know about them."

Maybe they're in hiding, afraid of being imprisoned or worse. Afraid of being ostracized like I've been my whole life.

"This isn't like what happened with you, Luna," Gabriel says carefully. "We knew everything when it came to Alexander back then."

Understanding grips me at her words, and the realization rushes from my lips in a faltering breath.

"Because of Alaric. Because he told you," I whisper.

I knew the Nephilim had helped imprison Alexander—he admitted that to me on the mountaintop overlooking Kandahār—but I never knew how deep that betrayal ran or how long he was working against the Gray. Or why, other than his desire to atone for helping to unleash Alexander's wrath on the world by unbinding him.

But now, knowing what I know about Alexander's infidelity, I can't help wondering...was Alaric's fear of Alexander's ambitions really his only motivation for trapping the angel under the Serapeum, or was something else back then guiding his actions?

Something like a broken heart.

As if reading my thoughts, Gabriel murmurs, "He did what he thought was right."

What he thought was right...

Like taking a dagger in the heart meant for me.

Tears flood my eyes. "He loved Alexander. You know that, right? They were...friends." I trip over that last word, my conscious fumbling with the partial truth leaving my lips. Because I know they were so much more than that. But that isn't my story to tell and it matters little now that Alaric is dead.

I stare hard at the Archangel, her face slightly obscured by my grief.

"Sometimes," she begins, her voice more gentle than I've ever heard it, "to save the people we love from themselves, we try to stand in their way...even if it isn't the right decision." There's a weight to her words, as if she isn't talking about Alaric at all, but about herself. The surprised look my father gives her only confirms that I'm not the only one who heard it—the longing and regret in her voice. He gapes at her, a silent question in his probing gaze, and when her eyes finally meet his, an entire conversation seems to pass between them in the space of a breath.

As I glance between them, I can see that whatever once made her choose the Creator over their love is no longer present. If faced with the same decision again, I have no doubt in my mind which way she'd choose.

A blush stains her fair cheeks again under the heat of my father's unwavering stare. It's so strange to see the Archangel this way—like a young, innocent schoolgirl experiencing her first love rather than an ancient celestial being capable of removing an enemy's head with a single determined swipe of her sword.

But as quickly as the redness flushes her skin, it fades and she looks at me again, her normally predatory gaze uncharacteristically consoling. "In Alaric's case, it was," she assures me.

"And in your case?" I retort. "Do you stand by what you did to me?" When she blinks in surprise, I add, "I know about the prophecy. That you entombed me because you thought I was the Destroyer." I allow a moment for this information to sink in before asking the only question that matters. The fear of the answer is a hand tightening around my throat, reducing the words to a whisper. "Do you still think that?"

"No," the Archangel declares with a fierce conviction that

makes me want to believe her. Heaving a shuddering sigh, she mutters, "Truthfully, I haven't believed that since Alexander first made his mark on the world."

"What?" Lucifer and I say at the same moment, and we share a startled glance before fixing Gabriel with the joint heat of our stares.

"If that's the case, why did you keep her in stasis?" Behind the Archdemon's biting words, I can almost hear another question there that speaks to the darkest depths of my heart, plucking at the strings of loneliness I felt for far too many years. *Why did you keep her from me?*

"I was afraid," Gabriel explains, a trembling breath passing her lips. Her focus on me intensifies, the hard edge to her dark gaze pleading. "When you were born, I locked you away out of fear that you would become the blight on this world the Creator spoke of, as some sort of divine punishment for having the audacity to love anyone more than I loved the Creator. But I was also afraid that if you *weren't* the Destroyer, then that meant you would become the Savior. And as history would go on to prove, Saviors have a tendency to become martyrs." Her voice catches, and an unexpected whimper escapes. She then gives a morose shake of her head. "I knew from the moment I first saw Alexander that he was dangerous. Had I freed you then, you would've been defenseless against him."

"She would've had us to protect her." Lucifer's comment is little more than a snarl, and when Gabriel gives him a patronizing look, whatever heat and love I saw between them only a few moments ago seems to vanish again.

She raises an imperious brow. "Against the entire Council?" She scoffs. "We've had this discussion. Keeping the world ignorant about Luna's existence was the only way to keep her safe."

The ire behind my father's eyes fades. "Even if it meant never setting her free?"

His words are soft—barely audible, even—and yet, they seem to ring through the room like a death knell, unnervingly loud and clear. Gabriel's face contorts, her expression wounded, but once again, she says nothing. And although her silence is its own admission of guilt, I can't find it in me to be angry at her. Maybe it's that frustrating sense of loyalty I still seem to feel toward her, or maybe I'm just beginning to grasp how difficult the situation really was. How isolated and alone she must've felt in her decision.

Which brings me back to why she did it. What did the Creator say that scared her so much?

"Gabriel, what did the Creator warn you about?" I ask, immediately regretting the flash of hurt that crosses her face when I call her by her name. Although guilt nips at me for causing that look, I don't feel comfortable calling her anything else. Not yet. "What exactly *is* the prophecy?"

Gabriel lowers her gaze for a moment, and when she finally looks back up at me, her eyes are laser-focused but distant, as if she's recalling the details of a long-forgotten memory. Suddenly, her expression grows stormy, and when she speaks, her voice booms through the airy room, giving the impression that the Creator is speaking directly to us, using her as His mouthpiece.

"'A child born of the Dark and the Light will threaten the sanctity of the planet. They will leave a trail of bodies and red flame in their wake and none, immortal or otherwise, will be safe. Until another, also spawned of the Light and the Dark, steps forward to challenge the one who seeks to destroy. Should they embrace their strength, the Savior will reign victorious and return peace to the Faithful and Fallen, healing a rift believed to be irreversible. But should they fail, the Destroyer will emerge triumphant and the human and celestial worlds will be forfeit.'"

When the final word rolls off her tongue, understanding strikes me hard and fast like a slap to the face.

Heal the rift.

"That's why He let me out," I breathe.

"He?" Lucifer asks. Beside him, Gabriel goes rigid, as if she knows what I'm going to say. Maybe she does. Maybe she's suspected the truth from the moment she realized I'm her daughter.

"The Creator," I clarify then to Gabriel, I say, "No one else knew where I was entombed except for you and Lilith, right? But the Creator—"

"He is omniscient. He would've known," she finishes,

sounding breathless.

Which means He also knew all this would happen. Hell, maybe He intended it to. Come to think of it, the Creator's involvement is also the only explanation for how I could've gone so long without drawing the attention of the academies, although, if I really am the Savior, I can't imagine why He'd want me so ill-prepared for the task. Wouldn't he want me trained and ready if I'm to take on Alexander? Unless—

My eyes widen as I recall Gabriel's conversation with Alaric when he first brought me to the Serapeum—how she had questioned why he didn't know of me sooner and how he had answered by saying my scent had been barely discernible, making it almost impossible to find me. Now, I can't help wondering if the Creator had a hand in that, too. If he hid me on purpose until the right moment. So that I would grow up far away from the ingrained prejudice of our world. So that when the time came and I crossed paths with Caleb, I would be drawn to him instead of repelled.

So that I would help him release Alexander since Gabriel never would.

The Creator wanted this to happen. He wanted Alexander free. He wanted my Dark side unbound. And He wants us to go to war—to see the prophecy to its completion, one way or another.

"What are you both trying to say?" Lucifer asks, a slight edge of irritation straining his tone.

It occurs to me that I've been silent too long, so I blurt out, "Lilith thinks the Creator is why I'm no longer entombed. That he purposely placed me in the mortal world and let me grow up believing I'm mortal—"

"Until He wanted you found," Gabriel cuts in, her voice the barest breath of a whisper.

The realization crossing my father's face sucks the warmth from his skin, and his expression hardens as he seethes through clenched teeth, "Which means He intended for all this to transpire."

Lucifer's rising fury is apparent, and I shrink back into the sofa, not wanting to anger him further, even though I know his outrage isn't directed at me. Still, I roll my lower lip between my teeth, hesitating a moment before finding the courage to speak again.

"I think the Creator… I think He *wanted* me to release Alexander." And although I know how much it will pain them to hear it, I add, "Had the circumstances of my childhood been different, I probably wouldn't have been willing to do that." Because it needs to be said. Because every step we've taken, every decision we've made, has been self-fulfilling, leading us down the very path the Creator seemingly wants us all on.

Had I grown up with parents who loved me, then Alexander wouldn't have been able to prey on my loneliness and deep-seated issues of abandonment and control me the way he did. Had I grown up knowing what I am, accepted in our world, he wouldn't have been able to use my feelings of isolation against me.

And then there's the matter of the divide. Had I grown up as a Light, exposed to such hate and divisiveness, I might have looked at Caleb the way the other students and teachers at the Serapeum all looked at him. Like he was beneath them. Like he wasn't worthy of a Light's love.

That thought turns my stomach.

Lucifer's brow furrows over eyes darkened with rage. "If you were the Destroyer the prophecy spoke of, I would understand why the Creator would want you to unleash Alexander. But if *he* is the Destroyer, then why—"

"You're forgetting one important part of the prophecy," Gabriel interrupts. Her face promptly falls. "The part where the Destroyer and Savior must meet in battle."

I nod. "And until we face off like the prophecy ordained, I can't do what it is the Creator really wants." When they both look at me in question, I sigh. "Remember what the prophecy said? About the Savior bringing peace to the Faithful and Fallen, healing the rift between them? That has to mean the divide."

Gabriel frowns. "I fear there are hidden meanings to the Creator's words that we are not grasping. Alexander is the Destroyer, I believe that, but he often spoke of erasing the divide—"

"Except he never wanted to heal the divide, he wanted to crush it," I counter. "He wants to remake the world as he believes it should be and rule over everyone in it."

Whereas I just want to walk this planet without anyone trying to shove me in a cage for being different. I want to love who I love without having to hide it. And I want peace between the Lights and the Darks. Real, lasting peace. No more bullshit fake truces. No more segregation. I want to bring our world back together…and heal it.

Even if I have no idea how I'm meant to do that.

"Lucifer?"

The unease in my mother's voice jerks me out of my thoughts, and following the direction of her panicked gaze, I glance at my father, startled by the sudden ruddiness of his cheeks. His hands are clenched into shaking fists on his knees and his eyes are pinned on a distant spot on the floor, unblinking but unfocused.

"The Creator waits millennia to try to make peace with his children and thinks He can use *my* daughter as some disposable pawn in his master plan?" With an ear-shattering roar, he jumps up from his seat, and his blue eyes blaze like twin flames seeking to burn and destroy. "If one hair on her golden head is harmed because of His scheming, I will storm the gates of Heaven and find a way to slay Him, consequences to all be damned."

"*Lucifer,*" Gabriel barks, her tone no longer worried but sharp-edged with warning. He blinks, shaken from his rising temper, and stares blankly at her for a long moment before looking at me. I'm not sure what he sees on my face, but it's enough to extinguish the last of his rage.

"Forgive me, Daughter," he says gently, stepping around the table between us and kneeling in front of me. Raising a hand, he touches my cheek again. "I did not mean to frighten you."

"You didn't," I whisper, although the lump in my throat and the trembling of my fingers says otherwise. But the truth is, I'm not afraid of Lucifer. I'm afraid of what he's capable of.

Of what he might do if something were to happen to me.

I don't know how to respond to such an overwhelming exhibit of love. I gaze up at him, lost for words. Rising, he shifts his hand to the top of my head, patting the crown of my hair.

"I believe some fresh air is in order, so I will take my leave for the moment."

"Father…" The song in my blood bonding us pulls at my heartstrings, and only half-aware of what I'm doing, I reach for him, grabbing his hand. I don't want him to leave. Not because I can't face Gabriel alone, but because we've only just been reunited, and because I'm so afraid that anyone who leaves me won't come back again, however irrational that may be—especially here where we're actually safe for the time being.

That fear has been with me ever since I was a little girl and is part of why I always pushed people away. If I didn't let them close, I couldn't hurt them….and, in turn, they couldn't hurt me. But now, I have so much at stake—too many people I don't want to lose—and anything could rip them away, tearing them from my life like a page from a book at any moment. That apprehension is stronger than ever, like rot in my heart. Rot that's only festered since we lost Alaric.

A warm smile tugs at his lips. "You and I have plenty of time to better acquaint ourselves. But for now, you and your mother have much to discuss. Later, we will go for a walk through the gardens if you like."

I manage a weak nod, loosening my grip on his hand. Then without another word, he barrels from the room, leaving my mother and me staring after him in stunned silence. Several tense moments pass before either of us find the words to speak.

"Would he really try to kill the Creator?" I ask.

Is such a thing even possible?

Gabriel's answering expression is grim. "I doubt he could, even if he wanted to. But you must understand. You are the embodiment of everything your father fought and fell for. He gave up Heaven for the chance to have love. To have a family of his own. And now that he has it, he's fearful of losing you. Of the Creator stealing you away—"

"Like he feels the Creator stole you?"

"Perhaps," she murmurs, knitting her hands together, her expression contemplative.

Silence encroaches again, the air between us heavy with so many unasked questions and thoughts I'm not even sure how to begin to voice. So, I settle on the easiest one. The one that's been bugging me most these past months.

"How long have you known you're my mother?" When she

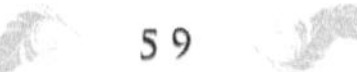

doesn't immediately speak, I continue, determined to pry an answer out of her one way or another. "Although the Council tormented me about it and the others kept saying it, I honestly didn't know for sure until you came for me in Kandahār. When I actually *heard* you call me your daughter. But you knew long before then…didn't you?"

Looking down at her lap, the Archangel nods. "That day you were eavesdropping outside my office—" She flashes me a look when I try to protest. "Don't deny it. I know you were."

I wither under her stare. "And that somehow made you realize I'm your daughter?" Doubt laces my every word.

"No," she says, glancing down at her hands again. "But after I caught you, I did something I'm ashamed of…and it was that action that made me aware of the truth."

I think back to those initial moments following her conversation with Alaric, trying to puzzle out what she means, but the answer eludes me.

"I looked into your mind," she confesses, and my mouth pops open as all the air rushes from my lungs in a whoosh. "I never intended to harm you. I only wanted to see what you heard."

I shiver at the notion of such an unwanted invasion, imagining phantom claws in my mind, sinking in and ripping out thoughts I never invited her or anyone else to witness. For some reason, it feels so much more personal and invasive than what Alexander did to me at the Serapeum—all those months he spent in my head, poisoning my thoughts to use for his own gain. Perhaps because I know her motivation for breaking into my mind wasn't coming from a place of malice or a sadistic need to force my compliance, like Alexander's reasoning when he broke into Caleb's—the horror of which still haunts me, the assault fresh in my memory like a nightmare I can never escape. She knew better, as a Light she lives by a strict moral code, and she did it anyway.

Because of that, I can't help wondering what other lines Gabriel has crossed with me...or may yet cross if she deems it necessary.

"What did you see?" I press, half hopeful and half afraid the answer will make me despise her.

To my surprise, tears glisten in her dark eyes. "Your birthplace. It was just a glimpse—there were no other discernible thoughts I could sense. Just that image, which I could see as clearly as I see you here sitting before me."

Shock slams into me, knocking the air from my lungs. My birthplace? But I didn't even know where I was born until Lilith told me back at the citadel—months after the encounter Gabriel speaks of. So, how could I have been thinking about it?

"I don't understand," is all I can manage in my confusion.

"I didn't either at the time," she admits. "But with the prophecy and everything else that's transpired, it can't be a coincidence. That glimpse I saw in your head was surely a message."

"A message?" As these words leave me, I realize I know what she's going to say before she even says it. "From the Creator."

She nods. "I can only assume He wanted me to know who you were so I would offer you aid…and so you would have the strength of your parents behind you for the battle ahead. A strong indicator you are the Savior if there were any lingering doubts."

I consider her for a moment, her words dragging me back to those dire moments under the Serapeum when she and I both seemed so close to death. "Is that why you called Lucifer to you? Because you thought the Creator would want you to?"

A brusque huff escapes her, and she presses her fingers into her eyes, wiping away the tears collecting there. "I didn't know what I was thinking except that he was the only person in the world I felt I could turn to at that moment—who I trusted to guard you and fight for you with the same determination that I would've had I not been injured."

The sincerity in her voice steals my breath, and I gape at her, for once allowing myself to see her as who she really is instead of as the terrifying monster I've built her up to be in my head.

As a terrified mother, desperate and alone, who only wanted to save her child.

"Everything that has led us here has been my fault, no one else's," she proclaims. "Your father never knew, Luna. You know that, right? He wasn't even aware you existed until the day Alexander was freed. He only wants to protect you, so, please…don't bear him the same ill feelings I'm sure you must have toward me. He doesn't deserve them. He deserves only your love and to have the time with you that I robbed him of."

Time he might not actually have, goes unsaid.

"And what do you deserve?" I ask, cocking my head to examine her more closely.

Gabriel peeks at me through her fingers, clearly not expecting this question. "I…" A grimace contorts her face. "I deserve your hatred. And his."

"But that's not what you want."

She blanches, letting out a throaty, humorless laugh. "Of course not. But what I want doesn't matter. Not after what I've put you both through."

While there's a part of me—a very large part—that agrees with her, the child still residing within me who is desperate for maternal love disagrees. She screams for me to make amends, and as that tamped-down voice hums in my ears, reverberating in my bones and everywhere underneath my skin, I can't help wondering if maybe this is the call of our blood, finally speaking to each other after all this time—our connection not permanently severed despite what Gabriel said about the bind. Maybe the spell she put on me all those years ago to keep us apart is beginning to fray as the mutual yearning in our hearts begs it to. As we take the first step to heal the rift between mother and daughter.

Or maybe, it was there this whole time and we were both too

deaf to hear it. Maybe that loyalty I feel toward her, even now, was the universe trying to tell me we are connected, even if our blood couldn't.

"I…understand why you did what you did," I say carefully, and as the words leave my lips, it sinks in just how much I mean them. What sacrifices would I make to keep Caleb safe? To keep him alive?

I would do anything, I muse, and as I stare into Gabriel's wide, surprised eyes, I recognize how much she was willing to do, how far she was willing to go to protect me.

How far she's *still* going.

"And I don't hate you, no matter how much you think you deserve it."

A strange air of discomfort overtakes the Archangel, as if she's not sure what to make of my admission. As if she's holding back the fleeting hope that I might actually find it in me to forgive her.

But the longer I look at her, the more I see the terror in the depths of her gaze, and it dawns on me that it isn't my forgiveness she needs.

It's her own.

"For what it's worth"—I keep my tone steady, even as my heart races a mile a minute—"I don't think it's my forgiveness you need, or even Lucifer's. I think you need to forgive yourself. Otherwise, how are we ever going to move past it?"

A skeptical breath fills the silence between us. "Is that what you want?" she asks. "To move past it?"

Do I want that?

Yes, a small voice in my head answers. The voice of that little girl still inside me who has waited her entire life for a mother.

"I'm willing to try." Then, with a delicate sniff, I add, "But *only* if you're nice to Caleb."

She lets out a stilted chuckle then sits up a bit straighter, lifting her chin with a dignified air. "*Nice* might be asking a bit much of me," she says, although an amused grin pulls at her lips.

The tension in the room melts away as I allow myself to envision the possible future before us. A future where I am her daughter and she is my mother and the loneliness, pain, and loss we've both suffered up until now no longer matter.

A future where I have the family and affection I've always wanted.

"Would you settle for civilized?" I counter, extending an olive branch.

To my immense relief, she takes it.

Her smile deepens. "I think I can do that."

four

CALEB

I STRETCH OUT ON the colorful silks swathing our bed, my fingers laced behind my neck. Luna is still with her parents, and my anxiety ratchets up as I wait for her. She's been gone a long time. I didn't want to let her go. Not because I don't think she needs to have a come to Jesus moment with Mom and Pops—she totally does—but because purple smudges have taken permanent residence under her normally dazzling eyes, and her skin is still too wan. She's an angel; she should be immune from the physical effects of grief, but she's not. In her suffering, she remains all too human.

The old wood of my door rattles with the sharp sound of a knock. Three precise raps that tell me Hammurabi is on the other side of the door. I appreciate his manners. Other first generations think they can waltz right into my private space. Ishtar, anyone? I don't bother to get up, a mantle of bone-deep exhaustion cloaking me. While Luna has sought refuge in sleep—which she probably doesn't even need—I spend my nights restless, nightmares of blood and death all wearing my grandfather's face haunting me. It sucks ass. I hate being on this emotional see-saw from hell.

"Come in," I call, my eyes flicking toward the door.

It creaks open, and my teacher steps in, hovering in the doorway, which is unlike him. Normally, he strides into a room as if he has every right to own it. His eyes rove over my sprawling form, face torn between disapproval and worry.

"You're still in bed," he accuses and I stiffen, glaring at him.

"So?" I challenge. "We've been here all of two days, and I've been taking care of Luna. My grandfather tried to kill me. Again. Alaric is dead. I'm entitled to laze about and recover if I want to."

Hammurabi crosses his arms over his broad chest. "I thought you were tired of playing defense and wanted to give offense a try."

Arching an imperious brow at him, I shrug. "I can plot in bed just as easily." I neglect to say that after my brave words to Hammurabi, thoughts of Alexander and what we're up against have plagued me, rendering me frozen and useless. "Besides, I'm sticking around in case Luna needs me after her meet and greet with the parents."

The Babylonian king's face softens. "The flower finally decided to confront them. Brave girl. Let us hope they don't smother her."

"With love or guilt," I say, rolling my eyes. "Since Alaric… died, she's been talking in her sleep, blaming herself for his death. She's literally wallowing in guilt over him—it's not good. Anyway, she doesn't need their guilt as well."

Hammurabi frowns. "Alaric's death belongs to neither one of you. The sooner you accept that, the sooner you can start being productive. Moping doesn't become you, boy."

I send him a fierce scowl. "I'm not moping. My mind still doesn't—I'm not right in the head, okay?" I confess bitterly, turning my face toward the ceiling.

He snorts. "Who is?" He shakes his head, sighing. "You've gotten your first taste of real pain, one of many in your long life, especially in these times." He crosses the room and shoves my legs aside, sinking onto the bed next to me, his elbows on his knees. "We are nearly immortal. The things I've seen and experienced…" Hammurabi shakes his head again. "My soul has so many scars, boy, it's nothing but a white-striped lump of flesh, but I endure, as will you. You'll endure because you love this world, and you love the things in it. You love your beautiful mother." I scowl at the way his voice caresses the word beautiful. "You love the flower."

I wonder what Hammurabi has endured over the years. I've never given it much thought, other than knowing he is scary and powerful and has seen a lot of shit because he's practically a dinosaur. He's experienced blood and battle and death. Maybe he's loved some mortals along the way, too, and lost them. I remember Lucifer's remark at the citadel, that he hoped Hammurabi would soon be curled up at Asmodeus's feet once more. The mighty king honest-to-the-Creator blushed at those words, which makes me wonder if there's something more than friendship going on there? But Hammurabi would never admit he has the hots for the Archdemon, even under threat of death. And I know better than to ask, unless I want some broken bones to go along with my broken mind.

I swallow hard, meeting his eyes, those ebony depths swimming with uncharacteristic sympathy once more. Ugh, give me hard-ass Hammurabi any day. Mr. Nice Guy makes me want to snivel like I'm a baby again, and it's not that I think grown-ass men shouldn't cry, but I hate being vulnerable around such a powerful creature. I know Hammurabi won't use it against me or deliberately hurt me, but I guess my experience with Ishtar has left a deep scar on my soul. According to Hammurabi, just one of many that will mark me the longer I live. Yippee! Something to look forward to.

"I know I need to get my shit together," I admit. "For Luna and for my mom, if not for myself." I shoot him a warning look. "Luna doesn't know that I'm not Super Caleb right now, 'kay? And she doesn't need to. She can't handle my problems, too."

He rolls his eyes at me. "I'm certainly not going to discuss your feelings with the flower over a cup of tea like an old village gossip. That being said, it's important not to hide from your lover. She won't thank you for it. She might even feel you don't trust her enough to reveal your true self."

I scowl at him. "If she asks, I'll tell her. If not, it's not her worry."

He huffs out an exasperated breath. "Children," he mutters.

"The big question is, do we even have a plan? Kali is doing us a solid, but we can't stay hidden here forever. What's our next move?"

A worried look flits over Hammurabi's stern features. "We are caught between the Council and Alexander, and if we remain, we'll be ground to dust. It is not an enviable position, to say the least."

"So, in other words, you have no fucking clue," I growl and stare at the ceiling once more.

In one swift move, Hammurabi rises, grabs my legs, and dumps me on the floor. I land with a soft thud on the many carpets and prop myself on my elbows, glaring at my teacher. He towers over me, fists balled on his hips.

"If we want to survive this, we all must work together, boy. As much as I regret it, you can no longer hide behind my shield. You and the flower must leave childhood behind now, Caleb. You are young but clever. I know you don't believe this, but hiding with your grandfather was the right choice."

"Tell that to Alaric," I spit like a venomous snake.

Squatting on his haunches, Hammurabi grips my chin, giving it a firm shake. "Alaric would agree with me if he were here. You managed to get the flower to her parents and give us a fighting chance. We would not have survived much longer without the Messenger and the Morningstar. Your plan was unconventional, but it is that kind of thinking we need right now. You may not want it, but you must take a seat at the table."

My gut recoils at his words. I'm going to be dragged kicking and screaming into this war, whether I like it or not. And I don't like it. I hate it. Yeah, I told Hammurabi I was tired of playing defense all the time, but I didn't mean I wanted to lead the offensive charge. I just wanted to be a good soldier and do whatever the hell Lucifer told me to do. No matter what Hammurabi says, the last time I planned anything, someone ended up dead.

My teacher arches an annoyed brow. "Boy, your doubts are so loud in your mind, I can hear them. Mourn Alaric. Take a whip and flog yourself until your blood washes away your guilt. Then you—what is it the young ones say today?—you get over yourself."

I sputter with laughter at his phrasing, the words sounding so bizarre escaping from his mouth.

His eyes soften. "Toughen your skin and heart now, Caleb. It will make the next blow easier, the next scar bearable."

"Wise advice," a deep voice drawls.

Hammurabi and I both whip our heads toward the doorway where Lucifer himself lingers in the frame. I can't believe we didn't hear him. If I wasn't certain he'd kill me, I'd put a bell on him. His deep blue eyes find mine, the antique gold of his hair managing to shine even in this dim light. The Morningstar indeed. I wonder if Luna is still with Gabriel. I hope she's all right.

Though Lucifer wears a cloak of friendliness, when those ancient eyes meet mine, my gut clenches. I think I'm about to experience the "if you hurt my daughter" speech. Honestly, I'm surprised he's waited this long. Of course, I've been like a pit bull where Luna is concerned, so he hasn't had a whole lot of opportunities to threaten to cut off my dick.

I shoot him a faint smile. "Hammurabi is as wise as he is old," I say, rising from the floor and smirking at my teacher. Just like the predictable asshole he is, he cuffs me on the back of the head. I chuckle.

Hammurabi shrugs at Lucifer, exasperation written on his face. "Children," he says, his voice resigned.

"King, may I have a moment with the child?" Lucifer asks politely. It sounds like a request, but I'm not fooled, and neither is Hammurabi. That dinosaur knows an order when he hears it, even one coated in silk.

Hammurabi smiles. "Of course. Don't go too hard on Caleb. The flower does love him so."

My chest warms at his words. Despite his gruff, grouchy exterior, Uncle Hammurabi always has my back. "I'm sure he'll leave bruises in places no one will see," I say.

Lucifer's brows raise in surprise at my quip, and Hammurabi strides away from me, muttering, "Boy has a death wish."

I grin. As soon as Hammurabi exits, quietly snicking the door behind him, my lips droop into a frown. "How can I help you?" This time, my voice is deferential because despite Hammurabi's words, I don't have a death wish. I'm not stupid enough to keep baiting the Morningstar. Grandfather taught me too well what kind of pain an angel can inflict. "Is Luna okay?" This comes out more of a growl than I intended, and I flinch inwardly.

"My daughter is a beautiful miracle," he says, offering me a blinding smile. "Though I resented your interference…I want to thank you for being brave and protecting her from us." His lips twist. "You were right. We would have overwhelmed her."

I give a cautious nod. "So, you're saying it's all good now?"

His wide chest heaves as he sighs. "We've taken our first glorious step. Time will eventually heal our wounds, and should the war go our way, we have nothing but time." His blue eyes narrow on me, calculating, and it takes everything in me not to squirm. "Have you thought about time, Caleb?"

My mind spins at his abrupt change of subject. "Um, like we're running out of time to defeat my grandfather and the Council?"

Lucifer gives a dismissive shake of his head. "No, have you thought about your mortality."

My entire body goes on alert, alarm bells blazing in my head at his words, but I have no idea why. I just know there's something here I'm not going to like. "I'm only eighteen, and if Alexander doesn't cut my head off, I'll probably live a few thousand years or longer."

He takes a step closer to me, and I battle the urge to cower away. The thing is, I actually don't think Lucifer wants to hurt me, but Gramps has messed up my head good and proper. Our eyes meet, and goddamn, I see Luna clearly in his face. Their beauty is staggering. Seriously, how did Gabriel miss the resemblance?

"Yes, you'll live much longer than these fragile mortals who surround us. You'll remain ageless while they grow old, becoming husks of their former selves until their return back to the dust from which they came."

I suppress a shiver at his words. "Okay, I'm not trying to offend you here, but you're seriously starting to creep me out."

"Luna loves you. Greatly. I know this," the Morningstar says, affection in his gaze as he speaks of his daughter. Meanwhile, I'm getting whiplash from his constant change in direction. "I started a war over love and free will, Caleb." He slides his hands in the pockets of his black trousers. "I have no desire to subvert your will or your love. I would sooner cut off my wings than violate my daughter's ability to choose, but I want you to understand what choosing you means for her, for the both of you."

Suddenly, I have an anchor in my gut, slowly sinking. His words are like floating puzzle pieces finally linking into place, showing me a picture I don't want to see. Not that it hasn't been knocking around in the back of my mind, that dread, but Luna and I are both so *young*. Fuck, even if she's technically old, she's still a baby, still brand-spanking new. We have years ahead of us. Literally hundreds of years, maybe thousands. But I'll still…

"Because I'll die?" I push past a tight throat. "Depending on how this war turns out, I hope that won't be for a long, long time."

"A couple thousand years at least," he says, nodding. "And that sounds like an eternity, and to you, I'm sure it is, but to someone who is eternal…" He shakes his head, a sad smile flirting with his lips. "My daughter is like me, I'm afraid. There have been others besides Gabriel, but none who held my heart captive the way she did. Still does, despite our… differences. Luna feels that way about you, child. She'll love you with all her eternal heart. And when winter finally claims you, it will break her."

I'm struck by the abrupt urge to vomit. I clench my hands into fists to guard against the nausea consuming me. My head spins. I close my eyes briefly. *Get your fucking shit together, Caleb.* I find my center by the ends of my fingertips, clinging onto my manufactured calm. My eyes snap open, meeting the blazing blue of the Morningstar's. I detect pity there, and it makes me want to destroy mountains.

"I'll break her if I walk away, too," I counter, my voice hoarse. Clearing my throat, I say more firmly, "I love her, and I'm not going to abandon her like everyone else in her life has for her own good." Lucifer flinches. Direct hit. I want to crow in triumph. I want to pay him back a little for shredding my life apart, but this isn't about him. "Yeah, one day I'll die, and that fucking sucks, but that doesn't mean I can't love Luna the way she deserves. And I will love her until she no longer wants me."

The Morningstar's wings materialize on either side of him, ebony and menacing. Every fiber of my being tells me to curl into a ball so the predator doesn't notice me. But I hold my ground. I only wish I had badass wings to flare out, too, so we'd both be strutting peacocks, circling each other. Lucifer's face turns cold until he resembles the beautiful statues Nephilim like to sculpt of him and place around the academies. He studies me, searching for any weakness, anywhere in my armor he might slip an emotional blade and gut me. I don't waver. I don't bat a fucking eyelash. He tilts his head, a slow smile blooming over his face like a sunrise, warming his eyes and making him golden once more. He gives me a nod, and I know I've passed some sort of test.

"I may not like you diverting my daughter's attention, but I can't fault your loyalty," he says. "Love her the way she deserves or face my wrath. Do we understand each other?"

Nodding, I say, "Perfectly."

His wings vanish, the inky feathers leaving trails of darkness. "Good. Luna will return momentarily. She and Gabriel have many things to discuss. There are deep wounds that need to be healed between them."

I almost choke on a derisive snort. "Understatement of the year," I mutter.

Mr. Bat Ears raises an eyebrow, his blue eyes gone a few shades colder. "Gabriel is Luna's mother. She loves her. To be with Luna, you must accept that."

My smile is anorexic. "I do, and you have to accept that I want to protect Luna from everything that causes her pain—even her mother."

Lucifer observes me through hooded eyes, and I fight the urge to fidget. He doesn't like my answer, but it's the truth. Yeah, Gabriel had her reasons but Goldilocks got hurt. And I don't like that.

"The time for either of us causing her pain is over," Lucifer finally says. "You needn't worry on that score anymore, child."

I chuckle. I can't help it. For all his immortality, it's clear the Morningstar is new to this whole dad business. "You will, and you won't mean to, but it's all part of being a parent. You'll fight and make up and love each other even more. Don't try to be perfect. It's not possible. Just be there. That's what matters."

Anger flushes Lucifer's cheekbones at first, but then he laughs. "You're quite wise for an infant," he says and I smirk. "It gladdens my heart to know you have a sharp mind as we face the upcoming war. You'll be an asset."

That sobers me the hell up. "It looks like you and Hammurabi are on the same page." My stomach sours. I don't want the weight of that responsibility, but I'm going to be saddled with it whether I like it or not.

"The king is superb at spotting talent," Lucifer acknowledges. "And I know my daughter would never be attracted to an ignorant boy. She's too intelligent."

"She's smart and beautiful, a lethal combo," I agree, then I frown. "Look, I'll carry my weight, and I'll do what you tell me to do, but like you said, I'm an infant. Don't expect miracles."

"You have a brain and good instincts, which means I can mold you into an effective leader and warrior. That's enough. Miracles are not required."

Ugh, I don't want to lead anyone anywhere, but I know arguing with the Morningstar is pointless. And stupid. Shoving my hands in my pockets, I rock back on my heels. "So, what's the plan now? We can't pretend to be Team Alexander anymore. Now, Gramps *and* the Council are after us. Hammurabi didn't give me much insight, which I won't lie kinda worries me."

Lucifer's smile is grim. "Now, I call upon my allies and all the favors owed to me. I am still the Morningstar, Caleb. I still command allegiance."

I believe him. I just hope it will be enough.

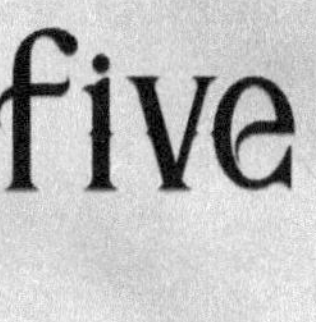

five

LUNA

I LEAVE AFTER SPEAKING with Gabriel, feeling significantly lighter than when I first entered the room, the apprehension of facing my parents replaced with a budding, albeit tentative, hope for the future before us. I still carry wounds that will take time to heal from, but the thought of that future eases the sting. Because I know, moving forward, I'm no longer alone.

Whatever comes next, we'll face it together.

And yet, despite that hope, the heaviness soon returns to my chest, weighing my every step with dread, making it easy—too easy—for the fear to catch up with me. I quicken my pace, hurrying toward the bedroom I share with Caleb, eager to escape the dark thought nipping at my heels—the understanding that the future I keep envisioning depends on what happens next with Alexander…and even more so on the Council's stance on Grays. What if the impending war changes nothing and I have to spend the rest of my immortal life on the run, always looking over my shoulder in constant fear of being imprisoned again? I don't want to live that way, and I certainly don't want to force that kind of life on Caleb or my parents, either. So, where would that leave us if that's all that awaits me? Would they remain by my side if the only future we could have together is one in hiding?

The heavy wooden door slides into view, and it takes everything in me not to run just to escape the daunting silence of the corridor sooner. In the hush, I hear every single one of my fears reflected back at me as if someone is screaming them, the unspoken thoughts echoing off the walls, which seem to shrink, closing in around me as the anxiety in my chest tightens around my heart. The sensation only eases when I feel the cool brass knob to our bedroom beneath my fingertips.

Grasping the metal, I throw the door open to find Caleb sprawled on the bed on his back, staring up at the ceiling. Although the sight of him immediately calms the chaos inside me, something about the blank expression on his face and the unnatural stillness in his body gives me pause.

His eyes shift to mine when I stumble into the room. "Hey," he says, launching himself off the bed and crossing the distance to me in two long strides.

"Hi," I whisper, my momentary worry forgotten, grinning up at him as he takes hold of my hands, his thumbs brushing over the backs of my fingers in a soothing caress.

If fear of the future is a poison, then Caleb—being with him like this—is my antidote.

"You were gone a while," he mutters, unable to hide the frown dancing along the edge of his lips. "I was beginning to get worried. How'd it go?"

I consider my answer before finally settling on, "Good, I think. A little awkward, obviously, but...it was a good start." And with time, dedication, and hard work, maybe my relationship with my parents will almost feel normal.

Although relief shines in Caleb's eyes, the concerned expression on his face lingers. "Did Gabriel behave?"

An airy laugh springs from my lungs. "Yes," I assure him. "And she even promised she'd try to be nice from now on."

He raises a brow, fighting a grin. "Try, huh?"

I shrug. "It was the best I could get."

He nods, but the faint smile slips from his face, replaced again by that unwelcome frown. I wait for him to prod me about my father—to ask me if we have the Morningstar's approval—but the question never comes. Maybe he's not as concerned about Lucifer's opinion as he is my mother's. After all, they're both Darks. They share common beliefs and viewpoints. Or maybe it's for that very reason he seems so on edge. Like he has to live up to some grand expectation to be more, to make some all-important mark on the world, just because of who my father is.

Biting back a frown of my own at the thought, I tug one hand free of his and press it flat to his cheek. When he leans into my touch, I say, "You definitely don't need to worry about my father, you know. He told me he's eternally grateful to you. I daresay he might even like you."

But those words don't seem to bring him as much comfort as I hoped they would because he pulls away, averting his gaze. Clearing his throat, he lets go of my hand and returns to the bed, plopping down on the mattress.

As I cross to the bed, I wonder what's bothering him—if Alaric's death is tearing him apart inside the way it suffocates me. Before, I was too wrapped up in my own grief to notice how exhausted he looks, like he hasn't slept in days. His face is drawn, as if something heavy weighs on his mind, although I can tell he's trying hard to hide it. He looks up at me and forces a roguish smile, acting like he's the same old Caleb when it's apparent he's anything but. I want to ask what's wrong, to encourage him to be open with me, but we've both been through so much—more than anyone else our age could possibly fathom—and it doesn't seem fair to goad him into talking when I'm not ready to talk about Alaric.

So instead, I sit down beside him and take his hand again, threading our fingers together. Whether it's the looming fear of his grandfather or Ishtar's betrayal or Alaric's death nagging at him, I'll be here when he's ready…just as he's always been there for me.

As if reading my mind, Caleb raises our joined hands to his lips and loosens his hold just enough to press a gentle kiss to the gold scar on my palm. I gaze at him over our fingers, and when our eyes meet, he lies back on the bed, pulling me with him until we're stretched out side by side on the blanket. A contented sigh brushes past my lips as he loops an arm around my waist and tugs me closer.

For a while, we stay like this. My cheek rests on his chest, his fingers grazing up and down the full length of my arm and occasionally skimming over my hip, sending small bursts of electricity arcing through me. It's soothing but dangerous, and I know if he keeps touching me like this, I won't be able to maintain control.

Suddenly, Caleb laughs under his breath, and it's only when I go still that I realize I've been fidgeting. Well, rubbing up against him more like. Not that I hear him complaining about it. He *did* say he always wants to have sex with me.

"So, what did you and your parents talk about?" he asks, to my disappointment, steering the conversation in a very unsexy direction.

I blow out a loud breath, feeling like I've been doused with ice water. Then flopping over onto my back, I tell him everything.

"Well, I guess it's good we're finally getting some answers," Caleb says once I've divulged the last detail, "especially where the prophecy is concerned."

His voice trails off at the end of that sentence, making me think there's more he wants to say. Propping myself up on my elbows, I look down at him, noting the way his attention is fixed intently on the ceiling again.

"But?" I prompt, my brows lifting.

He turns his head, his gaze drifting to mine, and for a long moment after, he just stares at me without saying a word, those beautiful dark eyes unblinking. I can practically see the wheels turning behind them.

"But I agree with your pops," he finally says, sitting up and swiping a lock of hair out of my face. "If the Creator really did set this all up, if we really are just pieces in some big cosmic game of chess and you end up hurt because of this shit with my gramps…" His jaw clicks when he clenches his teeth, his body stiffening as he lowers his hand, his eyes dipping down to the blanket beneath us. Shaking his head, he grinds out, "Then I'll be right there next to Lucifer, smashing down the gates of Heaven."

"Caleb—"

He shakes his head again, and his eyes snap back to mine, a stubborn pout contorting his lips. "Before you point out the obvious and say I can't fly, just know I will literally hitch a ride on your dad's back if I have to."

Biting back a laugh at that mental picture, I sit up and comb my hand through his hair. As my nails glide over his scalp, he sighs.

"It won't come to that," I murmur, trailing my fingertips down the back of his neck. "Why would the Creator have done any of this unless He wanted us to win?"

Exhaling, Caleb scrubs a hand over his face. "I have no clue,

Goldilocks. But—and I can't believe I'm saying this—I agree with your mom. She locked you away so you wouldn't end up as a martyr, and I won't let you become one, either. Fuck fate. *Fuck* the Creator's plans," he growls. Cupping my face, he pulls me to him until I feel his hot breath on my lips. "We are going to win this war, and you are going to get the future you deserve."

The future I deserve…

And what kind of future is that? I'm tempted to say. But I don't because no good can come of that answer.

After all, it would depend on who we're asking.

Frowning, I whisper instead, "I wish I knew how we're going to do that."

Caleb plants a barely-there kiss on my lips then collapses backward onto the bed again. As the mattress settles beneath him, I hear him mutter, "I'm sure we'll find out soon enough."

Fallen start arriving early the next day—half a dozen figures clad in rippling shadow, all claiming to be supporters of my father. As soon as the first one appears, Caleb and I are ushered into a large, open living space by a disgruntled Hammurabi, who it seems has once again been reduced to his role as our babysitter and herder. Despite his deep frown, I can tell he doesn't actually mind, his fondness for Caleb shining out in every interaction between them, even when he's smacking the younger Nephilim upside the head. And I can tell Caleb has a soft spot for the Babylonian king—hell, as intimidating as Hammurabi can be, even I find his presence comforting, which is much-needed these days given the frequent mayhem that seems to keep finding us. There's just something endearing about the old grouch.

My parents greet each of the new arrivals, although my mother doesn't receive the same warm reception from the Fallen as my father. They regard her like they might a snake, their eyes tracking her every move as if they fear she might attack as soon as they turn their backs. Still, they listen with rapt attention as my parents give a very brief—and vague— explanation as to why my father called them, and when Gabriel and Lucifer finally introduce me as their daughter, the Fallen stare at me not with the fear I expect, but with a thousand questions in their eyes. Despite admitting they heard rumors of Alexander's return, they seem less knowledgeable when it comes to Grays—as if they had no idea we exist. I wonder if this is the first time many of them have even heard of a Gray. Alaric said Alexander's followers all had their memories wiped, but what about those who didn't follow the Conqueror during his first conquest for power? Are their memories about what he is still intact, or was everyone—Light and Dark alike—given a clean slate in a desperate attempt to bury the past? Or maybe some never know the truth at all.

Either way, the newcomers don't turn tail and flee or threaten to turn us into the Council, which at this point, is really all we can ask for. Their respect and loyalty towards my father was all it took to guarantee their allegiance to our cause, though, I'm not sure how much help six Fallen will be when going up against Alexander, who has hundreds, possibly more, at his command…and the ability to resurrect any who are cut down on the field of battle.

I peer around the room, taking in the faces before me. To win the impending war against my fellow Gray, we need to be united, and yet, of our present group of allies, only two are Lights—my mother and Kali. Grief rises in my throat like bile when I think about how, if Alaric was alive, he would be here, too, standing with us, ready to fight by our sides. But he isn't, and it seems my mother doesn't command the same loyalty as my father. That, or she doesn't trust any Lights besides Kali to not run off and squeal to the Council should she attempt to involve them in our plan—assuming we ever actually come up with one. That thought only depresses me more. How am I supposed to heal the divide with so little trust between the two sides?

"Holy shit," Caleb whispers, and I follow his gaze from where he sits beside me in the middle of the U-shaped settee to the other side of the vast room where a towering figure steps out of the darkness drenching the distant corner in black.

A late arrival.

As the man emerges from the Shadow Road and steps into the light streaming in through the arched windows on my right, I notice his skin is a deep copper brown, and his eyes, which blaze orange, like glowing topaz, are decorated with black and gold paint, reminding me of ancient Egyptian paintings of royalty. Despite his modern clothing, he wears an elaborate choker made of what I suspect is real gold.

"Who is that?" I ask.

I glance back at Caleb, surprised to find him looking slightly star-struck.

"Abaddon," he answers, his tone almost reverent. "Headmaster of Machaerus Academy. Dude is a grade A badass, so having him on our side is a massive win. Plus"—he lowers his voice even more, leaning in to murmur in my ear—"the fact he's here means the Council isn't as united as we thought it was."

I pull back to meet his gaze. "That's good, right?"

He nods. "*Very* good. First, Asmodeus, then Beelzebub, and now Abaddon?" A smile spreads across his face as his eyes turn in the direction of the Archdemon again. "It means there's hope."

We watch, silent spectators to this reunion between Council members, as Abaddon approaches my father where he stands with my mother to the left of the sofa. "Lucifer," he says with a dutiful nod. His focus then shifts to my mother, and he looks her up and down with a contemptuous sneer. "Gabriel."

"Abaddon." The Archdemon's name rolls off her tongue like honey laced with venom. "Thank you for coming. I'd introduce you to our daughter, Luna"—she waves a hand toward me, and I instinctively shrink into the sofa, hoping to escape the latecomer's attention—"but of course, you already know all about her. You did, after all, aid in locking her in a cage."

"As did Asmodeus, who also helped to free her," Lucifer reminds my mother, placing a warning hand on her forearm. She stills at his touch except for her shoulders, which raise like hackles on a hissing cat, her brow furrowing over dark eyes. "Retract your claws, Gabriel. Abaddon is on our side."

Ignoring Gabriel's stormy glare, the Archdemon places a hand on his chest and once again inclines his head toward my father. "My allegiance is to *you*, Morningstar. I followed you into one battle, and I am prepared to do the same again. Give the order and I will take up my sword."

Lucifer grins, and his face is the very sun itself, momentarily dazzling everyone present. Especially me.

"Only words are needed today, Brother," he says, clapping Abaddon on the back. "Come. We have much to discuss."

"Is this everyone?" Abaddon asks as Lucifer steers him toward the sofa. "I fear you will need greater numbers than this if you are to take on the Conqueror's army. And where is Beele? I do not see him here."

"Beele?" I fail to stifle my shock at the nickname for the fearsome Archdemon. Beelzebub might resemble an adolescent on the cusp of teenagehood, but I have zero doubt he could take on anyone in this room and hold his own, if not come out on top. It's strange hearing him referred to in such an endearing tone, like someone might talk about their younger sibling. Or a puppy.

Caleb chuckles into his hand. "Well, that is just adorable. He must be the little guy's bestie."

I let out an unbidden giggle at that mental picture then immediately go silent when Hammurabi scowls at us from his perch at the far end of the sofa, giving a subtle shake of his head. If the others hear us, they don't comment on it, though I do catch my father watching me out of the corner of his eye from where he stands a few feet away, a grin tugging up one corner of his lips. Just past him, I notice my mother looks equally amused, though she's trying much harder to hide it.

Clearing his throat, Lucifer looks back at Abaddon, gesturing for him to take a seat before stepping past him and sinking onto the cushion beside me. "Beelzebub will show, of that I am certain. He has never failed me before."

Although Abaddon nods, he looks unconvinced, concern etched into his features as clearly as words printed on the page of a book.

"Do you come with any news of Asmodeus?" Hammurabi asks, drawing the focus of everyone in the room. "Forgive me for speaking out of turn," he adds, looking between my father and the other Archdemon, "but I have heard nothing of my mistress and fear for her safety."

My chest goes tight at the thought of the headmistress of

Babel. The last time we saw her, she was preparing to confront the Council alone while Caleb, Hammurabi, and I fled to Hilla and escaped into the Shadow Road. While in Kandahār—as glorified prisoners at Alexander's base—we heard she was imprisoned but any other news about the Archdemon has been sorely lacking.

"Anything you can tell us, Abaddon," my father encourages, the pleading edge to his tone only eclipsed by the fury riding every word. "I, too, fear for Asmodeus. She has risked much for my sake, and I cannot let her suffer any longer on my behalf."

Beside me, Caleb straightens, and he grabs hold of my hand, his palm sweaty with anticipation and a worry that's almost palpable with how close he sits. I taste it in the air, I feel it in the trembling of his fingers, and I find myself praying to the Creator that Asmodeus is safe and unharmed. For Caleb's sake more than anyone's, even her own.

A dark shadow dims Abaddon's vibrant eyes. "I'm afraid I must disappoint you both," he says, casting a forlorn glance at my father and then at the Babylonian king, although there's a split second where his gaze catches mine. There's something there in the way he looks at me, however brief. Something my gut tells me is blame. "She is being held in an underground cavern on Thwaites Glacier, entangled in chains which are spelled to frost over and burn her exposed skin with her own ice should she struggle. Her punishment for aiding your daughter is not a pleasant one, Lucifer, and it is not due to expire anytime soon. I fear the glacier will melt long before her detainment there ends."

My stomach plummets, and I fight the overpowering urge to throw up. Asmodeus isn't only imprisoned because she helped me, she's being punished for it—and horribly from the sounds of it. I shiver at the thought of ice against naked skin, imagining the worst kind of frostbite—of burns inflicted by cold instead of fire, unsure which is worse. I wonder if whatever cage she's being held in is also preventing her from healing, much like that terrible egg hindered me.

"If we know where she is, surely we can go get her out?" I whip my head back and forth, swiveling between Lucifer and Abaddon, my voice hitched up an octave as an all-too-familiar panic sinks in.

Caleb tightens his grip on my hand, and when I look at him, the expression on his face only stokes the embers of my growing hysteria.

"We barely escaped in one piece from the Council's last prison," he says, his tone gentle, as if consoling a young child after a nightmare. "And honestly, Goldilocks, as much as I want to help Asmodeus, I don't want you within a hundred miles of those assholes again. It's too risky."

Tears well in my eyes. "But there are more of us now. And it's *my* fault she's in there—"

On my other side, Lucifer touches my shoulder, and when our eyes meet, he brushes my cheek with his knuckles. "The burden of guilt rests with me, Daughter, not with you. Do not let it trouble your mind."

I shake my head. "But—"

"Worry not," he says over me, offering a genial smile. "I will ensure she is freed. But first"—his expression darkens—"we must discuss Alexander."

There's the delicate sound of someone clearing their throat, then, "I hope you weren't planning to start the party without me."

My gaze is pulled over my shoulder where it locks on a woman standing in the doorway, her figure draped against the door frame like a sumptuous courtesan holding court. A devious smile curls ruby red lips as eyes of obsidian peer around the room.

"Lilith," I breathe.

"Who invited the traitor?" Abaddon growls, rising from the sofa.

"I did," Gabriel barks, stepping forward. She crosses the room to her friend, who hooks an arm around her, pulling her in for a hug. My mother returns the embrace—a lot less awkwardly than I would've expected given she isn't exactly renowned for warm, fuzzy displays of emotion—then pulls away, fixing Abaddon with a glower. "She isn't allied with the Conqueror. Not anymore."

Abaddon scoffs. "Since when?" Behind him, the other Fallen all gape at Lilith, expressions almost spellbound, as if this is the first time they've seen the ex-Archdemon in person. After siding with Alexander and then losing her wings, I can only imagine Lilith probably didn't make many public appearances. For all I know, this could be the first time many of them have seen her for thousands of years.

Lilith leaves Gabriel's side, prowling into the room like a panther on the hunt. Sneering at Abaddon, she bites out, "Since recent events made me realize I was wrong about the prophecy." She looks at me then, and her face instantly softens, a sincere smile curving her lips. "Hello again, Luna."

I blink at her, taken aback by the pleasant coo of her voice and the warm, almost fond way she regards me, even if I got a brief taste of it in those final moments of our last conversation. Still, it's a staggering contrast to the antagonism she displayed for the most part at the citadel, and the difference throws me for a loop.

Confused mutterings fill the room, mainly coming from the Fallen and Kali, who it seems had no idea there even was a prophecy, let alone that Gabriel had lied about the details.

Abaddon, on the other hand, merely arches a brow. "Wrong?" he echoes, bemused. "The prophecy has always been clear that a Gray will be the Destroyer of our world. Even before we knew of a second Gray, you were adamant Alexander was innocent." Now, he fixes my mother with a furious stare that would make any lesser creature cower. "So, I do wonder how our dear Lilith could have misinterpreted the prophecy to begin with unless there is something you failed to disclose to the rest of us when you first delivered the Creator's warning. We all know you have always held her ear."

Pinching the bridge of her nose between her thumb and forefinger, Gabriel lets out a long-suffering sigh. Then, with a blink-and-you-miss-it glance at my father, she says, "It's time you all knew the truth."

The Archangel repeats the full prophecy with the same possessed look she wore yesterday when she revealed it to me, her eyes hazy with distance and her voice thunderous in the encompassing hush. Everyone in the room watches her with unbroken focus until the last word leaves her lips.

Once Gabriel finishes speaking, Lilith takes it upon herself to fill in the rest of the blanks, explaining our suspicion about the Creator's involvement and what that means for the prophecy…

And for me.

"The Creator is playing a dangerous game," Abaddon mutters, rubbing a hand along his sharp jawline. "To what end? To see us all united in Heaven again? Forgive me, but I will not surrender my freedom on Earth to be His slave again."

"I think—" I hesitate, unsure if I'm supposed to speak or if anyone even cares what I think. I might be an angel—and possibly the Savior the prophecy spoke of—but I'm not a leader, and no one here ever asked for my opinion.

I swallow under the weight of every eye in the room.

"Go on, Daughter," Lucifer encourages, lightly touching my

arm. "You are involved more than any of us, so if you have something on your mind, you should say it."

My teeth begin to worry my lower lip, but I catch the movement, not wanting to give the impression of weakness around such powerful beings—especially when the fate of the world rests on my shoulders.

Be brave, Luna, I chide myself.

"I think He just wants to see us all get along," I say, relieved my voice remains steady. "For the rift between our kind to be healed. Obviously, I don't know what He's *actually* thinking, but the Fall happened hundreds of thousands of years ago. Maybe He just wants to make amends."

Abaddon responds with a dubious laugh. "You are naive if you think such old wounds can be healed."

"Well, not with that attitude, they won't," Caleb mutters.

The Archdemon's orange eyes blaze like fire, and he glares at Caleb as if determined to burn him—to sear holes in his skin for his insolence. His mouth peels back in a snarl, and he rises, but his movements are halted by a fearless Hammurabi, who stands as well and crosses to Caleb, placing a protective hand on his shoulder, even though the Archdemon could destroy him if they came to blows.

Still, he remains by Caleb's side, protective and unmoving. Uncle Hammurabi, indeed.

"You speak of old wounds," the Nephilim retorts, "and yet, you have served on the Council with Lights for many long years now, Abaddon. You have worked together despite the divide. For the sake of the future and the welfare of our young, I think we can all stand to do the same. We are all capable of tolerance, at the very least."

"We are capable of more than that, King," my father agrees. "I, for one, am ready to put past hurts away." As he says this, he looks at Gabriel, his eyes on her face almost leering in their intensity, making no effort to hide the affection in his gaze. Although I witnessed glimpses of tenderness between them before—flickering remnants from the love they once shared— it shocks me to see him showing it so openly now, especially after how heated he got yesterday when we spoke of Gabriel's reasoning for keeping me locked away.

Then again, their rooms here are linked. Maybe they worked on their issues behind closed doors when I was no longer present.

"So, what's the plan?" Caleb presses, and when no one immediately answers, he lets out an exasperated huff. "I'm all for us holding hands and singing *Kum Ba Yuh* like some Whos on Christmas morning, but seriously, what's our strategy for dealing with my gramps? Because while we sit here clucking like a bunch of old hens, you can be sure as shit he's thinking about his next move."

"The Conqueror is past thinking," a familiar voice grunts, and my nose wrinkles at the sudden stink of smoke and sulfur flooding the space. Searching for the source of both, I shift on the sofa, my eyes widening when I catch sight of the small figure entering the room from the same dark patch of shadow Abaddon emerged from before.

Beelzebub hobbles into the light, one ice-blue eye swollen shut and blood oozing from a wound in his shoulder. A female Dark Nephilim with frosty white hair is beside him, and at first, I think she's helping him walk, until I realize it's his arm around her waist and not the other way around.

"The next move has been made," the Archdemon rasps, and I watch in stunned shock as my father and Abaddon both launch off the sofa. Caleb and I mimic the movement, jumping to our feet.

"Beelzebub!" my father shouts at the same moment Abaddon cries out, "Beele!"

Beelzebub stumbles, his fair skin black with soot stains, his clothes scorched and completely incinerated in places. The Nephilim beside him doesn't look to be in much better shape. If anything, she looks worse. Far worse.

"What happened?" Abaddon growls as Beelzebub moves the injured Nephilim to the sofa. Once she's deposited on the cushions, he straightens and looks up at my father.

"War is upon us, Lucifer." He grimaces then, and to my horror, a tear slides down his cheek, cutting through thick smears of blood and ash. "And Ashkelon..." he breathes, his youthful voice trembling. "Ashkelon burns."

SIX

CALEB

MY JAW TRIES TO connect with the floor as Beelzebub's words echo throughout the room. There's an honest-to-Creator tear running down his face. That freaks me out more than anything because Mighty B doesn't strike me as the emotional type. The Dark Nephilim tagging along with him reeks of smoke, and she's injured, her face wan, her breathing erratic. She clutches her chest and leans against the cushions, eyes shutting. I glance around, noticing everyone's face is a mask of shock. Considering I'm surrounded by beings who have seen some shit in their time, I know this is bad. Really bad. Ashkelon is gone. I can't believe Alexander would destroy a *school*. All that history gone. Ashkelon goes back to the time of Canaan. Did any of the other teachers get out? And what about the poor Nephilim kids? He wouldn't murder kids, would he? That goes against his whole savior MO.

"Even Gramps can't be that fucking crazy," I say aloud,

drawing everyone's attention. "Why? What does this gain him? And what about the students? The teachers?"

The miniature Archdemon's darkness gathers around him like a cloud of wraiths, concealing the angelic blood dripping from his wounded shoulder. Rage practically lights his eyeballs up. "There is no line your grandfather won't cross, boy. He sent his followers and his loyal hound, that bitch, Ishtar, to take the students." Well, at least he didn't kill the kids.

Beelzebub's eyes land on Lilith, blue depths practically spitting fire when he registers her presence. Then he stills, as if he understands what her being here must mean. He shoots an accusing look at the ex-Archdemon. "*You*. This is your fault," he hisses. "Ashkelon used to belong to you. He's making a statement with its destruction. He's punishing you for your disloyalty."

Lilith's posture stiffens, and she delivers a world-class fuck-you glare to the Archdemon forever locked in a pre-teen body. "You're a fool if you think this is the only school he'll destroy. Yes, he's making a statement. Nothing the Council has built is safe from him. He can and *will* conquer all. And he'll take our precious children and mold them in his image."

"Let us not forget the weapons he's sure to have taken as well from the Fall," Lucifer says darkly and I flinch.

"And it's not like we can make more," I mutter, and Luna jerks her head toward me, her brow arched in question, bewilderment etched across her face. "The knowledge to make angel-killing steel and the armor to protect against it was lost after the Fall. No one has ever been able to replicate it. Who knows why? Maybe the Creator made us forget so we wouldn't fight anymore. Fuck all good that did since we're going to war. If Alexander gets those weapons, we are seriously fucked."

Her eyes round with fear and she glances at her mother and father, as if waiting for confirmation of my words.

"He still has to find the bloodlines to match the weapons," Gabriel points out, her voice surprisingly soothing as her gaze slides between Lucifer and her daughter. The Messenger's icy demeanor is thawing and I wonder who's responsible. Lucifer or Luna? "We have a little time." Those last words are directed at the Morningstar, and his shoulders relax a little.

Beelzebub scoffs. "Not that much time, Messenger. Since when did you become an optimist? Has motherhood softened you?" A warning growl escapes Lucifer's mouth, but Beelzebub just offers a condescending smirk. "The Conqueror doesn't only have Nephilim on his side, but a fleet of Fallen who desire nothing more than to possess their weapons once again."

Well, shit. This *is* really bad. Baddie, bad, bad. A gasp tears from Luna's mouth, wretched and terrified. The room freezes at that pain-filled wail. My head whips toward her, and she clutches my arm, horrified eyes clashing with mine. She shakes her head over and over again, the motion jerky, her eyes like those of a cornered animal. My heart sinks. We've been working on her stability and making progress, but I feel like all that effort just ran off a cliff. I mean, yeah, what's going on sucks, but why is it triggering Luna?

Out of the corner of my eye, I see Gabriel and Lucifer take a step toward us, uncertainty lining their faces. Hammurabi huddles closer to us, eyes narrowed on Luna, his body tense as if he wants to beat somebody up for upsetting his flower, but he doesn't know who to punch.

I keep my voice soft, soothing. "What's up, Goldilocks? Talk to me."

She glances over at Gabriel before her eyes land back on my face. Guilt buries itself in her hazel gaze. "I—at the Serapeum, when Alexander first started talking to me, he showed me a vision of buildings burning. The schools. And you. You were burning, too. He said he was going to burn down the divide, but I thought he was being... I didn't think he was being literal." She shakes her head again. "Caleb, if I had known, I would've told you, but he played with my mind so much... I'm so stupid. I didn't think. This is my fault." Tears drench her cheeks, and I pull her into my chest.

"This is definitely not your fault," I tell her, keeping my voice firm, steady. "Gramps was majorly messing with your mind back then to serve his own ends. Hell, you were so brand-spanking new you didn't have a clue what he was showing you. Alexander is good at spotting his enemy's weakness and using it against them. You know that. You know how ruthless he can be." I stroke my hand down her back in a soothing sweep. My eyes lock with Gabriel, and I see fury burning in her dark stare.

I think she'd like a chance to smite my grandfather again.

"Alexander is a seasoned warrior, Luna. You stood no chance against him. You bear no blame," Gabriel says, taking those last steps toward us and placing a tentative hand on Luna's head.

"And after everything the Council put you through, Daughter, I'm surprised you've remembered what he showed you at all," Lucifer adds, coming to stand next to Gabriel. I start to feel a little claustrophobic.

Beelzebub gives a derisive snort that has me seeing red. "Is there anything else you've neglected to tell us?" he demands, upper lip curved in a nasty sneer. "Speak up before more schools burn."

I want to punch the little asshole in the face. Repeatedly. Hammurabi's angry hiss tells me he's right behind me in line.

Lucifer whirls on Beelzebub, wings flaring from his back, and the potential for violence sizzles along my skin. Luna burrows into my chest like she wants to disappear at the forever tween's scathing words while Gabriel turns fiery eyes on the Archdemon, and even stoic Abaddon appears surprised. The other six Fallen tense, eyes darting back and forth between the bigger players. Kali wisely backs up from the confrontation, maintaining a minimum safe distance.

Lilith just gives a venomous chuckle. "Careful, little one, or the Morningstar will finish the job Alexander started."

Inky darkness spills from Beelzebub. "Pardon me, wife of Adam, did you just have your school set aflame? Did you just witness loyal Nephilim getting cut down as your students were stolen by a madman? No? Then kindly fuck off."

"Don't you mean *my* school?" Lilith says, inspecting her nails.

Beelzebub's smile is vicious. "Oh, yes, *your* school. Before you betrayed us all and got your wings cut off for backing the wrong horse. Tell me, Lilith, are your wounds still tender?"

I barely have time to gasp before Lilith has her hands around Beelzebub's throat, and he coils his darkness around her neck, squeezing. She releases a hand and jabs her nails into his wounded shoulder. He gives a harsh grunt and backhands her, sending her flying away from him. I'm torn between disgust and awe at the display. These are our *allies*? It's so nice to see they're being grown-ups and getting along.

Lilith springs to her feet like a jungle cat, only this time Lucifer is there to restrain her. "Enough," he hisses at them.

Abaddon now leans over Beelzebub's shoulder, his orange eyes bright in the lingering darkness. He really does resemble the Nubian kings who used to rule Egypt.

"Warring amongst ourselves hardly serves our purpose," his deep voice rumbles.

Beelzebub pulls his power back, leaving the room brighter. He straightens. "Forgive my display of emotion. I've had a taxing day." His eyes flick to Luna, who now sobs quietly against my chest. "Though I may have been…harsh, Luna needs to tell us everything Alexander showed her, so we can save our schools."

"Hey, give her a minute. She's been through some shit," I

growl, tightening my arms around Goldilocks.

"She'll answer our questions later when she's not so distraught," Gabriel says, narrowing her eyes at Beelzebub.

"The flower is delicate right now," Hammurabi interjects in a withering tone.

"We're all distraught, and coddling her now won't do any of you any good, especially her," Beelzebub counters. "If she can't contribute to our efforts, then hide her away again. For her sake and yours because she'll serve as a distraction that will get you killed."

That's about enough of that. "Okay, jackass—"

"Don't speak about my daughter that way," Lucifer booms, advancing on the mini Archdemon who, to his credit, holds his ground.

Luna pushes away from me, hard, the abrupt motion causing me to sway. She's a helluva lot stronger than she looks. All that angel strength.

"Stop!" Luna screams, wiping her cheeks with the backs of her hands. "Father, just stop. He's right."

Stunned amazement wipes the Morningstar's face clean of rage, and my jaw sways in the breeze for a moment before I find my voice. "Like hell he is," I snarl. "Goldilocks—"

She holds up a slender hand. "I know I'm not the poster child for stability right now, but I have to learn to be part of the team, or I *am* a distraction to you all. A liability. We can't do what we need to do to defeat Alexander if you're all constantly worried about me." Luna takes a deep breath, lips trembling. I want to bite her lips then kiss them better. "And I have to learn to…share more. I'm not used to having people to share with." Her chuckle holds bitterness, and I see Gabriel flinch out of the corner of my eye.

Lucifer is the very embodiment of pride as he stares at his daughter. "You're made of steel, Daughter. Never doubt it."

Luna gifts him with a soft smile stitched with love. If I thought he was pride personified before, he now wears a golden glow at his daughter's tender expression. I sneak a glance at Gabriel, whose mouth pulls down. I guess it sucks when your kid so obviously has a favorite.

"I wish I could give you more details, tell you what school he plans to attack next, but he wasn't that specific. He just showed me our world on fire," Luna says, chin up, eyes steady on Beelzebub. "He said the divide must be destroyed, and I guess that's what he thinks he's doing. And now, you know everything I do."

"Why would he show you your lover burning?" Beelzebub questions, his eyes tapered into dubious slits.

A blush creeps over her cheeks at the word "lover," and I suppress a grin. We're not lovers. Yet. "To manipulate me into helping him. He knew how much I cared about Caleb, even then," she replies.

Warmth fills my chest. Warmth with a shot of guilt. I know Goldilocks and I are cool now, but it doesn't mean I've forgotten how I lied to her. Her eyes drift to mine, and I let her see how much she means to me. It's uncomfortable being this vulnerable, but it's worth it, especially when I see my love reflected back at me.

Beelzebub rolls his eyes, snorting. "Save me from young love. Though, grandson of the Conqueror, he may want to burn you in truth now."

I shrug, not caring anymore that Gramps wants to kill me. "There's certainly no love lost between us. It's not like he hasn't tried to fry my brains before."

"Your family is more dysfunctional than most," the little Archdemon agrees, and I almost like him for the understatement.

"If Alexander plans to attack all the schools, we alone can't stop him," Abaddon says. "We don't have the numbers."

Lucifer gives a grim nod and looks at Gabriel, whose expression is equally dark. "No, we don't. And we can't allow Alexander to take more children. Or more weapons." He then turns to Lilith, mouth compressed in a thoughtful frown. "You do realize what must be done?" He sighs as she stiffens. "Come, Lilith, we all voted to take your wings in punishment, and yet you're here with us. You haven't tried to kill me—yet."

Beelzebub looks between them, his eyes widening. "Ahhh," he says. "Of course."

"Indeed," Gabriel replies.

I glance between them all as Abaddon and the other Fallen slowly nod. Hammurabi scowls, but looks resigned, and Kali just releases a weary sigh, like she knows what's coming, but thinks it's a terrible idea. Well, I wish they'd share with the rest of the class. I hate feeling like the only dumbass who doesn't get the joke. Luna snuggles next to me again and raises her eyes to mine in question. I just shake my head.

I wave my hand in the air. "Hey, the babies over here are clueless. Care to catch us up?"

"Yes, I thought we just agreed information must be shared," Luna says, and I'm proud of the bite in her voice.

Lilith pins me with her glare. "The Morningstar is suggesting we bring in the Council to help us deal with Alexander."

"The Council who just imprisoned me?" Luna protests, a tremor racking her frame, and I grasp her hand tightly.

"We can't fight both the Conqueror *and* the Council," Lucifer tells her. "Right now, our interests and the Council's align. We both want to stop Alexander, and we need each other to do it." He gently extracts Luna from me, and I reluctantly release her. He takes her into his arms. "And I promise you, Luna, they'll never put you in a cage again."

"So, the old 'the enemy of my enemy is now my friend' bullshit?" I ask, crossing my arms over my chest. I'm sure Mammon will just love seeing me again.

"We must deal with one problem at a time. This is the best way," Gabriel says, her eyes retreating from Luna and meeting Lilith's. "You know it is, dear friend."

"I agree," Beelzebub says. "The burning of the schools will

spur the Council into action."

"So, are we all in agreement?" Abaddon asks, gazing around the room.

A chorus of "ayes" ripple across the space until only Lilith is left. "Yes, I agree," she finally says, her full lips twisting as if she's just ingested poison.

A hand lands on my shoulder. "Don't worry too much, boy. They can't be any worse than staying with your grandfather," Hammurabi says, but his words offer little comfort.

seven

LUNA

WORRY BITES AT ME like teeth on my skin as I stare through the window at the gardens below, my eyes fixating on the bountiful plant life in desperate search for a distraction. Vines creep over stone, taking root in the foundation through even the smallest cracks they find, like the invasive thoughts in my head always seem to find the cracks in my sanity. Shuddering, I rub my hands along my upper arms and squeeze, hugging my torso to hold myself together—the panic in my chest inflating with every breath, a balloon about to burst.

The decision is made. We're going to approach the Council, which means facing my captors again…as well as the very real possibility of reimprisonment should our meeting with them go sideways. Sure, I'll have my parents with me this time, along with some powerful allies to protect me, but the Council outnumbers us in strength. Not to mention, certain members will undoubtedly be seeking their pound of flesh after what happened during my escape.

Another shudder rips through me at the memory of Mammon's eyes—shifting from the lie of Alexander's contrasting ones back into their true crimson hue—his howl of fury and pain a lingering echo in my ears, scratching at my composure like nails on a chalkboard. As terrified as I am for myself at the prospect of seeing the Council again, I'm frightened for Caleb even more. He didn't just help to release Alexander, he broke me out of the Council's prison and cut off an Archdemon's wing. As much as I keep telling myself my parents would shield him—would treat him as an extension of me—I know these actions will not be forgiven, and there will be little they can do should the Council insist he pay for his crimes. What if the Council demands Caleb's life in return for asking for their aid? Regardless of their promise to accept him—to accept our love—would my parents hand him over for the chance to ensure a future for their daughter? I want to believe they wouldn't ever hurt me that way. But I also know the lengths Gabriel has gone to in the past and would go to yet again if it meant protecting me.

Swallowing past the rising lump in my throat, I shake that thought away. I wish we didn't have to go. I wish we could stay here forever, safe and undisturbed in this beautiful refuge. But I know that's not an option—not when Alexander continues to put other celestial lives at risk. It's only a matter of time before he finds us...or tears the world apart trying.

Ashkelon burning is an image in my head I can't escape. Although I've never seen the school—and can't pick it out from the images Alexander forced into my head—I imagine it as if I were actually there, my stomach twisting as guilt encroaches behind that ceaseless worry about meeting the Council. Back at the Serapeum, Alexander showed me his plan—he *showed* me he wanted to set fire to the academies and I...I did nothing about it. I didn't tell anyone. I didn't warn anyone.

And because of that, I'm as responsible for this chaos as he is, regardless of what my parents or Caleb think.

A hand brushes my shoulder, making me jump, and turning, I find Caleb standing behind me as if he somehow materialized from my thoughts, the liquid-like depths of his brown eyes scorching.

"You okay, Goldilocks? I didn't think it was possible to sneak up on an angel."

I force a small smile and shrug. "Just thinking."

"You're worried." Reaching up, he grazes a thumb over my cheek. "Your mouth gets all pinched whenever you're worried."

"Aren't you?" I breathe, trying not to let my voice wobble.

Exhaling, he retracts his hand from my face and redirects his fingers to his hair, brushing the thick locks back from his forehead. "Honestly? And I hope this doesn't tarnish my image too much as the coolest guy in the room, but I'm shitting bricks over here."

A smirk pulls at my lips. "Well, you're the only guy in the

room, so…"

He huffs out a laugh but says nothing.

Silence swells between us like a physical force; if I were to extend a hand, I'm certain I'd be able to touch it. The claustrophobic sensation it stirs within me reminds me far too much of the Council's cage—of near invisible walls and an endless landscape on the other side, taunting freedom and eternal confinement simultaneously. Because beyond those walls, there was nowhere to go, and that's how I feel again now. Like we're stuck in one frozen moment when all I want is to go back to our usual banter and not have this constant terror hanging over our heads like a guillotine, the blade always one second from falling.

My eyes scan over Caleb's features, and although he's much better at hiding it than I am, I can read the fear on his face. I can sense what he's afraid of as clearly as if he said it in words.

Reaching up to cup his cheek, I say, "I won't let Mammon hurt you. I promise."

What good is being an angel if I can't use this strength and power to protect the person I love? Caleb has always been there for me, has risked the wrath of Alexander and the Council for my freedom, and now, it's my turn to be there for him—to ensure he makes it out of the coming war alive, even if it means sacrificing my immortal existence for his mortal one. I don't want to think of a future where we aren't together, but if the cost for him surviving is my life, then it's a price I will happily pay.

An unfamiliar pain I've never seen before flashes across his face, which contorts into an expression that's somewhere between a frown and a grimace. Grabbing my hand, he gently pulls it away. "That's not all I'm afraid of."

My pulse picks up speed at his casual dismissal of my touch, and I shake my head, confused. "If you're worried about the Council imprisoning me—"

"It's not just that," he interrupts, the words soft. There's a strange edge to his tone that knots my stomach.

A million questions race through my head when he doesn't elaborate, and as the silence stretches again, I'm overcome by the sickening temptation to break into his mind—to reach inside his skull and pull out whatever thoughts he's so reluctant to voice. But I don't. I couldn't.

I wouldn't, I vow. Because I am not Alexander, and I will not use force to get what I want.

Blowing out a strained breath through his nose, Caleb finally puts me out of my misery. "Yesterday, after you spoke with your parents, your dad came here to talk to me."

"Oh," I mutter, not quite sure what to make of that. "Why didn't you tell me before?"

A sheepish look crosses his face. "I've been processing what he said, but now, with us leaving soon to meet the Council and everything so up in the air..." His eyes bore into mine, piercing, and the words that follow are equally sharp. "We need to talk about it, Luna."

We need to talk. How many times have I heard those words in my life? How many times did they preface the decision to abandon me—to thrust me back into a system determined to see that I would remain alone? How many times have they made me feel like I'm not worth fighting for? Like I'm unworthy of love?

Is that what this is? Is Caleb giving me up?

Did I get my parents back only to lose him in the process?

I blanch, feeling suddenly unsteady, like the whole world might tip to the side and throw me off into space, gravity be damned.

"Are you…" My throat thickens. "Are you breaking up with me?"

"What?" Eyes going wide, he reaches for me, his fingertips searing into my skin as his hands flatten on both sides of my face. When he next speaks, his voice is a growl. "*No*, Goldilocks. Never—"

"Then what is it?" I demand, hysteria creeping into my voice. As much as I'm trying to keep it together, I'm on the brink of freaking out. "What did he say to you?"

His fingers tremble against my cheeks. "I love you, you hear me? And I want nothing more than to get through all this bullshit with Gramps and the Council and spend a million lifetimes with you. But…" My heart buckles at that word.

"We'd love to help you, but…"

"We can see how hard you're trying, but…"

"We know what we said, but…"

But…

How many times have I been fed false hope for that single word to then rip it away?

"But what?" I rasp when he doesn't continue.

Caleb winces. "But…as much as I wish that, we're temporary. One day, sooner or later, I'll die, and you…" He shakes his head. "You won't."

I suck in a startled breath, unprepared for this conversation and hating that our current circumstances are forcing us to have it. Caleb's mortality has crossed my mind a few times, but never like this—never as an immediate problem to be solved. I suppose I assumed it was something we'd talk about eventually, but not yet. Not so soon into our relationship when our time together is only beginning.

"You say that like it's something we need to worry about right now." I gesture vaguely toward the doorway. "Look at Hammurabi. Look at Alar—" My chest tightens, and I stop myself before his name can fully form on my lips. Pushing past the pain in my heart, I continue, unashamed of the pleading note to my tone. "Look at any of the Nephilim we know who have walked this earth for *thousands* of years. We have so much time."

Do you? that unwelcome voice of doubt taunts me. *The Council may kill one or both of you, and if they don't, Alexander will certainly try.*

"Maybe," Caleb mutters, averting his gaze. "But do you want

to spend thousands of years with me only to spend thousands more mourning my death?" He looks back up at me and leans in, his voice low. "I will take however long I can get with you, Goldilocks. Ten years. Ten decades. Hell, I would take ten minutes with you if the alternative was nothing. Nothing will ever make me leave your side...unless you tell me to go."

"But I'm not telling you to go!" I shriek.

"I know," he says, nodding. "I know. But you need to understand what awaits us at the end of this. Because as much as I wish otherwise...we have an expiration date, baby. And as much as I want to be selfish and say fuck it, I can't knowing that it might hurt you. I would rather die now than leave you with that kind of grief because I know how much it would hurt me if the roles were reversed."

I claw at his hands, feeling the heat of his skin under my fingertips. "You say you'll take any time you can get with me... Can't you see I feel the same?"

Agony paints his face, his frown deepening. "I just don't want you to feel trapped. Talking with your dad made me realize it isn't about what I want. It's about what you need, and you need to know you have options. I need you to know you always have a choice."

A choice? As if I could ever envision a world where I wouldn't choose to be with Caleb.

"And you think us being together isn't my choice?"

He considers me for a moment then shrugs. "After everything

you told me about the Creator, I started thinking… If Lilith is right and He *was* the one who placed you in the human world, then what else is He responsible for? You said it yourself—all signs point to Him wanting you to release Alexander and trigger the prophecy, which means He also planned for us to meet. And if that's the case, then chance didn't bring us together, fate did, and I…"

Hearing my own conclusions spewed back at me this way, from Caleb's perspective, is like a knife twisting in my gut. The realization forming in my head only sinks the blade deeper. "You're worried your feelings for me aren't down to free will?"

Free will means everything to Darks—to Caleb—and if he believes what we have is in direct contradiction to that, then where does that leave us? Could he continue to love me willingly if he thought he never had a choice in the matter?

A strained laugh parts his lips. "For the first time in my life, I don't actually care. I'll take these feelings, regardless of where they came from, and I'll hold onto them for as long as I live. I meant it when I said I would take any time with you I could get. But you…Luna, you have forever. I just want you to be happy. *Always*. Even if that happiness isn't with me."

Anger tears through me, hot and fierce. Anger that Caleb could ever doubt my devotion to him. Anger that my father's words and the Creator's manipulations—however well-intentioned both might have been in the grand scheme of things—tangled together to poison him with such thoughts.

"Listen to me," I say slowly, "because I'm only going to say this once. The Creator might have drawn us together, but there isn't a single possible scenario where He could have *made* me love you. Don't you think if He had that kind of power, He would've stopped Lucifer from rebelling?"

Hope flickers behind Caleb's eyes, and I see his will to fight this—to be selfless when I would rather he be anything but—wavering just a little.

"I love you because of you," I persist. "Because I *want* to love you, not because fate or some deity neither of us have ever seen forced these feelings on me. And since what I said yesterday didn't convince you, let me say it again: regardless of what awaits at the end of this, I will always choose us…even if we don't have forever. I *love* you, and I would rather spend one Nephilim lifetime together than never be with you at all." I curl my fingers around his in a vise grip, willing him to hear me. To believe me. "I'm not afraid of your mortality, Caleb."

"Luna…" He exhales my name, muttering the word like a wish, and this time, when silence rises between us again, it's filled with a mutual desire and need that neither of us can ignore any longer. And understanding.

Understanding that we are meant to be together, and this love is our choice.

Stepping back, he tugs me away from the window, our eyes clashing as he brushes one hand against the side of my neck, his touch a kiss of skin on skin as it trails from the nape of my hairline to the dip in my collarbone, mere inches from my racing heart.

The caress of his fingertips sends a shiver rocketing through me, and it takes all the willpower I possess to not leap at him and attack his mouth with mine. To give into the animalistic urges inside me and take what I've wanted since the very first moment I saw him. His lips part, his tongue darting out to lick across the lower one, withering my restraint and tempting me closer.

An almost primal, base desperation pushes all inhibition and nervousness I might otherwise be feeling aside, leaving only the deep love and yearning I feel for him. I'm done wasting time not taking what I want, and I'm sure Caleb feels that way, too, especially when we have no idea what will happen moving forward. We might not get another chance if we don't seize this moment.

The column of his throat shifts when he swallows, and his dark eyes gaze down into mine, hooded and heady with the same lust rushing through me, overtaking every one of my senses. Lust we've both kept at bay for too long.

But no longer.

"I choose you," I murmur. Then rising onto my toes, I close the distance between us, slanting my lips over his. A perfect fit, as if we were put on this planet and molded to always come together. His arms snake around my torso, drawing me closer, and as his fingers travel upward, skimming under the straps of my tank top, I slide a hand under his shirt, teasing at the waist of his pants. His body buckles slightly and he lets out a strangled breath, pulling away just enough to look at me.

"We have time," he breathes, and I relish the sentiment, though I don't know if I believe it. I want to, but reality might have other ideas, as will Alexander. "We don't have to—"

I press a finger to his lips. "I want to."

His pupils blow wide as I slink backward, and hands shaking, I pull the tank top over my head before dropping it to the floor at my feet. Standing before him this way, I'm exposed, and as his attention falls to my chest, my cheeks flush, but I'm not embarrassed. I *want* him to look at me. To see me in this vulnerable way no one else has ever seen me before. To know that I want to give myself to him completely, now and for forever.

After appraising me for a moment, he reaches out and drags a knuckle along my side, a smile teasing the edges of his lips when I shudder. "You are so beautiful." The words are a throaty purr, and drawing me back into his embrace, he kisses me with fervor, every slide of his tongue against mine pitching me deeper into a euphoric haze I don't ever want to emerge from.

My hands reach out to grip the hem of his shirt, and when our lips break apart, I yank it over his head. I falter for a moment, appreciating the sight of his sleek muscles and the way the shadows of his aura dance across his bronzed skin in anticipation, begging me to touch him again. I comply, relishing the soft exhalation escaping him as I run my fingertips along his chest. Unable to contain myself any longer, I press a kiss to every single spot my fingers touch, eager to mark him. To claim him.

To make the world know he is mine.

Dragging his fingers through my hair, he lures my mouth back up to his, one big hand cupping my breast as his lips trail biting kisses along my jaw and throat. Then bending down, he hooks his arms under my legs and lifts me, pivoting until my back is facing the bed. Crossing the room in two great strides, he deposits me on the mattress, and I lie back against the blanket as he crawls over me on all fours, his black hair falling into his eyes as he once again looks down at me, taking in every inch of my naked torso. Bending down, he presses a feather-light kiss to the top of my stomach, and a sound that's half gasp and half giggle bursts from me unbidden.

Peeking up at me through thick lashes, he smirks. "Are you ticklish, Goldilocks?" I can't find the words to answer before he's kissing me in the same spot again, then lower, even more gently than before. Then lower again. With every kiss, my giggles lessen until the only sounds leaving me are near-silent and ragged.

When he reaches the waist of my jeans, he unfastens the button and hooks his thumbs into the belt loops before carefully tugging the denim down my legs, the scratch of the material against my skin an assault on my already overstimulated senses. I hear the low thud of the pants pooling on the floor after a moment, and I'm acutely aware of their absence as his lips graze my knees, my thighs, my hip bones, moving ever closer to where the heat building inside me is strongest.

"Caleb," I gasp, not even sure why I'm saying his name.

In the space of a breath, he's leaning over me again, his face close to mine and expression serious. All manner of teasing is gone from his tone when he asks, "Do you want me to stop?"

I jerk my head, too flustered to form a coherent thought.

He peers down at me for a moment, examining my face with intent as if checking to see if I'm really okay with us taking this next step. If only he knew how much I want this—want *him*. But I don't trust myself to say the right words, so instead, I press up onto my forearms and kiss him again, letting him know what I want with my actions instead of my voice.

He moans into my mouth when I raise a hand and brush it over his abdomen, dangerously close to his waistband, but the heat of his skin disappears all too quickly as he inches backward off the bed. I stare up at him where he looms over me, chest heaving, watching with wide-eyed wonder as he unfastens the button on his jeans.

As he frees himself, my gaze dips to his obvious arousal, and my cheeks heat further.

Climbing onto the bed again, he slides an arm under my back, pulling my chest flush to his. "We can stop at any time. Just say the word."

"What word?" I ask, breathless.

Caleb chuckles, dropping his forehead to my chest for a

moment before peeking up at me, his own cheeks rosy. "I was thinking a simple no would suffice. But if you must know, my safe word is unicorn."

I snort. "Unicorn?"

"Mmhmm." He leans in, brushing the tip of his nose against mine before licking across the seam of my lips ever so gently, as if asking permission to kiss me again—to slip inside and claim me the same way my body is dying to claim his.

I open my mouth for him, and as I swallow his kiss, he slides a hand over my thigh, making my insides quiver. When he touches me, I gasp and he devours the sound, kissing me deeply. But soon, his touches alone aren't enough. I want more. I *need* more.

I want him more than I need air to breathe.

"I'm ready," I whisper against his lips.

He draws back to look at me. "I love you," he rumbles, his voice thick. He clears his throat. "More than anything."

I smile at him, unable to contain my elation knowing we've finally put all doubt behind us, and the next time he kisses me, we join in a way we haven't before, his movements slow and careful, part pleasure and part pain. It's the most overwhelming sensation I've ever experienced, and with every touch, I feel undone, like I might explode if I don't find a release. The feeling is both stifling and exhilarating, and the nerve endings in my body all scream in unison, begging for more. More stimulation. More heat.

More Caleb.

For the first time since finding myself in this world of celestial beings, I can picture what Heaven must be like and I know this is it for me. Here, lost in the warmth of his arms, where I am happy and loved. Nothing will ever be better than this. Nothing will ever compare. And in this moment, I know I would give up my wings if it meant never having to live a single day without him. If it meant I could live a mortal life with him rather than an immortal one where he won't always be with me.

Tears slip from between my closed lids. Everything Caleb said about the future has evoked a fear I wasn't quite ready to face and a dread that this thing we have together will be but a blink of an eye in the endless tides of my existence. I hate myself for thinking it, for ruining this perfect moment with such distant worries, especially after my own protestations about not caring about his mortality.

And yet, I can no longer ignore the reality that time will eventually tear us apart. That one day Caleb will die and this love—this sweet, beautiful bliss—will be gone.

Stifling a sniffle, I bury my face in his neck and rest a hand against his side, determined to savor every moment we have. However fleeting they might be.

"Am I hurting you?"

It takes me a moment to realize Caleb has stopped moving, and when I lean my head back to look at his face, apprehension floods the dark depths of his gaze.

"You're crying—"

I shake my head, squeezing my eyes shut. "I'm just…"

Scared. I'm just scared.

Scared of losing this.

Caleb grips my chin with his forefinger and thumb when I try to turn my face away, keeping me still. "Luna, look at me," he pleads, and at the trepidation in his voice, I open my eyes, glancing up at his worried face through my tears. The intensity of his gaze makes my stomach flip flop. "We can stop whenever you want—"

"No!" I nearly shout. "Please," I beg when he begins to pull away, my hands grasping at his back, holding his body to mine. "I don't want to stop. Really."

Brow furrowing, he sweeps an errant strand of sweaty hair behind my ear. His thumb lingers on my cheek, grazing the skin, then moves to my chin again, pressing firmly. "Then what is it?" he asks, his breath hot on my lips.

A tear dashes from the corner of my eye.

I love you so much I never want this to end, and my heart hurts knowing that one day it will. That I'm powerless to keep you with me.

That's not true, that small voice reminds me, and I shiver with revulsion at the picture forming in my thoughts of Caleb's father right after I killed him. At the memory of how Alexander then resurrected him as if it was nothing. Another image follows the first, reminding me what I'm capable of.

The moth in the Serapeum.

No. I shiver again. *I won't do that.*

Why not? the voice prods. *Then you won't have to lose him.*

But it wouldn't be him. Not really.

I don't dare utter these thoughts aloud, so instead, I say, "I love you. I just really, really love you."

A grin tugs at his cheeks. "You are the best thing that has ever happened to me, Goldilocks, you know that? And this…" With an airy laugh, he dips his head again, his sable hair brushing my chest. "You don't even know how fucking happy I am right now."

"Really?"

At my disbelieving tone, he raises his head, his eyes blazing with lust and love. "Yeah," he purrs, his grin widening. "You feel so good, I could seriously stay like this forever."

Forever.

That word knocks the air from my lungs and strips me bare of the pleasure I should be enjoying right now instead of this suffocating, premature grief. I don't want to feel this way. I don't want to mourn an eventuality so far in the future it's almost inconceivable. And yet, now that I've been forced to face it, I do.

I mourn it more than I mourn Alaric.

When my face falls, Caleb's smile disappears, as if he's realized his mistake. Shaking his head, he says, "I'm sorry. I didn't—"

"It's okay," I whisper. "I just got overwhelmed. I promise I'm not trying to ruin this."

"You aren't," he says. Then he leans down, pressing his mouth to my ear. "I love you. Nothing could ever ruin this." His next words are a tantalizing hum just loud enough for me to hear. "Now, let me show you how happy you make me."

He shifts his face, capturing my lips in a bruising kiss, then moves his hips again, setting every inch of my body on fire. Each slow, deliberate movement is ecstasy, driving me toward an unfamiliar brink. And as I lose myself to his touch, I let myself forget my fears, if only for a moment.

eight

CALEB

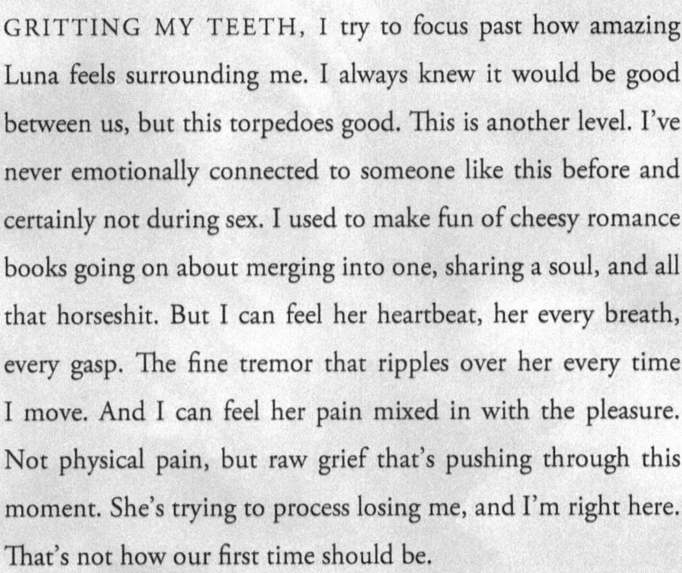

GRITTING MY TEETH, I try to focus past how amazing Luna feels surrounding me. I always knew it would be good between us, but this torpedoes good. This is another level. I've never emotionally connected to someone like this before and certainly not during sex. I used to make fun of cheesy romance books going on about merging into one, sharing a soul, and all that horseshit. But I can feel her heartbeat, her every breath, every gasp. The fine tremor that ripples over her every time I move. And I can feel her pain mixed in with the pleasure. Not physical pain, but raw grief that's pushing through this moment. She's trying to process losing me, and I'm right here. That's not how our first time should be.

I want her to forget her own name until *my* name is all she remembers. I want her to exist in just this moment. And I think I know how to do that. I grip her hips and roll, placing her on top of me.

The sudden move lands her firmly in the present. She blinks wide eyes at me. I squeeze her delicious butt and grin.

"What are you—"

"Do you trust me?" I say, even though I know the answer.

"Of course, I do. You know that," she says, biting her lower lip as her eyes track down my chest.

"Then take what you want from me," I tell her, sliding my hands down her thighs and back up again. "Take control."

That's what this is about. Luna feels like everything in her life is beyond her control. She's caught up in some bullshit prophecy, designated to be a savior, and she didn't ask for any of it. Now, with my mortality messing with her head, there's another element to add to the list of things she has no say over.

A blush stains her cheeks and streaks downward until it paints her beautiful breasts a pale cherry. Mmm. My eyes dash up to meet hers, and I let her see how much I want her.

"I don't know how to," Luna whispers.

"Yes, you do. You've imagined it a thousand times. I know you have because I think about you like this all the time." I smirk. "Have your wicked way with me."

It's as if my words free something inside her. Her wings burst from her back, swooping around us. I shudder as the velvety feathers brush my skin. She clenches my wrists and bends over me, placing my hands by my head. Her mouth fuses with mine as she begins to move her hips. Experimentally at first, then faster, her movements frantic. I groan inside her mouth. She feels too fucking amazing.

She releases my lips and falls back, her pupils swallowing the hazel of her irises.

Panting, she says, "Help me, Caleb."

I know exactly what she wants. I sit up and tangle one hand in her hair and kiss her again, the other hand sliding between us. She grinds against me as I move my mouth to run my tongue along her neck, her chest, and back to her lips while my fingers dance. Her moans are the sweetest music. She's not quite there yet, and I grit my teeth to hold on. No way am I coming before her.

My eyes open, snagging on her wings. I slide my hand up her stomach, causing her to whimper in dismay. My other hand slides from her neck and she cries out when my fingers sink into the luxurious feathers of her wings and caress the upper curve of muscle. My touch is firm, and she arches against me, crying out again as tremors rack her entire body. Her wings unfurl to their full span, pewter feathers glistening. A soft, golden glow encases her entire body, like the beginning of a sunrise. I growl and finally let go, my vision washing white. Honest to fuck ringing fills my ears as all my senses are wiped out by the best orgasm of my life.

I fall back and she sinks against me, her feathers splayed over us like a blanket. I'm trying to catch my breath, and I feel her chest rise and fall rapidly against mine. "Jesus, baby, you killed me," I say, grinning when her head pops up and her eyes meet mine.

"You killed *me*," she gasps as a flush colors her cheeks.

I shut my eyes against temptation and squeeze her against me. "We killed each other," I amend and feel her shift, her lips brushing mine in a tender caress.

"Thank you," she whispers, and my eyes pop open once more. She's so goddamn sexy when she's satisfied, her body all loose and pliant. Her eyes are clear and tender, missing the darkness that so often haunts her.

"For what?" I say, cupping her cheek.

"For making this perfect," she answers, delivering a kiss into my palm. "For getting me out of my head."

"Goldilocks, it was never going to be anything but perfect between us," I say. "I was always going to make sure of that." The way we felt together…perfect doesn't cover it.

Then it hits me like a sledgehammer. I just came inside Luna without a fucking condom. Me, Mr. Safe Sex. Fuck. Noticing my frown, Luna tenses, and I smooth my thumb against her cheek, soothing her.

"What's wrong?" she asks, her eyes locked on mine.

"With the sex? Like I said before, perfect. You own my dick," I say, and a shocked giggle escapes her. I smile at the sound then sober. "I just realized that we didn't use protection," I admit, watching her face. Her eyes widen and she sits up, stunned, pulling away from me.

Luna shakes her head, her skin paling. "I didn't even…oh,

my God, I…we can't…"

I sit up, too, and take her into my arms. "Good news is I doubt I knocked you up—I don't think. I mean, from what I've learned, Nephilim don't procreate easily with each other. That's why there are more human/Nephilim offspring. But we don't have a real big population, as you know. I'm not sure about angels, but I think the principle would hold. Anyway, best to ask your auntie Lilith. Whatever you do, don't ask Gabriel." My muscles tense as I imagine that conversation. "Though, she probably heard us and is plotting my death," I mutter and Luna turns red.

Then she relaxes a little and nods. "I'll ask Lilith about it as soon as I can." She blushes then at her eagerness, and I chuckle, chucking her under the chin.

"I knew it. I've created a sex fiend. I even made you glow," I tease, and her eyes go wide at that. Brushing a quick kiss across her lips, I say, "We just have to be careful, not celibate. But first, I need to be a gentleman." I gently untangle myself from her limbs as she looks at me with a questioning gaze.

Like all these ancient places, there's no shower, but I find a water basin and a clean cloth. I wring the cloth dry and return to bed. When Luna realizes what I'm about to do, her cheeks turn fiery.

"No, Caleb, I can do that myself," she shrieks in protest, hands trying to ward me off.

"You're cute when you're embarrassed, which considering

what we just did, is hilarious," I say. "Stop that and let me take care of you."

I clean us both up, and my eyes assess her naked body with a predatory gleam. She's flawless. I legit wish she'd never put clothes on again. She stills at the hunger in my gaze, her chest rising and falling rapidly once more. Grabbing her ankles, I pull her toward the edge of the bed and sink to my knees.

"Caleb, what are you—" she gasps, clenching my shoulders.

I glance up at her. "I said we just have to be careful, not celibate. And I want to make you feel good again. Are you okay with that?" She didn't let me spend nearly enough time here before. At her shy nod, I growl, "Sit up a little so I can touch your wings."

Her pupils blown, she obeys, trembling. I lower my head as my hands snake up, my fingers burying themselves in silky softness. "Fuck," she says, moaning, and I grin against her skin.

nine

LUNA

MY STOMACH IS A tangle of nerves as we walk along a dusty path lined with low-cut shrubbery, approaching a simple-looking rectangular building. Although somewhat unimpressive on the outside, the Queen's Bath in Hampi is exquisite and ornate on the inside. Covered walkways surround the four sides of a large sunken bath, decorated with beautiful arches and alcoves that form balconies over the empty space in the middle. It's now little more than a ruin turned tourist attraction, but once the structure would have been filled with water and used as a bathing spot for royalty.

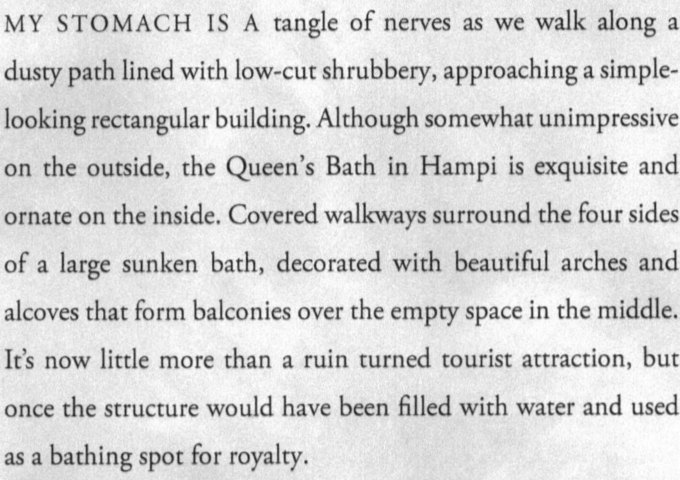

Kali suggested the bathhouse as a neutral spot for our meeting with the Council due to its proximity to her home at Virupaksha Temple, should we need to make a quick escape back to our temporary hideout. We're too vulnerable on the Roads, which provide little cover were we to end up in another lengthy pursuit like what happened after Caleb broke me out of my prison and Mammon chased us across the globe. This way, in the event our gathering doesn't go as planned, we're close enough to flee on foot. Unlike the Roads, the real world has plenty of nooks and crannies to hide in.

The downside is that this meant Kali couldn't join us to avoid compromising our refuge since the Council keeps tabs on all the Fallen and Nephilim and where they reside in the world—a countermeasure in case they ever need to do any damage control and alter human minds, my mother explained. While the logic behind the decision made sense, I can't help wondering if the ancient Light was relieved to be sidelined from our impending confrontation. Even with my parents, Caleb, and a frowning Hammurabi accompanying me, I know I'd sit this one out if I could. But I can't. They're all involved because of me, and this war is only occurring at all because of my misguided actions. Because I let Alexander out of his tomb without really understanding what I was about to unleash on the world.

Granted, the Creator intended for that to happen, so I can't help feeling He should shoulder some of the blame, but He's not the one down here on Earth who needs to clean up the mess.

Swallowing, I step through one of the archways lining the cloister forming the outer perimeter of the building and proceed down the narrow stone stairs into the spacious empty bath below. Overhead, the morning sun is blazing despite not even being at its highest point in the sky yet, and sweat prickles my skin, though I'm not sure if that's down to the oppressive heat or the fear gripping me—likely the latter since the other angels and Fallen present seem unaffected by the sky-rocketing temperature. Come to think of it, I don't think I've seen my mother look so much as dewy. Perhaps, unlike certain other mortal needs that confinement in the Council's cage forced me to abandon, I'm stuck with this one lingering habit. Physical proof of the terror I can never quite shake.

Even now, that terror coils around my lungs like a snake as my eyes dart in every possible direction, searching the ruin for any sight of the Council, but there's no one here apart from our small party of five—not even mortals. Then again, it is the off-season for tourism and the humidity is atrocious.

Although Beelzebub and Abaddon are on our side, along with at least a handful of other Fallen, my father stressed that it was vital we don't give the Council any reason to think we're calling them here to declare war. This meeting is meant to result in a truce, not give them further reason to hunt us, and the best way to achieve the desired result is for Abaddon and Beelzebub to partake in this exchange from the side of the Council and speak up for us when the timing is right to turn the remaining members in our favor. As for Lilith and the six Fallen who arrived yesterday to declare their support, they're lingering somewhere nearby out of sight, just in case we need them. I hope it won't come to that.

"Are we ready?"

Lucifer's lilting voice draws my gaze, and I glance between

him and my mother, who dips her chin, her expression and golden aura unwavering and resolute.

Behind me, Hammurabi grunts. "No time like the present and all that," he grumbles.

"Daughter?" Lucifer presses, his blue eyes burning with fatherly affection and concern. The shadows surrounding him writhe and dance, reaching out to me as much as the limits of their movements allow.

I try to swallow again, but my throat is almost painfully dry, the insides of my mouth gritty. It feels like I've been gargling sand, and I struggle to form a response as the snake around my lungs squeezes tighter.

Stepping in front of me, Caleb cups my face and bends down until his gaze is level with mine. When our eyes meet, I'm reminded of what we did last night, and the memory gets wrapped up in my panic until my body is a tempest of chaos and longing and heat, the emotions and sensations within me at war. "It'll be all right, Goldilocks," he murmurs. "I'm here. *We're* here. No one is going to take you again, I promise." His thumbs rub soothing circles on my cheeks, pushing down the inflating anxiety in my chest.

I drag in one deep breath then another, and on the third exhalation—the air pushing past trembling lips—I manage a weak but hopefully convincing nod. I turn my focus to my father, but he's no longer looking at me; he's looking at Caleb, envy written into the perfect contours of his face.

There's approval there, too, but the jealousy is what I notice most, though it isn't malicious or resentful so much as sad, as if seeing Caleb comfort me is just another reminder of all the time and bonding we've missed out on as father and daughter. I wish I could find the words to tell him that he's important, too—that I *need* him, too. That while he might not be the prime pillar of support I lean on, he is becoming a vital part of my foundation—the base the rest of me relies upon to stay standing. If anything were to happen to him, stealing away that beautiful song connecting us, surely everything that makes me what I am would crumble to the ground in ruin. I already lost one father figure. I can't bear to lose another.

And the truth is, that's what frightens me most, not just about meeting with the Council, but about this whole ordeal with Alexander. The Gray already stole Alaric from me. Who else am I inevitably going to lose before this war is over?

Pushing that thought aside before it can cripple me, I clear my throat and say, "I'm ready."

Lucifer, shaken free from his own silent musings, rolls up one sleeve of his charcoal button-up shirt then gestures for us to stand behind him before pressing a fingertip to a pale white symbol branded into his forearm just beneath the crook of his elbow. Low mutterings breach his lips, and déjà vu ripples through me as I recall a similar moment under the Serapeum when my mother, wounded and bleeding out on the stone in front of Alexander's tomb, called out to my father the very same way. Even their tattoos are identical—thin crescent moons, barely visible against their fair flesh. Just like then, apprehension pools in my unsettled stomach like curdling milk.

And just like then, the Council is sure to come.

We don't have to wait long. A couple of minutes later, a burst of bright light floods the sunken bath and the first angel steps from the radiant depths of the Blessed Road into the scorching Indian sun. When the blinding light fades and the figure's features slide into focus, it takes all my self-restraint not to recoil.

"Uriel," my father purrs with a respectful bow of his head.

The Archangel's golden aura brims with contempt as he locks eyes with Lucifer, but he says nothing, instead redirecting his gaze over his shoulder when the entrance to the Blessed Road once again opens and five other Archangels emerge from its glowing maw. Behind them, I sense movement in the shadows of the cloister and note dark, looming shapes filling the archways above us, surrounding the empty bath on three sides. My eyes jump between the Archdemons, catching and hanging on Mammon as I search the faces above us for Abaddon and Beelzebub. The fear sweeping through me hardens like ice in my veins when I notice Mammon's crimson gaze is locked intently on Caleb, his upper lip curling back in a snarl. He looks furious and I shudder, consumed by the thought of what danger I've put Caleb in by bringing him here. He didn't have to come. He could've stayed behind with Kali or waited out in the wings like Lilith. He didn't need to be here, front and center, a target to the Archdemon's wrath.

But it isn't in Caleb's nature to cower in fear, and I know I couldn't have made him stay behind even if I tried. Not that it would've changed anything. Regardless of Caleb's presence here today, he stole something precious from Mammon, and I doubt a truce with the Council will stop the Archdemon from leaping at the first opportunity to make him pay for it. My wings bristle under my skin at the thought, thrumming with restrained power.

When that time comes, I'll make sure I'm ready.

Tilting my chin up, I inch closer to Caleb until I'm also in Mammon's line of sight, meeting his furious gaze with a scowl and glaring at him until he breaks our battle of stares with a disinterested scoff. Relief floods my system—as temporary as I fear it may be—and remembering the task at hand, I peer through the shadows once more, finally glimpsing Abaddon among the Council, his poker face firmly in place. Beelzebub, on the other hand, is nowhere to be seen—a fact that hasn't gone unnoticed by the others on the Council who raise curious eyebrows and mutter his name softly under their breath in question to each other. If I wasn't so certain of his loyalty to my father, I might wonder if his absence is a sign he intends to stab us in the back.

"Brothers, sisters, thank you for coming," my father says, tugging me away from such thoughts, his soothing voice echoing through the empty space.

The tapping of shoes against stone draws my gaze, and my stomach turns as I force myself to look at the angel who orchestrated my mental torture in the Council's prison. Mammon might've been the one in my head, tricking me with his many false faces, but it was Uriel who held his leash. He and he alone tried to use my worst fears against me as a bargaining chip.

Hands clamped loosely behind his waist, the Archangel steps toward my father. "I assume, Morningstar, that you have not called us here to surrender yourselves or your daughter?"

Lucifer lets loose a soft, breathy chuckle. "Wishful thinking on your part, I'm afraid." Although I can't see his face, I can picture the easy smile he must be wearing. The calm, collected poise and confidence of someone who isn't afraid.

Which, of course, only infuriates Uriel.

The Archangel's own expression darkens, but before he can say another word, one of the other Faithful steps forward. The man's skin and hair are a stark lily white—made brighter by his simmering golden aura—and his blue eyes are so pale in color they look almost gray, closer in hue to ice than the sea. His hands are fisted at his sides, and two red patches spread across his cheeks like blooming roses, staining his features with the evidence of his anger.

"Then tell us, Brother, why have you summoned us if not to surrender? Are you declaring war?"

"Of course not, Amenadiel," my father assures him. "My intention is to bring us all together, not drive us further apart."

"Together?" Amenadiel retorts. His upper lip quivers as he spits, "You have *betrayed* us. You have consorted with Gabriel—a *Light*—and actively worked to undermine our authority." His eyes cut to my mother then. "And *you*...the bearer of the prophecy. How righteous you have acted all these years when in reality you harbored such a filthy secret."

My mother reels back as if she's been slapped but Lucifer just snorts, raising his face to the sky, and whispers, "Consorted..." so softly I'm not sure the others hear it. But I hear it, along with the blatant disbelief constricting his tone. It squeezes the word with a sorrow and heartache that are reflected in the wavering darkness around him, which sags as if pulled down by a heavy weight, making the shadows almost look like they're weeping.

Chest rising and falling with a sigh, he looks back down at the other celestials. "Tell me, were we not all Lights once?" he asks. "Were we not, at one point, all the same? This senseless division between our kind needs to end."

"Careful, Morningstar," Uriel warns, clicking his tongue. "You're beginning to sound an awful lot like Alexander."

"He is *nothing* like the Conqueror," Gabriel hisses. When she speaks, flashes of light crackle around her like bolts of electricity, and her irises glow an otherworldly orange I've never seen before. She marches forward, trying to push past my father toward Uriel, but Lucifer holds out an arm, stopping her.

She looks up at him, fury etched into her face like a chisel to stone, but he just shakes his head.

"Unlike Alexander, I desire peace, not war." There's a hard edge to Lucifer's voice that begs anyone listening to disagree. "And despite what I'm sure many of you might think, I do not wish to see another Fall. I only want the freedom we Fallen fell for all those long years ago…and the freedom to live that peace how I choose." He takes Gabriel's hand then, eliciting a number of shocked gasps from the Council, though no one looks quite as stunned as my mother, who blinks up at my father, confused. Her expression is an eddy of disbelief, terror, and doubt.

"With *whom* I choose," he adds, interlacing their fingers, and I can't suppress a smile as the fear in her face gives way to hope.

A hope that is quickly shattered when a dark-haired Archangel—*Serathiel,* I remember, recognizing her from that fateful day under the Serapeum—barks out, "Your blasphemous words are a mockery of everything we have worked toward for thousands of years. Need I remind you, Gabriel is not Fallen, Lucifer. She does not possess these freedoms you speak of—"

"Which is why our laws need to change," he bites back, his knuckles whitening as his grip on my mother's hand tightens.

A sudden movement to my left draws my attention, and a lean Archdemon with freckled, tan skin and inky black hair jumps down into the bath from the shadows of one of the archways above. His face is all hard planes and sharp angles, like those of high-fashion runway models, and his deep green eyes are hooded by thick sable brows. "Have you not already sullied this world enough with the one offspring you share?" He sneers, his eyes darting between my parents. "Or will you keep testing the limits of the divide and put us all in further peril? The prophecy—"

"The prophecy is why we are here, you ignorant fool!" My mother's outrage booms through the bath, and I can feel the tingle of the electricity that swirls around her again like static in the air. It presses against my skin, a pressure filling the space that threatens to shatter the stone underfoot and bring the whole bathhouse toppling down.

Caleb loops an arm around my waist, pulling me close to his side, and I'm certain he can feel it, too.

"If I am ignorant, it is only because you have made us so with your half-truths and deception," the Archdemon snarls.

"Enough!" Lucifer bellows, and a sudden chill clings to the air, banishing the overwhelming heat and making me shiver. Above us, the clear sky grows dark, and shadows stretch across the stone, laid atop the ruins like a blanket. It only lasts for a moment, but it's long enough to silence everyone present. "Neither I nor my daughter are the real threat you fear," he continues once the sky brightens again. "And we did not summon you to waste time slinging insults at one another. Though"—he stalks toward the Archdemon who last spoke, and this time, when the shadows descend, they congregate around where he pauses with only a few feet between them, lending menace to his tall form—"I will warn you, Belphegor, say one more negative word about my daughter, and it *will* be the last thing you say. She is a blessing to this world, and we are here to prove it."

"A *blessing*…" The Archdemon stares at Lucifer, mouth agape. "Have you lost your mind?"

"My goodness, I do *not* miss this," trills a familiar voice, and I glance up in the direction it came from, shielding my eyes from the sun—more out of reflex than necessity. My stomach flips when I spot Lilith sitting perched on the crumbling balustrade on the low open roof overhead, her legs encased in skin-tight black leather, dangling over the edge, crossed at the knee. A cunning smile twists her scarlet red lips.

"What is she doing?" I mutter under my breath.

I peer up at Caleb, catching his eye, but he just shrugs. "Fuck if I know," he whispers back.

Considering who Lilith sided with the last time Alexander started a war, her presence before the Council could endanger our chances of actually getting them to agree to a truce. That's why she was supposed to stay out of sight until *after* this meeting. Until *after* we convinced them Alexander is the real enemy to our kind, not me. Until *after* we had a chance to tell them the ex-Archdemon has switched sides.

"Lilith?"

I recognize the Archangel who speaks, noting the strawberry blonde tones of her hair and the way her delicate brow is furrowed as she stares up at the roof in disbelief. She was also there the day I released Alexander, but I can't recall her name.

Pursing her lips, she cuts her eyes to my father. "What is the *traitor* doing here, Morningstar?"

Lilith jumps down into the bath, landing with the steadiness and grace of a cat despite wearing dangerously thin stiletto heels. To my amazement, she doesn't even wobble.

Rising like a phoenix reborn from its ashes, she struts forward, waving an indifferent hand. "I could hear your senseless bickering from miles away. It's a wonder you haven't attracted the attention of every creature in the country."

A glower contorts the female Archangel's face. "Why don't you go back to whatever hole you crawled out of—"

"Sticks and stones, Raphael," Lilith simpers. Then, with a tinkling, mischievous laugh, she says, "Oh, don't look so put out. I promise, your words have positively *wounded* me."

"Remove yourself from this congregation, Lilith," Uriel warns, "or we will—"

"You'll what?" she challenges, pausing mid-step. "You'll take my wings?" When he says nothing, she rolls her eyes and crosses her arms. "I see nothing has changed. The lot of you are still sanctimonious bores. Seriously, Lucifer," she throws over her shoulder, "at this rate, the war will be over before you've even negotiated the damn truce."

"Truce?" The word leaves Uriel in a skeptical huff. "Is that why you called us here? Desperation has driven you to delusion, Morningstar."

"This is a trick," a deep voice growls, and my eyes snap toward the archway just above the Archangel's left shoulder. Toward Mammon, who has been unnervingly silent until now. An ominous shadow darkens the bloody hue of his gaze.

"I assure you, Brother, it is not a trick," my father says. "Nor delusion," he tosses at Uriel, unable to keep the frustrated bite from his words, "as I am hoping you will come to agree that a truce is in all our best interests."

Incredulity paints the Archangel's face. "How can there be a truce when you have broken our most sacred law? When you stand against the Council you swore to uphold?" His dark eyes flash behind Lucifer then, to where Caleb and I stand back with Hammurabi, not yet daring to utter a word. "The boy with you…he is of the Conqueror's blood, is he not? The one who aided your daughter in his liberation? Not to mention the *traitor* in your midst," he adds with a derisive sneer at Lilith, "who so loyally stood by the Conqueror the last time we were faced with such madness. So, tell me, Morningstar, how can you seek a truce with us when your allies of choosing have aided the enemy? Unless you, too, have joined Alexander and this is merely a ruse?"

"I have not joined Alexander, Uriel," my father snaps, losing his patience, the shadows around him vibrating. "I called this meeting because we must stand against him. *Together.* As for young Caleb, he is here for the same reason we are—to unite and overcome this threat to our world and our kind. And while it's true he helped to free Alexander, his only crime was being easily led. He was not alone in his actions, and he did not know what he was unleashing."

"So that excuses it?" Raphael asks through clenched teeth.

"No, but how can we punish ignorance?" Lucifer counters. "We neglect to teach our young of these dangers and then punish them when they break laws they knew nothing about. How is that just or right? Besides, thanks to both the boy and Lilith, we know where Alexander is hiding and have a better understanding as to his numbers. I am certain, as the Council, you are eager to possess such knowledge. Knowledge I am willing to share, should we reach an…understanding."

Mammon lets out a sharp laugh, the sound abrasive and cruel. "Or use to lead us all into a trap."

Whispers echo throughout the large space and my pulse hitches, racing under my skin until my heartbeat is everywhere at once. I clench my jaw, frustrated. The angels and Fallen argue like I imagined immortals would—like they have all the time in the world when time is the one thing we don't have. Lilith was right. This is getting us nowhere, and at this rate, Alexander will make his next move long before we make any progress with the Council. I glance toward the shadows of the cloister again, meeting Abaddon's watchful gaze. If there was an ideal moment for the Archdemon to intervene and put in a good word for us, it would be now.

With a barely perceptible nod in my direction, he jumps down from the ledge and crosses the empty bath to stand beside Uriel, drawing everyone's bewildered attention. "You are all willfully choosing to ignore the one question we should be asking," he says, looking at my mother. "You said you're here because of the prophecy, Messenger. So, what of it? What tidings from the Creator do you bring to us now?"

She hesitates, and I watch her side profile as she looks up at my father, noting how she licks her lips and the way her throat shifts when she swallows. Is she nervous? The thought is almost laughable, but then, I suppose unearthing a several-thousand-year-old lie that has affected the lives of literally all of our kind is bound to rile up some nerves.

With an encouraging nod, my father squeezes her hand and she nods back, letting out a deep breath. "I do not come with new tidings…but old ones." At the confused mutterings of the Council, she says, somewhat louder, "I have not been forthright with the full extent of the Creator's warning. When I told you of the prophecy those long years ago, I only delivered half of His words. The truth is, He spoke not of one Gray but two. A Destroyer and a Savior…destined to meet in battle, which will ultimately decide the fate of our world."

Everyone is silent for an uncomfortable moment, and I follow the glances shared between a handful of the Council members, searching for any sign of intrigue or the barest hint that they're open to the possibility presented before them. To my dismay, a sharp laugh breaks the tense hush.

"And you expect us to believe your daughter is this Savior?" Amenadiel asks with a dismissive titter. "Why should we accept your words as truth when you have just admitted to *lying* about the prophecy—a deception you have kept up for nearly as long as we have been on Earth?"

"I lied to *protect* our kind," Gabriel seethes, a flush of indignation sweeping up the back of her neck. "I was pregnant when the Creator first delivered the prophecy, and the timing of it made me believe it was His way of punishing me for faltering in my faithfulness to Him." There's a fleeting pain in her tone that clenches my heart—that makes me worry she will never be able forgive herself, not only for her actions with me but with Lucifer—but she forces it behind her usual icy persona. "I knew my daughter wouldn't be born a Light, that she would be different, having the blood of both factions, and as such, I feared she would grow to become the Destroyer the Creator spoke of. So, I did what was necessary and I locked her away where she wouldn't be a danger to us."

To my horror, there isn't a single sympathetic face in the bathhouse. To think, these unfeeling angels are the ones responsible for shaping so many young lives.

Gabriel continues, undeterred. "Then, millennia later, Alexander appeared…and I began to have doubts. But even then," she growls, "I did not release her."

"Then who did?" Serathiel presses, arching a dubious brow.

"If the child was locked away as you say, then how is it she stands before us now if you did not release her?"

Every eye turns and settles on me, and I still under the combined weight of the Council's inscrutable gazes. I know I'm supposed to be strong—that I need to prove I'm a force to be reckoned with, on equal footing with the immortals before me—but I can't seem to force myself to speak. To stand up for myself, even though I want to.

To my surprise, Lilith is the one to speak for me. She crosses the bath and stands to my left, throwing her arm around my shoulders like we've known each other forever. I suppose, on some level, that's true.

"Because the Creator did," she explains. "Can't you see? He wanted all this to happen. He released Luna without anyone knowing and made it damn near impossible for anyone to find her in the mortal world…until the moment came when He wanted us to."

"Like a Dark transfer entering the Serapeum on a mission to find and free his grandfather," Gabriel adds.

Uriel balks. "You are implying the Creator *intended* for these children to meet and release Alexander?"

"I had assumed that was obvious, yes," Lilith answers, a sweet, mocking smile upturning her lips.

"But why?" Raphael asks, exchanging panicked glances with Serathiel. "Surely, He would desire another war between our kind even less than we do."

"He doesn't. But a war between the Destroyer and Savior is the only way to unite our kind again…and we believe that is His intention," my father grinds out, the words rife with the same bitterness I heard in his voice when he swore he would go to war with the Creator should anything happen to me.

"Unite…" Uriel rolls the word on his tongue for a few seconds before understanding dawns, and a harsh, accusatory scowl mars his features. "You mean destroy the divide."

"No, not destroy. *Heal* it," I blurt out, finding my voice. Panic strips my senses raw, but I persist, and closing my eyes, I recite the one part I remember verbatim from the prophecy. The one part that haunts my every thought with a daunting purpose I feel too small to live up to. "'Should they embrace their strength, the Savior will reign victorious and return peace to the Faithful and Fallen, healing a rift believed to be irreversible. But should they fail, the Destroyer will emerge triumphant and the human and celestial worlds will be forfeit.'"

Lids fluttering open, I lock eyes with Uriel, who stares at me, his expression unreadable. His dark eyes scan my face with keen perusal before fixing on my parents again. "How convenient that would be for you all, wouldn't it? Tell me, Messenger, why should we believe your words now when the tidings you deliver, claiming to be gospel, would serve to benefit only you and those you hold dear? And if what you speak of is, in fact, true, then how do we know your daughter is the Savior and not the Destroyer the Creator spoke of?"

"For fuck's sake, haven't you already been through this once?" Caleb groans, pushing sweat-slicked hair back off his forehead. "My grandfather wishes to rule us, not free us. Does that sound like a Savior to you?"

Belphegor snorts. "And we're supposed to believe this *girl* is the Savior? You'll forgive me for having my doubts as to this measly whelp's ability to go to arms with Alexander."

"Which is why we called this meeting," Lucifer states, his calm, level tone completely at odds with the violent, murderous thrashing of his aura. If such a thing were possible, I'm certain the black and violet tendrils of shadow would lash out and choke Belphegor into silence. "Not just to beg for a truce… but your help."

Uriel narrows his eyes at my father. "And if you're mistaken about the girl? If we offer you aid and neutralize Alexander only to discover she is the real threat? If you are wrong and she is the Destroyer, you will have doomed us all."

Terror trickles down my spine, and I shiver as I'm finally forced to acknowledge the one fear I can't bring myself to face. That it isn't only this war, or imprisonment, or Caleb's mortality that frighten me, but that everyone I care about is wrong about who I am. *What* I am. Caleb. Alaric. My parents. Even Hammurabi, who had no reason to fight at my side but has stood by as a loyal protector, even at the risk of his own safety. I never wanted or asked for any of this, but at least by being the Savior, there was a glimmer of hope. A shred of peace in believing I am good and not the monster I spent seventeen years believing myself to be. But if I'm not...

If I *am* the Destroyer...

Then I deserve every second of eternal punishment Caleb rescued me from.

Out of the corner of my eye, I track Gabriel's movements as she pulls free of my father's grip and crosses to where Uriel stands a short distance away, silent judgment rolling off the Archangel in waves. Reaching over her shoulder, she pulls her sword free from the invisible scabbard on her back but makes no move to attack the Archangel. Instead, she slowly drags the sharp edge of the blade along her palm, opening the skin until blood drips onto the cream-colored stone.

Then, lifting her chin, she holds out her hand.

"If that proves to be true, you can have her...and we will no longer stand in your way."

ten

CALEB

GABRIEL'S WORDS HANG IN the air along with the scent of her blood, and rage fogs my brain. What the actual fuck? She did not just offer up Luna on a silver platter to the Council. A rabid wolf has better maternal instincts than she does. Goldilocks stills next to me, her muscles locked tight, and I hurt for her.

"Are you out of your goddamned mind?" I snarl at Gabriel, anger pounding through me as I take a step forward. I don't give a shit that she's an Archangel and I'm just a lowly Nephilim. Or that the entire Council is witness to my anger. You don't offer your kid up to your enemies. That's just *Parenting 101*.

Luna places a delicate hand on my forearm, stopping me. "It's okay, Caleb," she says, giving me a faint smile.

A chiding huff escapes Hammurabi's lips. "Boy, calm yourself. No one is taking the flower anywhere because she's not the Destroyer, and we all know that, especially her mother."

My eyes clash with Gabriel's, and she gives me a grim nod. Okay, maybe she has to say that bullshit for the Council to take her seriously. I still don't like it, but I snap my mouth shut. United front and all that. Reaching out to Luna, I squeeze her hand, but she's already relaxed. Guess she has more confidence in her mom than I do.

My gaze shifts to Uriel, and I scowl. The Archangel was a big player in Luna's psychological torture, so I hate him on sight. He sneers as he regards Gabriel's sword. "I find it ironic that for all your insistence that you're not here to declare war, you've certainly arrived armed for one."

Gabriel releases a scornful laugh. "As if you didn't arrive armed as well. Stop with your useless stalling. Are you going to accept my offer or not? I won't make it again."

Uriel pulls a blade out of thin air—or maybe his ass. Something has to be wedged up there to account for his shitty attitude. He cuts open his palm and holds it out to Gabriel. His eyes hold a hint of malice. When she clasps his hand, he says, "Betrayal is no longer an option now, Messenger."

Ah, now, I get Gabriel's oath and some of my anger loosens. Her eye-roll is epic as she draws her hand away. "It's just like you to state the obvious."

Raphael's eyes flick to me for a moment, then she glances at Gabriel. "Now that the dramatics are out of the way, I'm curious. Do you always allow little Darks to speak to you in such a disrespectful manner?" Her lips curve into a condescending smile.

"This little Dark managed to cut off the mighty Mammon's wing," Gabriel purrs. "Why don't you think on that before you speak about matters you don't understand."

Raphael's eyes widen, and her head whips around to meet Mammon's now blazing red gaze. The hulking Archdemon is framed by one of the bathhouse's delicate pointed arches, but there's nothing delicate about him. The heat of his fury is blistering, and it takes everything in me not to step back. The lanky Archangel pivots to study me.

"Well, I guess you really are the Conqueror's blood, although Alexander would've taken his head as well as his wing. Lucky for Mammon, you're not Alexander," Raphael says to me, then her smile turns poisonous. "But I think being unable to fly is worse than death, so maybe he's not so lucky after all."

I blink. Wow, the Council is so full of love and sunshine for one another. I'm really getting the warm and fuzzies just being around them.

Lilith tosses her hair and gives Raphael a bored look. "Oh, it's so good to be back amongst you again. How I've missed the malice and backstabbing all in the name of world order."

"Enough," Lucifer hisses, arms crossed over his broad chest. His shoulders stiffen, and I'm sure he'd like to bust a few heads. "To stop Alexander, we must work together, unless all of you relish being under the yoke of the Conqueror. No? Then let's play nice, shall we, like the good little angels we all used to be."

His head jerks toward Mammon. "And don't get any ideas, old friend, about killing the boy. He's under *my* protection."

"And mine," Gabriel says, shocking me. After my outburst, I wasn't expecting the back up. I give her an apologetic smile when she looks over her shoulder.

"And mine," Luna declares, twining her fingers through mine. Damn, I didn't think she could get any hotter, but protective Luna just proved me wrong. Man, do I love this woman.

Mammon's lip curls as his eyes peruse Luna, but he tilts his head in deference to the Messenger and the Morningstar. "As long as we have a truce, he's safe enough from me."

I don't believe him, but Lucifer just gives him a nod. Hell, they've known each other since the beginning of time, so I guess the Morningstar can tell when Mammon is lying. I hope. But then again, even if he's lying, would it matter? We still have to work together.

Hammurabi mutters out of the side of his mouth, "Keep eyes in the back of your head, boy."

Sweat trickles down my neck, and it's not just from the oppressive heat. Well, that confirms it. Mammon is lying, and I have to make sure I'm never alone with the murderous asshole.

"Now that we've all decided to play nice, perhaps we should wait for Alexander to make a move," Raphael suggests and Uriel nods.

Out of the corner of the bathhouse, where the shadows are thickest, darkness pools out like an inky puddle spreading across the stone. The liquid puddle rises, swirling, and out steps Beelzebub. I grin. Man, that is the second dramatic entrance that little dude has made in as many days. "My, my, I suppose your intel isn't up to date," Beelzebub says. "I thought your spy network was better than that, Raphael. How disappointing. The Conqueror *has* made his first move. Ashkelon lies in ruins at Alexander's hands, and he's taken the children *and* the weapons." Stunned murmurs ripple around the open space, but the ancient tween ignores them. "I was lucky to escape with one of my loyal Nephilim after we were ambushed. We must act now and swiftly to protect the other academies before he targets them, too. I think even we can all agree that Alexander amassing weapons from the Fall is quite terrifying."

Uriel frowns. "Why didn't you report this to us immediately?"

Beelzebub sneers at the Archangel. "I went back to look for survivors and to see if any children had managed to hide. I don't know how you Lights run your schools, but Darks don't leave their people behind."

Uriel growls at him, baring his teeth, and the Archangels visibly bristle at little B's words. Here we go again, but to my surprise, sanity prevails as Uriel manages to overcome his anger and ask, "Why destroy the schools? Why not just take the weapons and the children? That kind of destruction can draw unwanted attention from mortal eyes."

Luna lifts her chin and stares her tormentor down, and pride puffs my chest out. Lucifer is right: she's solid steel. "He wants to burn the divide. Literally. He wants our kind united again, but not in a true alliance—not as equals, at least not to him. He just wants us united enough so he can rule over all, regardless of if we're Light or Dark. If we're all banded together in fear, he doesn't have to worry about an uprising from either side. Considering this isn't the first time he's tried this, I thought that would be obvious," she says, mimicking Lilith's earlier statement.

I hide my smirk at her snark. Go, Goldilocks.

Uriel gets his panties in a twist at her mocking tone. "Perhaps it's obvious to you, Gray, because you think like the Conqueror."

"Or maybe because she exhibits intelligence," Lilith shoots back with a saccharine smile.

I can't help it. I hold my other hand out, making a fist and presenting it to the saucy ex-Archdemon, but she just gives me a blank stare. I sigh. But Luna gives my knuckles a tap, grinning. Lilith rolls her eyes at both of us.

"Just so you know, you were equally awesome," I tell Goldilocks in case she doubted.

"Oh, I know," she says pertly, which makes me want to strip her naked again as soon as possible.

Uriel opens his mouth, his lips twisted into a snarl, but Gabriel interjects smoothly, "Whether he's bothered by unwanted attention from mortals or not, our children are in danger—as are we once those weapons are dispersed. We need to evacuate the schools and empty the armories and museums."

Serathiel, clad in a fitted suit, black hair clipped short, scowls at Gabriel. "Yes, we must act swiftly. This is a potential disaster for us and the world."

Beelzebub barks out a laugh. "Way to state the obvious, Sister."

Lucifer ignores the pissy tween and says, "Yes, we must act now and form teams to evacuate the schools. You must return Asmodeus to the fold. We need her."

Leviathan, a massive Archdemon who is the size and breadth of a sumo wrestler without the fat, chuckles at Lucifer's demand. His blue-black hair is pulled into a half ponytail, highlighting his inky eyes, which are so dark and liquid they border on creepy. "I don't think so, Morningstar, not until you prove that this isn't some elaborate ruse to save your daughter. We need something from you to cement our alliance."

My jaw drops as I regard the overgrown Archdemon. I guess Gabriel bleeding and swearing a fucking oath wasn't enough. I glance at Luna who rolls her eyes. "Of course they do," she mutters, and I suppress a laugh.

For the first time since we've begun these negotiations, I see Hammurabi get pissed. He delivers a death stare to Leviathan, and I can almost spot steam curling from his ears.

"Asmodeus is one of you," he spits. "She does not deserve to be imprisoned because she had the wisdom to see what Luna really is."

Wow, he actually said Luna's name. He's furious.

The angel of death, Azrael, who's been silent this whole time, cuts in. "I always had a touch of envy for Asmodeus for possessing such a loyal hound," he says, and Hammurabi stiffens at the insult. Asshole. Too bad Azrael didn't keep his trap shut. "But we don't trust you. Your motives are suspect at best and selfish at worst." His dark eyes focus on Luna, his reddish-brown skin gleaming. I think the Native American tribes based their pantheons on him. "Evacuate your respective schools and Babel and bring us the Nephilim and the weaponry. Then we'll release sweet Asmodeus." He sits back, eyes darting to meet those of the other Council members.

"Agreed," Uriel says, "and that means you return your swords to us, too." His last words are directed at Lucifer and Gabriel.

"How shall we fight Alexander then? With harsh language?" Lucifer retorts. "We can't evacuate our schools with our power alone. We need angel-killing steel."

I almost laugh at how the Council members collectively flinch. Mammon, however, just stares at me, hatred and menace emanating off him like cheap cologne.

"Having just battled Alexander, I know we can't go into the academies unarmed. Perhaps a compromise? One of you can travel with us, sword in hand, and aid with the evacuation. That way you can witness for yourself what's happening and keep us in check, as you so love to do," Gabriel offers with an icy smile.

Raphael's grin holds razor blades. "As you so loved to do as well, Messenger. Don't be a hypocrite. It doesn't suit you, and you did more than keep us in check. I thought deception was more your lover's forte, but you wear it well." Gabriel's face darkens, and I straight up think she's going to slap a bitch when Raphael adds, "But that is acceptable to me. I'll accompany you."

Mammon's ruby gaze latches onto mine. "And I'll accompany you, Lucifer."

Beelzebub bares his teeth at the larger Archdemon. "That's not necessary. I'll accompany the Morningstar. It's my right to seek vengeance."

I wonder if the Council has any idea about little B's real loyalties, but as my eyes pass over their faces, I realize they don't have a clue about Beelzebub's alliance with Lucifer. Damn, the spymaster is good. Luna catches my eye, and I know she's thinking the same thing. I'm glad no one is questioning B's real motives to go with Lucifer because I plan to hitch a ride with them to help with Babel's evacuation—I've got friends there—and I'd rather be with the pissy tween than the murderous Mammon.

"Not to point out the obvious," Luna says, drawing the eyes of everyone. She swallows bravely before continuing. "But shouldn't you begin the evacuation of your own schools, too? We don't know where Alexander is going to strike next." Her eyes dart to Raphael. "How are you going to do that if you're with my mother?"

"Well, I suppose I shall have to persuade Gabriel to stop by Mount Sinai and aid me in escorting my little flock to safety. I would certainly remember such generosity," Raphael says, her message clear.

Gabriel scratches her back and Raphael might be more hesitant about locking Luna away again. Whatever, we have to take what we can get from this group of assholes. We need them to defeat Alexander, but no matter what happens or what Gabriel promised, no one is locking up Luna again.

eleven

LUNA

SILENCE ENGULFS THE SUNKEN bath as the Archangels and Archdemons exchange sullen nods. The Council might not be fond of this new peace between us, but reluctant or not, it's a truce, and I take some comfort in the safety this ceasefire will bring. Now, at least for the moment, we only have one enemy to worry about instead of two. And maybe, with the Council's help, we can eliminate the threat hanging over all our heads before too much damage is done.

"What of the Gray?" Mammon calls out, his voice grating, cutting into the hush like a serrated saw through bone. I shudder as every eye swings toward where he hangs back in the shadows above, thick brows drawn low over that gleaming red gaze. "Where will she be while her parents are preoccupied with the evacuations?"

"With me," my mother announces before I even have the chance to consider that question. I've been so worried about this meeting, I didn't spare a thought for what would come after it. Or what part I'd play beyond my fated role as the prophecy's Savior—and that's what the Council will expect me to be or I'll find myself with a one-way ticket back to an eternity in that glass egg. Either that or they'll just kill me to avoid me becoming a second Alexander. Gabriel might have bought us some time—and allies—with her promise to Uriel, but that time will mean little if I don't figure out what I'm meant to be doing. Regardless of what anyone expects of me, the real trouble is, I don't know *how* to be a Savior, and I certainly don't know how I'm going to save anyone, let alone the entire world. I can't even seem to save myself. Hell, at this point, I'm little more than a piece on a chessboard, being moved around by one side or another with no apparent free will of my own.

Mammon's gaze narrows on my mother. "You expect us to trust—"

"I gave you a blood oath," Gabriel interrupts. Though her words are a growl, her voice is clear. "That should be proof enough I won't go back on my word." A soft, humorless laugh parts her lips as she peers down at her hand, the sliced skin already stitched back together. "I couldn't now, even if I wanted to."

"Worry not, Brother," Raphael says, giving the Archdemon an impatient look. She slinks across the space toward my mother, and her slow steps remind me of the orderlies back at the hospital who would always hover nearby in case one of the patients needed restraining. Pausing an arm's reach from Gabriel, Raphael snaps her eyes over her shoulder, locking me in the heat of her stare, as her lips twist into an unnerving smile. "I will keep an eye on the little bird."

"Then it is agreed," Uriel barks, his commanding tone putting an end to any further objections. He turns in a circle, taking in each Council member's face. "Depart to your respective schools and evacuate the children and retrieve the weapons at all costs. Once the task is completed, we will reconvene." His eyes cut to Lucifer. "Your next actions will determine the veracity of your claims here today."

I blink, glancing between the glowering Archangel and my father, feeling like I'm missing something. Beside me, Caleb clears his throat.

"Reconvene where, exactly?" he asks, sounding just as confused as I am.

Gabriel scoffs, flipping her raven hair over her shoulder. "A location that will be disclosed, I assume, once the Council is adequately convinced this has not all been some elaborate ruse."

"Indeed," Uriel says, plastering on a forced smile that raises the hairs on my arms. "For your sake, let us hope that is not the case, Messenger. And that, this time, your warning has not come too late."

There's a beat of silence, then a flurry of movement erupts around us as the Archangels and Archdemons vanish into their respective Roads. Of those not accompanying us, Uriel and Mammon are the last two to leave, and as the Archangel steps into the blinding glow of the Blessed Road, he shoots one final warning glare at my mother before his dour countenance is swallowed by light, and the opening seals behind him like a zipper. Mammon lingers a moment longer, his eyes burning like flames in the shadows. They dart between my face and Caleb's as he steps back into the embrace of the darkness.

A breath whooshes out of my lungs once the Council is gone until I remember Raphael is still here, her watchful gaze looming over our party, and my heart rate escalates once again. Licking my lips, I look at Gabriel out of the corner of my eye then back at the other Archangel, waiting to see who will make the first move.

Raphael spares a split-second glance in my direction, giving a delicate sniff of disdain, before pinning the full weight of her gaze on my mother. "Time waits for no one, Messenger. Let us be off." Turning slightly, she trails a hand through the air, as if feeling for that invisible zipper. At the touch of her fingers, radiant light pours across the sand-colored stone, opening the Blessed Road.

Smirking, the Archangel steps back from the entrance and gestures with a dramatic sweep of her arm for Gabriel and me to enter.

I shake my head as understanding sinks in. "But Caleb—" I begin to protest, finally registering that by going with my mother and Raphael, Caleb and I will be separated. As a Dark, he can't travel the Blessed Road, and I know Gabriel would never let me go with him on the Shadow Road. Nor would Raphael, who is looking for any reason to distrust us. The only alternative is Caleb meets us at the Serapeum, but there's no way in hell I'll let him take the Shadow Road alone—not when Alexander's minions could be out there lying in wait. Which leaves only one option.

He doesn't come at all.

Crossing the distance between us, Gabriel brings her mouth to my ear, lowering her voice to a barely audible whisper. "I cannot shield him on a Road I'm unable to travel," she murmurs, echoing my thoughts. "*You* are my concern, Daughter." Then, slightly louder so Caleb can hear, she adds, "Caleb will be safer with his fellow Darks." I don't ask if that's because she would leave him behind in a heartbeat if doing so meant protecting me.

Swallowing, I follow her piercing gaze to my father, who nods, as if he can sense my concern. But although I trust him— trust the song humming between us—the thought of leaving Caleb behind with him doesn't bring me any peace.

Tears blur my vision. "We said we'd go together," I whisper, turning to look up at Caleb, remembering the night at Babel after he rescued me and how he said we wouldn't be separated again.

With a frown, he brushes his knuckles against my cheek,

stroking me gently. I sigh at the touch of his fingers on my skin as he leans in, touching his forehead to mine. "I know, and I wish we could, but..." He trails off, tensing his jaw, as if he wants to say something else but thought better of it. He remains this way for a moment then says, "Don't worry about me, Goldilocks. I'll be fine. Just...stick to your mom like glue, you hear me?" I don't miss the warning edge to his tone, which only makes the snake around my heart coil even tighter.

"Worry not, little Dark," Lilith coos, stroking a hand through my hair. I almost forgot the ex-Archdemon still stood beside me. "I will keep an eye out for our dear Luna," she says, winking at me when I look over at her.

Gabriel arches a dubious brow at that, and Lilith gapes at her, affronted.

"Oh, you didn't think I would stay behind, did you?" Nostrils flaring, she hisses under her breath, "Someone will need to watch both your backs, and I don't trust Raphael as far as I can throw her." As she says this, she directs her dark eyes to where Raphael lurks by the Blessed Road entrance, watching us.

My mother lets out a resigned sigh and nods. "I'll be glad to have the help."

Lilith's lips peel back into a mischievous grin. "Nothing will scare the little Lights into the Blessed Road faster than a Fallen on their doorstep."

Heart racing, I glance at my mother then Caleb. "If Lilith is coming, then Caleb wouldn't be alone on the Shadow Road.

He could come with us," I plead.

My eyes flash to Lilith, whose mouth splits into a simpering smile. "I suppose he could tag along if he likes. Don't worry, boy. I don't bite. Much."

"As fun as *that* sounds," Caleb begins, shooting a finger gun at Lilith, "I'm going to follow G's suggestion and go with your dad, Goldilocks. I have friends at Babel, and I need to make sure they're okay."

"You don't have to go at all, you know," I breathe, desperation forcing the words out in a rush. "You could go back and wait with Kali." *Where it's safe.* I don't say that last part aloud.

Caleb's mouth pinches into an even deeper frown until the look he gives me borders on a scowl. "Is that really something you think I'd do?" He cocks a wry eyebrow, and I feel myself flush.

"No," I say quickly. "…no. But if Alexander is there—"

"He'll what? Kill me?" Caleb snorts. "Tell me something new." He rolls his eyes, but I wince at his words—at the fear they instill in me with every breath and with every moment that takes us closer to crossing paths with his grandfather again.

Caleb must notice my expression because his hands are on my face again in a heartbeat, and he's bending down until our eyes are on the same level.

"Hey, look at me," he murmurs, brushing the warm pad of his thumb over my lower lip. "I'll be okay, I promise. Besides, good ol' Hammurabi will be with me, won't you?" He flashes a look to his left, and I follow his expectant gaze to the Babylonian king, who crosses his arms over his broad chest and nods.

"I will watch out for the boy," he rumbles.

"As will I," Lucifer seconds, stepping forward.

Caleb moves back as my father approaches, surrendering his place before me—perhaps out of respect for the Archdemon or to give us some space to say a proper goodbye. Tears prick my eyes at the thought. We've had so little time together, and I can't help fearing it's all we'll have. That this will be the last time we see each other, the song in our hearts destined to go silent.

As if sensing my fears, Lucifer draws me into his arms, pulling me into the comforting warmth of his chest. "We will be together again soon, I swear it," he whispers in my ear.

I want to believe him. I *need* to believe him.

Otherwise, the terror might consume me.

"This is all very touching," Beelzebub grinds out in a growl, "but can we leave now?"

"As much as I hate to agree with you on anything, Brother," Raphael drawls, examining her nails with a bored expression plastered on her face, "waiting for you all to finish mooning over each other and say your farewells is getting tedious. Let's get on with business, shall we?"

Lucifer breaks our embrace, and I glance at Raphael before looking over at the tiny Archdemon, who glares at us like a sulking child on the verge of a temper tantrum. If he wasn't so frightening, I might find it funny.

Sighing, Lucifer meets my gaze again and presses his palm

to my cheek. I rest my hand on top of his. "Be safe," I whisper back, squeezing his fingers.

Nodding, he turns toward my mother. "Look out for her," he pleads. "And look after yourself." A strange energy passes between them like heat, and I watch—torn between happiness and discomfort at the lust in their gazes—as the sparks of their distant past reignite.

Gabriel tilts her chin up, her gaze fierce. "You know I will."

They stare at each other for another long moment, then Lucifer retreats, making for the nearest stairs leading up into the cloister and the thick shadows within. Beelzebub tags along behind him, barking for the others to follow.

A heavy weight presses down on my chest as the reality of the moment fully sinks in, and heart racing, I glance at Caleb, who gravitates toward me again and clutches my hands.

"You better come back to me," I rasp, my voice hoarse. It's a command and a plea rolled into one.

An easy smirk lifts the edges of his lips. "Like anything could ever stop me."

But despite his playful tone, I can tell by the way his aura squirms, pressing tight to his frame, that he's just as uneasy about being apart from me as I am from him.

Tugging free of his grasp, I rise onto my toes and fist my hands in his velvet-soft hair, yanking him toward me until our lips are touching. The move is a bit rougher than I intend but I can't control the panic swelling in my chest. I just need to hold him close for a moment—to brand him on every inch of my soul so I never forget what he smells and tastes like. So I can carry at least that much of him with me.

Not caring that we have an audience, I deepen the kiss and breathe in, letting Caleb's nearness, his touch, flood every last one of my senses. And for this fleeting moment, it's as if we're the only two people in the world. As if nothing and no one could ever tear us apart, even though I know that's not true.

Behind me, my mother clears her throat. "Come now, Luna," she says gently, placing a hand on my shoulder.

I don't even realize tears curve down my face until we pull apart, and Caleb brushes the moisture from my cheeks. "See you soon," he murmurs, and there's a promise in his voice that comforts me, even if my trepidation still lingers far too close to the surface.

He pivots, turning to follow my father, and I watch his retreating figure for a moment before shifting my focus to the ancient Nephilim falling into stride beside him.

"You be safe, too, Hammurabi," I call out, my throat thick.

The Babylonian king looks back and gives me a curt nod. "You, too, little flower," he says, and I swear he offers me the smallest glimpse of a smile.

I watch, my fear like a lead weight in my stomach, as the pair ascend the stone stairs and vanish into the Shadow Road behind my father and Beelzebub.

"Caleb will be all right," my mother assures me, her voice

caught somewhere between a consoling croon and the hard-edged reservation she always wears like armor. "Your father will make sure of that."

Nodding, I let her guide me away, and together, we approach the Blessed Road entrance where Raphael waits for us, tapping her foot. Lilith flanks me on my other side but pulls back before we get too close to the light.

"I suppose that's my cue," the ex-Archdemon says, and with a salute to my mother, she saunters away in the opposite direction, tracing the other Darks' steps toward the stairs. "See you at Mount Sinai," she calls over her shoulder, then she, too, disappears into the shadows.

A shudder races through me at how alone I feel now with only Gabriel beside me, all our other allies departed. Apprehension hardens in my gut as my eyes turn to Raphael, not exactly a friend or a foe, but certainly not someone either of us can trust.

Lips pursed, the Archangel glowers at us. "Took you long enough," she grumbles when we finally step over the threshold of light into the Blessed Road.

Immediately, I'm consumed by warmth, and the touch of the Road's radiance on my skin as we walk, passing marker after marker, takes my mind back to the last time I traveled this path…and forces me to picture the person who was there at my side. The crushing memory of Alaric's face is a weight on my chest I can't take on right now. Not when the anxiety building under my skin already threatens to pin me to the ground.

"What's Mount Sinai like?" I ask, eager for a distraction from the thoughts that seem determined to keep me confined in my panic.

Although Raphael is the headmistress of Sinai and best positioned to answer my question, I look to my mother, my brow raised in question.

Behind us, keeping several paces back to make sure we don't attempt an escape, I hear Raphael jeer, "Yes, Gabriel, do tell us what *my* academy is like."

Gabriel shoots a scathing look over her shoulder then mutters, "Far more isolated than the Serapeum."

Raphael snorts. Clearly, that answer wasn't sufficient.

Rolling her eyes, Gabriel expands, "There is a human monastery at the base of the mountain… Sinai resembles that but is much larger in scale and far grander. It truly is a sight to behold," she finishes, her voice mockingly reverent.

"You sound envious, Gabriel," Raphael coos. "Or perhaps you're just feeling the loss of your own academy?"

That stops my mother in her tracks.

"Loss?" I echo, pausing beside her.

My eyes shift to Raphael, who practically purrs as she says, "Your mother has broken the law, little bird. As has your father. And neither have been present to oversee their academies since you freed Alexander." Her lips curve into a menacing grin that's all teeth. "The Council obviously had no choice but to fill those positions with more *worthy* candidates."

Malice drips from every syllable uttered, and my heartbeat thunders in my ears as I contemplate the severity of what Raphael is saying. Of course, I knew my parents were on hiatus from their academies—how could they run their schools when they were physically on the run from the Council? But I never really took the time to consider the bigger picture of what their absence would mean. How could I? Since the moment Caleb cut me out of my prison, everything has happened so fast. I've barely had time to process most of it.

"Does that mean you're not on the Council anymore?" I ask, the words nearly choking me as I gape at my mother, though her eyes—always so sharp and alert—avoid mine. Her silence only compounds my fears, and dread sinks into my bones when Raphael lets out a low, cold laugh.

"That remains to be seen, doesn't it? The situation is rather… *gray*…at the moment. Not as black and white as it was," she taunts, roughly pushing between us. Stumbling, I whip around, glaring holes into the Archangel's back as she continues a few steps ahead—just far enough to encourage us onward but not enough to risk giving us space to flee. Not that we could…or would. The blood oath my mother made with Uriel would likely backfire on us if we tried, and besides, we need the Council's help. Running from them now would be counterproductive. "Come," she crows when Gabriel and I don't resume our forward march. "Sinai draws near."

Still, neither of us move, my feet rooted to the soft, airy

ground underfoot despite the required urgency of our mission. Chest heaving, I snap my eyes to Gabriel, watching her blank, stony face with a growing alarm that rings deep in my bones.

Only Council members preside over the academies, which means if someone has taken Gabriel's place as headmistress… that same person will also inevitably supplant her on the Council, just like Beelzebub replaced Lilith all those years ago when Alexander was imprisoned. While part of me has recognized that my parents' rebellion against the other Archangels and Archdemons has put a strain on their positions, I never considered just what it would mean if they were no longer part of the Council. Or the consequences that would come from their expulsion. Those effects might not impact my father too greatly, but my mother…

"If you're off the Council, does that mean you'll have to go back to Heaven?" My voice is reedy, my tone hollow, and my airways tremble with the returning threat of tears. The only Faithful allowed to remain on Earth are those in charge of the Light academies. If that no longer includes Gabriel, then what's stopping the Creator from calling her back?

It would be almost karmic, I suppose, to have my mother ripped away from me when I'm just finally coming around to the idea of embracing her in my life.

"No," she bites out, the protestation gruff. Glancing up at me, she reaches out, grabbing my hands, and her fingers are cold around me despite the warmth of the light engulfing us.

"Even if it's what the Creator demands, I won't make the same mistake. Not again."

I gape at her, taken aback by the vehemence in her voice… and by the sheer sincerity of her words. She couldn't have made her meaning clearer if she had outright declared her intentions to stay. Hell, she just practically said she's choosing me over the Creator. If there was ever a moment when I sensed Gabriel's affection for me, this is it. And it's enough to make me weep, my eyes pricking with tears of joy. But the moment of honesty and feelings bared passes quickly, and before I know it, Raphael clears her throat and we're trudging forward, progressing the rest of the way to Mount Sinai in total and unnerving silence.

It takes far less time than I imagined it would to return to Egypt—this time to the mountains southeast of Alexandria, not far from the border to Israel—and as we step out of the Blessed Road, exchanging one expanse of bright light for another, I breathe out, the air all but torn from my lungs at the sight of the immense palace before us. There's no other way to describe the grandiose structure built into the mountain face. My mother was right—it does resemble a monastery, but it's so much more than that. And as my eyes trail over the golden roof tiles glinting in the late morning sun, there's a moment when I could swear the Creator is here with us, His presence reflected in the imposing and otherworldly facade of this place, as if we're in Heaven itself.

"Wow." That one word escapes me in a gasp as I step through

the freestanding archway preceding the steep stairway leading up to the entrance.

"Impressive, isn't it?" Raphael asks, a satisfied smirk on her lips. But she doesn't wait for me to answer before continuing onward toward the towering doors up above. Although I'm a good distance away from them still, they give me déjà vu, and I'm struck with a momentary flashback to the first time I approached the Serapeum. Even if everything else looks different, this one aspect—and the uncertainty writhing within me—is the same.

Except…Alaric isn't here.

Swallowing the returning thickness in my throat, I move to follow her, then pause when I hear Gabriel hiss, "Any trouble on the Road?"

I shift my gaze over my shoulder, confused why she would be asking me this when we were together on the Road the whole time, only to find Lilith walking beside her a few feet behind me. I'm not sure how long the ex-Archdemon has been here or if she arrived at the mountain before us, but I'm relieved to see her all the same. My nerves settle a little knowing Gabriel and I have at least one ally here at Sinai.

"None at all," Lilith responds with a sigh, sounding almost disappointed. Her eyes flash between us as we ascend the stone steps. "You?"

Gabriel shrugs. "A little. That is if you count Raphael's incessant chatter," she says dryly.

The ex-Archdemon chokes out a coarse laugh. "I think I'd rather cross blades with every member of the Council at once than fall victim to that."

Silence sweeps over us, and my attention jerks back to the top of the stairs when the doors boom open, the sound a deep rumble echoing through the mountains, the glinting gold parting before us like the Red Sea. Given this mountaintop is said to have been where Moses received the Ten Commandments from the Creator, I can't help wondering if he really existed…or, perhaps, *still* exists. Maybe he's a Nephilim like Hammurabi and Gilgamesh and the others I've met over the last several months. Figures that once existed to me only in history books and myths.

I'm about to ask Gabriel when a woman with bronzed skin and a chin-length obsidian bob emerges from the doorway, her steps clip-clopping across the stone like hooves as she hurries forward to greet Raphael. She falters when she sees us, her brown eyes taking in each of our faces before settling on the Archangel.

"Headmistress, you have returned…with guests," she says once we reach the top of the stairs. The woman's tone is droll and her upper lip curls back in disgust as her gaze settles on Lilith.

Raphael waves away her unspoken concerns. "Unfortunately, we come with bitter tidings, Hatshepsut. We must evacuate the school."

This seems to get the Nephilim's attention. "Evacuate? Why?"

"The potential danger I confided in you about, that I told you to prepare yourself for…it is here. The Conqueror is free again and he has declared war," Raphael says in a low voice filled with warning, and my brows lift at her words. Considering Alexander has been amassing an army for months, it's surprising so many still don't know he's on the loose. Even the Fallen we met with in India said they only heard rumors about Alexander's return, nothing more. I guess the Gray has been covering his tracks well. "We must escort the children to safety and empty the museum at once. The weapons cannot be left behind."

Hatshepsut's lips press into a taut line, and she peers over her shoulder back into the school, staring into its quiet depths for a moment. When she finally looks back to question Raphael further, her voice is equally hushed. "War? You know this for certain?"

"If you require proof, why not visit Ashkelon?" my mother suggests, the words snide. "It's little more than ash and cinders now thanks to the Conqueror."

The Nephilim stumbles back a step, disbelief seeping into the features of her face like spilled ink on paper. She looks to Raphael, her pupils blown wide, and in her stricken expression, I glimpse the one question she's too afraid to ask aloud: *Is this true?*

The Archangel can only nod. "Quickly, Hatshepsut," she commands, placing a hand on the Nephilim's upper arm.

Her touch seems to jerk Hatshepsut out of her shock. She startles, dipping her head, before turning and hurrying back inside the school.

"She's another first generation, I take it?" I whisper to Lilith as we watch the Nephilim's retreating figure. There's something majestic about the way Hatshepsut carries herself, making me all the more certain she's played a larger role in history than whatever her current position is here.

An unexpected smile touches the ex-Archdemon's lips. "And she was the first woman to rule over Egypt. I quite admire her for that."

A flood of respect fills my chest alongside the internal groan trying to quash it. "So, a pharaoh. Why am I not surprised?" Seriously, are all first generations royalty of some kind?

Except Alaric, a small, melancholic voice in the back of my head reminds me.

Stamping it out, I glance at my mother. "What now?"

She shrugs. "This is Raphael's school. I am sure she will give us our orders and tell us where we can all best be put to use." She offers the Archangel a sardonic smile.

Raphael's mouth pinches at the corners. "Messenger, you are to remain in the entrance hall to oversee the children. Hatshepsut will see to it that the other teachers are alerted and the students are sent down here to be organized for immediate evacuation." The Archangel's gaze cuts to Lilith, and she looks her up and down as if she isn't quite sure what to do with the ex-Archdemon. "Lilith…I don't really care. Just don't get in anyone's way. As for Luna, she will come with me to the museum to secure the weapons."

Gabriel's ire erupts with the fury and rage of Mount Vesuvius. "If you think I'm going to let you go anywhere alone with my daughter—"

"We are short on time," Raphael interrupts, "and I do not trust that you won't spirit her away at the first opportunity should I leave you two alone. Nor do I trust Lilith with the students. At least, not unsupervised."

My mother can only bare her teeth before Lilith plants a hand on her shoulder. "Worry not, Gabriel. I will accompany Raphael and Luna to the museum in your stead. Ensure she doesn't traumatize the poor dear." She gives Gabriel a pointed look, which brings whatever reaction that was boiling inside my mother to a less violent simmer.

Clenching her jaw, my mother stares at her friend for a moment before sucking in a breath through her nose. "Two eyes, Lilith," she growls.

"If we are quite finished here," Raphael snaps, "we have work to do and little time to do it."

The Archangel beckons for me to follow, and I share a fleeting glance with Gabriel before tailing Raphael into the school, Lilith following closely at my heels. As we proceed into the palace that is Mount Sinai Academy, I examine the gilded doors in passing, but up close, I can see that the gold and size are the only two things they have in common with the entrance at the Serapeum. Instead of a depiction of the Fall like in Alexandria, here the surface is carved with intricate patterns that I can't make out at first, the lines too tied up in one another to form a clear, discernible picture. It's only once I'm in the entrance hall and I peer over my shoulder, taking them in from a distance on the other side where the pattern is repeated, that it dawns on me what I'm looking at. The lines seem to come together before me, forming…not exactly a shape—especially with the doors still standing open, cutting the completed image in half—but a concept. A feeling of utter beauty.

I don't know how I know it…but something in my gut tells me I'm right.

Maybe because I've seen it, I muse. Nearly eighteen years ago, when I was let out of the tomb my mother locked me in.

"Is that…?"

"The Creator," Raphael answers without slowing her pace, her tone reverent. "As He is perceived by our eyes."

I'm not sure what to say to that, so I say nothing at all as Raphael leads us through wide passageways with high-vaulted ceilings and broad, multi-colored windows, which look out over the mountains. This academy is beautiful—more so than the Serapeum—and there's a heightened feel to the very air we breathe, though that may just be the elevation. I'm not used to being so high up. I don't have much time to appreciate its splendor, however, as the Archangel beckons us to move quickly.

Every hallway we hurry through is empty, and I wonder if the students are all in class at the moment—or on their way now to the entry hall, if Hatshepsut has begun the evacuation. I haven't heard any sounds that would suggest she has, but then she might be trying to avoid a panic. Or outright chaos. That would surely only complicate things. I haven't given much thought to what it will be like leading so many people through the Blessed Road, most of them children, and all of them likely to be scared and very, very confused.

My mother's words to Lilith when we arrived reverberate in my ears, and a sickly dread pools in my stomach. I can only hope we don't run into any trouble, either here or on the Road.

Raphael slows her gait as we approach a set of glass doors, and past the transparent panes, I glimpse white stone bookcases and rows of marble tables run through with veins of glimmering silver and gold. Though it takes my breath away, the library pales in comparison to the sky-scraping grandeur of the one in Alexandria. The thought of my one safe haven at the Serapeum brings me back to a less complicated time when I would spend late nights in a hidden nook between the bookcases with Caleb. Then, my only real worry was that my powers were manifesting in a manner unbefitting a Light.

Now, however, the weight of the world seems to rest solely on my shoulders.

The handful of students present scatter at Raphael's scolding command, leaving the library empty for us to explore. As expected, the main room leads through to the museum, and like in Alexandria, this space is dark, lit by low-hanging hurricane lamps to avoid degradation of the treasures within. Curiosity pulls my gaze to each of the display cases standing in tidy rows, but I don't glimpse any moths inside, or any monuments to the Nephilims' history. Only weapons.

The same weapons we've been tasked to secure.

I startle at a loud *thud*, my heart jumping up into my throat as I look down at the open trunk by my feet, then up at Raphael, who glowers at me.

"You're rather jumpy for a supposed Savior," she scoffs.

Lilith emits a low, threatening snarl, but Raphael just rolls her eyes.

"This will unlock the exhibits," she says, gesturing to the cases around us with one hand while pressing a dull brass key into my palm with the other. "Remove the weapons and put them in these trunks. That shouldn't be too hard for you. And do be quick about it. We're short on time." She points to a second trunk at the edge of the room before stomping off toward another door in the corner. "Oh, and Lilith?" she calls, pausing at the threshold to glare at us. "I'm aware of everything that happens in this room, so I'd think twice before you try anything, or you'll find yourself missing another appendage."

Lilith mutters something unintelligible under her breath. The only word I make out is "Bitch."

We set to work, moving quickly, unlocking each case and removing the weapons to be secured someplace safe—or at least out of reach of Alexander, which is better than nothing. The task is easy, and although I know these blades can't actually cut me except when branded by their owners, it's unnerving to hold them, to be near them. To know, in the hands of the right person, the steel could cut through my skin when no mortal weapon has that power. The thought sends a violent shudder up my spine. The Council might not wish me dead at the moment, but who knows how the other Lights and Darks who haven't sided with Alexander will feel once the truth of what we are is revealed and my existence becomes public knowledge. All it would take to get rid of me is a single one of these weapons and the right bloodline to wield it.

My eyes drift to the door in the corner, watching the shadows for movement, as I inch a bit closer to Lilith. I don't know when I began finding comfort in the ex-Archdemon's presence. It's insane given how little I know her, but she really does feel like family now—like what I imagine an eccentric aunt would be like if I had any experience to draw from. Or, if not family, then at least someone I know I can depend on, even if some of the others on our side still view her as a traitor.

Traitor... That word feels so hateful, so demeaning, like *crazy* always has for me. Does it pain her to know what the Council thinks of her? To know even other Darks see her that way? As someone not to be trusted for a single error in judgment made millennia ago?

I frown. The ostracism I've witnessed her facing reminds me far too much of what I experienced myself back at the

Serapeum…and at every other school before it. Except, she has to bear the added burden of being without her wings. Surely, that alone was punishment enough.

My hands still at that thought, and I suddenly find myself thinking back to our meeting with my father's allies, hearing Beelzebub's voice in my head, of all people. What was it he said about Lilith's wings?

My stomach drops as the memory sharpens.

"Lilith," I prompt, and she looks up at me, arching a brow. "Something Beelzebub said yesterday is bothering me."

"Oh?" She sounds mildly intrigued but only just.

I chew on my lower lip for a moment, not wanting to dredge up bad memories, but needing to understand. To make the pieces in my head fit together. To make the questions burning inside me make sense. "About…" I hesitate, swallowing around the lump in my throat. "About how the Council voted to take your wings." When her expression doesn't so much as flicker, I croak, "Surely, that would've included my mother?"

Lilith nods, though she doesn't look as upset as I imagined she would.

"So, why help her then?" I press when she doesn't speak. "Why don't you hate her, too, like the rest of them? Like you hate my father?"

While the ex-Archdemon has never come straight out and said she hates Lucifer, her meaning was clear enough when we first spoke at length back in Kandahār, and she told me of my origins. But my mother is just as much—or was, at least—a part of the Council. If being stripped of her wings is why Lilith has no love for my father, surely, the same feelings should apply to my mother, regardless of any pre-existing friendship.

"I don't hate her," Lilith begins, speaking slowly, "because she didn't *want* to do it. Hell, she didn't even want to vote. She planned to abstain, but I wouldn't allow it."

"Why?" I ask, jarred by this revelation. Not because I believe Gabriel to be cruel, but because everything I'm learning about her is making me realize she's the opposite. That the cold demeanor she wears like a layer of ice is just to hide her pain. To push people away. But not to hurt them.

To protect herself.

Lilith shrugs. "Because Council decisions must always be unanimous, and I knew no good would come of her refusal to participate. Her abstaining certainly wouldn't have changed my fate. If anything, it might've very well led to her being placed on the chopping block beside me. You know, guilty by association and all that." Clicking her tongue, she looks down at the trunk and carefully wedges in a bronze-hilted broadsword. "I believe that's part of why she volunteered to be Alexander's warden, you know. I think she felt responsible for what happened to me. Yet another burden she carried." She murmurs this last part under her breath.

"She wasn't mad you supported Alexander?" I ask, my voice rife with disbelief as I shove another sword into the trunk. I struggle to envision Gabriel not feeling at least somewhat betrayed about that decision.

Lilith lets out a sharp laugh. "Oh, she was irate. And she attempted, on countless occasions, to make me see reason. I almost relented once or twice, but I couldn't let go of my certainty that Alexander was the Savior from the prophecy, a belief I very much regret now. Fortunately for me, just as she never stopped loving your father despite him choosing free will over Heaven, Gabriel never stopped loving me despite my decision to side with Alexander. She was quick to forgive me."

"And my father?" I press. "When we first spoke in Kandahār, you didn't seem to think much of him. I guess I'm just trying to understand why when it was his side you chose during the Fall."

Lilith purses her lips. "To be clear, I did not choose Lucifer, though I can admit our motivations at the time aligned. I told you about Adam. *He* was my choice. And I live with the outcome of that decision to this day." She shakes her head, letting out a soft sigh. "As for my feelings toward your father, any bad blood between us arose after the Fall. I didn't actually dislike him at first, though—and I'm loath to admit this—I was jealous of the bond he shared with your mother as it reminded me of what I so desperately wished to have with Adam. When Lucifer's rebellion offered me that possibility, I took it, but despite our different allegiances, I *never* abandoned Gabriel. Not like he did. Once she discovered she was with child…although I knew he wasn't aware of you, part of me resented Lucifer for leaving Gabriel in that position. For forcing her to go through her pregnancy alone. For leaving *me* to pick up the pieces of her shattered heart. And it was shattered. Gabriel might have ended things between them when she chose to side with the Creator, but I think part of her always hoped Lucifer would find his way back to her, regardless of the divide, the same way I did. In her eyes, as unlikely as she knew it would be, having him only as a friend was better than not having him at all, but he shut the door on that option." Her eyes darken with sadness, and she averts her gaze as she layers two more swords into the trunk. "Then there was the matter of my wings. While the Council agreed that I should be punished for supporting Alexander, it was the Fallen who would determine how that punishment would be enacted. Darks decide on Dark business, Lights on Light. That has always been the way." A long beat passes before she adds, "The Darks agreed my wings would be forfeit and your father was the executor of their will, though in hindsight, I suppose it was the more merciful retribution when the alternative was rotting for eternity in a tomb. At least, I still had my freedom."

Although I suspected Lucifer might have had something to do with Lilith losing her wings, hearing her confirm it only floods my chest with an aching sense of remorse.

"I'm sorry," I whisper, not sure what else to say.

Lilith snorts. "What for? You did not steal them from me. And in truth, I find myself unable to hate your father as I once did. Not now that I can see how blind I was in my choices. I was foolish, and I have only myself to blame for the consequences of my actions."

"Um…speaking of consequences…" A flush heats my skin, circling around to the back of my neck. If there was ever the perfect segue to ask about unprotected sex, this is it. "How easy is it for angels to get pregnant?"

Lilith's outstretched hand freezes mid-motion, and she looks up again, staring hard at my burning face. I'm about to dive behind the nearest display case to escape her unfaltering scrutiny when a wide grin splits her lips.

"You are smart to come to me about this and not your mother," she says through a chuckle, returning to the task at hand. "She may very well kill the poor boy."

My heart trips on the terror surging to the surface, the panic behind it squeezing the air from my lungs. The twin daggers in my grasp clatter to the floor at the thought of Caleb at my mother's mercy, a victim to her maternal wrath.

"You won't tell her?" I squeak, not quite sure if I'm asking or begging for the ex-Archdemon's silence.

Lilith arches a brow. "And risk finding myself in her warpath? No, thank you. Even I am not immune to your mother's temper."

I nod then tentatively pick up the weapons I dropped, carefully lowering them into the trunk, before moving on to the next display and doing the same again. Lilith mimics my movements until both trunks are full to the brim and the surrounding cases are empty.

"Is that everything?" I ask.

"Seems like it," she mutters with a glance around the cavernous room. An exasperated sigh parts her lips. "Let's go inform Raphael we've finished."

"Okay."

Closing the lid, I lock the clasps on the second trunk then follow Lilith across the dimly-lit space toward the door in the corner where we last saw Raphael. As we move, neither one of us utters a word, and in the tense hush, my thoughts drift to Caleb. The sooner we finish here, the sooner we can move on to the Serapeum. And the sooner we evacuate everyone there, the sooner he and I can be reunited. As concerned as I am about the innocent students at the academies, that's all I want—for today to be over and to find myself in the comforting warmth and safety of his arms.

"Um, Lilith?" The ex-Archdemon looks down at me with a hooked brow. "You never answered my question. You know, about..." I trail off, feeling the returning heat flood my cheeks.

An amused titter escapes her. "You needn't worry. Female angels can...self-actualize, so to speak, which is why our kind doesn't procreate very often. Think of it as natural birth control. The males will spread their seed, but the women, well, unless they want it—"

My heart seizes at her words, and I falter, stumbling to a standstill.

Lilith continues, oblivious that my perception of my birth has been torn to shreds by that one simple statement. "Nephilim and humans don't have that option, of course, which is why there are far more of them than there are us. Their procreation lies in the hands of Mother Nature and luck. But angels?" She shakes her head. "The Fallen are more inclined to parenthood, but you'd be hard-pressed to find a single mother among the Faithful besides Gabriel. Come to think of it, it's actually quite rare for two angels to produce an offspring. I can count on one hand how many times I've actually seen it happen."

She only now notices I'm no longer beside her, and she pauses, glancing back at me with a worried crease to her brow.

"Luna?"

My heart drums so loudly in my ears I barely hear her say my name. Genuine concern twists her features, and she crosses back to me, placing her hands on my shoulders.

At her touch, I peer up through a thick haze of tears. "So, you're saying…my mother *wanted* me?" My voice breaks, and Lilith lets out a strangled breath as understanding dawns in her gaze.

Pain and remorse go to war on her face, and for a horrible moment that feels like an eternity, she doesn't answer. Then, when I don't think I can bear her silence any longer, she smiles—not in a sarcastic or devilish way, but with an honesty and affection that touches my soul.

Her smile spreads to her eyes as she lightly grips my chin between her thumb and forefinger. "I'm *saying* if she didn't... you wouldn't be here, Luna."

twelve

CALEB

ADRENALINE PUMPS THROUGH MY veins and not just from Luna's desperate goodbye kiss, her lips a hot brand upon mine. Though that kiss keeps me warm on the cold Shadow Road. That and all the memories of everything we did last night until early morning. My skin flushes hot, then my eyes hit Lucifer in front of me, and I feel the icy sting of the Road once more. I hope he's not reading my mind because he'll definitely smite me, and he's got his sword out and ready. Hammurabi walks directly behind me, and Beelzebub brings up the rear. Soon, we approach the marker to Babel. My heart pounds in my chest and my skin feels clammy. Shivering, I thumb the dagger resting in a leather sheath strapped around my leg. Hammurabi gave it to me before we left. It won't kill an angel, but it'll provide me some protection.

Lucifer turns to me then, blue eyes stormy. "Young Caleb, you and Hammurabi will have to direct us once we get inside.

Though I've been a guest at Babel, she was never mine, so I don't know her the way you two do."

I raise a brow, my heart suddenly thudding in my ears. It sounds like he's asking us to look for survivors, not prepare for battle. "Do you think…do you think Alexander has already hit Babel?"

The Morningstar's face has all the softness of chiseled stone. "The Great has a way of being one step ahead of us, and unfortunately until the Council fully commits to our cause, he has greater numbers. Babel was your home, and I understand how much you care for the people there. I want you to be prepared for the worst."

"Your friends will be safe, boy," Beelzebub cuts in. "Your teachers on the other hand… Most of my Nephilim didn't make it out alive."

I glance back at the slight Archdemon, who wears lines of grief etched into his youthful face. I know all his Nephilim were like Hammurabi, ancient and powerful and wise. To lose such beings leaves a permanent scar on the world. They are irreplaceable. Hammurabi looks disturbed by Beelzebub's words, and I wonder how many friends he's lost that he's not talking about. He's not exactly Mr. Feelings. Oh, he can dish out solace and sympathy, but I don't think he's comfortable taking it. Giving him a manly pat on the back seems lame and inadequate, so I just shove my hands in my pockets and keep my mouth shut. Maybe sparing him from my sputtering platitudes is comfort enough.

"If Babel burns, the boy and I will lead the way," Hammurabi says to Lucifer, his expression stony. "We must save as many of our brethren as we can."

I give a grim nod. Even if Alexander managed to take Shalina and Rafe, they'll be fine. Well, maybe fine isn't the right word. They'll be safe enough until the brainwashing begins. But Gramps will try to charm them first before he resorts to breaking their minds to get what he wants.

As Lucifer reaches the marker for Babel and steps off the Road, I steel myself for what is to come and follow him…into bright sunshine and cerulean skies. The scent of citrus trees and jasmine curls around my nose, and I breathe in the paradise that is the Hanging Gardens. The scent of home. The Tower rises before us, flawless. I spot students trudging up the stairs toward the entrance, oblivious to the danger set to fall upon them like a hammer. But…there is *no* danger right now. I can't sense anything. Granted, I'm a second generation Nephilim, so I could be missing something, but I'm pretty damn sharp. My eyes dart to Lucifer and Beelzebub, who stand still as statues, sampling the air. I meet Hammurabi's gaze and he shakes his head. He doesn't feel anything, either.

"They're not here," Lucifer says, eyes finding Beelzebub.

The mini Archdemon nods. "No, they're not. Let's make haste. Just because they're not lurking in the shadows at the moment doesn't mean they won't pop out of one soon."

"Come," Lucifer says, and we make our way toward Babel,

the Morningstar masking our presence until we reach the stone steps.

Two first-years gasp as we appear in front of them, Lucifer allowing his massive ebony wings to swing on either side of him. The girls stare at him, rather dazed, like they've just spotted their favorite celebrity, and he lives up to all the hype. One of them looks positively punch-drunk. Yeah, yeah, the Morningstar is a golden god. We get it.

But I can't say I blame them for their infatuation. He *is* the original rebel after all. And it's not like he goes around touring schools so Nephilim can fawn over him.

"Children," he says to them, his voice a velvet rumble. "I have a task for you. Don't ask questions, just obey me. Do you understand?"

Dark Nephilim generally would balk at such demands, but when you're faced with the Morningstar, you shut the fuck up and do what you're told. The young girls nod at him, their expressions dazzled.

"What do you need us to do?" one of them asks, stepping forward. "We're your servants."

I roll my eyes and barely restrain myself from making a gagging gesture.

"I need you to round up your first-year classmates and evacuate them from Babel. Take them to the Hanging Gardens and wait for me there." Lucifer's eyes land on mine. "Caleb, go with them and help. Hammurabi, seek out your

Nephilim teachers and explain the situation and aid Caleb in the evacuation effort. Beelzebub and I will find whomever the Council put in charge of the school and place defensive wards. Babel will not burn on our watch."

At the word "burn," the two girls manage to roll their tongues back in their mouths, a touch of fear now brimming in their eyes.

"B-Burn?" one of them repeats, and I shoot her a confident smile, trying to project calm.

"Hey, didn't you just hear the Morningstar? He's not gonna let that happen. You heard the man—let's start rounding up the students. I'm Cal—"

The other one focuses on me and pipes up, "We know who you are." I blink, staring at her. Her entire face flushes. "You're at the top of your class and…" She trails off lamely, and I smother a laugh.

Huh, I guess my reputation must precede me seeing as I haven't been a student here since the beginning of the school year when these girls would have only just been starting at Babel. That will definitely make everything easier. "Good, you can tell me your names on the way." I give the two Archdemons and Hammurabi a brief salute and then hurry up the steps, the two girls practically tripping on my heels.

Dahlia and Inma prove to be good little helpers, rounding

up the first-years with all the skill of cowboys lassoing cattle. It doesn't hurt that I'm there, a final-year student barking orders when kids get a little mouthy. It also doesn't hurt that rumors about Lucifer and Beelzebub being in the building have already spread like wildfire, lending credence to our story. But then again, they did experience a Council invasion two weeks ago, even if they weren't directly involved. Those war horns are fucking loud. Asmodeus is gone, and I know that raised all kinds of questions, and while things appear normal on the outside, there's a ripple of unease in the air I can feel.

Darks are naturally curious, but I guarantee no one's answering any of their questions about their headmistress's disappearance. I don't know the Fallen who's taken Asmodeus's place, but whoever they are, they have massive shoes to fill, as the Archdemon is beloved by the student body. Sure, she's terrifying, but that doesn't detract from her popularity.

Once we've pretty much emptied out the first-year dormitory and classes, I turn to the girls. "Go wait outside with the others. I can take it from here."

Inma shakes her head, her curly hair a cloud around her face. "No, Caleb. You can't evacuate everyone by yourself."

I sigh, deciding not to put up a fight. I'm not too proud to admit when I need help—most of the time. "Fine, start getting out the second-years, but I'm heading to the final-year dorm by myself. Those lazy asses will still be in bed. I'll meet you on the third year floor in fifteen with some help," I promise.

At their nods, I bound up the stairs and into the familiar corridors of my dorm. Final-year students have the privilege of starting class later in the day, so most of them sleep in or do the walk of shame from being out all night. We have a curfew, but that doesn't mean we abide by it. I head straight for Rafe's door. Not bothering to knock, I thrust the door open.

Big mistake. I see Rafe...well, thrusting, and the face that stares over his shoulder in horror and shock looks familiar. Shit. It's Shalina. Ugh, someone blind me right now. I've seen Rafe's ass. Who doesn't lock the door while getting busy? I spin around, staring out the now open door, wishing I could bleach my mind clean.

"*Caleb*?" Rafe's incredulous voice says behind me. "What the fuck are you doing here?"

"Knock much?" Shalina growls. "I didn't think voyeurism was your thing, pervert!"

I make a gagging noise, debating on whether to get Hammurabi to wipe my memories right now. "So much for you two hating each other. Guess you had to work out all the negative energy somehow." I smirk at Shalina's outraged hiss.

"What are you even doing here? Aren't you supposed to be with the stuck-up Lights stroking harps or some shit?" she demands.

"Yeah, about that... You two need to get dressed. Now. We have to leave Babel," I say, cautiously peeking over one shoulder. Thank the Morningstar the sheet is now covering all the important bits.

Rafe stares at me like I've started spouting Enochian, then he laughs. "Okay, what's really going on, Caleb? Did you mess with some Light's mind, and you've pissed off Gabriel, so now you're on the run?"

Wow, I guess everyone really is clueless about what's going on. The Council locked that down tight. I pick up his discarded pants off the floor and hit him in the chest with them. "Listen, I haven't been at the Serapeum for months. I've been with—I'll tell you all about that later," I say, shaking my head. "I'm here with the Morningstar himself, and we've got to leave. *Now.*"

Shalina and Rafe exchange a look. "The Morningstar?" Shalina says. "Does this have anything to do with Asmodeus being taken away?"

There's a reason she and I compete for the top spot in school. "Yes, it does. Schools are under attack, so I'm here with Lucifer, Hammurabi, and Beelzebub, trying to get your asses out of here before that happens."

"Hammurabi is with you?" Shalina asks, her eyes round. "He just disappeared around the same time as Asmodeus, and no one is saying a damn thing. Ishtar has been gone for months, too."

"Who the hell is attacking schools?" Rafe demands. "Caleb, you're not making any sense."

I sigh, rubbing the bridge of my nose. "Okay, short-short version. I released my grandfather, Alexander the Great, from his tomb in the Serapeum with Ishtar's help. Turns out, he's actually a Gray angel, and now he's on the warpath. He's burning schools and taking students for his army. I've been with him most of the time until Luna… Yeah, no time for that. Anyway, he might be on his way here, so we need to get the fuck out, okay?"

Both their jaws literally drop as they stare at me like I've gone insane. Rafe recovers first.

"Is that why you were chosen as the exchange student? Because of Alexander?" he asks, proving why he's also a fierce competitor for best in show.

"What is a *Gray* angel?" Shalina asks, her normally glowing brown skin pale. "Is it…what I think it is?"

I hold a hand up, staving off more questions. "Ishtar played me pretty hard," I admit bitterly to Rafe then shake my head. "And yes, Shalina, a Gray angel is exactly what you're thinking, both of the Dark and Light. I swear I'll give you all the details the minute we're out of the danger zone. Unfortunately, Babel isn't safe for us anymore."

As I say those words, sourness churns in my gut. Babel has always been the epitome of *safety*. It's our home. And my grandfather wants to burn it to make a point.

Shalina edges off the bed, taking the sheet with her, and for the second time that day, I'm seeing way too much of my best friend. Rafe growls at her as he stabs his legs through his pants, and I give them my back once more.

"You sound like a stark raving lunatic," Shalina says, and I hear her shrug on her clothes. "But I believe you."

"Me too," Rafe says, "but as soon as we're out of here, you're going to spill every last little detail, including who Luna is."

So, he caught that. I nod. "You'll be meeting Luna soon enough. And she'll blow your mind," I promise.

Rafe and Shalina help me drag all the final-year and third-year kids outside. We might have had a real struggle on our hands, but good ol' Uncle Hammurabi showed up and threatened to bust heads if asses didn't get on the move. I love that sourpuss. Plus, once everyone got a load of Lucifer and Beelzebub, they stopped grumbling real quick. I don't recognize the Fallen with them—the one who took Asmodeus's place. He's tall and rangy, towering over Beelzebub and managing to look Lucifer in the eye. He doesn't look too happy to be between the two Archdemons, but he's outgunned.

I recognize some of my other teachers like Blue Jay, who shows up in Salish mythology as a trickster god. Along with Ishtar, he's a master at mind manipulation and illusion, and he earns his reputation. His black eyes find Hammurabi, and I see relief flit across his face.

I push my way to the front with the Babylonian king, Shalina and Rafe trailing in my wake. Lucifer watches us approach, turning away from the Fallen. The stranger looks at me and Hammurabi, lips pursed with displeasure. I guess Lights aren't the only ones who have sticks up their asses. I ignore him, focusing on Lucifer.

"We've gotten out all the students," I report, resisting the urge to salute.

"There is no one left," Hammurabi confirms, eyes mournful. "Babel is now a shell, empty and alone."

I shiver at his words as I look back at the ancient tower standing proudly in the sun, defiant, just like its former inhabitants. My chest tightens at the thought of those lively halls gone silent.

"She won't be that way forever, my friend," Lucifer soothes, but Beelzebub gives a derisive snort.

"Unless we stop Alexander, she will be. Let us hope he doesn't burn the school down out of spite. I do believe he's just that petty," Beelzebub says, and I see rage reflected in his eyes. I know without a doubt if he gets the chance, he'll take off my grandfather's head himself. We just might need to find him a box.

"If that is true," the Fallen says with an arrogant tilt of his head, silver hair gleaming in the sun, "then shouldn't we be going? We present a rather large target out here." His condescending tone raises my hackles, even if I happen to agree with him.

"Sagar," the mini Archdemon says with a cutting smile. "Just because you've been temporarily promoted, it doesn't mean you have a seat at the table. Asmodeus will be with us soon enough. Remember your place."

Damn, the tween is starting to grow on me. I smirk at the Fallen—Sagar. Lucifer wears a long-suffering expression on his face as he listens to the biting exchange. Come to think of it, despite the Morningstar being the original Archdemon, I've never really heard him get into the petty politics of the Council. Yeah, he's all about it now because they threaten Luna, but he doesn't go on and on about hierarchy. Even when he confronted Alexander, it was more about scolding Gramps for having the audacity to think he could make Lucifer a puppet in his war. I guess when you've led the Great Rebellion, you don't have to prove shit to anyone anymore.

"You two are like Egyptian street cats fighting over scraps, puffing yourselves up to look bigger," Lucifer says, and I stifle a laugh. "Let us forget the power games for a brief moment and focus on safely removing these children from harm's way, shall we?" He gives Beelzebub and Sagar both a withering glare before turning to address the Nephilim strewn across the steps of Babel in clumps like patches of weeds.

"Dear children," he begins, projecting his voice until his smooth baritone rings out around us. Then his eyes snag on a few of the teachers, and he smirks. "Well, no matter your age, you're all children to me."

I see Hammurabi roll his eyes, and I have to say, I've never met someone less child-like.

Lucifer's face hardens. "I apologize for tearing you away from the shelter of your home, but Babel no longer represents a safe haven for you. None of our academies, Dark or Light, are safe anymore. An old threat to our world has emerged, and I refuse to allow you to be pawns in his war."

Murmurs ripple over the crowd, and I know everyone is dying to start peppering Lucifer with questions, and they only abstain because he's the Morningstar. And he's scary. They're afraid, too. Their orderly word has been turned upside down. We Darks might bend the rules but we rely on them to keep us secure.

"We first go to Megiddo, and then we'll take you somewhere safe." Lucifer's eyes soften as he takes in all the young faces before him. "Look at all of you, dying to drown me in your curiosity, but I'm afraid it will have to wait." His battle mask slides back on.

We all trail behind Lucifer like ants in a nursery rhyme. Once we're back on the Shadow Road, paranoia settles under my skin again. We're traveling with close to four hundred kids to Megiddo, and as fast as Nephilim can move, I still feel like we're a herd of tortoises shuffling along. I'm in the middle of the pack with Hammurabi, Lucifer leads, and Beelzebub and Sagar guard our backs. I think Lucifer put them together as punishment for their earlier sniping. Teachers are strewn throughout, offering protection. It doesn't feel like enough, and I hate this vulnerability chafing at my skin.

It's not like the Nephilim kids are delicate butterflies who'll be forever maimed if something brushes against their wings. Hell, the third and final-year students will put up a decent fight, especially if they have strong bloodlines. But they're just kids. They fight simulated battles in a carefully controlled environment. They're not worried about dying.

I know because until a handful of months ago, I was just like them. Now, I've wounded two angels and was in the middle of a major brawl and barely survived.

Shalina's slim hand on my shoulder shakes me from my somber mood. I meet her green eyes and suppress a groan. The interrogation is about to begin. Well, I was expecting it, and I owe them an explanation.

I glance at Rafe, who looks like he's been biting his tongue this whole time. I roll my eyes and wave a hand. "Ask."

But before Rafe can open his mouth, Shalina holds up her hand. "Start at the beginning, with Ishtar."

I give her a bitter smile, well aware that the two of them love Ishtar, too. So, I spill about Ishtar's plan and how she convinced me—quite easily, fool that I am—to release my grandfather.

"She's obsessed with him," I tell them, "at the cost to all others around her. Her first loyalty is to him, and if you're not prepared to bow before the king, you're her enemy. She had no problem throwing me away."

Rafe and Shalina look deeply troubled by my words. "Is

Alexander really bad news?" Rafe asks.

"Well, he's a Gray angel. How can he be good news?" Shalina says with all the prejudiced contempt she can muster.

"Cut that bullshit out right now," I hiss, taking her by surprise. "Being a Gray has fuck all to do with it. Gramps has a Messiah complex. He thinks being a Gray makes him the rightful ruler of us all, and that he can smash down the divide between us. Problem is, he doesn't care how much destruction or death he causes to reach that goal. Get me? Luna is a Gray, and she's as sweet as pie. She doesn't care about power and just wants us to stop being assholes to each other. She's the best of both worlds."

Shalina's brows rise at my venomous tone, and Rafe cocks his head to the side. "You mentioned Luna before. Who is she?"

"There's *another* Gray," Shalina says at the same time.

I glower at Shalina as I say, "Luna is my…girlfriend." I hesitate over the word, not because I'm commitment phobic, but because calling an angel your girlfriend seems so lame. Like it's not an adequate enough word to describe what Goldilocks means to me. "We met at the Serapeum."

"There was another Gray just wandering around in the *Serapeum*?" Shalina asks, voice shrill.

"You have a *girlfriend*?" Rafe demands.

Well, it's clear where both their priorities lie. Hammurabi hears our voices and shoots me a warning glance across the body of Nephilim crowded on the Road. I give him a sheepish shrug and glare at my best friends.

"Cut the dramatics," I say. "Luna just thought she was a Light Nephilim—she didn't know she was a Gray, not until later. Her Dark side had been repressed. Anyway, we became friends, and it turns out she's a Gray. And an angel."

"You're banging an angel?" Rafe asks, glee and admiration in his eyes.

"I'm going to punch you in the face," I threaten, and I'm not joking.

"I'll join you," Shalina says, giving her lover a poisonous glare.

He throws his hands up. "Sorry, but this is just too good. Plus, you liked her when you thought she was a *Light*. That's some Romeo and Juliet shit right there."

I roll my eyes and give them a brief rundown on what happened at the Serapeum, finishing up with who Luna's real parents are. That leaves them both speechless and I chuckle, enjoying a nice moment of quiet. It doesn't last long.

Shalina's eyes narrow on the front of the crowd, as if she can see through them to get to Lucifer. Nephilim can see well, but we don't have X-ray vision. "The Morningstar...and Gabriel?" She looks like she's about to be sick. "How...*what*?"

"Hey, Ishtar and Gilgamesh have been sleeping together for years," I say. "He defected to Alexander for her, so it does happen." I mean, it rarely ever happens—at least that we know of.

"Ew," Shalina gasps, and Rafe gives her an irritated glance.

"Baby, I didn't realize you were such a prejudiced little prick," he says, frowning, and she glowers at him. "We're Darks. We're meant to break rules, and Lucifer is the original rule breaker. And Gabriel is hot, even for an ice queen."

"And this happened before the Fall," I point out. "But Rafe is right. When did you become so narrow-minded, Shalina?"

"I'm sorry, Caleb, but I don't remember you being all Team Light before you left," Shalina counters. "You sure weren't advocating for us all to just get along."

Point scored. "You're right. Meeting Luna changed a lot for me. I never realized how…petty we all are to each other. I don't agree with my grandfather's methods, but he's right about one thing. We gotta bridge this divide between us. All this hatred, what good is it doing us? What are we so scared of? And with Alexander going all Conqueror, we're going to have to somehow get along, or we're not going to survive."

Shalina frowns, rubbing her hands up and down her arms. "I never thought of it like that. Coming together to defeat a common enemy. I guess…we have to, don't we?"

Rafe slings an arm around Shalina, looking more relaxed. "Besides, Luna is half Dark so that makes her one of us."

Warmth soothes my tension at his words. It's not like I'd give up Luna for them, and I'd straight out kick their asses if they disrespected her, but it's a relief to know I don't have to lose my friends.

A small smile tugs on Shalina's lips. "You're right. She *is* half Dark and Lucifer's kid. How bad could she be?"

I grin at them both as we edge closer to the marker for Megiddo. As the kids ahead of me go through, my eyes wander to Hammurabi, and he nods, letting me know to keep my guard up. Babel was a cakewalk, so I choose to be optimistic about Lucifer's school.

The acrid smell of smoke assaults me when I step from the Road, dashing my hopes for an easy evacuation. Screams echo around us, and I look at where the school is supposed to be. Megiddo belches black smoke and scarlet flames. My heart sinks as I take in the destruction.

"Caleb, look," Rafe breathes, pointing.

My eyes round as I see soldiers in black Kevlar armor herding the Nephilim kids into the streets. A battle cry rents the air, and my head snaps toward that enraged bellow. Lucifer has his wings out and his sword drawn. He soars up the hill, Beelzebub following.

Oh, shit. It's on.

thirteen

LUNA

THE EVACUATION FROM MOUNT Sinai goes smoothly. Shortly after securing the weapons, we return to the entrance hall along with Raphael, where we find Gabriel, directing the students with the help of Hatshepsut and a few other of the academy's teachers. When the first generation Nephilim catch sight of the trunks in our hands, they relieve us of the responsibility, leaving Lilith and me empty-handed and with little else to do but part ways and return to our respective Roads. As Mount Sinai is a secondary academy, most of the students have experience with the Blessed Road, which streamlines the process. But it doesn't quell the obvious panic looming among the hundreds of Nephilim whispering in hushed voices to each other, their questions and murmurs of dread carrying to my ears where I walk at the front of the crowd with Raphael and my mother.

I can understand their unease. Uncertainty plagues our every step, and there is no answer any of us can give—no reassurance—that will assuage their fears. If only we knew something of the war to come or what to anticipate next from Alexander.

If only I knew what the Creator expects from me.

Once again, a sense of helplessness gnaws at my thoughts. *No…not helplessness,* I realize. Because I'm not. What I am is powerless. Powerless to act beyond the role and path decided for me by fate.

A scornful breath escapes me. I wish I knew what the hell I'm meant to be doing.

I peer at Gabriel out of the corner of my eye, exchanging one weighted thought for another. We haven't said a single word to each other since we reconvened at Sinai. While things have always been awkward between us, now the tension is exacerbated, and what's worse, it's completely my fault. I'm acting weird and I'm sure she can sense it. That's the only explanation for why she avoids my gaze, even though I know she can feel my eyes on her face.

I frown at the croon of Lilith's voice in my head again, and though it's not loud enough to drown out the terror clawing at me, it's persistent enough that I can't ignore it any longer.

I was wanted. I wasn't some unplanned accident—a burden Gabriel got saddled with—like I assumed. I was *wanted.*

And for some reason, knowing that breaks my heart.

It's not that I ever thought Gabriel didn't care for me. After all, she wouldn't have gone to the lengths she did to protect me from the prophecy if she didn't. But to hear that I wasn't some unwelcome mistake, that she actually *wanted* me, that I wouldn't exist at all if she hadn't, on some subconscious level, desired a child with Lucifer…

I shake my head at the thought, unable to imagine the pain she must have endured when she chose to lock me away. For so long, I've battled my own anger and resentment about what she did to me, but now…now, I'm struck with a heartache and sympathy that fills every inch of me like water rushing into my lungs.

My mother wanted me. She wanted me and she lost me, just like she lost my father. And though she vowed she would defy the Creator before being separated from us again, I can understand now why she seems so terrified to embrace our reunion, embrace *us*. She hides behind her guilt, but the reality is, she's afraid. Afraid of having her happiness snatched away.

I part my lips to say something—*anything*—but no words rise to the surface. I can't bring myself to tell her I know. To tell her I also wanted her, more than any child could ever want a mother. I want to say it, but I don't. I can't.

Because the truth is, I'm afraid, too, and saying those words only makes it all the more likely I'll eventually lose her. It's too late to push away my father or Caleb, but Gabriel…I can keep her at a safe distance. I can shield my heart from this one potential loss.

For now, at least.

The journey from Mount Sinai to the Serapeum takes only minutes using the Blessed Road, and before I know it, I'm stepping out of the encompassing light of the celestial path back into the warm Egyptian sunshine of the mortal world. Raphael and my mother emerge with me—followed by the students and teachers from Sinai, who remain by the entrance to the Road, awaiting our return from a distance just in case the academy isn't safe—and together, we approach the Serapeum, sharing the unspoken hope that Alexander hasn't already been here.

Unlike the last time I stood in front of the academy like this, I don't need to look past its glamor to see the structure's true magnificence. Now, with the bind lifted, I see it more clearly than ever.

My stomach twists. I'm not sure how I feel about being back here. This place has served as the setting of so many of my worst memories, but at the same time, it's also home to some of my fondest. Like meeting Caleb. And growing close with Alaric. Plus, if I hadn't ever come to the Serapeum, who's to say I would've ever found out what I am? If I had remained in Maine in the hospital, or even attended a different academy, I likely still wouldn't know what a Gray is…or who my parents are, for that matter. Looking at it that way, the good that came out of my attendance at the Serapeum far outweighs the bad. And yet…

"It's strange to be back," I mutter, placing my foot on the bottom-most stair as Raphael and my mother ascend on each side of me. Above us, I glimpse the familiar golden doors carved with a depiction of the Fall. Although I can't see the image fully from here, the details are carved into my memory, although some are sharper than others. Like the face of my father. Looking back at when I arrived in Alexandria, the moment I walked through these doors was the first time I felt something between us—not the song of our blood, but a connection. I just didn't realize what that connection was.

"It is for me as well," Gabriel admits. "Especially now that I can see how blind I was to what was right before me."

"Blind?" While I know she's talking about me, I don't entirely know what she means. I don't hold it against her that she didn't realize I'm her daughter when I was a student here. How could she have? The song between us was severed—*is* severed, even if I swear I can feel the tingle of it trying to return.

Her eyes shift to mine, and the barest smile quirks the edges of her lips. "You look so much like your father. Only a fool wouldn't have noticed."

A malicious chuckle escapes Raphael. "She's his reflection. You were a fool, indeed, to fail to notice the resemblance."

"Or in deep denial," Lilith mutters, trudging up the stairs on my mother's right side where a moment ago there was nothing but air. The ex-Archdemon is beginning to make a habit of popping up out of nowhere.

Raphael gives a dramatic eye-roll, but Gabriel ignores her, scowling at Lilith, who laughs. "Don't give me that look. You know I'm right."

My mother grumbles under her breath, but she doesn't protest as we continue to the top of the stairs. Like at Mount Sinai, the doors open at our approach, but unlike at Mount Sinai, no Nephilim or angel steps out of the school's depths to meet us. Whoever's in charge here must not know we're coming.

"No welcoming party this time, I see," Lilith comments, arching an imperious brow.

"Are we supposed to be welcomed?" I ask. No one came to greet us when Alaric brought me here. Then again, it was his job to escort new students to the academy, and if any of those other arrivals were anything like me, meeting another Nephilim or even Gabriel within moments of stepping foot in this place would've been one mind-blowing interaction too many. Especially when I was already grappling with the bombshell he tossed into my lap that I wasn't actually human. Given Alaric's kind nature, he probably didn't want the experience to be any more overwhelming or confusing for me than it already was. The focus had to be on calming me, not overstimulating my already fragile mind.

"Not if we were entering a Dark school," Lilith says, "but the Lights *thrive* on pomp and circumstance. After Sinai, I merely assumed we would receive the same warm welcome here." Her tone drips with sarcasm.

Raphael crosses her arms, tapping a forefinger against the crook of her opposite elbow, a glower darkening her fair face. "It is *not* pomp and circumstance," she retorts, glaring at the ex-Archdemon. "It is good conduct to send someone to greet important arrivals, just as it is considered good conduct to not enter another Council member's academy without their permission. At least, not unless they're expecting you."

Her words make me think of Caleb and my father. I'm not sure who the Council put in charge of Babel in Asmodeus's absence, but I doubt the unknown Fallen is expecting their arrival either, though I can't exactly see that stopping Lucifer. I only hope they don't encounter any problems—from Alexander or otherwise.

"The Lights here clearly have to work on their manners then," Lilith scoffs before strutting forward, sauntering through the open doors without a care in the world.

"What are you doing?" Raphael snaps.

Lilith waves a dismissive hand over her shoulder but continues walking. "Whichever of your trained dogs you put in dear Gabriel's stead isn't officially on the Council yet, are they? Besides, we do not have the leisure of time to care about manners."

Raphael gives a haughty sniff. "I...concede you have a point," she grinds out before reluctantly tailing Lilith over the threshold.

My mother and I follow closely behind, and as we take the path from the entrance hall to the administration office, my eyes scan the details of the school as if this is the first time I've seen them. It's all so familiar and yet somehow foreign—or maybe it all just feels so different because of how much I've changed since I last stepped foot in these halls over half a year ago. Either way, I feel out of place, like I don't belong.

Then again, I never really did.

"How is it Hatshepsut knew we were coming at Sinai but no one was aware of our arrival here?" I muse aloud as we pass through the cloister into the long hallway of classrooms. I keep my voice low so as not to interrupt the muted din of lectures on the other side of each door. At least if the students are all in class, the evacuation should move quickly.

"Think of the academies as living entities of sorts," Raphael says, a surprisingly patient drawl to her words. "Each one is attuned to the angel or Fallen who oversees it. They know when we are there. They know when we are gone. And they know when we return, as will those who we trust to help run them. I suppose you could say they speak to us, in a way."

"Interesting, then, that no one came to greet us, wouldn't you agree?" Lilith sneers. "It's almost like the Serapeum doesn't approve of Gabriel's replacement."

Raphael bares her teeth in a growl, but before she can utter a scathing word in response, my mother cuts in, "That's enough, both of you. We have more pressing matters at hand."

Picking up her pace, Gabriel charges ahead, leading the way into the administration office at the end of the corridor, never once faltering in her determined advance as she pushes through the set of glass doors. I race to keep up, brushing past Raphael and Lilith, who are locked in a battle of glares.

As I near the office, I hear a familiar voice squeak, "Headmistress!" and I peer through the glass to see Evangeline jumping up from her desk. Remembering herself, she clears her throat and amends, "Gabriel. You're back." Relief glistens in the blue pools of her eyes, which snap to me as I step into the office. "I hope—" she begins before gasping out, "Luna! I..." She shakes her head, glancing between us, visibly rattled. "What—"

Gabriel holds up a hand. "Your questions will have to wait, Evangeline. We need to speak with Zerachiel immediately."

Zerachiel?

I didn't think my mother knew who took her place as headmistress. Then again, she entered the Serapeum once before, uninvited and unannounced, to retrieve her armor and sword before coming to my rescue at the citadel. She could've easily discovered who is running this establishment in her stead at that time. Either that or the school somehow told her, if the academies really do speak to their caretakers and the Serapeum still sees Gabriel in that role.

"O-Of course," Evangeline says, her cobalt eyes darting between Gabriel's face and the black door in the corner. "I'll just—"

"I'm afraid we don't have time for pleasantries or polite conduct," Gabriel interrupts with an apologetic smile at the Nephilim, crossing the room to her old office. She hesitates for a moment before grasping the handle, giving a soft snort at the large silver Z imprinted into the wood in place of her own sigil. Then, with a dignified lift of her chin, she throws open the door.

"What is the meaning of—" The booming male voice falters mid-sentence, and I pause behind Gabriel, peering over her shoulder into the spacious office at the angel I presume to be Zerachiel. Violet eyes stare, dumbfounded, at my mother. "Messenger," he breathes, rising from his seat, long chestnut hair brushing his shoulders. "I'll admit, I didn't expect you to show your face here, but then, you were always a bold one. I assume it was you who purloined your sword and armor from the museum?"

She shrugs. "It is not theft if they are rightfully mine."

His aura contorts as he leans forward, placing his hands on the desk that once belonged to her. "Give me one good reason why I shouldn't contact the Council and turn you over."

Although I can't see her face, I can easily imagine the icy smile forming. "Because the Council is here with me," she retorts, her tone somehow both frigid and scalding.

As if on cue, Lilith and Raphael appear at my side, and I watch the contempt on Zerachiel's face transform into unease as the latter steps past me and Gabriel into the office.

"Hello, Zerac," Raphael purrs. "Enjoying your time on Earth, I take it?"

Straightening, he glances between the two Archangels and Lilith, confusion written into the furrowed crease of his brow.

"I…don't understand," is all he says.

"And we're short on time," my mother huffs. "So, here's the abridged version."

The shock that Hatshepsut displayed when she learned about Ashkelon pales in comparison to the horror stripping the color from Zerachiel's face. Learning about the fate of the Dark academy is all the convincing he needs, and over the course of the next twenty minutes, we split off into groups—my mother, Evangeline, and Zerachiel scouring the library and securing the weapons in the museum, while Raphael, Lilith, and I knock on dorm room doors and visit every classroom, urging students to proceed to the entrance hall of the school for immediate evacuation. The Nephilim all react to our presence with audible confusion, though it's Lilith who bears the brunt of their poorly concealed shock the most. They gape at her with the same question in each of their nervous gazes—why is a Fallen in a school strictly for Lights?—but they seem to know better than to question her and obey without hesitation when she tells them to move. Fear of the unknown is a powerful motivator and outweighs whatever distaste they have toward Darks.

Once every last room has been checked, we join the rest of the school, preparing to re-enter the Blessed Road and finally make our way to the Council's rendezvous location. The teachers—some of whom I recognize, like Vesta, and some I don't, like Gilgamesh's replacement for *History of the Fall*—corral the students alongside my mother and Raphael, herding them into manageable lines.

I watch them work, standing off to the side of the entrance hall with Lilith—ever the outcasts—beside the white marble statues of the seven Archangels, counting every second with building unease. Curious eyes keep looking my way, and I spot recognition in some of those glances, though it seems uncertain, as if the onlookers aren't quite sure they know who I am.

"Is that...?" I hear someone say in a thick, Southern accent, and goosebumps pimple my skin as a shiver of dread rolls through my body.

I know that voice. It tormented me for months. And sure enough, I spot Lisbeth and a gaggle of girls walking past us, gaping at me like I've taken the form of a hydra and I just sprouted several heads.

My eyes sweep over the crowd, looking anywhere but at the girls who bullied me mercilessly when I was a student here. The last thing I want is to give them the satisfaction of knowing I can hear them. Still, I can't stop myself from watching them in my peripheral vision, clinging to every word.

"Holy shit, it is," Ellie mutters before shaking Lisbeth's shoulder and pointing to the front of the crowd where my mother is overseeing the students. "And look, Gabriel is back, too."

Lisbeth doesn't take her eyes off me—I can feel them burning into the side of my face—or lower her voice when she says, "Hey, does Lunatic look kinda different to you?"

Different?

Without meaning to, I glance at them, and Ellie recoils.

"C-Come on," she stammers, a genuine terror in her voice. She tugs on Lisbeth's arm. "Let's go."

As she pulls the other girl away, Lilith whispers in my ear, "They can sense it."

"Sense what?" I ask, finally tearing my gaze from the group as they hurry to join the shifting lines now proceeding through the open doors. When I peer up at her, she places a hand on my shoulder.

"That you aren't like them. Not anymore."

She jerks her chin, gesturing for us to follow the crowd, and as we make our way back out of the school and down the steps into the afternoon sunshine, I mull over her words. I know I'm not like them—I never have been—but I never realized how different I am now until I saw that fear in Ellie's eyes. I used to think Gabriel was terrifying—before I knew who she was to me and, if I'm honest with myself, even after—but it's what Caleb once said to me that sticks in my head now. That angels are beautiful and terrible and can frighten the wits out of even first generation Nephilim.

Is that why Ellie was so scared? Because I give off a sense of otherness that I didn't possess when I was bound? If so, I wonder if Caleb senses it, too. If I seem different at all in his eyes to the meek, bullied girl he met at the Serapeum.

Would it matter? I ask myself. Angel or not, immortal or not, Caleb loves me. So long as I have that, I suppose I don't really care.

My eyes drift to the bottom of the stairs where the students are ushered into the Blessed Road by their Nephilim teachers before they, too, vanish into its radiant depths. I hurry down the steps toward my mother, who waits by the entrance with Zerachiel and Raphael.

"That's the last of them. Now, where are we going?" Gabriel asks in a hushed voice, her heated glare on Raphael. When the Archangel doesn't immediately respond, Gabriel growls, "We've proven our sincerity, Raphael. Surely, you can see that."

"And if the threat really is as great as you say, we shouldn't dally," Zerachiel says.

Raphael's eyes flash with annoyance at the other angel's words, but after a moment, she nods. "Indeed," she agrees, sounding somewhat begrudging. Then, clearing her throat, she adds, "Of course."

Closing her eyes, the Archangel draws in a deep breath and tugs her blouse sleeve down over her shoulder, pressing her forefinger to the white Enochian symbol branded into her now-exposed upper arm—similar to the one my mother possesses on her forearm, though the character isn't exactly the same. Her eyes flutter beneath their lids for a moment before they slide open again.

"We're to reconvene in Derinkuyu," she says in a careful voice, keeping the words just a breath above silent. Her stern gaze snaps between us then fleetingly across our surroundings and back.

My mother exchanges a quick glance with Lilith, who touches a hand to my shoulder before retreating toward a half-broken pillar nearby and the slip of darkness puddled underneath it. She vanishes into the Shadow Road without a word.

With our mission completed, we don't delay our departure, and my mother, Raphael, Zerachiel, and I hasten to join the Lights in the Blessed Road. Once again, Gabriel and I head to the front of the crowd—the combined student body now a staggering eight hundred, plus a few dozen teachers—while Zerachiel heads to the back, stating his intention to keep an eye on his pupils. Unlike when we traveled to the Serapeum, Raphael doesn't join us this time, either, instead opting to check in with her teachers from Sinai. I hope the fact that she's no longer hovering over us like a vulture means she trusts our intentions and plans to join our cause against Alexander. Or, at the very least, stop trying to force me back into a cage.

Once Gabriel and I are out of the Archangel's earshot, I turn to her, lifting a questioning brow. "Derinkuyu?"

"An ancient underground city in Turkey," she answers. Then, with a nod of approval, she adds, "A sensible place to hide so many innocent souls."

I'll have to take her word on that.

"And she knew that's where the Council wants everyone to meet just by touching her tattoo?" After Caleb freed me from the Council's prison, I stood witness as Asmodeus gifted Alaric one of these sigils, and while I remember what she said about how they work, I still don't fully understand the process—even if the thought of a celestial cell phone is probably the least bewildering thing I've witnessed since the day Alaric brought me to the Serapeum.

Gabriel tugs on the collar of her shirt, pulling it down over her shoulder and revealing an Enochian symbol on her upper arm, identical to Raphael's. I knew about the crescent moon on her forearm—the symbol she used to call my father to her side shortly after I released Alexander—but I never knew she had more than one of these brands.

"With these, we can call each other to our locations. This sigil is for everyone on the Council, though I haven't dared to use it in months, and I doubt anyone would answer me now if I tried."

"Like how you called Lucifer to you under the Serapeum?" At her surprised expression, I say, "I saw the Enochian symbol on your arm."

Her mouth hardens into a grim line, and her eyes cloud with the memory of that day. She probably didn't think I was coherent enough in my pain to notice. "Yes," she murmurs after a moment. "Though that sigil isn't true Enochian. None of the ones we use to commune are."

I blink at her, confused. "They aren't?"

She shakes her head. "This"—she tugs up her shirt sleeve, revealing the thin, crescent moon tattoo—"is a sigil your father and I created for our personal use. And this"—she repeats the gesture with the other arm, exposing a symbol a few inches above her wrist that resembles an X—"is mine and Lilith's. Many of us do that, you know—come up with our own sigils when we desire private communication—otherwise anyone, Fallen or Faithful alike, could brand themselves with the same symbols and…eavesdrop on the connection in a sense. Even the Council's sigil is an altered form of an existing Enochian letter." She points now to the E-shaped brand on her upper arm. Then righting her shirt, she glances at me. "Think of these variations like angelic slang. They're all based in the pure language but you won't find them in any alphabet."

I snort. "I wouldn't be able to find them regardless. Enochian isn't taught anymore, remember?"

Gabriel gives me a pointed look. "Not in the schools, no. But I could always teach you. Or your father could," she amends when I just stare at her, rendered speechless by the offer. "I'm sure he'd be happy to."

I mull over that notion, imagining myself learning the language of my lineage, one piece closer to being whole. To becoming who I was always truly meant to be. It warms my chest, and yet, the idea quickly sours, turning my stomach.

"You don't think the Council would have something to say

about that?"

My mother's responding expression is defiant. "They can say whatever they want. Despite what they think, you are not Alexander."

Tears prick behind my eyes and I nod, desperately hoping she's right. That my actions in the war to come will prove that we haven't made a huge mistake and misinterpreted the prophecy. That I really am the Savior and not the monster destined to destroy this world. That I'm a force for good, even if I don't quite believe it. Otherwise, Gabriel will have no choice but to follow through on her bluff and help the Council lock me away again.

Shaking that thought away, I change the subject. "Asmodeus gave Alaric a sigil."

"An…unheard of gift for a Nephilim," Gabriel says, but I notice she doesn't sound surprised. I suppose she wouldn't be. She was with my father when Alaric met up with him while I was at Babel with Caleb—before we found out about the tracker in my head, and everything went to hell.

"So he said." I clear my throat, swallowing the rising lump of emotion that always grips me when I think of the Nephilim. "When Asmodeus was telling him how to use it, she called the connection an echo, but I don't really understand what she meant. How exactly does it work?"

Gabriel considers that for a moment. "Well, when Raphael touched her sigil, the others branded with that same symbol would've felt it. Through that connection, she could've either informed them of her location or discerned theirs, if they were open to it, which, clearly, someone on the Council was, or she wouldn't have received an answer. The communication…" She falters, searching for the right way to explain it. "Well, it comes to us in pictures, so yes, I suppose you could call them echoes, as it's quite similar to echolocation."

"So…we're basically human-shaped bats?" I peer over my shoulder, imagining my outstretched wings, and immediately begin to wonder if Alexander had it all wrong when he called me a dove.

Gabriel chuckles, drawing my gaze again. "Hardly. Many creatures use echolocation, and last I checked, neither one of us resembles a whale."

"Raphael kind of looks like a shrew," I mutter. "In certain lights."

An amused smile tugs at Gabriel's lips. "I don't think that's the insult you intend it to be." When I arch a bemused brow at her, she shrugs. "What? Shrews are…cute."

Cute? Did Gabriel really just call something *cute*? A shocked gasp escapes me. "That might be the nicest thing I've ever heard you say."

Her grin widens. "Don't tell Raphael. Our entire relationship is built on mutual loathing."

A smile of my own forms at that, and I revel in the comfortable silence that falls between us, relishing how normal this feels. Well, not the whole escorting nearly one thousand scared Nephilim to a safe haven part, but the mother part. The being someone's daughter part.

Turning to face her, I open my mouth to say something—to finally tell her everything that's been floating around in my head over the last few hours, to cross the final chasm between us despite the risk to my heart and sanity should I lose her—when a shrill cry in the distance chills me down to the bone and all but freezes the blood in my veins. Gabriel and I whip around at the same moment, scanning the mass of Nephilim for the source of the scream. Panic rises through the crowd, the students' terror a mirror image of my own.

"What's happening?" Fear is a hand around my windpipe, choking the words to a rasping breath, and its grasp only tightens when flames of the deepest blood red erupt along the Road, scorching across the full breadth of the path behind us.

The screams become widespread now, and the terrified Nephilim try to run—to flee the unknown danger and reach the nearest marker, regardless of where it might throw them out in the world—but the fire seems to sense their movements, blocking their every attempt at escape and building around the large group like a fiery pen intended to trap us like sheep. The only route of escape is ahead, but the flames are moving quickly, and it won't be long until that path is blocked.

It's just like in my nightmares and like in the visions Alexander tormented me with at the Serapeum. Angry crimson flames roar around us, hungry and ready to devour the world.

Gabriel's hand flies to my wrist as I whisper, "He found us," and before another coherent thought can form, she grabs my shoulders and roughly turns me to face her.

"Listen to me," she hisses, her gaze piercing. "Run ahead now while you can, leave this Road, *hide*, and once the coast is clear, contact Lilith." As she speaks, she shoves up my shirt sleeve and clamps her hand around my forearm, her grasp like a vise. I wince at the slight burning sensation that follows then stare at my skin, amazed, when she pulls her fingers away to reveal the same X-shaped Enochian brand she showed me on her own arm only moments ago.

"What?" I shake my head, glancing between her fierce face—a resolute devastation burning deep in her eyes—and over my shoulder toward the flames, which grow bolder and larger as screams ring out around us. The Nephilim scramble toward us, trying to reach that sole available route of escape, their fear of this unfamiliar threat palpable, like the scent of rot in the air. Any moment now, they'll trample us in their terror, but I don't move despite my mother's plea. I glance around, my eyes alert, searching for Alexander. He must be here. Only a Gray can create red fire and I sure as hell didn't start this inferno. But in a sea of nearly one thousand Nephilim, he is a needle in a haystack, and I see nothing but chaos.

Past the screaming, I catch the grating sound of swords clashing, and I wonder who else is here on behalf of Alexander—

how many Lights he's managed to sway to his side since we left Kandahār and are now attacking their own kind. *No, this isn't just an attack, it's an ambush,* I realize. He knew we would come this way. Maybe he even planned for us to and attacking Ashkelon was just the catalyst to corner a larger herd on the Road.

I look back at my mother as the horror of another realization sinks in. She wants me to run—to leave her and everyone else here to die. Or worse, leave them to become chained puppets in Alexander's conquest for power.

"No—" I begin to protest as she shouts over me, "This isn't a debate! Go *now*!"

The seconds slow to a standstill, and all the blood rushes to my ears, drowning out the screams and fighting. My eyes track a movement over Gabriel's shoulder, and I let out a gasp as flames rise up like a wall ahead of us, cutting off our only path of escape. That's when I finally see him: Alexander emerging from the fiery depths, descending on Gabriel from behind, his dagger upraised to smite her.

"Mom!" The warning tears from my lungs with the force of a thunder strike, and I only have a split-second to embrace the blood song between us, finally freed from the cage of our hearts as that one all-important word leaves my lips, as if saying it aloud has somehow broken the spell cast over us. No, not a spell. A *bind*.

A fleeting happiness spreads across Gabriel's face as this realization hits her as well, but it's instantly dampened by the understanding that something isn't right—that I didn't call for her out of affection but fear. Noting the direction of my petrified gaze, she begins to turn to face our enemy, but her movements come too late. Alexander's blade already descends and she'll never react to the threat and reach her own weapon in time to stop him from cutting her down.

But I can.

Swallowing my fear, I hurl myself forward, reaching for the pommel of Gabriel's sword where it sits in the invisible scabbard on her back. I can't see it, but I can sense the steel as it rings out like the tings of a tuning fork, calling to me, just like it did the first time I saw it in the museum at the Serapeum, even if I didn't understand why at the time. Sensing my desperation, it guides my hand until my fingers wrap around the cool metal, and as I pull it free—pushing Gabriel out of the way—the bronze hilt and steel blade reveal themselves, gleaming in the light of the Road. The sword vibrates under my touch, and as I lunge toward Alexander, meeting his dagger in a clash of metal on metal, it yields to me even as I feel the full force of his blow reverberating all the way down to my bones, the steel holding steady despite my inexperience in battle…and despite Alexander's clear intention to kill. His strength is formidable, and if I was a Nephilim, I have no doubt he would've cut right through me. But, as I'm learning, I have strength of my own, and with the sword in my hand, I feel stronger than ever. This sword is the power of my bloodline, and like Gabriel before me, this weapon is mine to wield. Because I am not just a Morningstar.

I am my mother's daughter.

"Hello again, little dove," Alexander purrs before jumping back several steps, out of reach of my weapon. I lunge forward again, but he just clicks his tongue, retreating farther. "There will be time for that yet," he says, flashing me a bone-chilling smile, which he then directs with pure venom at my mother. He dips into a low, mocking bow. "Until next time, Messenger."

He thrusts out a hand, extinguishing the flames ahead, then vanishes from the Road.

Shell-shocked, I stare at the spot where he stood only seconds ago, trying to piece together what just happened. Beside me, Gabriel climbs to her feet.

"I'm sor—" I begin to say, expecting her to berate me for stealing her sword—or at least for endangering myself—but she just pulls me into her arms, hugging me so tightly I can't finish the sentence. The song in our hearts rings like a church bell, tolling in my ears, making me feel complete in a way I never expected or imagined, and I know she hears it, too, because she hugs me tighter. Her aura blazes around us like she is the sun itself, swallowing me whole, and my fingers slacken, dropping the blade to the ground, before curling around her back.

We stay that way for a moment, and when we finally part, I notice the flames that barricaded the path behind us have been extinguished as well, returning the Road to normal again. The screaming and clang of battle have both ceased, and as far as I can tell, no one seems to be injured or any worse for wear—a fact we confirm with Raphael, Zerachiel, and the Nephilim teachers from Sinai and the Serapeum after we gather and do a head count. To my dismay, I was right. Lights have joined Alexander and a dozen or so first generations attacked the students. But what's strange is that no one is missing, no one is hurt, and most peculiar of all, none of the weapons were taken.

So, what was the point of that ambush other than to terrify us?

"What the hell was that about?" I growl in a low voice to my mother when we resume our forward march to Derinkuyu a short while later. Her sword has been returned to its rightful place on her back, though my fingers tingle, mourning the loss. Or maybe I'm just realizing now how important it is that I learn to defend myself, not only against those who would seek to do me harm, but most importantly, against Alexander. "Why didn't he fight back?" I find myself asking, confusion leaching into my tone. Not because I wanted him to—he would've killed me if he had—but because his inaction doesn't make any sense.

Gabriel shakes her head. "I don't know. But whatever the Conqueror's reasoning, it doesn't bode well for us."

fourteen

CALEB

THE GREAT TEMPLE IS halfway gone. I mean, archeologists and tourists already think it *is* gone, but now it actually resembles the ruins people come to gawk at in wonder. Made out of mud bricks, it's much more vulnerable than other ancient sites that have the fortune to be hewn of stone. The tall gates with their sentry towers writhe in orange and scarlet. I can't tell how many of the palaces are on fire, but they couldn't have escaped unscathed—not with this much smoke.

My throat burns and I cough, eyes watering, but I still manage to spot a few bodies lying on the steps in front of the temple like broken dolls. I know in my heart they aren't students but brave teachers who tried to protect their charges. How old were those Nephilim? How many gaping holes are left in the world now that can never be filled? I can't imagine how many treasures were inside Megiddo that we have lost.

Treasures and weapons.

"Boy," Hammurabi hisses in my ear, and I whirl to face him, startled out of my immediate horror. "Draw your dagger and follow me. We join the Morningstar in battle."

I glance back at Rafe and Shalina whose eyes brim with terror. I try to give them a reassuring smile, but it comes out more like a grimace. Hammurabi barks orders to the Babel teachers, and they herd their charges together, going for safety in numbers. I notice Sagar stays with them, instead of joining Lucifer and Beelzebub. But I guess they are *his* responsibility now, and he has to protect them. Besides, it's not like he can take them anywhere—those assholes on the Council have made sure of that, holding the location of the safe house hostage until we finish with the evacuations. Steeling myself, I leave my friends and sprint toward my grandfather's troops, heart pounding in my chest like a battering ram.

Hammurabi and I run past the burning gates and straight into the chaos. Smoke surrounds us, and my eagle eyesight tries to punch through the wall of gray. The bright light of the Morningstar can't be denied, and I see Lucifer in all his golden glory swing his silver sword in a vicious arc. A moment later, a head rolls down the stone-paved street, stopping when it meets the toe of my boot. The face of the Nephilim is forever frozen in a state of shock.

Some of Alexander's Nephilim yank kids into the Shadow Road as fast as they can while others face the fury of Lucifer and Beelzebub. But once the students see the Morningstar, they begin to fight back. Hammurabi flashes me a savage grin and wades into the melee, blades flashing. I follow him into the scuffle, but I'm not trying to cross swords with more experienced soldiers. I'm just trying to snag as many kids as I can. While the Babylonian king attempts to relieve an enemy Nephilim of his guts, I swipe two young first-year students—a boy and a girl—and shove them toward the gates.

"Run!" I scream. "Teachers from Babel are outside and can help you. Go to them." They look at me, expressions shell-shocked. "Move!" I order, voice like a whip, and they turn from me and flee into the haze.

I whirl around, trying to find other students I can help. One of Alexander's Nephilim recognizes me, and her aquamarine eyes fill with hatred. She abandons the group of kids she was herding along and comes at me. I feel her power. She's a second generation like me, but she's older. Much older. And shit, she has a sword. I dodge her first strike, coming in close and kissing my blade to the underside of her ribs. She roars, and I dance out of the way, keeping my distance and looking for an opening, but it's hard in all this smoke. I cough, keeping my eye on her as she fades in and out of sight.

Then she's suddenly on my right side, sword heading straight for my shoulder in a diagonal slash. I raise my knife in defense, but tendrils of inky blackness whip past me and wrap around the Nephilim. She's lifted in the air and slammed into the burning walls over and over again until her broken, bloody body goes limp. The tendrils release her and she slides to the ground. The whole thing was over within a matter of seconds. My terrified eyes find Beelzebub, who gives me a bored nod.

"You were taking too long," the Archdemon drawls. "Go help the children."

That is one seriously scary forever tween.

I pivot, eyes darting around for any other stragglers I can poach from Gramps. Two charred bodies rest near Lucifer's feet as he gently pushes a group of students toward the gates. The kids rush past me, alarm plastered onto their faces. In the distance, near one of the ravaged palaces, I see a tall figure standing motionless, staring at me. I still and gaze back. He's an old Nephilim. Really old. I can sense his power from here. A gust of wind momentarily clears the murkiness, and my raptor's vision picks out the details of the man's face. High cheekbones, amber eyes.

My head rings like it's been hit with a sledgehammer. I blink and blink again. Is that…Alaric? But he's dead. I mean, we saw him straight up get murdered. Sourness settles in my gut. Unless…did Grandfather resurrect him? Could someone as old as Alaric even survive that with his mind intact? I start toward him, and he breaks eye contact, vanishing in a mushroom cloud of smoke. When it clears, he's gone.

Is this some sort of trick? Was some shape-shifting Nephilim imitating Alaric? I shake my head because that's not possible. Only Mammon has that ability. And what would be the purpose of imitating Alaric if I'm the only one who saw him?

A flaming beam cracks and swings toward me. Shaking myself from my daze, I leap out the way, barely avoiding being crushed. The intense heat and screams tearing through the air bump me back hard into the present. I want to give chase and hunt the Nephilim down until I'm certain he's really Alaric, but I'm here to save kids. The mystery of Alaric will have to wait, no matter how painful that is. I spot another small cluster of teens who have managed to escape their abductors. I take a step forward, only to stagger back, one hand going over my heart.

No, this can't be happening. I didn't think it was possible, but…I hear it. In my blood, in my mind, sweet notes of family like a saxophone solo in a Blues piece. I focus on the group of young Nephilim until my eyes zero in on a petite girl with straight black hair and huge brown eyes. I can't see much of my dad in her, and if I had to bet, I'd say she's of Japanese descent. She stops running and stares at me, too. She's about fourteen, and a swell of protectiveness crests within me, which seems ridiculous because we haven't even officially met yet, but she's family. *Family.*

She's also a huge target. Alexander would love to get his dictator hands on his granddaughter. Prime clay for molding. I again shake myself out of my stupor and hurry toward the kids.

"Hey!" I call as I run. "I'm with Lucifer. I'm here to help." My eyes snag on my sister once more. My *sister.* She's looking at me, too, her large eyes practically popping out of her head like a deranged cartoon character. I feel you, kid.

"You're my brother," she blurts out, and I wince as the other students stop and stare at me.

"It sure looks that way, Sis," I say smoothly, "and as I'm trying to rescue you from being kidnapped by the big bad, let's save the family reunion for later."

Hammurabi clips me on the back of the head, and I turn around, glaring at him. Blood paints his face, but I don't see any wounds, so it's not his blood. "Move it, boy. The Morningstar says we're done here."

I glance behind me, spotting Lucifer and Beelzebub strolling toward us. Scarlet stains Lucifer's blade, and a few bodies litter the ground in his wake. Rage glows in the Morningstar's eyes, and I shiver at the violence there. He's still craving blood. Not that I blame him. By my count, we've managed to save some of his students, but not all of them. I turn back to the kids and make a shooing motion.

Hammurabi barks, "*Move*," and they hurry their asses down the hill, me trailing behind.

My sister keeps darting glances at me over her shoulder, and I wonder if she's trying to figure out if I look like our dad. It's not like she's ever met him. Unfortunately, yes, I do look like my pathetic father, but I wear his features better than him, if I do say so myself.

A bigger crowd awaits us, and I'm happy to see that our numbers have increased substantially. We haven't exactly doubled in size, but we're close. Fuck you very much, Gramps. I find my way to Shalina and Rafe, my sister practically tripping over my heels. I gently reach back and tug her to my side. My friends study her with open curiosity.

"Who the hell is this?" Rafe asks, eyeing the younger girl up. "Don't tell me you picked up another fangirl."

The girl twists her mouth in disgust. "Ew, this is my brother, dick," she grits out, and I snort.

Shalina's brows raise in surprise, but she grins. "Yep, she's your sister all right."

I glance at the girl and chuckle. Just what I need, a sarcastic mini-me to torment me. "I'm Caleb," I say to her. "You wanna tell me your name? It'll make things easier."

"You think?" She tosses back her hair. "Aya," she says. "Do you know if you're my only brother?"

Whelp, she didn't wait to open that can of worms. "Not even close. Dear Dad spread his seed a lot from what I've heard." Her eyes widen at my words. "But you're the first sibling I've ever met."

"He's a manwhore then. So, are there enough of us to make a baseball team?" she asks, crossing her arms over her chest.

I nod. "It's definitely a possibility. He's like the Bob Marley of Nephilim."

Her brow crinkles, and she gives me a questioning look. Right, kid doesn't know who Bob Marley is.

The tall presence of Hammurabi looms over us. "This is

hardly the time or place to speak about your father's breeding habits." He delivers a ferocious glare to me and Aya. "Or did the burning buildings and dead bodies not offer you clues that we're in danger?"

Aya flushes. "I was just asking—"

"Did I give you permission to speak, girl?" Hammurabi hisses, and my sister's jaw snaps shut. I swallow my protest at the Babylonian king's harsh words because he's right. Now's not the time or place for twenty questions. "We're at war. Gossip later. Fall in line. We're crossing into the Shadow Road now."

I look ahead and see Lucifer vanish, and kids start entering the Road in pairs. Sagar is near us in the middle of the pack, and scary-ass Beelzebub remains at the rear of the train, bleeding darkness. It's creepy as fuck, and I'm not sure what the inky spill does, but I wager it's something horrible and painful.

"He's cranky," Aya whispers to me, and I grin when Hammurabi throws over his shoulder, "I can hear you, small child. And this is me being perfectly reasonable. Ask young Caleb what it looks like when I lose my temper."

I flinch. "He's fond of the whip when you really piss him off. You do know that's Hammurabi, right?"

My sister shrinks behind me a little, and I muffle a laugh, meeting Shalina's amused eyes over Aya's head. Hammurabi only believes in physical punishment when you've really fucked up and decided to meddle with the mind of a human or something. But my sister doesn't know that. Best for her to treat the king like the scary asshole he is.

After a few minutes, it's our turn to jump into the shadows. I breathe a little easier when we land back in the cold, charcoal-gray world of the Shadow Road. Well, we're not really safe here, but Alexander's minions burned Megiddo to the ground and looted what kids and weapons they could. It's not exactly a victory, as we have a sizable chunk of the student body with us, but the weapons from the Fall alone will make it worth their effort. Gramps can lure even more Lights and Fallen with the promise of glory and slaughter.

Aya slides up to me again, keeping her voice low. "Are we allowed to talk now?"

"Sure, as long as we don't attract too much attention to ourselves," I say. "What do you want to know, kid?"

Rolling her eyes, she digs into my ribs with a bony elbow. "What the hell is going on, obviously. I mean, our school is attacked, and this Light finds me and tells me to run, that I can't let them take me. He singled me out. Why? And since when do *Lights* help Darks?"

I stare at my sister, unable to comprehend her words for a moment. I feel like my head has been shoved underwater and everything sounds muffled and distant. Sniffing out bloodlines is a rare talent, and the only one I know who possessed such a skill was Alaric. I replay seeing that powerful Nephilim through the smoke. Those familiar amber eyes. In that moment, I thought it was impossible. That my mind was messing with me—or that someone else was playing a cruel trick. Or maybe my psyche conjured up the kind, patient Light to assuage my guilt.

I was wrong on all counts. He's not some mirage or trick, and even if Gramps raised him from the dead, he's alive with his sanity seemingly in check. But what will Alexander do when he finds out Alaric isn't exactly Team Conqueror and is carrying out his own agenda? Obviously, he's not blatantly giving Grandfather the middle finger, as he was there with Alexander's forces, but I'm terrified of what will happen to Alaric if Alexander discovers the Light is helping his blood to escape him. The memory of phantom fingers ripping my mind open washes over me, and I shudder.

Nephilim can take a lot of punishment, but that doesn't mean we don't suffer under the brutality of the pain, and I know firsthand how brutal Gramps can be. Maybe that's the reason why Alaric hasn't contacted us yet, because he's afraid of the agony Alexander can and will inflict. That's the only explanation I can think of because he'd never willingly turn his back on Luna, and he's got that nifty Bat Signal. Then again, maybe he's tried and Grandfather found out.

"Caleb!" Aya's loud hiss interrupts my frantic thoughts.

I glance at her, noticing her scowl. "What?" I say, my tone unintentionally harsh, and she shies away from me. I can't bother to apologize, though, because knowing Alaric is alive and trapped with my grandfather has left me shaken. In my gut, I know if he could've, he would've returned to us. He loves Luna too much to abandon her.

I watch Aya square her shoulders. "Do you know the Light who helped me?" she whispers.

"Yes, I saw him die," I say, and her mouth forms an O of surprise. "Or I thought I did. He's one of the best people I've ever known. And now he's..." I shake my head, bitter at my helplessness. Oh, God, this will kill Luna. She'll be happy he's alive of course. She loves Alaric. But the thought of him with my grandfather might send her spiraling. She understands all too well what Alexander is capable of.

"He's what?" Aya persists, fingers clamping my wrist with surprising strength. Fourteen-year-old girl or not, she's still a second generation Nephilim.

I give her a bleak smile. "He's at the mercy of our grandfather."

She cocks her head at me. "We have a grandfather? Who?"

"Alexander the Great. Ever heard of him? I wouldn't get too excited," I say when I see the expression of awe on her face. "He's responsible for burning down your school and killing your teachers. He was looking for you. He wants all those of his blood gathered to help him in his great war."

She shakes her head. "Great war? But he's a *Nephilim*. How is he going to fight angels?"

My laugh holds no humor. "Because he's not a Nephilim and your blood is a little purer than you thought."

"He's an *angel*?" she breathes, and I resent the sparkles in her eyes. I guess she skipped over the whole great war and burning down your school bits.

"A *Gray* angel," I say. "And again, don't get too excited. The whole burning and pillaging thing."

"What's a Gray angel?" she demands.

I never have the chance to answer as two Nephilim pop onto the Shadow Road and snatch two Babel kids in front of Rafe and Shalina and vanish. Shalina screams and I grab Aya's wrist, plastering her against me. I draw my dagger with my free hand, terror pounding through me.

"Stick close to me!" I shout to Rafe and Shalina as more screams echo on the cold Road. "Whatever you have to do, don't let them take you!"

Hammurabi's battle cry cuts across the mayhem like a cleaver, sending icy ripples over my skin. The teachers react to that sound like a call to arms. They form a perimeter around the kids, clashing with enemy Nephilim. But they're outnumbered and more students disappear off the Road.

A first generation Nephilim pops up next to me. He's a big brute, with neon blue eyes and a shaved head. I don't recognize him from my time at Alexander's citadel, but his eyes light up with triumph when he sees me. Like he's just won the lottery. A malicious smile curves his lips, and I know he's going to kill me. There is no dragging me back before Gramps. I've crossed Alexander one too many times. The Nephilim draws a blade and strikes. I barely manage to raise my own dagger in time to avoid having my carotid artery severed.

I shove Aya away from me so I can have space to maneuver. The battle around me quiets until it's nothing more than a dull roar, and it's just me and him. And then we dance. But he's better than me. And fast. So fast he's a blur. I dodge and parry, but in seconds, I'm bleeding from slashes across my chest and arms. He ducks under a strike and tries to bury his knife in my armpit, but I slide back at the last minute, earning a deep wound across my deltoid. Fuck. I won't last long at this rate.

He knows it, too. A vicious smirk spreads across his lips. I gasp for breath, my thoughts full of Luna. I can't die here on the Shadow Road like this, not when my Goldilocks needs me. Life can't be that cruel. But I'm slowing down, despite my supernatural healing abilities, and I take another slice across my opposite side. I pant and the Nephilim laughs, and I think I hate him more in that moment than I have ever hated anyone. He's going to take me away from Luna.

Then the Nephilim topples over, and I shake my head, trying to clear my mind. I look down. Rafe has tackled him from behind, trying to pin him to the ground. But he's stronger than Rafe and manages to rise to his knees only to meet Shalina's fist as she punches him in the face. Once, twice, three times, and his nose cracks. Then my *sister* delivers a bone-crunching kick to his ribs. Still, the asshole doesn't go down, bucking against Rafe's hold. A savage scream rips from his lips. If he gets his knife hand free, someone is going to die.

I have to get my shit together and end this. My gut roils as I take a step forward. I stabbed Gabriel, and I cut off Mammon's wing, but I've never killed anyone. But Hammurabi is busy, and Lucifer and Beelzebub aren't coming to save me. Alexander's soldier won't hesitate to murder me or possibly my friends. Not after what they've done to him. I shut my guilt down, lock it away tight. There'll be time to mourn my innocence later but not if I'm dead.

I straighten, the pain in my body already dulling. Two determined steps bring me right in front of the struggling Nephilim. His eyes meet mine, and his movements become bestial as he reads my intent. He manages to get one leg under him, dragging Rafe up. I don't hesitate. I don't falter. My long fingers clamp onto his bald head in a ruthless grip, and I draw my blade across his throat until the metal meets bone. He can't heal from this. Blood sprays, saturating my face and clothing. I know I'll never forget the shock in his eyes for the rest of my long life.

Rafe lets go and the body thuds to the ground. I sink to my knees. The taste of copper coats my tongue like a slimy film, and I vomit, heaving and heaving until there's nothing left. Shalina's hand grips my shoulder while Aya kneels next to me, running a soothing hand over my back. Rafe stands in front of me, quiet.

I spit out one last time and rise. My ears pop as the sounds of battle roar back in. There are patches of kids missing, creating gaps in the line. We have to get off the Road to wherever the hell the Council is. We're sitting ducks out here.

Darkness spills from the back of the line, encroaching on us like a nightmarish tidal wave. Aya screams but I don't even flinch. Beelzebub has unleashed the beast. Within seconds, I'm blind. This isn't natural darkness. There isn't a sliver of light. I feel like I've been dropped in a vat of tar, and it's drowned my senses.

Just as I adjust to the suffocating blackness, bright liquid gold bursts across my irises, burning them. Momentarily blind, I tighten my grip on Aya's hand, clenching it. She gropes my arm, molding herself against my side, trembling.

I hear another roar—from Lucifer this time—then silence. Tears stream down my face, and I blink rapidly. Shapes form in my vision and finally color returns. Well, what little color that is found on the Road. My jaw drops when I take in the scene before me.

Alexander's soldiers whittled about a third of our numbers. But with Lucifer and Beelzebub's shocking display of power, the last of the Conqueror's warriors who attacked us lie dead around us, their bodies mangled.

A blood-coated Hammurabi finds me, his countenance grimmer than usual. "We're safe for now, boy. Let's not tempt fate by lingering." He turns from me, shouting, "Move!"

I gently nudge a shell-shocked Aya, and we shuffle along behind the thinned crowd, Rafe and Shalina trailing us.

fifteen

LUNA

WE EMERGE FROM THE Blessed Road into a subterranean labyrinth of volcanic rock. Tunnels branch off all around me, leading into nooks, other passages, and down, deeper into the bowels of the Earth for nearly three-hundred feet and at least eighteen levels. In terms of space, it's definitely fit for purpose, and considering the underground city was created to protect its past inhabitants from war, I suppose my mother was right: it *is* a sensible place to serve as a safe haven for the thousands of Nephilim crowding its depths.

I had never heard of Derinkuyu before today, so I absorbed whatever information I could glean from Gabriel on the Road. That way I would know what to expect once we got here and actually be prepared for once. Still, despite her descriptions, I didn't anticipate how truly ancient the site is, or how I would almost be able to *feel* all the years of history in the rock underfoot, as if the memories of the people who once walked

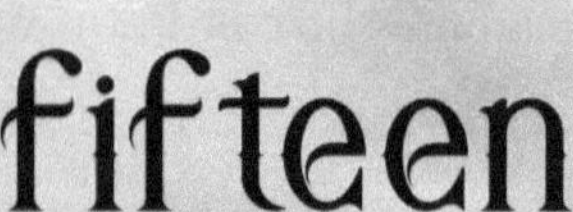

through these caverns linger to this day, like ripples in water from a stone thrown a long time ago. The ghostly hum in the air makes me wonder if, in thousands of years, this moment will also be remembered. If our kind will look back on this day and see the one bright spot in the darkness or if they'll only recollect our fear. I desperately hope it's the former—that they all remember what transpired here the way I see it now.

As a turning point.

I'm not sure I could've ever envisioned it—what it would look like to see so many Lights and Darks together in one space. Bodies flood the tunnels, the students from the other academies spilling over into every available side room, and as Gabriel ushers me forward toward a wider cavern up ahead, I notice how the opposing auras around me form a checkered pattern of black and gold. In every other respect, the Nephilim are the same, united not only in their celestial blood, but against a common foe. Not that the students know that yet. I glance behind me at the horde of Lights we brought with us from Sinai and the Serapeum, taking in so many confused faces as they all shuffle forward through the passage behind us, uncertainty and a clear disdain for their new living situation stamped onto their features. They mutter in terrified whispers to each other much like they did on the Road, voicing questions I don't know how to answer. My mother doesn't attempt to answer them, either.

"Gabriel!"

The sound of my mother's name grabs my attention, and I

look ahead, spotting Lilith cutting her way through the crowd, hurrying toward us and barking at any Nephilim who dares to get in her way. When she reaches us, she throws her arms around Gabriel, pulling the Archangel into a fierce hug.

"You're late," she growls. She then takes a step back to look at both of us, her dark eyes scanning our faces. "Did something happen on the Road?"

"Alexander," is all Gabriel says.

The ex-Archdemon's expression turns hostile. "What happened?" she asks again, this time through clenched teeth. The muscles in her jaw pop with each word.

"Nothing," I mutter, shivering at the recollection of crossing blades with the Gray. Of how close I came to certain death… had Alexander actually been inclined to fight me. "That's what's so weird about it. He blocked the Road, spent all of five seconds attacking us, and then he just vanished. He didn't even *try* to steal the weapons."

Lilith's eyes swing to mine and hang there, uncertainty burning in the dark pits like black flames. Then, brows raised, she shoots a questioning look at my mother, who scrubs a hand over her face.

"Has Lucifer returned?" Gabriel asks.

My stomach flips at the thought of seeing Caleb—of imminently being in his arms again—but my rising excitement is quashed when Lilith shakes her head. "Not yet. But the others have."

Gabriel doesn't quite manage to hide her own disappointment, giving a jerky nod. "Then let's find them and, together, maybe we can figure out what Alexander is planning."

"Yes, let's," a familiar voice coos, and we turn to find Raphael standing behind us, her thin arms crossed over her chest. "Don't mistake this to mean I trust you. I *don't*," she adds with a steely glance at me. "But neither am I foolish enough to ignore the obvious threat the Conqueror poses. He did not harm any of my students today…but next time might be a different story."

To my surprise, my mother places a consoling hand on the Archangel's shoulder. "We stopped him once. We can do it again."

"For good this time," Raphael asserts, and I shudder at the insinuation behind those words—not because I want to spare Alexander or believe he deserves it, but because I know that one misstep, and I'll be treated with the same disregard.

After all, the Council won't make the same mistake twice.

My father, Caleb, Hammurabi, and Beelzebub still haven't returned by the time we find the other Council members and recount our run-in with Alexander on the Blessed Road. Raphael and Zerachiel testify to the truth of our words, adding their own accounts—although Uriel could have just as easily asked any of the eight-hundred-plus Nephilim who were there if he did have any doubts. To my increasing unease, no one has any explanation for the ominous encounter, and the lack of insight only makes me more anxious about where Caleb and the others could be. Why aren't they back yet? Are they okay?

Are they alive?

Tears burn the backs of my eyes as I shake that unwanted thought away, and swallowing, I focus only on the passing stone as a first generation Light Nephilim I don't know leads me, Lilith, and a group of young, terrified students from the primary academy at Mount Nebo down several levels, deeper into Derinkuyu, to the rooms we've been randomly assigned during our stay here—however long that may be. The ancient city will serve as a makeshift dormitory for the foreseeable future, but I hate being so far underground. It's claustrophobic and reminds me of how it felt to be encaged in that egg.

I wanted to stay as close to the surface as possible where the air is fresher—at least until Caleb is back and can find creative ways to distract me—but my mother wasn't having it. She told me to go with Lilith and get some rest, as if I could while this worry eats at me. Meanwhile, she stayed behind with the Council and the Nephilim who serve as teachers and staff at the academies to aid with organizing the students until the others return—though not before verbally sparring with Uriel and demanding he release Asmodeus, reminding them of their agreement. I was stunned by my mother's insistence regarding the Archdemon, but then Asmodeus is important to Lucifer, and I know Gabriel was sticking her neck out for his sake. To get his friend back in one piece. If my father was present to witness her dressing down the Archangel, he probably would've swept her off her feet and kissed her then and there.

A few of the other Council members made the point that the deal wasn't considered upheld until Lucifer returned, but Gabriel wasn't having any of that, either. Though I could see it pained her to say it, she asked them what they would do if my father and Beelzebub didn't return at all. Would they leave Asmodeus in her prison and willingly choose to be down three allies instead of two? No one had a response for that. Except for Uriel, who, in a clipped tone, told one of the Archangels—Azrael, if I remember correctly—to go "attend" to the Archdemon. Code, no doubt, for *bring her back.*

Relief scorches my insides at the thought of seeing Asmodeus again, burning away some of the guilt I carry from leaving her behind at Babel. I've barely been able to escape the mental picture of her in that frozen prison—a prison I'm responsible for putting her in—but knowing she'll be free and reunited with us soon helps chase it away, just a little. I can only imagine how my father and Caleb will feel when they see her again. And Hammurabi, who I suspect harbors something a bit stronger than just respect for the Archdemon. My gut tells me he'll be the happiest of them all.

Our group thins as we deliver the students to their rooms until it's only me, Lilith, and the Nephilim leading us, who keeps casting wary glances at the ex-Archdemon out of the corner of his pale eyes. As a Light, I imagine he's only heard stories of Lilith, and not complimentary ones I'd wager. But if his behavior bothers her, she doesn't show it. Instead, a diabolical amusement shines in her black gaze, and a jaunty whistle leaves her lips as we descend into the bowels of the city.

While Derinkuyu isn't masked by a glamor like the academies, appearing to my eyes as the old world ruin it is, the cave system has been updated since its last known human use thousands of years ago—the Council's handiwork, I assume, in the event of a scenario just like this one. While not lavish, the rooms are each fitted with a bed and wash basin as well as a door that locks, ensuring the privacy and comfort the students will undoubtedly need during this time of upheaval. Not only to make them feel safe from Alexander…but also from each other.

Because, as united as we are in our terror, it's going to take much more than forced proximity to bring the Lights and Darks together. To make them accept one another and finally put this ancient feud behind them. But this animosity didn't originate with the Nephilim—they just inherited it from the Faithful and Fallen. The rest of us have a chance for a clean slate if we just make the choice to leave the past in the past.

I only hope the students here will come to see that.

"Your rooms," the Nephilim leading us says, pausing before one door and gesturing across the passage to another. He throws one last nervous look at Lilith then departs with a hasty nod at me, scurrying back the way we came.

"I better not have a roommate," Lilith calls after him as we watch the Nephilim flee like a dog with its tail between its legs. Then, with a devious smile, she says to me, "Not unless they give me one as handsome as yours."

My nose wrinkles. "Hands off, cougar," I grumble.

As Lilith barks out a laugh, I push open the door and, with an uninterested glance at the sparse furnishings, I cross the small space and drop face first on the bed. The mattress is hard but I don't care. I couldn't sleep even if I wanted to.

Rolling over onto my back, I stare up at the low ceiling. The creamy stone is pockmarked with thousands of dips in its surface, each one representing a moment I fear I'll spend here waiting for Caleb to return.

Nerves prickle under my skin, and I fidget against the soft blankets, so close to coming undone now that the adrenaline of my encounter with Alexander is wearing off. I hate this. I hate not knowing what's going to happen. I hate not knowing where my father and Caleb are or if they're okay. And above all, I hate how helpless I feel. How, despite fate's plan for me, I still seem like little more than a child, wrapped up in a battle intended for adults.

"Your thoughts are so loud, I can hear them from here," Lilith trills.

I lift my head and glare at the ex-Archdemon where she lounges in the doorway, her feet crossed at the ankle and one shoulder propped against the stone frame.

"Does it bother you?" I ask through my teeth, sitting upright.

She arches a barely interested brow. "What?"

My eyes dip to the ground, and I cross my arms, hugging them tightly around my chest. "That you've gone from being a valued member of Alexander's army to being my babysitter. I'm sure this wasn't what you had in mind." I don't mean to take my sudden bad mood out on Lilith, but she's here, and I need something to distract me. Plus, this question has been eating at me, and as much as I want to trust her, I can't really see what she's getting out of being here. Choosing our side won't get her wings back. Not that choosing Alexander's would, either.

Lilith snorts. "Am I not valued here?"

I look up at her, stunned. "That's not what I—"

"I know." Sighing, she walks over to the bed and plops down on the mattress beside me. Her hands knot in her lap. "I wouldn't blame you, you know. For thinking me fickle."

I shake my head. "I don't think that. But...I don't want you to feel indebted to me, either." I hesitate, rolling my teeth over my lower lip. Lilith blames herself for misinterpreting the prophecy and aligning herself with Alexander, but I don't want guilt or some unspoken need for repentance to be why she's helping us. "I don't want you to be here because you feel like you have to be or because my mother asked you to."

Lilith flashes me a humorless grin. "No one forces me to do anything, child, and if Gabriel had that much sway over me, I wouldn't have joined Alexander in the first place."

I open my mouth then promptly close it again as her words sink in. She has a point.

"I'm here with you because I *want* to be, Luna," she says. "That might not mean much given my past alliance with Alexander, but I am still capable of thinking for myself, and this is where my heart is telling me I should be. As for your other comment, you hardly need a minder, but your parents and I don't trust the Council, and we agreed that it's best you aren't left by yourself, just in case. Your parents are expected to aid the Council in their current endeavors, which means they can't be with you at all times, whereas my absence will hardly be noted. Around others, you have the protection of visibility, but we'd rather not take any chances when you're alone."

My breath catches. "Do you think they'd try anything?"

Lilith shrugs. "Hard to say. I would hope not, seeing as Alexander's recent penchant for arson only supports our claims about the prophecy." She looks at me with a supercilious hook of her brow. "Snatching children and burning down schools isn't very Savior-like of him, is it?"

A frown tugs at the edges of my lips. "There's nothing very Savior-like about me, either."

"That's not true." When I try to look away, Lilith grabs my chin, and although I try to avoid her gaze, her eyes are like magnets, drawing the focus of mine. "I have known your parents for a very, *very* long time, dear girl. So, believe me when

I tell you that you possess the best of both of them. There isn't a malevolent bone in your body, and I know I'm not the only one who can see that." She snorts. "Even Uriel and those other tight-asses on the Council would be hard-pressed to deny it."

Although her confidence in my moral virtue is reassuring, it doesn't change how frightened I am of the unknown path before me. A path I'd be leading who knows how many innocent people down toward their potential demise.

"What am I supposed to do, Lilith?" I ask, my eyes filling with tears. "How can I possibly fight him and win?"

"With help," she breathes, taking my face in both hands. "You are *not* alone."

A small, hiccuping sob escapes me. "I don't know how to fight with a sword. I can barely control my flame! Not to mention, Alexander's numbers are greater. And he'll—" I wince at the memory of Caleb's father, his screams silenced, his body unmoving on the floor of the citadel…and of how easily he rose again. "He'll just bring them back if they fall."

This notion doesn't seem to worry her nearly as much as I think it should. Her expression remains unchanged as she counters in a level voice, "Battles have been won with worse odds."

Worse odds? I choke back the urge to laugh. Our odds are about as bad as they can get, especially if the future of our kind and the preservation of the entire world is dependent on me.

"That's not very comforting," I grumble.

She shrugs again, lowering her hands from my face. "If it's comfort you're after, I'm certain that lover of yours would be all too happy to oblige." An impish grin slides across her features, and she chuckles at the rising heat on my cheeks.

I groan. "You're going to give me shit about our sex talk literally forever, aren't you?"

"What else are aunts for?" Lilith smirks then stands, ruffling my hair. "Have faith, sweetling. When the time comes, we will prevail. Of that, I have no doubt. And in the meantime, I can teach you a thing or two about wielding a blade."

I sober at her words and nod. That's definitely one offer I'll be taking her up on. Because someday soon, I'll have to fight Alexander, and while I doubt I'd ever be able to outmatch him in physical combat, I want to make sure I'm capable enough with a weapon to not be helpless against him, either.

"Ow." I gasp, my eyes snapping down to my forearm when a strange burning sensation sears into my skin, as if I've accidentally pressed against something hot. Pushing my sleeve up, I gape at the Enochian sigil my mother branded into my arm, the edges of the white symbol shimmering like a fresh coating of snow reflecting the light. "It's...*glowing*," I whisper, bringing my arm up to my face to get a closer look. The burning has subsided—either that or I just fail to notice it anymore past my awe.

"Gabriel is calling us to her," Lilith murmurs, and I look up to find the ex-Archdemon staring down at her own sigil, identical to mine in every way, from the shape of the tattoo to its location on her forearm. Her brow creases. "Something must be happening upstairs."

"My father? Caleb?" I choke out, bolting upright, my pulse leaping under my skin.

Lilith tugs down the sleeve of her silk crimson blouse. "Let us hope," she says, but there's an apprehensive edge to her tone that only feeds my unease.

Neither of us says another word as we retrace our steps to the top level of the city. Lilith doesn't even question how I got the sigil—not that it would take a genius to work out why Gabriel gave it to me—nor does she seem bothered by sharing a connection previously reserved for only her and my mother. I don't anticipate the rush of emotion that follows this thought or how her unspoken acceptance makes me feel.

Loved, I realize. It makes me feel loved, like I matter to the ex-Archdemon as something more than just an instrument in a prophecy.

The top level of Derinkuyu is packed with fresh bodies, replacing the horde of students already funneled into the lower depths of the city. My eyes dart between the faces before me, but it's hard to pick out any features I recognize in the overwhelming mass, the Dark auras of the Nephilim combining into one solid blanket of shadow.

Spotting my mother's golden light through a break in the crowd, I push forward into one of the larger caverns, Lilith close at my heel, and as we squeeze past the students, my nose wrinkles at the distinct burning smell filling the space. I stumble, fear freezing my steps as my gaze catches on the scorch marks on some of the Nephilims' clothing.

My stomach plunges into my feet. Was another academy attacked?

Was Babel attacked?

It's strange to think I was only just there—that a place I took shelter at only a few weeks ago might no longer exist on this planet. But what troubles me more is that Babel was Caleb's home and he might have had yet another thing he loves— or wanted to love—stolen from him. First Ishtar, then his grandfather, or rather, the dream of a father figure, since he never really had him.

Still, how many more losses must Caleb endure? How many more can he take?

"Students from Babel and Megiddo," Lilith says in my ear, as if reading my thoughts, and placing a hand on my shoulder, she urges me ahead until we're standing side by side with my mother.

The troubled expression on Gabriel's face does little to comfort my nerves.

"Any sign of them?" I manage in a meek whisper.

"Not yet." Her lips press into a hard line, and I can tell she's trying to keep it together—to mask the fear I know she's feeling. But I see it, simmering deep in her eyes, just like I glimpsed it that day under the Serapeum. Except this time, it isn't me she's afraid for.

It's my father.

"He'll be here," Lilith assures her.

My gaze hangs on my mother, and the longer I watch her, the more it sinks in how much we have in common in this moment—both of us waiting here, silently worrying for the safety of the men we love…even if Gabriel's too proud to admit her lingering feelings for my father aloud.

Suddenly, the muttering around us falls silent, and beside me, I hear my mother's breath falter when a familiar crown of golden hair appears over the crowd. Bodies part before us as Lucifer steps into the room, and my attention snaps away from my mother as I find myself caught up in my own relief, which plows into me like a tidal wave.

"Father—"

I'm nearly to him before I'm even aware my legs are moving. Bemused Nephilim step out of my way, and whispers of surprise pass through the watching crowd as I leap into his arms, throwing mine around his neck. As he hugs me back, the song of our blood shouting out in glee at our reunion, the bewildered whispers around us grow louder, and it occurs to me—somewhere in the back of my head where I can still think clearly—that it must not be common knowledge yet that the Morningstar has a child.

My hold on him tightens as tears streak my cheeks.

"Luna." He lets out a strained breath, hugging me tighter. "Are you all right?"

With a strangled laugh, I pull away, taking him in. He looks like he's been to Hell and back, and while he doesn't appear to be hurt, I can't ignore the smattering of blood painting his clothes. Whose blood is it? "I'm fine," I promise. "Are *you* okay? What happened? Babel—"

"Still stands unscathed, thankfully."

A heavy weight lifts off my chest at his words, and I exhale, thankful they got there in time—that Caleb's home remains intact. Surely, with the students and weapons removed, Alexander has no reason to destroy it—

My breath catches at that thought. If Babel is fine, then the students whose clothes were burnt had to have come from somewhere else.

"And Megiddo?" I dare to ask, glancing at the scorch marks and ash staining his shirt. My eyes flick up to his face, and although his jaw is tight, his expression stoic, his gaze is grief-stricken.

"Not as fortunate, I'm afraid," he murmurs.

Tears swim across my vision. "I'm so sorry."

I can't even begin to imagine how he feels or what it must be like to see thousands of years of love and devotion destroyed in one day of violence. As powerful as angels and Nephilim are, it makes me far too aware of how fragile some of us are, too. Of how easily our world can change in a moment. Of how much hangs on the prophecy…

And of what we all stand to lose should I fail.

"We will rebuild," Lucifer vows.

Sniffing, I dab at my eyes with my shirt sleeve. What happened to Ashkelon and Megiddo is my fault. They would still be standing if I hadn't—

I bite my tongue, trying to curtail that thought. I can't go down this road. I can't think about the lives that were lost or how the blood of innocent Nephilim is on my hands because I was foolish enough to release Alexander. I can't let the guilt consume me or I'll never find the strength to fight. To be the Savior we need to stop him.

"Where's Caleb?" I rasp. I need to see him. I need to wrap myself in his arms and hide away in our room for however many hours it takes for him to make me forget everything.

I glance past Lucifer's shoulder, but I don't see any familiar faces in the crowd behind him. Caleb *is* okay, isn't he? Surely, my father would've said if something happened to him.

Lucifer touches my arm, drawing my gaze again. "He's here. Or will be any moment now. Students are still entering from the Road. But he's *safe*, I assure you of that," he says, his voice soothing my frazzled nerves. "And probably looking for you as we speak."

Another wave of relief washes over me as the same three thoughts circle through my head on a loop—*Caleb's okay. He's here, somewhere. He's alive*—only pausing in their endless merry-go-round in my skull when I notice Lucifer's attention drift over my shoulder, and it dawns on me that Caleb isn't the only one here searching for someone. Lucifer is looking for Gabriel—*at* Gabriel. I can sense it, and the unabashed longing in his gaze only confirms my suspicion. A knowing smile curves my lips, and I step back farther, moving out of his path. We've had our moment and I'm not the only person in his life.

Nor am I the only one he loves.

"Like you were looking for Mom?" I say softly.

His brows reach for his hairline. "Mom?" he echoes, spluttering slightly. His eyes snap back to mine, and I don't miss the shock I glimpse in them. Or the overwhelming pleasure behind it.

The smile slips from my face, and I glare at him. "Don't change the subject," I warn. "And don't even *think* about making fun of me. This is all weird enough as it is."

Chuckling, he holds up his hands in surrender. "I wouldn't dare. Though…am I correct in assuming you two have reconciled your differences?"

I consider that for a moment then nod, and the way his face lights up in response makes every second of my discomfort worth it.

"She'll probably never admit it," I whisper, following his gaze, which has once again inched toward Gabriel, "but she was worried about you."

"Oh?" He cocks a golden brow. "She told you this?"

I snort. "Of course not."

"Then how do you know?" There's an uncertain pang in his tone that hits me straight in the heart. But in it, I also hear hope.

"Well, for one, she told me she wouldn't 'make the same mistake again.'" I draw out these last words, hooking my fingers into air-quotes for emphasis. Caleb is definitely rubbing off on me, and not just in the bedroom. Lowering my hands, I shrug. "But aside from that, I guess I can tell because I know how it feels to love someone the way I know she loves you."

Lucifer gapes at me, as if he's not entirely sure he heard me correctly, but the moment of hesitation passes quickly, and standing a little bit taller, he straightens his shirt. "Go. Find Caleb," he says with a wink. "I have some unfinished business with your mother."

He turns, making a beeline for Gabriel, and all around, I notice the way the Dark Nephilim stand in silence, watching the scene unfold like an audience in a movie theater. All that's missing is the popcorn. Their palpable confusion and shock makes me bold, and fighting back a grin, I call out, "Hey, Dad?"

Lucifer turns at the sound of my voice, his blue eyes blazing bright, and I wonder if he relishes the startled gasps filling the room nearly as much as I do. A smile, brighter than any I've ever seen, lights up his face. "Yes, Starlight?" he asks.

I warm at the endearment, returning his smile.

"Thank you. For keeping Caleb safe." And I mean it more than I could ever mean anything.

My father frowns. "I'll admit," he begins, his tone unnervingly hesitant, "with everything that transpired at Megiddo, I did not keep as close an eye on him as perhaps I should have." My heart jackhammers against my ribs at those words, and I feel a strange mixture of sympathy and fear—of sorrow for everything my father lost today and an overpowering unease as my mind spins in circles, trying to comprehend what he's saying. I'm about to ask what he means when he quickly adds, "You needn't worry. Beelzebub tells me Caleb held his own." A contented grin shapes his lips and he beams again, my own personal sun. "That boy is strong. You've chosen well."

My heart swells at the pride in his voice, and with a nod, he turns again toward my mother, his long stride crossing the space to her in only a few steps. Although I could easily hear what they say, I choose to tune them out, stepping back and immersing myself into the throng of students to give them privacy—or as much as they can get with so many spectators.

I weave through the crowd, searching the faces around me for Caleb, pausing only once to look back at my parents. I choose the right moment. Gabriel flushes as Lucifer takes her into his arms, and when he kisses her, she kisses him back, the divide—and past hurts—between them finally healed.

sixteen

CALEB

I'VE NEVER BEEN SO happy to be underground before. Blinking, awe fills me at the sight of my surroundings. Although I haven't gotten around to visiting yet, I recognize Derinkuyu from photos I diligently studied in art history. This isn't exactly how I imagined ticking the place off my bucket list one day—on the run from a megalomaniac—but I take comfort that this ancient city has provided refuge for those in need for thousands of years.

Ironically, we jump into one of the Christian chapels where a fresco of vengeful angels draw swords and point at the demons writhing in the pit below. I think one of the gray, leathery-looking beasts is supposed to be Lucifer himself. I snicker. The Morningstar has gone ahead and Beelzebub leads our procession out of the chapel. I think of Lucifer's golden curls and smirk. Grotesque demon, my ass.

I wonder if Luna is back with Gabriel and Raphael. Does

Alexander have enough Lights on his side to attack them on the Blessed Road? I don't think he'd venture out of his fortress yet, not until he's at full strength, but Gramps isn't exactly predictable or sane. My heart thunders in my chest, and I want to push past everyone to get to Beelzebub, but it's not like he has any more information than I do at this point. By the speed in which he's leading us into the maze of corridors, I know he's just as anxious as I am for more information.

I need to see Luna, kiss the hell out of her, then disappear to our room for a few days or a couple of hours at the very least. She's an angel, I know that she's almost impossible to kill, but she's not a match for Alexander, and I need to see with my own two eyes that she's okay.

Aya clings to me, her nails digging into my biceps and yanking me back to the here and now. Her eyes round as she takes everything in. "Where are we?" she demands.

Shoving down my worry, I smile at her. "Derinkuyu, ancient city in Turkey. Don't let the Christian art fool you. This place has been around since the Hittites."

"The who?" She smirks at me. "You're such a nerd."

"No, little sis, I'm just smart. Maybe you should try it sometime," I counter, chuckling as she scowls. "Besides, this is all part of Nephilim history, and I know firsthand that our history can and will come back and bite us in the ass." Especially when you let your daddy complex persuade you to release a monster into the world.

"He is a nerd," Rafe says, coming up beside me, "but he's not wrong. Damn, I've always wanted to visit this place. Not while running for my life, obviously."

As we file into a wide corridor, Shalina gazes around in wonder. "Me too. If I wasn't so terrified, I'd go exploring."

"I'm surrounded by nerds," Aya mutters.

Shalina glances at Aya. "Children are best seen and not heard."

I snort. "Give her a break, Lina. She's just a kid." Aya gives me side-eye, which makes me laugh harder. This is just the distraction I need to keep my head from exploding worrying about Goldilocks. "What? You're a baby."

"I helped you kill that guy," Aya points out. "I'm not a baby."

That sobers me the hell up again. And I'm reminded that my skin is tacky with dried blood that pulls at my flesh every time I move. Rafe and Shalina both fall silent, looking everywhere but at me. They helped, sure, but I'm the one who took his life. My intestines knot themselves into one giant ball.

Aya bites at her lip. "I'm sorry, Caleb."

"That's okay. Kids say stupid things." My voice is sharper than I intended and she flinches. I turn my attention to Rafe and Shalina. "This place can hold up to twenty thousand people, so we'll have plenty of room. But, um, fair warning. You'll be staying next to Lights."

"Excuse me?" Shalina says, almost tripping over the uneven stone floor. "We're going to room with *Lights*?"

"I got no problems with Grays," Rafe says, "but I don't know about Lights, man."

"You'll conduct yourself as a student of Babel and follow the rules," Hammurabi interjects, bumping into Rafe's shoulder. "The Conqueror is after us all. There is no Light or Dark to him, just potential pawns for his war. I understand it's a bitter pill to swallow, but swallow it we must."

Shalina pouts but one look at Hammurabi's hard face has her giving a hasty nod. Rafe dips his head, too.

"I still have my whips, and I don't mind making an example of children who are foolish enough to step out of line in a time of war," Hammurabi rumbles.

"Yes, sir," Shalina and Rafe say, straightening.

"Yes, sir," Aya squeaks, pressing herself against me.

"I'm cool with everyone these days," I tell him, and he rolls his eyes.

"I'm aware, boy. The lovesick looks you exchange with the flower are enough to make me ill." He strides ahead of us as I narrow my eyes at his retreating back. He pauses and looks over his shoulder. "I'm sure the flower is well. She's proven she's not so easily bruised."

I give a curt nod, swallowing hard. I hope he's right. I watch as he barks orders at students to move along.

"Big bro's in lurv," Aya taunts, grinning at me. Rafe and Shalina laugh. "As your sister, you have to let me meet her, so I can decide whether to give my approval."

"The only person whose approval I give a damn about is my

mom's and she loves Luna," I tell Aya. "But nice try."

"She met your mom, bro?" Rafe asks in surprise while Aya says, "You know your mom?"

And for the second time, an uncomfortable silence descends on us. Shit, that means Aya's mom just dumped her at Nephilim daycare and never came back. I always knew I was lucky Mom didn't do that to me. That she stuck it out, even though she had a half-immortal kid with superpowers. Aya literally has no family in her life but…me. No pressure there.

"We're going to catch up with Hammurabi," Shalina says, eyes darting between Aya and me. "Come on, Rafe."

"I've missed that old asshole," Rafe says, and he and Shalina speed up, leaving me alone with Aya.

Well, not alone, as we have scared students milling around us. I wince, feeling bad for them. Their entire world has been ripped to shreds in a matter of hours. At least I had slightly more time to adjust. I sigh and focus on Aya.

"You don't remember your mom at all?" I ask cautiously. Sometimes, human mothers keep their Nephilim children for a little while before giving them up. I don't know what's worse, for Aya to have no memory of her mom or to have bits and pieces stuck in her brain, tormenting her.

She shakes her head. "Nothing, not even a feeling of her being there. A smell. For a long time, I hoped my dad would come at least." Her laugh is bitter. "Clearly, that never happened."

"Dad's a piece of shit," I tell her. "He doesn't care about any of us. I wish I had better news for you."

"You've met him?" she demands, big eyes hard on mine.

The memory of me bringing the whip down on my father's back is seared into my brain. I give a reluctant nod. "Yeah, I did, and I wish I never had. It didn't give me the closure I thought it would."

Her eyes go bleak, as if she held out some small thread of hope, no matter how thin, of our father coming into her life and filling the enormous void there. "And Alexander?"

I grimace. "Grandfather cares, but not in a way you want. He wants to build a dynasty and use his blood to further his glory. We're all just tools to him. Pampered, well-cared for tools if we obey him, but tools nonetheless." She still looks skeptical, like maybe that doesn't sound that bad as long as she gets a grandpa out of the deal. "I didn't exactly get in line and go along with his 'take-over-the-world plan,' and he almost killed me for it. And Luna." And I thought Alaric. But it doesn't seem like that's true...

"So, basically our whole family sucks?" she says, resentment lacing her words.

"Hey, I'll have you know most people consider me fucking amazing," I tell her, pleased when a small smirk twists her lips. "And I'm totally willing to share my mom with you, but be prepared to be spoiled and fed really, really well. And don't even think of saying no when she tries to ply you with seconds."

Tilting her head to the side, Aya studies me for a moment.

"You mean that? You'd let me meet your mom?"

I nod. "Yep. Not right now, obviously, with a war on and all, but the moment it calms down, we'll take a road trip to New York. I promise."

She blinks shiny eyes at me, her brash attitude gone, making her look like the young girl she is. "Thank you, Caleb. That's… thank you." She frowns again. "Are there really more of us? Other brothers and sisters out there?"

I huff out a laugh. "I guarantee it. I'm pretty sure we'll be meeting them sooner rather than later, though I can't promise they'll be as amazing as I am. Few are."

She rolls her eyes. "Maybe they'll be more modest."

It's my turn to roll my eyes. "Nephilim? Modest? You *are* young." I loop her arm through mine once more. "Come on, kid. I need to see my girl and make sure she's all right."

Now that I've taken care of Aya the best way I can for now, my whole focus—and worry—returns to Luna. I mean, she was with her badass mother and the eternally annoying Raphael so odds are she's perfectly fine. Not to mention scary Lilith treats Goldilocks like her new favorite niece and will no doubt crush anyone who tries to harm her. But Gramps wasn't considered a military genius for nothing. No matter your arsenal, you'd be a fool to underestimate him.

We wind our way through the tunnels until we come into a larger room, which appears to be a shared communal space. There, her golden mane shining, is my Goldilocks, not a hair out of place, weaving through the crowd. A panicked expression has taken residence on her beautiful face, quickening my steps. As if she can sense me, her head swivels my way and our eyes clash. My steps falter as I take her in. Relief flashes in the depths of her gaze, and her eyes sweep over me from head to toe, searching for injuries. I know my mortality worries her, but I haven't got a scratch on me. Physically. My soul is a little worse for wear.

Then her relief vanishes and panic floods her expression again. I glance down at myself and frown. Fuck, she's freaking out because I'm covered in that dead Nephilim's blood, and she thinks it's mine. I desperately need a shower. I stride toward her, long legs eating up the distance. I can hear Aya scurry along behind me.

Luna meets me, reaching for my hands and clenching them, but holding herself back, as if she's afraid she might hurt me. "Caleb, what happened? Where are you hurt—"

I drag her against me, folding my arms around her back. "Shh, baby, I'm fine," I croon. "This isn't my blood."

She gazes up at me, tears glistening in her eyes. "Are you sure you're okay?"

I want to banish the worry and doubt in her voice, so I sweep her up, one arm hooked under her ass. Her legs wrap around me as our mouths clash in a desperate kiss, tongues dueling. She's okay. We're okay. I feel her tremble, and I try to control my own shaking. A whoosh sounds as her wings spring free, and I stroke one thumb over the beginning arch of a wing as I break our kiss and bite her where her slender neck meets her shoulder. She shudders, and I want nothing more than to carry her to our room and stroke her wings until she comes.

"Caleb," Luna admonishes me, breathing ragged. "People are staring at us."

I glance up to see a delightful ruby flush stain her cheeks. I smirk. "I haven't given them anything to stare at. Yet. Embarrassed of me?" I tease and she frowns at me.

"Of course not. I just…" She blushes again. "I can't control myself when you touch me like that," she whispers, burying her face in the crook of my neck.

My body tightens at her words, and at this rate, I'll embarrass myself in front of all the gawking Nephilim. Not that I have anything to be ashamed of, thank you very much.

"Yeah, well, I can't control myself when you touch me, either, baby, so we're even," I murmur into her hair before gently unwrapping her legs and placing her on her feet, smooth as butter. "Has Lucifer seen you already?" I ask. Mentioning Luna's father douses my lust just as well as ice water.

She nods. "Yes, right before you. He's with my mom now."

I raise a brow at the ease with which she calls Gabriel "mom." Something good must have happened on the trip between the two of them. I stroke her cheek, happy for her.

A wolf whistle pierces the charged air, slicing through our tender moment. I jerk my head around to see Rafe standing behind us, grinning at me and giving me a slow clap. "Damn, that was quite a show. Now, all we need is dinner."

Shalina is next to him. She rolls her eyes at Rafe, but mischief glimmers in her gaze when she turns to me. "Caleb was always one to put on a good show."

I slide my arm around Luna's shoulders, taking care with her wings. "Um, considering the show you two put on for me this morning, you owe me dinner for the next year."

Shalina glowers at me. "Voyeurs don't get free meals."

Luna arches a brow at me. "Voyeur?" Her eyes dart back and forth between us, clearly lost.

"Voyeur?" I choke out. "I'm lucky my eyes didn't melt out of my sockets. And who doesn't lock the door, for fuck's sake?"

A body wriggles under my free arm, and I look to see Aya staring at Luna, an awestruck expression on her face. "Your wings are beautiful," she breathes. "They're *gray*. I didn't know angels could have gray wings."

She's not the only one staring at Luna's silver feathers, but Goldilocks is too intent on Aya to notice. Her eyes narrow as she studies my little sister, Rafe, and Shalina, then she turns a questioning gaze on me.

"I'm his sister," Aya says before I can give a proper introduction. "But don't get pissed that he's never introduced us before. We just met." She smiles at Luna, clearly already won over. "I can't believe my big bro landed an angel! You better hope you're good enough for her," she adds, her dark eyes sliding to mine.

I glare at the suddenly annoying presence by my side. "Pipe down, little sis. Didn't we just have a conversation about how awesome I am?" She knows me for five whole seconds, and already she's butting into my love life. I think I took being an only child for granted. "This annoying child is Aya, and those two hypocrites are Rafe and Shalina."

"Sister?" Luna breathes, stunned amazement in her face. "But how? I thought…" She winces, her face darkening.

I know what she's thinking. She's remembering killing my father. My theory is when she killed my dad, the deal he made with the Darks became null and void, and now all his kiddos can find each other.

I nudge Aya with my elbow harder than necessary and give Luna a bright, teasing smile. She doesn't need any more dark thoughts. "I'm sure I'll meet many more brats who make my life difficult soon."

"I'm not a brat," Aya protests, scowling at me.

"If it walks like a brat, and talks like a brat—"

"Caleb," Luna scolds but she's grinning, and my heart feels like it's made of helium. "It's so nice to meet you, Aya," she says, turning toward my sister, and her warmth reminds me so much of Lucifer. Aya practically melts under the beauty of her smile. "It's nice to meet you, too, Rafe and Shalina. I just wish it was under better circumstances."

Before Rafe can open his mouth and bust my balls, an

excited ripple rolls over the front of the crowd. Hammurabi is suddenly behind me, gripping my shoulder. I glance back at him, noticing his intense expression.

"I'm so glad you're safe," Luna says to him.

"Thank you, little flower," he replies, and I grin at his affectionate nickname.

"What's going on?" I say as I feel Luna huddle closer to me. Aya presses against my other side. I think Hammurabi scares the shit out of her. Rightfully so, the old grouch.

"I'm afraid to hope," he breathes, which has Goldilocks shooting me a look of concern.

"Hope for what?" she asks him, one small hand reaching over me to cover the Babylonian king's.

It's a testament to how far their relationship has come that he doesn't throw off her hand or even flinch at her touch. He gives her an indulgent smile. "Asmodeus, child."

Shock reverberates through me, but Luna doesn't look surprised, and I see a mixture of hope and guilt reflected on her face. I know she blames herself for Asmodeus being taken, even though it wasn't her fault. Aya just gazes at me with round, confused eyes, poor kid. I honestly didn't expect the Council to return the Archdemon so soon. I see the Babel students swarm around a figure, which just shows how scared they are, because Asmodeus isn't the give-you-a-hug-and-cookies type. Yes, she loves us, and we love her, but she's still terrifying. Rafe and Shalina rush forward, but I hold back because Hammurabi isn't moving. I don't understand why. I know for a fact he's happier to see the mistress of Babel than anyone if I've been reading the room right. Maybe he's just giving the kids their moment.

A small crack in the crowd appears, and I see Asmodeus's hair, otherworldly in its garnet sheen. Her green eyes meet mine for the briefest of moments before they latch onto Hammurabi. Her lips curve at the sight of him—a warm, relieved smile— then she's swallowed by the mass of bodies once more. What does he mean to her exactly? Does the Babylonian king now occupy the place Ishtar used to hold? Or is their relationship different? There's no doubt a deep affection lies between them.

"I never understood why she let Ishtar live," I mutter to myself, but of course, Hammurabi and Luna hear me. Luna's brows raise at my odd question, which literally landed out of nowhere.

"Ishtar? Like *the* Ishtar?" Aya pipes in, but I ignore her.

Hammurabi just gives a sad shake of his head, expression grave. "When you have lived as long as Asmodeus, there are few things that you treasure, that you love. Ishtar was one of those things."

My heart clenches at his words for a moment. I know I will be one of those things for Luna. The same way she'll be for me—if I'm lucky to live a long life and Alexander doesn't kill us all first.

Asmodeus breaks away from the students and strides toward us, her steps so light I can't even hear them. She eyes Luna's hand, still offering comfort to Hammurabi, and Goldilocks snatches it away, as if she's been caught touching something that isn't hers. I smother a laugh because I don't see jealous possession in Asmodeus's eyes, only a pleased expression that grumpy old Hammurabi finally got with the program.

Hammurabi steps forward and offers a deep bow. "It's so good to see you again, Mistress." His rich baritone rings with unnamed emotion, and I fidget a little, feeling like I'm interrupting a private moment. Luna's hand finds mine and squeezes. Aya has practically burrowed into my side at the sight of Asmodeus. Smart girl.

Asmodeus flicks long ivory fingers. "None of that, old friend," she says. "It brings me joy to see you safe." Reaching out, she clasps his shoulder. Their eyes meet, and then she acknowledges Luna and me. "All of you. I knew, King, you would not fail me. You never do." Her gaze lands on Aya who squeaks. "It seems you've made a new friend, Caleb."

"Sister," I say, and the Archdemon's eyebrow arches. I grin at her. "We're damn happy to have you back." I was worried about her, especially considering how vicious the Council is.

"I failed to keep you safe," Hammurabi says and her eyes narrow.

"Nonsense," Asmodeus scolds him. "I'm the mistress of Babel. It's my job to keep *you* safe."

"I'm so sorry. I should've stayed to help," Luna blurts out, and I hear her guilt. "I could have—"

Asmodeus holds up a hand, silencing her. "Child, you couldn't have." Her voice is surprisingly gentle. "You would've just been captured again. I knew the three of you would end up exactly where you needed to be."

I snort. "I'm glad you were so confident."

Hammurabi growls at me in warning, but Asmodeus chuckles. "Haven't I always said Babel students are superior? Clever Caleb, of course, I was confident in your ability to survive."

Luna shivers. "Let's hope we can survive the upcoming war."

Asmodeus nods. "Yes, child, let us hope we can all come together and defeat the Conqueror once and for all."

seventeen

LUNA

"WE NEED TO TALK. Alone," Caleb whispers in my ear once Asmodeus departs a few moments later, spouting an excuse about wanting to find my father, with Hammurabi following at her heels. Although the Archdemon seemed no different than the last time I saw her, I can't help wondering if her imprisonment affected her as much as mine impacted me. Then again, I was in that hell for four months whereas Asmodeus only had to endure the Council's torture for a matter of weeks. To an angel who's walked the Earth since the Fall, that length of time must have seemed like a heartbeat.

"What about your sister?" I whisper back, glancing down at the girl practically nestled into his other side. At the sound of my voice, she blinks up at me with starstruck eyes, and I offer her a shy smile.

Caleb follows my gaze and shrugs. "She can hang out here with Rafe and Lina." Raising his voice for the others to hear, he says, "You guys don't mind watching over Aya for a bit while I catch up with Luna, do you?"

Aya reels back, visibly appalled by the suggestion. "I'm fourteen, not four," she grumbles. "I don't need a babysitter."

Before Caleb can comment, Rafe huffs out, "I see how it is. Stick the friends with babysitting duty so you can ditch us to go bone your girlfriend." With a dramatic sigh, he drapes a languid arm across Shalina's shoulders. "And here I was hoping we could find a dark corner to finish what we started earlier." A salacious grin forms on his lips as he waggles a brow at her, but she just rolls her eyes and sighs.

Caleb lets out an affronted gasp and slams his hands over Aya's ears. "Children are present!"

"Shove off, you big idiot," the younger girl growls, slapping his hands away. Her dark eyes then shoot daggers at Rafe and Shalina, who both chuckle under their breath. "Again, for those who need the reminder, I am *not* a child. And I know what sex is, thank you very much."

I watch with quiet amusement as Caleb wrinkles his nose.

"You do *not* know what sex is, and as far as I'm concerned, you're going to die a virgin," he tells her. Then shaking his head, he clears his throat and says, his tone almost comically authoritative, "Aya, stay here. And don't you dare sass me about it. You're my responsibility now. You two"—he jabs his pointer and middle fingers at his own narrowed eyes then shifts his hand, directing them at Rafe and Shalina—"behave yourselves. I'll be back soon."

Grabbing my hand, he tugs me away from the group, and as I stumble after him, I give his sister a small goodbye wave, somewhat unnerved by the devious smile curving her lips. We barely make it five feet before Aya's voice projects through the busy cavern behind us.

"Don't be upset if he doesn't last long, Luna. Boys his age never do," she calls after us. "I'm sure he'll get better."

Caleb falters, throwing a glare over his shoulder, and I swear I hear him grumble, "The audacity," before he trudges ahead, once again pulling me after him, even though he has no idea where he's going. "If this is what having siblings is like, I want to be an only child again."

I glance at him, biting back a laugh, though my cheeks are unbearably warm—not from embarrassment but from the thought of having sex with Caleb. We've only just taken that step in our relationship, and it's only happened once, but at least I can safely say he has nothing to worry about in that department.

I grip his hand tighter, grinning to myself, and since he has no idea where to go, I quicken my pace to get in front of him then pull him toward the archway up ahead, which leads through into the adjacent passage. We weave through the Nephilim in our path, and we're about to step out of this room into the next one when—

"Going somewhere?"

I instantly recognize the voice that coos from the shadows, and a second later, Lilith steps into our path, a sly obsidian brow hooked upward.

Beside me, Caleb growls, "Damn, Lilith. Lurk much?"

He rakes a trembling hand through his hair—the sable strands filthy with ash and blood—and as I watch him out of the corner of my eye, I focus on the low thud of his racing pulse as it slows back to normal. Although he would never admit it, whatever happened at Megiddo has made him jumpy.

I clear my throat, drawing the ex-Archdemon's attention. "I was just taking Caleb down to our room so we can talk in private. Where are my parents?"

I peer past her shoulder, squinting my eyes with intent, as if my parents will manifest in the passage behind her if I look hard enough.

A grin tugs up the corners of her lips. "Having a reunion of their own."

I grimace at the insinuation in her tone. The last thing I want to think about is what my parents get up to together behind closed doors.

"Nice job, by the way," she adds with a wink. "I don't know what you said to your father about Gabriel, but it clearly worked. How very *Parent Trap* of you."

I blink at her, confused. "I don't know what you mean—"

"Wait, you know what *movies* are?" Caleb cuts in. He shakes his head, his mouth agape. "And here I thought all angels were technologically challenged."

The ex-Archdemon crosses her arms. "I have been in exile for thousands of years. I had to spend that time doing *something*." She looks us both up and down and shrugs. "Well, what are you waiting for? Come along."

She turns her back toward us, beckoning over her shoulder for us to follow, but Caleb doesn't move.

"You aren't coming with us," he asserts, though the comment comes out more like a question.

Lilith glances back at him and snorts. "Wipe that scandalized look off your face, child. I am merely walking you to your room. I have no intention of staying to watch." She flashes a teasing smile, though it takes a moment for me to grasp her meaning.

"W-We aren't—" I stammer, but I fumble the words, a blush burning its way across my cheeks again. Well, we aren't going to our room explicitly for *that*, though I certainly won't complain if it happens again while we're there.

Lilith clicks her tongue. "Methinks you doth protest too much, Luna," she says, wagging a scolding finger. "Just remember what I said. Now, let us be off."

"I don't—" Caleb begins to say, but she cuts him off with a warning glare.

"And save your questions," she growls.

I can feel Caleb's eyes on my face, his confusion almost palpable, but I can't bring myself to look at him. The heat in my blood has reached boiling point, and if I meet his gaze, I might erupt.

Thankfully, the walk through the many levels of Derinkuyu gives me time to cool off, and by the time Caleb breaks the silence again, my thoughts have shifted elsewhere, my anxiety ratcheting higher as I wonder what he'll tell me about Megiddo once we're alone.

"So…we need you to escort us, why?" he asks once we're several levels down.

"My parents and Lilith don't trust the Council," I murmur, taking care to keep my voice low, my eyes darting between the many wooden doors lining the passage. Although I don't hear anything on the other side of them, I can't say for certain if the rooms beyond are actually empty…or if anyone inside might be listening. "They think it's best if I'm not left alone…just in case."

To Caleb's credit, he doesn't puff his chest out and try to act like he could protect me from the Council. He's not a fool, and he knows even a seasoned Nephilim like Hammurabi would struggle in a fight against someone like Mammon. Hell, it took four of us to hold the Archdemon off when Caleb sprung me from the Council's cage and I'm an angel. Lilith, on the other hand…

"If those smug shits try anything on my watch, they'll live to regret it," she vows.

Caleb raises a brow at me. "I don't doubt it," he mutters.

We walk the rest of the way without saying a word, and upon reaching our room, I grab the handle, pushing the door open without delay. I jerk my head for Caleb to enter then hurry in after him, relieved we'll finally be alone in a moment. I've missed him, and I need him to hold me without a hundred eyes watching us.

"I'll wait for you in my room," Lilith says from the doorway, glancing across the hall at an identical door less than five feet away. "Let me know when you wish to rejoin the others. I have little doubt the Council will be calling a meeting again now that everyone has returned, so keep in mind, you may not have long."

I nod.

"Oh, and Luna?" she calls just as I'm about to close the door. "Because of the stone, these rooms are well-insulated. It also makes them virtually soundproof, so you needn't worry about being too loud." A wicked grin forms on her lips. "Just thought you'd like to know."

Caleb laughs under his breath as I slam the door shut with more force than necessary. "Lilith has really settled into protective aunt mode, hasn't she?" he asks as I slump against the wood. His lips tug into a lopsided grin.

I heave a sigh, pressing a hand to my forehead. "Who knew having a family could be so exhausting?"

He snorts. "Try exasperating." But as he says this, his smile lingers, and I can sense happiness behind his false veneer of annoyance.

Caleb, who has spent his entire life disconnected from the Nephilim side of his family, finally has someone he's tied to through his angelic blood—someone not only outside Alexander's influence but who, from the brief encounter I witnessed between them at least, seems just as eager to accept him as her brother as he is her as his sister. The one silver lining to come out of the evacuations.

That thought sobers me, and pushing away from the door, I cross to him, gently taking his hand. "Was it bad?" His warm brown eyes search mine, and bracing myself, I whisper, "Megiddo."

The smile finally slips from his face, and he nods. "Yeah," he says, and for the first time, I notice the trembling in his fingers and the lack of color in his cheeks. Unless, of course, you count the dried blood, which still stains his skin.

Releasing his hand, I cross to the brass wash basin a few steps from the foot of the bed—the only means of washing we've been provided in this ancient place—and dunk the small cloth hanging over the side into the tepid water.

"May I?" I ask, turning to face him and raising my hand, the sodden fabric clenched tight in my fingers.

His gaze darts to my hands, and he snorts. "So much for modern plumbing," he grumbles. When I arch a brow, he nods, his eyes shuttering.

Returning to his side, I carefully drag the damp cloth across his left cheek. The blood flakes off at my touch, but there's a pain in his expression that surfaces. That I can't wipe away.

"Caleb?" I hedge when he doesn't speak. He swallows loudly

then swipes his tongue across his lower lip. It wobbles slightly.

"I…" he begins, his eyes opening slowly, and there's a dreary emptiness in his gaze that tells me everything I need to know about the horrors he encountered today.

I move the cloth to his other cheek, but his hand flies up, touching mine, and I freeze.

I can't stop myself from asking—from needing to know what's troubling him so I can do whatever it takes to banish it from his thoughts. "Caleb…what's wrong?" I breathe, my heart racing.

And then, to my heart-wrenching horror, he breaks.

"I killed someone." A single tear cuts down the cheek I just cleaned, which he hurriedly brushes away. "They deserved it," he adds before I can respond, as if he feels the need to justify it. "He would've killed us if I hadn't, and I—"

"You did what you had to," I protest, lowering my hand and the cloth from his face. With my free hand, I twist my palm, threading our fingers. "All that matters is that you're okay. When we saw Alexander—"

"Wait, what?" His eyes blow wide, and he gapes at me, his expression dancing between horror and disbelief. "What do you mean you saw Alexander?"

His voice is breathy, his tone saturated with panic, and I berate myself for not breaking the news more gently, especially considering the hell he's already been through today. The shock on his face is apparent, and I wish I could take it all back—erase that fear—but I can't. Just as I can't take away the trauma he'll carry for taking a life. A trauma I know all too well.

"On the Blessed Road," I explain. "On the way here after evacuating the Serapeum. He and some first generation Lights intercepted us."

A shadow crosses the planes of his face. "I was afraid of that. I guess that means Gilgamesh has been recruiting," he muses.

My answering frown is bleak. "It seems so."

"Was anyone injured?"

I shake my head. "Well, Alexander *tried* to kill Gabriel," I correct myself, "but I stopped him—"

"Wait," Caleb says, interrupting me for the second time. I blink up at him, taken aback by the unexpected anger I glimpse in his gaze. "What do you mean, you *stopped* him?"

I spend the next few minutes recounting what happened on the Blessed Road. The whole time, Caleb stares at me with stunned incredulity, saying nothing.

When I finish, he takes my face in his hands and leans in. "As badass as that sounds, Goldilocks, you could've *died*," he breathes, the words hot on my lips.

"I know." I keep replaying that moment, and the realization of how close I came to death sits just under the surface of my skin at all times now, like an itch I can't scratch. And yet, I'd do it all over again to avoid the alternative outcome I'd be faced with if I hadn't acted. "But he was going to kill Gabriel. If it was your mom, what would you have done?"

He opens his mouth and then immediately snaps it shut. He can't argue with that. After all, we both know he wouldn't hesitate to defend his mother if her life were in jeopardy. Hell, he didn't hesitate to protect her from a thirsty Hammurabi.

The worry creasing his brow only deepens. "I don't like this. Alexander wouldn't attack for no reason—everything he does is calculated and deliberate." He pulls away from me and begins pacing the room, scrubbing a hand over his face, one cheek clean and one still dirty, almost like he's wearing war paint. "He's a military strategist, for fuck's sake."

"Maybe it was a distraction," I consider. "To delay us and stop us from helping at Megiddo." I know I'm grasping at straws, especially since the Darks didn't ask for our aid, but I can't figure out what other motivations Alexander might have had for intercepting us.

Caleb pauses mid-step and throws a dubious look over his shoulder. "I mean, yeah, assuming the Roads follow a similar path, you would've passed through Israel to get here from Egypt, but it still doesn't really add up. Like, how would you even know Megiddo was being attacked from inside the Blessed Road?"

"The sigils?" I suggest. "Gabriel told me the Council has one they all use to commune with each other, and she also has one just to contact my father. Maybe Alexander knows that."

"Maybe." Caleb looks only slightly more convinced than he did a moment ago. Plopping down on the edge of the bed, he bends forward, resting his head in his hands. "I don't know. Something about all this doesn't feel right."

A sinking feeling twists my gut at those words, and I find myself hoping Caleb is wrong—that the ambush on the Blessed Road really was just a diversion and not a sign of something worse. Because if he isn't, then that means Alexander's appearance today was an omen, a warning of what's yet to come. And I can't help fearing that—whatever that something is—we won't be ready for it.

"Luna." Caleb's voice shakes me free of my thoughts, and I glance at him, not realizing my concentration drifted. He sits straight now, his face no longer obscured by his hands, but when our eyes meet, the sensation in my gut only worsens.

"There's something else," he says, a slight, unnerving tremor distorting his tone. "Aya said a Light was at Megiddo, that he warned her to run before Alexander's followers could take her. Just her…like he knew who she was."

My brow furrows as I try to make sense of what he's trying to tell me. *A Light?* Why would a Light be at Megiddo?

He jerks his head, wincing, one of his eyes fluttering closed for a moment as if he's in pain. "I saw him when we arrived at the school, but it was chaos, and I thought I was seeing things—"

"Saw who?" I cut in, an all-too-familiar panic swelling inside me. "What are you talking ab—"

"Alaric," he whispers. The misery in his voice when he says that one word is reflected on his face. He licks his lips, staring at me with wide eyes. "Luna…I saw Alaric."

I freeze, and for a long moment, I'm not even sure if I remember to breathe. It's not possible. I *saw* Alaric die. I watched Alexander plunge his knife in his chest, and I saw the light of life leave his eyes. It's not possible.

Alaric is dead.

"But he's…" I trail off, barely able to form a coherent thought in my shock. If Alaric is dead, Caleb couldn't have seen him at Megiddo. Not unless—

My knees buckle, and I stumble forward a step, as if I'm the one who's been stabbed in the heart. Caleb jumps up from the bed and launches forward to catch me, his warm arms forming the safety net I need to keep me afloat as the waters of grief rise again to drown me.

As he pulls me close to his chest, I manage through a sob, "Did Alexander…" But I'm unable to bring myself to finish voicing that thought, even if I hear it on repeat like a constant scream ringing in my skull.

Did Alexander resurrect Alaric?

"No," Caleb says, but his answer struggles to penetrate the haze of my mind as the memory of our brief time at the citadel comes rushing back. In my head, I see his father again and as I watch him die—and then relive how easy it was for Alexander to raise him, it takes every ounce of self-control I possess to keep myself from retching…or weeping.

Although I didn't stick around to see what became of Caleb's father after his resurrection, I do remember the eerie emptiness in his gaze—how when he rose from the stone floor, he looked at me with zero recognition, even though I had just killed him.

I didn't want to admit it then, but I understand now why resurrection is forbidden among both the Lights and the Darks. It *is* unnatural, and I want to cry picturing Alaric that way, like an empty vessel for Alexander to manipulate and control. And on the off chance he did come back as himself, what was stopping Alexander from wiping his memories—or at least any recollections he had of me?

What if Alaric no longer knows who I am?

"No," Caleb says again, firmly this time, tilting my chin up with his finger. "I mean, it crossed my mind for a hot second, but if that was the case, why would he help Aya? I don't know all the ins and outs of resurrection, but it can't be that different to how we Darks give life to inanimate objects. It's all based in the same root premise, and I feel like Alaric would be beholden to Alexander or something, like those objects are to us. It *is* magic at the end of the day, and Alexander would be his tie to the living world."

Although my head is foggy with shock and grief, Caleb's reasoning makes enough sense to reach me. He has a point. In Kandahār, Alexander made it perfectly clear he planned to use Alaric's talent to track down his other grandchildren and bring the rest of their bloodline into the fold. If Alaric *was* under Alexander's command, he would be hunting Caleb's siblings down, not warning them to run.

As if we share one mind, Caleb adds, "If Alaric was in any way being controlled by my gramps, he wouldn't have just let her go."

My mouth puckers into a grimace, the words sour on my tongue as I choke out the only other explanation for how Caleb could've possibly seen Alaric if he wasn't resurrected. Because if Alexander didn't bring him back from the dead, then that can only mean…

"So, you think he's been alive this whole time?" That thought is a sledgehammer to my lungs, and I gasp around tears, "That we left him…"

That *I* left him.

My knees go weak again, and slipping out of Caleb's arms, I sink to the floor in a near catatonic heap, my mind a whirlwind of unwanted memories, which assault me with merciless abandon. Again, I see Alexander's dagger, buried to the hilt in Alaric's chest. Again, I see the Nephilim glance at me with a devastating relief in his eyes—relief that I was physically unhurt, even though my heart was breaking.

"We didn't know," Caleb whispers when a strangled sob escapes me. Crouching to the floor, he plants his hands on my shoulders. "We didn't know, Goldilocks. This isn't our fault."

You're right. It isn't our fault. It's mine.

Hot tears burn my cheeks, and a full-body shudder wracks me down to my marrow. Alaric took that dagger to the chest to save *me*. He sacrificed his life for *me*. And although logic keeps screaming at me that we couldn't have saved him—that Caleb is right, that we didn't know—I still can't help blaming myself for this outcome.

My fingers snake into my hair, gripping my skull, as I jerk my head side to side. Everything bad that keeps happening is my fault. Alexander's freedom. Alaric almost getting stabbed to death. The destruction of Ashkelon and Megiddo.

How can I possibly be the Savior when the blame for all of these terrible occurrences rests on my shoulders?

"No," I persist, the word like broken glass in my mouth, cutting me. "No, he can't be alive. If he was, why would he stay with Alexander? Why wouldn't he come find us?"

Why wouldn't he come find me?

"Maybe he can't." Caleb's tone is unnervingly gentle, like every word is an egg he's taking care not to drop. "I doubt my gramps let him hang onto his phone."

I sink my teeth into the inside of my cheek, biting back the influx of emotion I feel rising in my throat. "But he has the sigil, remember? He could contact my father." Hell, he could have contacted him at least a hundred times by now. And yet, he hasn't.

Frowning, Caleb touches a hand to my cheek, sweeping his thumb across my wet cheekbone. "Something must be stopping him. Trust me, Alaric is not Team Alexander. If he's in his right mind, then he has his reasons for not leaving."

I nod. Caleb's right. The trouble is, Alaric *has* a good reason to stay. Because even after everything, he loves Alexander...

And if he isn't careful, that love will get him killed. For good, this time.

As Lilith predicted, the Council does call a meeting, and less than an hour later, I, along with thirty-three other angels, demons, and Nephilim, sit cramped together in one of Derinkuyu's more secluded caverns, perched in a ring of wooden chairs that seem to have materialized out of nowhere. I have no idea who found the time to furnish the place before our arrival at the underground city, but they seem to have thought of everything—including how many chairs we would need to host the extra guests.

Aside from the fourteen Archangels and Archdemons in charge of the academies—still including my mother and father—Zerachiel and a Fallen I don't know are here, along with one chosen Nephilim per each member of the Council, with the exception of my mother, who chose to bring two. In addition to Evangeline, she also invited Kali to the meeting, and after everything she did to help us in India, it's a relief to see her here—a familiar, kind face among so many that still look at me as if I can't be trusted just because I'm a Gray.

I regard the unfamiliar faces with curiosity. I can only

assume the unknown Fallen is the one who temporarily stepped in for Asmodeus at Babel. I peer around the room, taking in the many faces around me, recognizing some of the first generation Nephilim joining our meeting. On Caleb's right side, Hammurabi sits tall and stiff beside Asmodeus while Evangeline grins at me between my father and Kali, who sits next to Gabriel, my mother a beacon radiating stern silence on my left. Hatshepsut is here as well, accompanying Raphael, and the tall woman beside Beelzebub is the same injured Nephilim he brought with him when he escaped from Ashkelon, though I can't remember learning her name. Aside from those five, I only recognize one other Nephilim in the room. She watches me from the other side of the oblong circle, her dark eyes swinging back and forth between my face and Asmodeus, as if waiting to see which of us will come at her first.

Nzingha.

I tense in my chair, my fingers wrapping around the edge of the wooden seat, which begins to splinter beneath the force of my grip. Because of her, we had to go to Alexander for help to get the Council's tracker out of my head. Because of her, Alaric—

Drawing in a deep, cleansing breath, I chase that thought away before it can form. I need to focus. I can't let her get to me, even if I would love to rip her to shreds for betraying us.

We're all allies now, I remind myself, but even as this thought crosses my mind, I find myself glancing at the glowering hulk of a man beside Nzingha. Mammon's aura is a menacing shroud of hate, his burly arms crossed over his chest, those red eyes staring daggers at Caleb, who sits impressively still under the Archdemon's scrutiny in the seat beside me on my right.

I have zero doubt Mammon would ignore the truce and attack Caleb if given the chance. If there weren't at least two Archdemons, one Archangel, a Gray, and a grumpy Nephilim who would stand in his way, I have no doubt he would try right now. But Caleb won't always have this much protection around him, and that's the time I worry about most—about what awaits once this truce is over.

I'll be there, I vow, releasing my grip on the seat of the chair and reaching for Caleb's hand. He grips mine back when I squeeze his fingers. *And I won't let anything happen to you.*

Someone clears their throat and I glance to the left as Uriel rises to his feet. "Two academies have fallen," he announces, his tone crestfallen. A beat of silence follows these words, then when the moment has passed, he adds, "I suppose it could've been worse."

"Of course *you* think that," Beelzebub seethes, his small hands balled into shaking fists in his lap. He looks about as restrained as I feel, which doesn't say much for our shared lack of composure. "It wasn't Light schools that have been burned to the ground."

Uriel's upper lip peels back in a snarl, and he opens his mouth to fire back what I'm sure is a scathing retort lacking any form of compassion for the Archdemon's loss. Fortunately, my father's voice booms through the space, silencing the Archangel before he can utter a word.

"For once, can we conduct a meeting without resorting to petty squabbles? Two schools lost is two too many, regardless of if they are Light or Dark."

"Lucifer is right," Abaddon says with a respectful nod toward my father as Uriel sinks back into his chair. "And if the Conqueror is willing to raze our academies, what else is he prepared to do? What extremes is he willing to go to? The danger to our students aside, the glamors would have been destroyed when Ashkelon and Megiddo burned. It will not be long before the mortals take notice, assuming they haven't already."

Caleb lets out a harsh, humorless laugh, unafraid in this company of more powerful beings. "I was there when he turned Gilgamesh, and Alexander's whole speech persuading him to 'come to the Dark side' was about how we won't have to hide anymore once he's running the show. He *wants* the humans to know we exist. For all we know, the attack on the schools was just the prelude to our big coming out party."

An unsettled murmur spreads through the room as the Faithful, Fallen, and Nephilim all exchange worried glances. I don't like that look or how afraid they all seem by the prospect of our kind being revealed to the humans. Then again, while our species is superior in strength, mortals vastly upstage us in number, and the last thing the angels and Fallen want is a repeat of the early days of the Nephilim when many were lost to prosecution and terror. There are only so many places left on Earth where our kind can hide. Blind ignorance is what keeps us safe.

"No one is asking the obvious question," Mammon interjects, and beside me, Caleb tenses as those crimson eyes rove over his face before shifting between the others in the room. "Why Ashkelon and Megiddo? Why those two schools of all the academies?"

To my surprise, Caleb is the one who answers, though his voice is soft, barely a whisper, and he only says one word. "Aya." When everyone looks at him, he clears his throat and adds, louder now, "My sister is a student at Megiddo. The Darks attacking the school tried to take her."

"Then it isn't just *any* student the Conqueror is after," Uriel muses, and his gaze turns stormy as he looks at my father. "Did you know about this?"

I watch Lucifer with bated breath as my mind turns over the same question. Caleb once told me the Archdemons made a deal with his father to hide his kids from each other so they wouldn't unite and hunt him down—a deal that came in the form of a blood bind, similar to what Gabriel did to me. A bind that I can only assume broke the moment Caleb's father died at the citadel, however brief that death may have been. When *I* broke into his mind and killed him.

Caleb and I have barely had time to talk since we got back from evacuating the schools, so we haven't even been able to really broach the topic of him having a sister—or that my father would've known about her. The whole "Alaric is still alive" bombshell dominated the little time we've had together.

"About the Conqueror's grandchildren?" Lucifer asks, his lilting voice yanking me from my thoughts. "Yes, though it would be foolish of any of us to think that was Alexander's only motive. He may wish to locate his descendants and broaden his dynasty, but we all know his real priority is building an army, and for that, he needs bodies and weapons. Weapons that can actually harm us."

He's right. Alexander might want to unite his family, but he's not sentimental enough to actually care whether they live or die. What he truly cares about is gaining devoted followers, and he probably figures blood relatives are the easiest Nephilim to persuade to join his side. It's like dominoes—turn one and others will follow. The vast numbers he already commands are proof enough of that.

I glance at Caleb. He doesn't look angry or accuse my father of withholding the information about his sister from him. After all, he knew he must have siblings out there in the world, and he knew the Archdemons had put a bind on them—though how they detected them to begin with is a mystery to me unless the Darks have someone in their ranks with a gift like Alaric's.

I quickly dismiss that thought. If there *was* someone else out there who could sniff out bloodlines, Alexander wouldn't be sending Alaric to the academies to track down his grandkids.

Surely, he wouldn't trust him not to attempt an escape. No, I have a feeling that's a one-of-a-kind talent, which means the Archdemons have another way of recognizing Caleb's bloodline. A detection ward, perhaps, built into every Dark school?

Filing that question away in the back of my mind to ask my father about after this meeting, I direct my focus back to Caleb. I can't imagine how he must be feeling, how something that was so distant and untouchable for so long can suddenly be so present and real. And while anger doesn't illuminate his gaze, he does look afraid, like he now has so much more to lose.

"How would the Conqueror even know where to find his grandchildren?" Abaddon asks. His deep, rumbling timbre draws my attention. "From what you have told us, Gabriel, the only Nephilim we know of with the ability to detect bloodlines is dead. And even if Alaric *were* alive, the bind on their line should prevent such detection."

A lump forms in my throat at these words, and I flash a quick glance at Caleb only to find him already looking at me, his eyes wide with the same fear I'm certain he sees reflected in mine. He hasn't told anyone else what he told me about Alaric, and this is why. Too many questions would be raised. Questions about Alaric's allegiance. And given that Alaric was the one who removed the bind on Alexander in the first place, the Council would have justification to wonder where his loyalties lie, even if in the end he helped them imprison the Gray. I have no doubt someone like Uriel would suggest Alaric might regret that decision.

I swallow, turning my eyes back to Abaddon, trying to keep my face calm and composed. Even though I want to shout it from the rooftops, the Council can't know about Alaric. Not yet. Not until we have tangible proof he's alive…

And that he isn't willingly helping Alexander.

"Unless the bind has been broken," Belphegor considers. "How else would the boy know of his sister?"

All eyes focus on Caleb, then on my father, as if searching for an explanation. But before either can speak, Leviathan asks, "What about the boy's father? It is he, after all, who makes us aware of his spawn."

I blink, taken aback by the Archdemon's cavalier statement. Could it really be that simple? No detection wards at the schools? No complex magic? The Archdemons know about Caleb and his siblings because his father told them?

Well, that's one mystery solved, I muse. My jaw clenches and my free hand once again grips the edge of the chair seat so hard it cracks. Caleb once told me his dad never sticks around to raise his kids. But this—this agreement his father has with the Archdemons—implies he at least sticks around long enough to confirm if whoever he's sleeping with at the time has a bun in the oven. Like Caleb's mom. Caleb's wonderful mom whom he left to deal with pregnancy all alone.

Asmodeus snorts, rolling her eyes at Leviathan. "Yes, right before he frolics off to make another sperm deposit elsewhere."

Beside me, Caleb is unnervingly silent, and as the Archdemons discuss the matter, I watch him out of the corner of my eye, searching for a reaction. Aside from a slight tightening of his lips, there is none.

"I highly doubt the boy's father is aiding the Conqueror on this matter," Abaddon drawls. "Have we forgotten why he bargained for the bind in the first place? His children nearly killed him once. He wouldn't risk facing their wrath again, especially now that their numbers could almost certainly populate a large village. No," he mutters, shaking his head. "If the bind has somehow been broken, it's far more likely he would make himself scarce."

"But he was at the citadel, wasn't he?" Gabriel asks. She's the only Light to enter the conversation while the others all glance between the Darks as if they're watching a game of tennis. "Hammurabi, you told us as much when recounting your time there."

The Babylonian king crosses his arms. "As a prisoner," he clarifies. "I do not believe Alexander had any intention of bringing him into the fold."

"It wouldn't matter if Alexander's controlling him," Caleb says.

My brows draw together and I blink at him, confused. Caleb and I both know his father has nothing to do with how Alexander is finding his siblings. Alexander made his intentions clear when we were at the citadel, and Caleb spotting Alaric at

Megiddo only confirmed it. So, why…

The answer crosses my mind as Caleb's eyes cut to mine, and I realize he's giving the Council a scapegoat, something to draw their focus—and blame—away from Alaric. I give a quick nod, urging him to continue.

He clears his throat. "The bind on our line is definitely broken because I *felt* my sister at Megiddo and—"

Leviathan holds up a hand, cutting him off. "For the bind to be broken, your father would have to be—"

"Dead. Yeah," Caleb says in a blunt monotone, interrupting him right back. I'm grateful he purposely leaves out the part about me being the one who killed him. "But he didn't stay dead for long. Alexander resurrected him, and, like a true villain, is now probably pulling his strings like an evil puppeteer."

"And sending him to hunt down his bloodline," Lucifer mutters. He hums softly under his breath then nods to himself before exchanging a grim look with the others. "I believe Caleb may be right. When our paths last crossed, Alexander was quite insistent he would not hesitate to resurrect any who follow him. He has always been obsessed with establishing an empire, and it is very likely he would kill his own son just to raise him again if doing so could help him achieve his goals."

"Resurrection?" Amenadiel says, aghast. "Surely, he wouldn't dare use such a power. It is unnatural!"

"We should not presume to know what the Conqueror is willing to do," Gabriel growls. "Nor should we underestimate him or his attachment, however shallow, to his bloodline. Clearly, there are many elements at play here."

"Are there others, then?" Serathiel chirps. Her attention turns to Beelzebub. "Did the Conqueror have any kin studying at Ashkelon?"

My stomach dips at the question, and Caleb's hand tightens around mine when Beelzebub nods.

"A boy of sixteen. Though he was not found among the wreckage, so we assumed he was taken by the Conqueror's allies to add to his ranks like so many others. Or he's…" He trails off, and his shining blue eyes shift to Caleb.

Dead, they seem to scream in the silence.

The hand wrapped around mine goes slack, and I risk a concerned glance at Caleb, noting the haunted look in his eyes and the waxy, wan tone to his skin.

"Does it even matter?" Azrael scoffs. "We are speaking of adolescent Nephilim. They hardly pose a threat to us."

A mortified laugh rips from Serathiel's throat. "I certainly hope you aren't suggesting that you would take up arms against children?" She balks, and I know she must be thinking of her own young students at the primary academy at Petra.

"Age matters little in war," Belphegor snarls. "And if they join the Conqueror, then they *are* the enemy. Besides, our softness toward the Nephilim may be precisely what Alexander is hoping for. They are a weakness he will use against us."

"He's right," Lucifer says, his tone stiff. I glance over at him to find him already looking at me, and I can't help wondering if he sees *me* as his weakness—the one vulnerability in his armor that Alexander will try to exploit. "It's likely Alexander knows we will do everything in our power to avoid going to war with our students, and he may even present them as a bargaining chip to force us to submit to his rule. Though, I doubt there are many who would side with him willingly. These are scared children we speak of, not seasoned warriors. We must take that into consideration and not judge too harshly those who may act under coercion."

Uriel frowns and rubs his large hand over his chin. "War with our students should be avoided at all costs, but we must also consider the greater good. We cannot let the safety of a few sway us from defeating this threat."

Serathiel flinches. "Our students *are* the greater good, otherwise what have we been working toward all these long years? Why construct the academies if we do not do everything in our power to protect those we have dedicated our lives to? We cannot let the Conqueror make a mockery of our legacies any longer. We must make the safety of the children a priority… until doing so is no longer a viable option."

"We do not have time for this," Gabriel says, her expression hard. "Whatever Alexander's intentions are for the children, the more immediate risk is our exposure. The preservation and secrecy of our kind has always been paramount to this Council. We must act before Alexander reveals us to the world or worse."

"What then do you propose, Messenger?" Uriel asks, his words patronizing and snide. He sneers. "What course of action would *you* have us take?"

Her jaw clenches, and I can practically hear her teeth grinding together with derision. Her dark eyes flit around the room, jumping between the many faces around us. "We must rally those loyal to us and strike first before Alexander can enact whatever other devious plans he has for us. We cannot sit idly by any longer, not when another devastating attack could be imminent."

"We have the advantage of knowing where he is," my father agrees. "This may be our only opportunity to get the drop on him."

"And with us on the defensive, surely the Conqueror will not expect our swift retaliation," Asmodeus adds. "Plus, we can take this opportunity to try to get the children out safely and perhaps retrieve some of our lost weapons while we're at it. Given what they mean to us and the strides Alexander took to steal them, it's likely he will keep both very close."

I peer between my parents and Asmodeus, gauging the mutual agreement stretching across each of their faces, but I'm unable to ignore the uneasy weight forming in the pit of my stomach. They're right—this may be our only opportunity to turn the tables on Alexander—but all I can think about is that smug look he gave me and my mother on the Blessed Road. He's up to something, I know it...

And once again, I can't help fearing the worst is yet to come.

"Or maybe that's exactly what he expects." Everyone looks at me, but I hold steady, refusing to flinch and refusing to blindly agree with this plan just because it was my parents' idea. Or maybe I'm just speaking out of fear—out of my terror of returning to the citadel, which serves as the setting in many of my nightmares. That and that awful egg I wasted away in for months. I swallow the rising lump in my throat. "Alexander *knows* we know where he is," I point out. "And that's assuming he's even still in Kandahār."

"She's right," Lilith says from where she sits beside Asmodeus. "We could be walking into a trap. We need to consider the risk."

"Do not make the mistake of believing you have a voice on this Council, Lilith," Uriel growls, spitting her name like a curse. "You lost that right when you chose to side with Alexander the last time we were in this predicament."

A cruel, mocking laugh parts her lips. "And yet, I know Alexander better than any of you. I would think you'd want to use what information I possess about him to your advantage."

"That's assuming we can trust anything you say, *snake*," he bites back.

"Enough," Gabriel hisses, glaring at Uriel before offering an apologetic look at Lilith. "The reality is, the risk is just as great if we choose to do nothing. And if his next move exposes our kind? What other option do we have but to act?"

She holds Lilith's gaze for a moment, and in the silence

between them, I sense an unspoken conversation—some deeper meaning to my mother's words. It isn't just exposure she's worried about but something else…and I realize that deeper meaning is me. Because every moment this war is drawn out is another moment that leads me closer to becoming a victim of the prophecy my mother has feared since the days of the Fall. A fear that led her to lock me away as a baby so she wouldn't have to lose me. A fear she's faced with again now and had to experience firsthand on the Blessed Road when Alexander had the chance to kill me in front of her.

As much as I don't like it, I accept that she's right. The scales are already tipped in Alexander's favor, and by doing nothing, we would only be giving him more time to unbalance them further. I don't like it, but what other choice is there?

I bite my lip, holding back the sudden burn of tears, as another thought strikes without warning.

If we go to Kandahār, we might find Alaric.

If nothing else, surely the risk is worth that?

"Let us not forget that taking up residence here was always a temporary measure," Beelzebub says, his youthful voice echoing through the cavern. "We cannot remain in Derinkuyu forever, so let us take advantage of this opportunity and be done with all this."

"We would be foolish to squander what might be our only chance to take the Conqueror by surprise. We know Alexander's location when he does not know ours. It is not often we have been able to say that," Raphael agrees, her tone lacking its usual acidity. I'm shocked she's managed to stay silent so long. Usually, she injects her opinion at the first available opening.

"And if the Conqueror *has* left Kandahār?" Mammon presses. "What do the traitors here suggest we do then?" His upper lip curls back in a contemptuous snarl as he glares across the cramped space at my parents.

But before either of them can answer, Caleb blurts out, "Then we figure out where he's relocated by searching the citadel." My eyes dart to his face, and I'm relieved to find the anguish in his gaze replaced with a fierce determination, which he directs at the scowling Archdemon, as if to say, *I'm not afraid of you*, even if I see the truth in the jerky movements of his aura. After a moment, he looks at me, and when he squeezes my hand again, I know we're thinking the same thing. That if Alexander and his forces aren't in Afghanistan any longer, then maybe we can at least find some clue about Alaric. Some confirmation he really *is* alive…

And if so, where we might be able to find him.

"Either way, we need to end this. Quickly," my father stresses. "Before any further damage is done." There's a pain in his voice as he says these last words, and my chest tightens when it dawns on me he's talking about Megiddo.

Once again, his eyes find mine, and as I stare into their shining depths, it occurs to me that he and my mother are driven by fear as much as I seem constantly hindered by it. They want this over because dealing with Alexander and removing the threat hanging over our heads is the only way to ensure not only my survival, but the safety of the Nephilim they've been charged with the task of caring for—a role that has consumed their lives for hundreds of thousands of years.

"Then our decision is made." Uriel stands, and the others all follow suit, as if sensing the impending conclusion of our meeting. "Send out messengers and call on your allies," the Archangel urges, and the angels and Fallen exchange weighted glances with their Nephilim companions as he says, "We leave at dawn."

eighteen

CALEB

I STARE DOWN AT the last place on Earth I want to be. Alexander's fortress rests below, as harsh and forbidding as I remember. The sun beats down on us, warming the cool mountain air. Pain slices my skull as I remember Gramps cracking my mind like a nut—something that might happen again if we meet today. I shake it off. Now is not the time to lose my shit.

Luna crouches next to me, and we wait for Uriel—I still hate that asshole—to give the signal. Gabriel and Lucifer should be in charge. Hell, put Hammurabi as general, even if he's just a Nephilim, but Creator forbid the Council take orders from someone who isn't an angel. The three of them have actually been inside Alexander's lair. But nope, before we left Derinkuyu, that dick Uriel insisted he lead because he's still unsure of our loyalties, thinking Lucifer and Gabriel will just run off with Luna if shit heads south. I hope when this is over, the Morningstar and the Messenger beat his ass. They have lots of scores to settle with him. I'll lend a hand.

Hammurabi flanks my other side, and Lilith remains behind Luna. I glance over my shoulder, seeing the Council—including Gabriel, Lucifer, and Asmodeus—perch on the sharp cliffs like birds of prey, along with other Fallen allies. They're unnaturally still, and it reminds me of just how *other* they are. I mean, I have celestial blood, but sometimes angels seem so alien to me. I know Luna is an angel, too, but she's so young that she hasn't evolved into what they are. At her core, she remains human. Her wings are tucked under her skin, as she's not adept at flying yet, though her parents have promised to teach her.

I wonder how much Lilith hates being down here with us, not because we're Nephilim, minus Luna, but because she must really miss her wings. An evil grin paints my face. Mammon is down here, too. Somewhere. He's keeping his distance, being watched by both Hammurabi and Lilith. He can kill Hammurabi but Lilith is a different story. Every once in a while, I feel ice slide down my spine, and I know he's watching me. I might make it out of this war alive only to be murdered by that shape-shifting psycho.

Luna is restless beside me, practically bursting with unease. She can't be easily hurt physically, but mentally she's vulnerable, and facing Alexander isn't good for either of our sanities. Lucifer and Gabriel don't like that Luna's on this mission. They didn't come right out and say it, but I know they wanted her to stay behind where she'll be safe, but they can't exactly suggest that. They have to convince the Council Luna is the Savior, so whether they like it or not, she has to come along to give truth to their claims. The Council will turn on her in a heartbeat if they think they're being played, and her parents know that.

Nephilim surround us, waiting on Uriel's signal. The angels and Fallen are the cavalry and we're the infantry. Once our scout reports back to Uriel about Alexander's numbers and the locations of his guards, we'll slip into the Roads and pop out and attack.

"This is wrong," Hammurabi murmurs beside me, his eyes fixed on the citadel.

"What about this fucked-up situation is right?" I whisper back and he elbows me. Hard.

"Where are the Conqueror's sentries? It's too quiet," he says, and my eyes dart around.

"We're still waiting for our scout to come back. Let's not panic just yet," I counter, frowning. "Gramps probably doesn't think we have the balls to attack him in his secret headquarters. Even if he knows we're with the Council, he's probably banking on the fact that they can barely agree on lunch, let alone battle plans." As those words leave my lips, I really hope they're true, but doubt gnaws on my gut. I understand why the Council chose to make this move, but I don't like this plan, not that I would ever say that aloud—I don't want to call attention to the universe and give us more bad luck.

Hammurabi shakes his head. "Boy, you know better than anyone that Alexander is never unprepared. We should have killed at least a couple of his soldiers by now. He wouldn't let the mountains go unwatched."

Luna gazes at me with worried eyes. "But with everyone the Council has called in to help, we have the larger force now. We can counter him, right?"

"We hope," Hammurabi says, and I wish for once Mr. Sunshine could try to be positive, although I secretly agree with him. Gramps is too fucking smart to get caught with his pants down.

"Creator be, King, you're full of optimism as always." Lilith's tart voice echoes behind us. "But in this, I fear you may be right. It is too quiet for my liking as well."

Terror blossoms inside me, and I see my trepidation reflected in Luna's hazel eyes. Like a jab to the face, it hits me again how *young* we both are. Two babies on a battlefield. Well, no matter what Alexander has up his sleeve, we'll be forged in battle today. And we're potentially not the only kids here. I have a younger brother who might be down there somewhere, but I can't let myself linger on that too much. It's a distraction I can't afford.

My eyes flick back to the fortress. With my Superman eyesight, I can pick out a few figures moving along the top of the outer wall, like two tiny dots creeping along.

"Ha!" I crow to Hammurabi, who immediately growls at me to shut up. "I see two sentries on the wall right now, so someone is keeping watch. Maybe we got lucky and missed their rotation in the mountains." Even to my ears, that sounds lame, but anything is possible. I hope.

"That proves nothing, child," he chides me. "And you can't possibly be that naive."

Luna, voice hesitant and unsure, asks quietly, "If he suspects we're coming, what do you think he has planned?"

The Babylonian king shakes his head. "That I don't know, little flower, but I am certain that whatever the Gray plans, you are his top priority. And the boy."

A shudder runs over me. By priority, I think Hammurabi means we're first on Alexander's kill list—Luna for interfering with his savior status and me for betraying my blood.

A Nephilim pops out of the Blessed Road and scurries up the cliffside like a mountain goat, whispering into Uriel's ear. I tense, watching the Archangel's expression closely, but his features remain flat. Man, that prick has a good poker face. He nods at the Light Nephilim and calls to us, "We go."

My balls shrivel at those two words, and I can feel bile creeping up my throat. Fuck me, I don't want to go down there. I'm no coward, but this is the big leagues, and I'm not ready to come up from the minors. I glance at Luna, and her creamy skin has gone wan with fear. *Be brave for her, Caleb.* My lips crash onto hers as I give her a desperate kiss, then we let the Shadow Road swallow us.

A few moments later, we emerge inside of the outer wall

framing the main courtyard. The plan was to split our forces and subdue the Nephilim in each section of the citadel, securing the students we find, if any, and killing the enemy until we reach Alexander. Hammurabi and Lilith are in charge of the first layer of defense while babysitting Luna and me, though there is no doubt that Goldilocks and I are here to slaughter as well. I'm not comfortable with that part, and I know Luna isn't, but Uriel and the Council insisted anyone helping my grandfather is to be killed and anyone showing his people mercy might suffer the same fate. There are no second chances, and in some cases third, I guess. Gilgamesh's face flashes across my vision for a moment, and I swallow. He's a self-righteous dick, but I can't say I want him to die. Ishtar led me astray, too, but I guess that's not entirely fair. I was there when Alexander persuaded Gilgamesh to the dark side but still. He's the King of Uruk. When he's dead, all that history and knowledge will die with him.

"Caleb, come on!" Luna's urgent tone hooks me back into the present.

Hammurabi and Lilith lead the charge up the wall, and we follow. I draw my dagger, but as I look at the Nephilim guards we're about to clash with, my heart thunders in my chest. Grandfather's Nephilim—all first generations—don't draw their swords. They don't react at all to the incoming threat of an ex-Archdemon and her band of warriors barreling their way.

A tall woman with blue hair marks our progress. Her eyes find mine, and a grin slashes her face, like she's a funhouse clown luring kids to their doom. It's creepy as hell. "The Conqueror sends his regards," she says, and she jumps off the wall, her comrades following.

I rush to peer over the wall, Luna at my side. The Nephilim all vanish into the Shadow Road. The foreboding presence of Hammurabi hovers next to me. I glance at his grim face, mouth pulled into a scowl.

"I hate that you were right," I tell him through gritted teeth—I hate that I was right, too—my eyes sweeping around the walls. Nothing. We're alone here. My stomach clenches. Even if Gramps suspected we were coming, how did he know we were coming today of all days? Does he know the Council better than I think and expected a swift retaliation, or do we have another Nzingha situation on our hands? My gut roils.

"I hate it as well," Hammurabi replies, staring at the ground.

"Now what?" Luna says, an edge of hysteria coloring her voice. "We're back to square one. What will the Council do if we don't find any clues and can't figure out where they went? If we don't know where Alexander is, will the truce be void? Will they try to take me again?"

"That's never going to happen," I tell her, clenching her hand. I'll fight to the death to keep her from being locked away again. And so will her parents.

"No, it won't," Lilith chimes in, placing a hand on Luna's

shoulder. "Now, we secure the perimeter and find your mother and father." She points back to the courtyard. "Children, wait there."

I scoff at her command but take Luna's hand and jump off the wall. We both land as nimble as cats. Lilith, Hammurabi, and a handful of Nephilim comb the walls, only meeting us once the outside is clear. Then, together, we head inside, the interior cool after being out in the blazing sun.

Eerie silence permeates the corridors. It's not just the absence of sound that's unsettling, it's the fact everything is gone. All the creature comforts and civilized touches Alexander added have disappeared. It's like no one has been living here for several months.

Beelzebub steps from the shadows, a frown painted on his lips.

"It appears as if we've missed the party," he says, and his eyes briefly clash with Lilith's. "It's almost as if a little bird whispered in Alexander's ears that we were coming. A poor, flightless bird with a proverbial ax to grind."

I don't even fight my epic eye-roll. Here we go again, but to my surprise and utter pride, Luna speaks before an obviously pissed-off Lilith can.

"Stop," she hisses. "Lilith wouldn't betray my mother. She wouldn't betray *me*. I understand you're angry—we all are— but this is why Alexander is one step ahead of us. We can't stop fighting with each other."

Lilith gifts Luna a smile ripe with affection before rounding on Beelzebub. "Indeed. Perhaps if some of us would remove our heads from our asses, we wouldn't be so blind to the truth."

I choke on air and even Hammurabi's mouth twitches. The other Nephilim have taken a few steps back from the scary duo, but I'm over this dumbass fighting.

"Hey, can we get our shit together and focus on the big picture here?" I demand, managing not to piss myself as Beelzebub and Lilith turn their rage toward me. "You two don't like each other. I get it. There's history I can't possibly understand, but my gramps is now out there in the world, planning and plotting, and we have no idea where he is. Luna and I can't be the goddamned grownups in the room." My eyes skip to Hammurabi who growls, "Stupid boy," under his breath.

When I turn my back on the two predators, Asmodeus is there, garnet hair shimmering. I manage not to scream, retaining my street cred, and from the amusement glinting in her eyes, I'm pretty sure she heard my last comment. I give a slight bow of my head to the mistress of Babel, positive she's there for Hammurabi. Those two don't stray far from each other since she's returned. I still haven't quite been brave enough to give him shit about it.

"Let's go find your parents, Goldilocks," I say, tucking her hand closer to me as I step around Asmodeus and walk away.

She and I agreed before we left Turkey that we'd try to sneak away to find clues about where Alaric is when we had the opportunity. We haven't told anyone he's alive—a lone

Nephilim being held against his will isn't exactly on the Council's priority list—and now that the superpowers in the room are in a bitch fight, it seems as good a time as any to make ourselves scarce.

Luna leans against me and whispers, "That deserves a standing ovation."

I snort. "Just don't let them kill me, okay? And speaking of standing ovations, I enjoyed your smackdown of Baby B."

Goldilocks shoots me a horrified look. "Shhh, he might be able to hear you." Her head swivels, and her eyes dart over her shoulder.

"Like I said, don't let them kill me." And that pissy tween just might be spiteful enough to do it.

A giggle squeaks from Luna but abruptly dies as we travel deeper into the building. I expect to find at least traces of the kids Alexander stole because kids are messy, but there's nothing. Not even a stray sneaker.

"Should we go to Alaric's room first?" Luna asks, and I hear the catch in her voice. The tears she's trying to swallow.

I nod, caressing her fingers with my thumb. "Yeah, let's hope he's left us some clue."

My hope fades when I push open the door to his old room, ushering Luna in before me, and see just an empty chamber. No traces of Alaric remain, but we dutifully search the walls and crevices for anything. Some sign that he left behind.

"There's nothing here," Luna says, and this time she doesn't bother to hide her tears. They pool in the corners of her lovely eyes.

I pull her into my arms, and she sags against me, as if she can no longer bear her weight. "Hey, this doesn't mean we won't find anything, okay? We've got more rooms to search. Don't give up just yet." My words come out confident, though I'm anything but. I fear Alaric is lost to us for now, but I can't say that to Goldilocks.

Her sigh is heavy against my chest. "Okay, let's keep looking."

"Did the little mice think they could escape the cat so easily?" Lilith purrs from the door, startling us both.

Heart hammering in my chest, I glare at the ex-Archdemon. "We're basically on the set of a horror movie. Was sneaking up on us really necessary?"

Her smile holds a hint of malice. "Just as necessary as you taking it upon yourself to scold Beelzebub and me. You should remember to respect your elders."

Score one for her, but I choke back a laugh when Luna retorts, "Not if they don't act like elders."

Lilith arches one perfect brow at Luna then snorts. "Point taken. Why are you children here?"

"We're searching for clues as to where Alexander might have gone," Luna interjects quickly. "That way the Council can't accuse me of not helping."

"Then I'm happy to aid you. Shall we continue?"

We move on to my room, and Lilith checks out a different

room across the hall. My chamber is stripped bare. It's like my time here—our time here—was a bizarre dream or nightmare. Goldilocks squeezes my hand tightly but doesn't speak. I don't, either, although I'm having a screaming freak-out in my head. How did they manage to evacuate so quickly? When did they decide to blow town?

And the million dollar question: how did they know when we would come?

Hammurabi was right. We underestimated Alexander the Great, military genius. Well, it's not that I don't know what Gramps is capable of, I just wanted this to be over. I wanted it over so badly that I was willing to go along with the Council's plan, even if I never really believed we could take the Conqueror by surprise. Besides, it's not like we had any better ideas. This was the only plan that made sense. The best option in a sea of shitty scenarios.

And I don't really think the Council—the Light side—really understand, despite Gilgamesh's defection, that it's not just Darks willing to pledge their allegiance to the Great. Lights are, too. For fuck's sake, they make it a point not to talk about Gilgamesh, like burying their heads in the sand will make the Lights switching sides to Team Conqueror go away. Maybe there are other Lights sick of the divide, too. Or hell, maybe they're tired of Darks having all the fun and want a little free will of their own. The honest truth is we can't see one another as we really are. We're stumbling around looking for the forest but the damn trees keep getting in our way.

I sigh as I look around my barren room. "Let's give it a thorough once-over just to be sure," I say and Goldilocks nods.

She takes the left side of the room, and I take the right, my eyes scanning over the walls and along the floor. I'm about to call it a day when my eyes snag on something folded on the stone. It looks like a piece of light-colored leather, but it's irregular, the edges jagged in places. Crouching down, I rest on my heels and reach for the leather, unfolding it. There's a marking on it, and my brows kiss my nose as I frown.

"What do you have?" Luna calls and I shrug.

"I'm not quite sure…" My voice dies as my stomach lurches, and I taste bile as I drop the piece of leather like it's on fire. No, not leather. Skin. Alaric's *skin*. That marking was the sigil Asmodeus gave him to call Lucifer.

Horrified, I take a step back. What the fuck is Alaric's skin doing in my room? And who cut it off of him? Did Alexander see the sigil and carve it from Alaric in a fit of rage? But that can't be right because the skin was deliberately planted in my room. There's no other explanation for why it would be here. Maybe Alaric sliced it off himself and left it for us to find, to let us know why he hasn't contacted us. But why cut off your only means of communication? My head spins.

Luna's small hand slips into mine. "Caleb, are you okay? What's going on?"

I point at the dried patch of skin on the floor. "Alaric left us a clue," I whisper, wincing at the way my voice shakes.

Our gazes clash and alarm is written on her face. She releases my hand and takes a step forward.

"No!" I yell, yanking her back. "You don't need to see that."

"Why? Alaric left it behind for us. We have to take it with us," Luna says, jerking out of my hold.

"For fuck's sake, Goldilocks, don't. It's his—"

But she's so desperate for news of Alaric, she moves with angel speed, stunning me, and picks up the skin. Her brows furrow in confusion before her eyes round in terror, and a cry of pure horror escapes her lips.

"What is *this*?" she demands, clutching the skin. Tears stream down her cheeks, and my heart aches for her.

"You know what it is, baby," I say, shoving my own fear in a box marked "shit I have to deal with later with a qualified therapist." I do my best to keep my voice calm, soothing.

"Alexander *cut* it off him?" she snarls, rage overtaking her dread. She shoves the skin toward me, and I fight the urge to recoil.

I shake my head. "I honestly don't know, Goldilocks. But if he did, I can't imagine he would want us to find it, which means Alaric must've left it here. For us. For *you* to find."

Footsteps echo and I whirl around as Lilith rushes into the room, face battle ready. She slows when she doesn't see any obvious danger, but her body tenses when she sees Luna's expression. "What's happened?"

Luna holds up that gruesome slice of Alaric. "This is Alaric's *skin*. It has the sigil Asmodeus gave him on it. He left it in our room for me to find."

For a moment, the ex-Archdemon's jaw slackens and she blinks. I've never seen the glib Lilith at a loss for words. This might be funny if it wasn't so goddamn tragic.

"Luna, Alaric is dead," Lilith says gently.

"Um, yeah, about that," I say, shoving my hands in my pockets. "I saw him at Megiddo. He found my sister and sent her away before she could be taken."

"And now, we know why he hasn't contacted us," Luna growls. "Because Alexander cut this off him!" Her enraged screech makes me flinch.

Lilith's eyes dart to Luna's folded fingers. A myriad of emotion flicks across her face too fast for me to follow. Maybe when you're as old as she is, nothing surprises you much anymore. "I see. Hmm, perhaps we should tell your mother and father about this?"

I don't know what they can do about it but Luna nods. "Okay," she says.

I expect her to drop Alaric's skin, but she slips it in her pocket, and I shudder. I don't tell her to put it back, though. Even if it repulses me, I get why she's taking it.

As we make our way to the makeshift throne room in silence—Lilith said Lucifer and Gabriel were headed there—Hammurabi catches up with us, but Asmodeus isn't with him.

If possible, his grim visage has gotten grimmer. He doesn't even lecture me about my bad behavior with little B so I know he's just as spooked about this place as I am. And he doesn't even know about the little gift we found.

I spot Lucifer outside the doorway the moment we turn into the corridor leading to the throne room. The enormous doors are thrown open, resembling a sinister maw waiting to devour us. The Morningstar's mouth is a slim slash and his expression is troubled. His eyes find Luna's and the worry—the fear there—makes my heart clench.

"Starlight," he calls. "Halt. I don't want you to come in here." Gabriel slides in by his side, and the two of them create a formidable blockade.

What the fuck is in there? How many horrible surprises are we going to face today? If the two of them are scared enough not to let us pass, then it must be really bad. I tuck Luna against me as I stare at the space between Lucifer's and Gabriel's bodies.

"What's in there?" Luna asks, and I can hear the slight tremor vibrating her voice. Then she straightens, pulling away from me slightly. "If it has to do with me, I want to see it." Her shoulders square, and I'm damn proud of her. She's being braver than me right now. I don't want to see anything that can possibly hurt my Goldilocks.

Gabriel frowns. "Luna—"

Luna gives a violent shake of her head, golden hair swinging. "No, I'm part of this war now." Her eyes dart to me. "*We're* part of this war. How do you expect me to go up against Alexander if I can't even face a possibly upsetting thing in a room? I can't be that fragile. I won't be."

I can't help it. I give her a slow clap. And I admonish myself for being a chicken shit in this moment. She's right. We have to start handling things.

"Well said, flower," Hammurabi says, his praise making Luna's cheeks pinken. She gives him a shy smile. I do believe she's quite fond of Uncle Hammurabi.

"We can't clip her wings when she needs to fly," Lilith points out, and the irony of her wing comment isn't lost on me.

Her parents, however, attempt to shoot lasers out of their eyes, as if they'd like to burn the Babylonian king and Lilith to ash. Hammurabi doesn't even flinch, taking his role as our de facto guardian seriously. Plus, I know Asmodeus would inflict serious damage to anyone who dared to hurt him. Lilith just shrugs, giving them a bored look.

"Dad," Luna says, her voice uncharacteristically sharp. "Let us pass."

Lucifer searches her face as if testing her resolve. Sighing, he steps aside. Gabriel's eyes narrow at him, but she moves as well, albeit reluctantly.

Goldilocks takes my hand, and we stride through the door, the Morningstar, the Messenger, Lilith, and Hammurabi following at our heels. Like the other rooms in the citadel, this, too, is empty, the open space amplifying every sound. The absence of the large stone bull might as well shout out that the seat of power has been moved. Well, it's empty except for that asshat Uriel, Raphael, and villain-of-the-week Mammon. Three of my least favorite people. They hover around the dais, murmuring to each other. As the rest of the great chamber is bare, whatever upset Gabriel and Lucifer must be there.

Mammon pivots toward us, his red gaze latching onto Luna. For a moment, I see pure malice glint in his eyes, then the emotion smooths over into indifference. Uriel and Raphael turn as well, but unlike the terrifying shape-shifter, I don't see any ill will when they regard Luna. Their expressions are a mix of concern and puzzlement. Their movement has opened a straight path to the dais, and I see Gramps has left something behind.

Luna's first golden gown Alexander forced her to wear to dinner during our time here drapes across his throne, a sword skewering the fabric where her heart would be, pinning the silk to the marble. My own heart thunders in my chest until I can hear its frantic dashes in my ears. I clutch Luna's hand in a crushing grip, my other hand curling into a fist.

This is a dire warning. Luna threatens the Great's power, and he doesn't tolerate threats. It's also a clear message. The time for taking Luna into the fold is over. He's no longer interested in having her as an ally. The next time we see Alexander, he'll kill her.

He didn't threaten the Council—he threatened *Luna*, establishing just how important she is. And how shaken he is by the prophecy. He will crush fate and anyone else standing in his way.

I feel Luna trembling next to me, and I fight the urge to take her in my arms. But I can't do that here, not with three predators in the room, watching our every move. I have to take my cue from her, but my heart aches for her. She doesn't deserve to be caught up in this prophecy bullshit, tasked to take on Alexander the fucking Great. It isn't fair. She can't die. I won't let her. The Creator didn't release her from stasis just to let her be killed by the Conqueror. I have to believe that. I clutch to that thought like a life raft in the middle of a stormy ocean.

I hear her swallow in the silent room. Then she gently frees her hand from mine. I raise a brow at her as our eyes meet. Determination and courage radiate from her gaze and I nod, willing to follow her lead. She walks toward the dais, stopping a few feet from the handle of the sword. She grasps the pommel, knuckles white from the force of her grip.

"No!" Uriel shouts as she yanks the sword free.

White-hot heat sears my brain, and agony screams along my nerve endings, setting them on fire. The last thing I hear is Luna crying out my name in panic before I fall head first into the abyss.

nineteen

LUNA

A RUSH OF WHITE noise floods my ears as the sword slips from my fingers, clattering to the floor by my feet. The echo of the blade as it strikes the stone is like a siren on the edge of hearing. I'm aware of it, but it's so far away, almost imperceptible past the panic assaulting my brain.

I snap my horrified gaze between the faces of these people—some family—I recognize so well, now reduced to mere writhing bodies on the floor before me, their expressions stricken, stretched into silent screams, and complexions drained of color. Their auras thrash wildly, the tendrils of shadow and light lashing out, as if attempting to detach from the bodies they surround.

I don't understand. All I did was wrench the sword from Alexander's throne. Ignoring it wasn't an option—not once I noticed the way the blade had been purposely positioned to stab through the heart of the first golden dress Alexander made me wear during the brief but horrible time we spent in this place. When I saw it, red washed across my vision—a blinding rage swaddled in an even more crippling fear, both born of how helpless this entire situation keeps making me feel—and it was all I could do to grab the pommel and yank the sword free. If I hadn't, my fire would have surely erupted and burned through the entire room along with everyone in it. If I hadn't, something terrible might have happened—like what I did to Caleb's father—and I would have been unable to stop it.

And yet, something terrible happened anyway. Because of me. Because I grabbed hold of that sword. *I don't understand.* It took little effort to free the blade despite the steel being firmly rooted in the marble, but then, I'm a full-blooded angel and I often forget I'm stronger than the mortal I once believed myself to be. With one tug, it lifted easily from the crack, which ran along the full length of the seat, the damage to the throne obscured by the golden fabric until the moment my arm jerked back and the dress, now freed as well, slipped from the stone. I don't know who the weapon belongs to. None of our bloodlines or else Alexander wouldn't have left it here—and that's assuming it's even a weapon from the Fall. I didn't notice any Enochian symbols etched into the steel but then I didn't take the time to look. The details didn't matter in my anger. Nothing mattered except grabbing that pommel.

I heard Uriel's alarmed protest as my fingers wrapped around the grip, but it was as if I wasn't in charge of my body—as if I was being controlled by the anger and fear I've spent so much of my life victim to. As if I was back at the group home when I was five, and then at the Serapeum, and in every other awful memory where I couldn't stop the evil inside me from being unleashed. Except this time, it wasn't my fire I set loose but a promise.

A silent vow to stop Alexander, no matter what it takes.

The anger that overtook me has since disappeared but the fear remains, joined now by confusion, which rises like a wall around me until I'm trapped by it, unable to move. My airways tighten. I can still feel Caleb's name on my lips, though I can no longer find my voice to scream it again.

I don't understand. That's the only thought I can manage. It spins through my head on a loop, surges through my body like a poison in my bloodstream, robbing me of sense. This shouldn't be happening. How is this happening? These are celestial beings before me, angels and Fallen and Nephilim more powerful than anyone or anything I've ever encountered.

Except Alexander, I find myself thinking.

And if my exclusion from this nightmare is any indication…

Except me.

That comprehension is the needed jolt to my heart to set me free from my terror, and stumbling forward, I reach out a hand to nothing and no one in particular, unsure what the hell I should do. The seconds tick by one after another, and my heart pounds in my ears as I attempt to process what I'm seeing. Caleb, my parents, Lilith, Hammurabi, the Council members…no one in the room is unaffected.

Except me, I consider again.

But why? Because I was the one who pulled the sword free, setting off the trap Alexander laid for us? Or because I'm a Gray? It can't be because I'm an angel as the Faithful and Fallen in the room aren't immune to whatever is happening—to whatever cruel magic is attacking their bodies and minds from within.

I clamp a trembling hand around my mouth, choking back a sob. Knowing Alexander, he intended for this scene to play out exactly the way it has, with me as the sole survivor of this attack, cripplingly aware of my own helplessness. I'm no match for him—this proves that. Just as it proves I'm sure as hell not the Savior. I can't be. Not when everything I do only leads to chaos and pain.

The worst part is I only have myself to blame. The sword was the powder keg but I was the spark. *I* set this off. *I* caused this…

And I have no idea how to stop it.

Tears cut lines down my cheeks as I drop to my knees, my hands curling into fists on the stone. This is just like what happened to my foster parents and to Caleb's father when I tore their minds open, the memory of their convulsing bodies a mirror image of the violent seizures now gripping the others. Out of the corner of my eye, I glimpse my mother, her back ramrod straight even as she thrashes against the hard floor, but my gaze quickly turns away, my focus drawn to one more than the others. Because as much as I doubt this attack could actually kill an angel—it will likely just keep them in a never-ending cycle of torment, effectively removing them from this conflict—I know it can kill *him*.

A strangled cry escapes me when I spot blood dripping from Caleb's nose. I shake my head as the tears come faster, harder. I can't let him die.

Not like this.

"I won't let you!" I cry, scrambling across the ground toward him. His head is limp when I pull it into my lap, his eyes shifting back and forth beneath their closed lids, and his skin is cold—so cold—almost as if he's already dead. "I-I don't know how to help you," I stammer, but as those words leave my lips, my eyes spring wide, and I realize that's not entirely true.

I witnessed this exact pain on Caleb's face two other times—both of which were here at the citadel—when his grandfather broke into his mind. First, to teach Caleb a lesson, and then, with the intention to kill.

But Alexander isn't here now and I can't fight the invisible hold he left behind. Not unless I attack it at its source.

A horrified gasp fills my throat, and as I stare down at Caleb, understanding dawns. This is why Alexander laid this trap—because he knew I won't be able to do the one thing that needs to be done to stop it. I don't have the control. I can't do it without destroying the person completely. And yet, there's no other way.

Sweat rises across my palms, and my pulse jumps under my skin, ratcheting higher, as I peer at the others, trying not to freak out over the wasted seconds as I assess each of their faces in turn. The effects of the spell are working more slowly on the angels than they are on the Nephilim. Hammurabi doesn't look to be in a much better state than Caleb, despite being several millennia older, while the angels haven't even started to bleed yet, though their expressions are agonized, revealing their pain.

Swallowing, I force my eyes back to Caleb, my fingers twitching against his cheeks. If I break into his mind, he might die, but he'll die for certain if I choose to do nothing. Tensing, I flatten my hands to the sides of his head and close my eyes. If there was time, I would try this first on Uriel or Mammon—someone I don't care about just to be sure I can do it—but there isn't. And their lives aren't in jeopardy. Not the same way Caleb's is.

My lips push out a shaking breath, and then I inhale again, concentrating as much as I can in my growing hysteria.

Be calm, I tell myself. *Focus on Caleb.*

My temples throb as I extend my thoughts outward, mentally reaching past the confines of Caleb's skull and breaching the boundaries of his mind, which relent to me easily, like a door opening. I expected more resistance but there is none, and suddenly, it doesn't feel like I'm breaking in at all but like he's welcoming me. Like he's okay with me being in here. Like he trusts me not to break him. And I won't. Unlike with his father, my focus is singular. I don't think about the past. I don't think about what I might do if I mess this up. I don't think about anything else except Caleb, and as I dig deeper, I smile at the memories unfolding before me. Everywhere I look, I glimpse my face—I see *me* the way Caleb sees me, and as I take in each memory, it dawns on me just how much he loves me. How much I consume his entire soul the same way he consumes mine.

"Caleb," I whisper, and I feel a tear drip from my chin as the memory of our first kiss plays before me as if it's happening all over again. I didn't notice it at the time—his happiness in that moment—but I sense it now…just as I sense his fear and worry that he'll never get to kiss me again. That he'll die here, trapped in the horrors of this malicious spell cast by a man who claims to want to see our world united when, in reality, he is doing everything possible to tear it apart.

I won't let that happen, I promise, pushing deeper into Caleb's subconscious, trailing that fear like a path of breadcrumbs. But as I descend, it occurs to me that what I'm sensing isn't breadcrumbs at all but a string—an invisible thread connecting one thought to another.

That thread leads me into a place of darkness, of sorrow and twisted recollections where nothing is clear, and all I'm aware of is pain. It's a strange, murky place, and the images around me are fuzzy and distorted, almost shapeless in the encompassing gloom. This isn't what I imagined Caleb's mind to look like, and dread squeezes my heart as I try to separate the tumultuous thoughts—as I try to figure out how to help him.

Panic shoots through my veins like adrenaline, and I can feel sweat beading along my hairline and dripping down the back of my neck, my body still convinced it's mortal in the throngs of terror. I'm running out of time—I can sense that in Caleb's increasing convulsions, can *smell* it in his blood, which flows faster and surely from more than one orifice now, draining him of life.

"Come on," I hiss, forcing myself even deeper. It feels like hours have passed in his head when it can't have been more than a minute or two, but even so, that's a minute or two too long.

Desperation claws at every inch of my skin. Why can't I find it? The source of Alexander's spell should be in here somewhere…shouldn't it? Shouldn't I be able to see what's causing this distress inside Caleb—see what's physically tearing him apart? Because this isn't the true state of his mind; this dark, cold place isn't the Caleb I know. No, this is Alexander's doing and whatever magic he cast is responsible for this pain. I just can't separate the chaos around me enough to see where it is and stop it.

Something catches my attention then, like a glint of light in the corner of my eye, and again, I notice the pull of that thread—that peculiar string tying Caleb's thoughts together.

My stomach swoops, and I feel the thrum of magic so close now I can taste it. I sense both Dark and Light at work here— Gray magic. Alexander's magic.

That's it. Heart racing, I feel for the string and tug on it with all the strength I can muster, trying to undo the spell, to free Caleb from this mental anguish. But the thread is tangled and for every pull, another section of string seems to take its place.

A scream of frustration rises in my throat. How am I supposed to save him if I can't even unravel the spell?

Because Alexander doesn't want you to save him, a voice says in the back of my head.

I do scream then, yanking as hard as I can on the thread. This time, it snaps, but my momentary relief is overshadowed by the comprehension that whatever magic is in here still lingers. The connection hasn't been severed…but why?

And that's when I realize…it isn't a string. It's a web.

"A spider's web," I breathe, horrified.

As these words leave my lips, several threads manifest before me, shooting off in different directions, and as I follow each one like a branch in a tree, I finally grasp why this spell is so cruel.

They're all tied together. Everyone who was in the vicinity when Alexander's trap went off is linked, their minds connected by the threads in the web. I can feel them at the end of each string, and so long as they're joined, I will never free Caleb from this misery…or anyone else.

Violent sobs rack my chest. I can't do it. I can't save them because saving one means saving them all, and I can't be in eight minds at once—

A gasp rips from my lungs, and suddenly, I find myself…

standing? I blink, confusion throwing off my center of balance. I'm in the middle of the throne room, staring down at my family and the Council members, who remain on the floor, trapped in the nightmare of Alexander's magic snare.

My gaze shifts. *I don't understand.* A moment ago, I was on the floor next to Caleb. A moment ago, I was in his head, but now…

The air rushes out of my lungs, and I stumble back a step. There, not far from the dais, I spot Caleb, blood seeping from his closed eyes and ears now as well as his nose…and beside him, I see me, kneeling with his head in my lap just like I was only seconds before.

I stagger forward, my heart a stampede of confusion and horror, and unsure what else to do, I reach out a hand, then quickly wrench it back with a small, alarmed cry. I peer down, my mouth popping open in shock. I turn my hand over, gaping at the flagstone floor, which is clearly visible through my palm, as if I'm an incorporeal being. As if I'm nothing more than a ghost.

I glance up again, focusing on Caleb and the other me—the physical me—noting the strain on my face and the sweat dripping down my temples and neck as my hands tremble against his head. How is this possible? How could I be over there but also here, outside my body?

My eyes spring wide, and I let out a gasp as the answer hits me like a wrecking ball to the chest. Swallowing my fear, I turn on my heel and dash across the floor to my mother. I don't feel the stone against my legs as I drop to my knees, nor do I feel the silky touch of her hair as I press my hands to her head, but that doesn't matter. All that matters is that I can do what needs to be done to save her.

To save everyone.

Breathing out, I close my eyes, and just before the lids slide closed, I see myself, repeating this same exact gesture with the others in the room. My fingers catch in the sweaty strands of Caleb's hair, my awareness abruptly shoved back into my physical body, but now, I also feel myself with my parents, with Hammurabi and Lilith, and even with Uriel, Raphael, and Mammon, my focus and mind split eight different ways—a piece of my soul cast out to each one of them like a lifeline at sea.

As I work, I feel a sense of control I've never known before. I don't question how I'm able to do this or if it's something the others are capable of. I don't question or think about anything except finding the threads tying them all to one another.

One by one, I find those threads—reaching out and working together with the projections of myself to untangle the knots—until finally, the web comes undone, slipping through my fingers as if it never even existed at all. When the last string falls away, I blink my eyes open, retreating from all minds until I'm only in mine, and with bated breath, I watch the now still faces around me, silently begging for them to wake up.

The first to rouse is my father, who sits up with a look of bewildered dismay on his face. Shaking his head as if to clear it, he crawls across the floor to my mother, who wakes a few seconds later. Her dark eyes immediately seek out mine.

"How?" she breathes, clambering to her feet. "How did you do that?"

Her question stuns me because it implies that she knew I was there in her head…and in the others' minds.

"I…" I trail off, unsure how to answer. Before I can form a coherent thought to explain what I did, the others begin to wake until the angels and Fallen and Hammurabi are all standing around me in silence, exchanging strange, perceptive glances. All except Caleb, whose eyes remain closed, though the erratic movement behind his lids has ceased.

I lick my lips and touch my hands to his shoulders, shaking him slightly, but he doesn't stir.

"Why isn't he waking up?" I croak, snapping my eyes to my mother. Her gaze is uncertain, and to my increasing dread, she says nothing. "Why is he still asleep?" I press, looking now at my father then Lilith.

In the space of a heartbeat, Hammurabi is beside me, touching a finger to Caleb's pulse. "He's alive…but he's young compared to us, flower. And the tie to his ancestral blood is weaker. Whatever devious spell we just walked into has taken a tremendous toll."

What does that mean? I nearly shout, but I can't find the words.

"He'll be all right, Starlight," my father assures me, stepping forward and crouching on the other side of Caleb, where he lies unnervingly still on the floor. "Look, he's already beginning to heal."

A quiet, hiccuping sob escapes me as I follow my father's gaze to Caleb's face. Sure enough, the bleeding at his nose and ears has stopped. Still, that brings me little comfort.

"We should leave this place," my mother murmurs, looking the perfect picture of health despite the hell her body experienced only moments ago.

To my surprise, Lilith, Uriel, Mammon, and Raphael remain completely silent. They say nothing, though the weighted looks they keep throwing at me speak volumes in the tense hush.

"Come," my father urges, and rising, he scoops Caleb off the floor as if he weighs nothing. With his body limp in Lucifer's arms, Caleb looks like an oversized, sleeping child. "We will find nothing else of use here."

"I will reconvene with the others and direct everyone back to Derinkuyu," Uriel says, his expression unsettled. "Raphael and Mammon will accompany you back to the city."

I blink stupidly at him as the Archangel departs the room. That's it? I just saved his life and I don't get so much as a thank you?

I half-expected Uriel to berate me for touching the sword—for setting the trap off in the first place—since it's clear to me now there was magic encasing the weapon, the tingle of which I feel still on my hands, like the touch of static electricity. But he didn't. He said nothing. He *did* nothing except look at me as if my actions here were somehow sacrilege. Maybe they were. Maybe breaking into another angel's mind is the worst sort of crime, and by doing it, I unwittingly added to the list of reasons the Council already distrusts me.

Hammurabi glances at the doorway Uriel just left through and frowns—probably at the thought of leaving without Asmodeus. But then his eyes shift to Caleb, limp and so pale in my father's arms, and the worry stretching across his face pulls him after Lucifer into the Shadow Road without further hesitation.

"Come, flower," Hammurabi croons over his shoulder, his gruff voice a needed tether to sanity.

Neither my mother, nor Raphael protest when I stumble into the Shadow Road after my father and Hammurabi, Lilith tagging closely at my heels. No one is separating me from Caleb right now and I know my mother understands that feeling better than anyone, her desire to stay by my side etched into her face at all times. As for Raphael, the Archangel has reason enough to believe we wouldn't try anything at this point, and we have Mammon tailing us to ensure it. We need the Council's help more than ever, and besides, where else can we go except back to Derinkuyu?

I walk between my father and Hammurabi, occasionally reaching out a hand to brush my fingers through Caleb's hair, hoping my touch will be enough to wake him. It isn't.

"He will wake up, Luna," my father says, and tears blur my vision when I meet his gaze.

"How do you know?" I breathe, my voicing breaking. "What if I took too long to stop it? What if—"

"Don't do this to yourself, little flower," Hammurabi cuts in. "What you did…" He shakes his head, scrubbing a hand over his beard. "If it wasn't for you, we would be dead. Well, the boy and I would be, at least."

"And we would be trapped in that nightmare until Alexander draws his final breath, severing the spell's connection," my father mutters, a slight pinch to his lips. "Which, given the fact he is immortal, may have been a very long time."

"I think I scared Uriel and the others," I whisper, risking a nervous glance over my shoulder at Mammon, who follows like a skulking, hungry dog in our wake. He keeps his distance, tracking my movements with those ominous eyes, his focus shifting between watching me and staring hard at my father's back—at Caleb, who lies helpless in his arms. If there was ever a moment for Mammon to strike, to seize his chance at revenge, this would be it.

A shudder rolls through me at the thought, and I inch that little bit closer to Caleb, ready to protect him here and now should it come to that. I didn't just dive into the deepest recesses of his mind and pull him free from his grandfather's sadistic booby trap only to lose him moments later to Mammon.

"Perhaps," my father considers, and it's only when I meet

his gaze again that he adds, "None of us have seen that kind of power before."

That stops me in my tracks. "No one?"

Lucifer pauses only long enough to look over his shoulder then gestures with a tilt of his head for me to keep walking. "No one," he echoes. "Breaking into the mind of one angel or first generation Nephilim would be a tremendous feat for any unskilled in the art, but to break into several simultaneously?" His expression darkens. "The Council has a tendency to fear what it does not understand."

Like Grays, I almost say aloud then stop myself. After all, where Alexander is concerned, the Council's fear is more than justified.

"Surely, this is proof," Lilith murmurs, walking on the other side of my father. Until now, she has been unusually contemplative since stirring from the effects of the trap.

"Proof of what?" I ask, glancing at her.

Her eyes find mine in the grayness of the Road. "That you *are* the Savior…and you have the power to challenge Alexander and defeat him."

Those words are a weight on my shoulders I don't know how to carry, and silence grips us the rest of our journey, none of us daring to utter a word. Upon reaching the marker for Derinkuyu, we step out of the Shadow Road into the city. It's quiet within, disconcertingly so, and empty, as if we're stumbling into the premises late at night rather than in the middle of the day.

I glance around, narrowing my eyes, searching for any sign of the Nephilim we left behind. Bowls and plates lay across every available surface, as if abandoned mid-meal, but the students they belonged to are nowhere to be seen. My eyes shift, and I spot a small discarded shoe in the middle of the floor, forgotten by its owner.

"Where is everyone?" My voice wavers, and a shiver of trepidation spreads under my skin.

To my left, Gabriel and Raphael appear, stepping out of the shining golden light of the Blessed Road. They immediately sense that something isn't right, and my mother is beside me in seconds, signaling for silence with a long finger to her lips. When she grabs my hand, I glance back at my father—at Caleb still lying limp in his arms—and to my relief, he follows me as I trudge after Gabriel, trying and failing to swallow the lump in my throat. She leads me through the passages until we reach the large cavernous space where we reunited with Lucifer only yesterday. That moment the three of us experienced here, of happiness and pure bliss...

It will be forever tarnished by the horror that now paints this room.

"Evangeline," my mother gasps, and I watch, outraged, distressed, disgusted—more emotions than I can even count racing through me—as Gabriel releases my hand and runs forward, dropping to her knees beside one of at least a dozen unmoving bodies strewn across the stone floor. Tears spring to my eyes as she rolls the Nephilim onto her back, but it's clear, even at a distance, she's dead, her face and blue shirt spattered in blood.

Hammurabi, Lilith, Raphael, and Mammon rush past me, checking the other victims, but the outcome is the same with every last one.

"They're all dead," I breathe, staring at the terrible scene of bloodshed before us. The first generation Nephilim—teachers and other staff from the academies—who volunteered to stay behind to watch the children while the rest of us went to Kandahār have been brutally slaughtered, but how? By whom? Most of them I don't know, but some…

I stifle a sob when I glimpse familiar copper hair, noticing one of my teachers from the Serapeum—Vesta—among the casualties. I didn't even know Vesta was here, and now, she's gone, snuffed from this world like a flame in the wind. We might have had a rocky relationship but I never wanted her to die.

"How…" At my father's strangled breath, I turn, no longer able to hold in my tears. "How did they know where to find us?" he whispers.

I don't have to ask whom he means because only one person we know could have committed such a barbaric atrocity. Only one person could've given the order for such needless death.

But how did Alexander find us? I thought we were safe here.

I thought we were hidden. I thought—

And that's when I see it. The symbols painted in blood on the wall.

It's written in Enochian, that much is clear, but I can't read it and part of me—a very large part—is certain I don't want to know what it means.

"Luna?" a small voice squeaks, and my heart jumps into my throat when I catch sight of Aya in the distant doorway, her head of dark hair poking around the stone arch. Seeing her releases me from the spell of my shock, and I sprint across the room, taking her in my arms.

"Are you hurt? Where is everyone?" I ask, cupping her face in my hands.

There are sticky streaks on her skin from tears that have fallen and dried, and at my question, fresh ones follow the tracks, carving new lines down her cheeks. Her face crumples. "They took them," she sobs, burying her snotty nose in my chest. "They killed the teachers and took them."

"Who?" My tone is pleading, but when she lifts her head, her eyes catch on something behind me, and I know at once she's seen her brother, who remains asleep in my father's arms.

"Caleb!" she shouts then lets out a heart-wrenching cry when she tries to run to him only to find a dozen dead bodies in her way.

Grabbing her by the shoulders, I pull her out of the room. "He's fine," I say quickly, though the words come out weak and unconvincing, even to my own ears. Maybe because I still struggle to believe it myself and probably won't until he wakes up. "He just needs rest. Is there anyone else here or is it only you?"

She takes a long moment to process my words, and in the seconds I wait for a response, I pray she isn't the only one here. That she hasn't been left to face this horror alone.

"Aya?" I press, and she jolts at my voice, shaking her head.

"T-There are others," she manages, her voice weak. "On the next level down. Rafe and Shalina and a few other kids I don't know. A teacher from Babel found us and we hid. His gift is illusion and he...he used it to hide us so they wouldn't see where we were."

I let out a shaking breath. At least Aya, Rafe, and Shalina are safe. I don't know how I would've broken that news to Caleb if they weren't.

"That would be Blue Jay," a familiar voice says, and I turn to find Hammurabi standing behind me. A troubled look crosses his face. "Where is he now, young one?"

Aya trembles. "Down—down a level. With the others."

My brows lift at that, and my voice comes out harsher than I intend when I snap, "Then why are you up here all on your own?"

Aya flinches, and I mentally berate myself, pulling her in for another hug. "I'm sorry," I whisper into her hair. "But you shouldn't take risks like that. What if, when you came up here, it wasn't us but whoever took the others? What if they had come back for you?"

Alexander's forces already tried to kidnap Aya once, and even if they didn't come here specifically for her, I have little doubt they would try again if they knew she was here.

"I felt him," Aya mutters, a sheepish look crossing her face when she peeks up at me with tear-filled eyes. "I felt Caleb and so I snuck away. I needed to find him. I needed to know he was okay."

I stare at her for a moment, confused. "You…felt him? You mean your blood song?"

Aya nods, and I glance at Hammurabi, somewhat baffled by this revelation. I remember the first time I felt that song connecting me to each of my parents, and I can feel the melody even now despite being a room away from them, the chords a thunderous choir in my heart. But as the space between us grows, the song gets softer, duller, until I can't hear it at all. So, how did Aya feel Caleb from a whole level below us?

But as I ask myself this, I remember the look on Caleb's face when we talked about Aya and how readily he embraced her as his sister. Embracing my family hasn't been as straightforward for me, and although we've already made huge strides, we still have a long way to go to put the past behind us. Maybe our blood is aware of that. Maybe the song is more sensitive for Caleb and Aya because there's nothing hindering their connection—no guilt or traumatic separation. Just a fearless and willing acceptance.

Aya sniffs, wiping her nose on her sleeve. "Are you mad?"

The whimpering way she asks me that breaks my heart, and shaking my head, I pull her in even tighter. "Never," I promise. "I'm just glad you're safe and I know Caleb will be, too."

"Come, child," Hammurabi interrupts, extending a large hand to Aya. "I need to speak with Blue Jay. Perhaps you can take me to him and the others."

I blink at the hulking Babylonian king, taken aback by the unexpected gentleness in his tone. I've seen glimpses of this side of him before but never like this. But then, he is a teacher, and this is a traumatic thing for a child to see. It's no wonder he would want to do anything to lead her away.

"Thank you," I whisper as he walks past, and he gives me a curt nod before trailing Aya down the nearby steps to the next level down.

Curling my quivering fingers into tight fists, I turn back into the room to find my parents, Lilith, Raphael, and Mammon gathered together, staring up at the bloody message on the wall.

"What's it say?" I try to keep my voice steady as I cross the space to my father, who—to my immense relief—hasn't relinquished his hold on Caleb.

Lilith's brow furrows in bemused consternation. "More or less, it says, 'Thank you,'" she begins, hesitating a moment before adding, "'for the inspiration.'"

"What is *that* supposed to mean?" Raphael asks, her pert nose wrinkling in frustration.

I stare hard at the Enochian symbols, repeating Lilith's words in my head. *"Thank you for the inspiration."*

The inspiration? What inspiration? And how the hell did they track us here—

My breath catches in my chest, and I go completely still until even my heart seems to cease its thundering rampage. Suddenly, I'm transported back to the Blessed Road, my memories a slideshow of horror as I relive the moment Alexander intercepted us. I didn't know what he was up to then. I assumed it was a diversion, and my gut tells me I was right about that, but only now do I realize how wrong I was about what he was distracting us from.

"He tracked us here," I whisper, and once again, I hear the clashing of swords on the Blessed Road. There were first generation Lights there who had joined Alexander, and at the time, neither I, nor my mother, nor anyone on the Council could understand why they made such an effort to corner us. Why they would attack without actually harming anyone.

But now, I know exactly why they did it, and what's worse is we gave Alexander the idea. The *Council* gave him the idea.

"Thank you for the inspiration."

"Luna?" my mother prompts me, and a tear slides down my

cheek as I turn to her.

"It's all our fault," I choke out, and she shakes her head, clearly not understanding the message the same way that I have. She wouldn't—she wasn't there when we went to Alexander for help.

She wouldn't know we gave him the weapon he needed to hit us where it would hurt most.

I swallow then force out the words, "He put trackers in the students' heads." I want to lay the full blame on the Council for this and shed myself of any guilt or culpability. I want to blame them for ordering Nzingha to put a tracker in my head back at Babel. And I do blame them. I blame Uriel and Mammon and their malicious vendetta against Grays. I blame them for being so caught up in their prejudices and allowing their fear to escalate this conflict. But although they were the perpetrators of this nightmare, I can't escape the blame I carry for presenting the idea to Alexander. For offering myself—and a tool he could use against us—on a silver platter. And I can't escape how foolish we all were to think evacuating the schools would be enough to keep everyone safe.

Turning my eyes back to the Enochian symbols, I reveal the devastating truth. "We did this. *We* led Alexander here." *We're all to blame for this.*

And now, the children and weapons are gone.

twenty

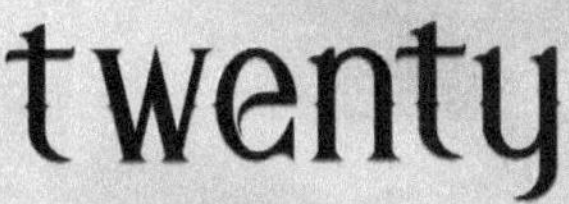

CALEB

I BLINK MY EYES open, shocked I haven't crossed the River Styx into the afterlife. My whole body feels like a bruised piece of meat, and I just lie there for a minute, happy to be alive. My angelic blood worked overtime to heal me, but I welcome the pain because that means I get to see *her* again. My Goldilocks.

Tilting my head, I seek her out, drawn to the glowing light in the otherwise dim room. She's slumped in a chair near the bed, palm open, ruby flame dancing above her pale skin. The flame hovers for a moment before splitting, forming complex patterns and motions. I prop myself on my elbows, astonished by Luna's newfound control. The fire then bounces from palm to palm, the small fireballs arcing back and forth as if Goldilocks is a master juggler giving a performance. The globules speed faster and faster until all I can track is a ring of scarlet. Then Luna folds her fingers and the fire vanishes. My eyes squint as they adjust to the sudden absence of bright light. A weary sigh spills from her lips. I know she's not tired from that display, as spectacular as it was. For us, that's just parlor tricks.

Then I realize she hasn't noticed I'm awake and is probably worried about me. Giving myself a swift mental jab, I say, "Damn, baby, that was amazing. How are you doing that?" Her head snaps up, stunning eyes widening when she sees I'm vertical. Kind of.

"Caleb!" She rises from the chair and collapses on the bed next to me, her arms sliding around my waist, her nose burying itself in my chest. She holds me for a moment, inhaling my scent, then says, "I don't know how I'm doing it. It just feels… easier now. Like things are clicking into place. What happened in Kandahār must've unlocked something inside me."

I stifle a flinch and wrap my arms around her. She smells like sunshine and wildflowers. She smells like home. "I was scared shitless there for a moment, Goldilocks," I confess into her silken hair. "I didn't know if I'd get to come back to you. But I felt you there in my mind, trying to help. I was grateful you were there, even if it was my end." I don't mean for those words to pop out, but that dance with death was too close for my liking. That old bastard can find another partner.

A tremor ripples over her slender frame, telling me just how terrified she was of that prospect, too. "I thought for a moment that I'd lost you, and that Alexander had finally won," she says, her own confession stark with pain and fear. She lifts her face from my chest, tears pooling in her eyes. "It wasn't just you. It was everyone."

I blink, confused. "What do you mean?"

"When I removed that sword, I triggered some sort of magical…bomb that hit *everyone*. Angels, Fallen, Nephilim. Alexander wanted to wipe out his enemies in one fell swoop, and I walked right into his trap." Anger and bitterness paint her words. I run a soothing hand through her hair. Then she grins, surprising me. "He used both his Dark and Light powers against us, and he didn't think I could figure out how to undo it. Stupid little girl who knows nothing about her powers. But I did, Caleb, I did figure it out. I saved *you*." She kisses me then, an eager clash of lips and teeth and tongue.

When we finally part, we're both gasping for breath.

"I couldn't let you die. I wouldn't let you. You have no idea how terrified I was—you had blood coming out of your mouth and nose and eyes. And I remembered how Alexander had almost killed you before…" A full-on shudder racks her frame. Her hands cup my face. "I knew my parents were in trouble, too, and I was worried of course, but I…I love you more than anything in the world. I refused to lose you. Alexander wasn't going to take you from me."

My lips seal over hers again, tongue delving into her mouth. I tear away from her, my breathing erratic, but manage to say, "You saved me, baby. You're my fucking hero. Thank you. I'm so proud of you. How did you do it?"

Her mouth drags down in a pensive frown as she explains

how all our minds were ensnared in a magical web. "I could see you all lying on the floor, and I—I don't know how—but I somehow slipped out of my body. It was like I instinctively knew what to do, and when I realized the threads had to be severed at the same time, I…duplicated pieces of myself."

I reel back, stunned. "You *what?*" I've never heard of that before, and if the Faithful and Fallen can do that, they never talk about it, that's for damn sure.

She hurries on. "I know that sounds crazy, but it's the best way to describe it. I cut the threads connecting you, and you all woke up. Well, you didn't, but the rest of them did. If I were mortal, you would've taken a decade off my life."

I digest what she's just revealed. "Do your parents know how you did that?"

Luna shakes her head. "No. They seemed pretty shocked actually. *Everyone* seemed pretty shocked. I'm guessing it must be a Gray thing. Only I—and maybe Alexander—can do it."

She finally mastered her power all on her own and beat the Conqueror at his own game and saved all those assholes on the Council. If that doesn't show beyond a doubt she's on their side, nothing will. "You've just proven that you're a force to be reckoned with. You broke the *Conqueror's* spell. Do you understand how amazing you are?"

Her cheeks flush a pretty rose, and I want to strip her bare and celebrate life in the most primal way possible. But I still see that impossible weight of melancholy dragging her down.

I tip her chin up with a finger. "Hey, you're officially Wonder Woman. What's wrong?"

Grief floods her eyes. "Remember when I told you I saw Alexander on the Road, and I couldn't understand why he was there? He could've killed me but didn't. I crossed swords with him, and he let me walk away..." Luna shivers, and I rub my hands down her arms. Her gaze latches onto mine, and dread fills me at the desolation I see there. "We underestimated him. Again. And now...the kids are gone. He *stole* them," she whispers.

For a moment, my heart stops, and I can't comprehend her words. "Stole them?" I parrot, shaking my head. "What do you mean? How? He doesn't even know where our base is." Against my will, my voice rises, booming across the small room. "*Aya*. Did they take my sister? What about Rafe and Shalina? All the teachers?"

My heart seizes as tears track down her face. "Aya is fine," she says, and relief is like a dam, bursting inside me. I've barely had a minute with my sister, but I care about her. She's family. "Rafe and Shalina and Blue Jay managed to hide, along with a handful of others, but..."

"But?" I prod, desperate for more information. Maybe this is all an illusion, and I'm not really here with Luna right now. Maybe I haven't woken up yet, and I'm still lost in the nightmarish confinement of my own mind.

"But Alexander managed to take most of the kids and slaughtered the teachers." Her voice is low, scratchy, as more tears roll over her smooth cheeks.

Her words are a gut punch. Rafe and Shalina weren't the only friends I had at Babel. And my teachers…those powerful first generation Nephilim…some of them are now gone. They were a bunch of hard-asses, sure, but wonderful hard-asses who loved their students. And I loved them. I want to throw up. I want to kill someone. Preferably Gramps. But this still doesn't make any fucking sense. How did Alexander know we were here? But then again, how did he know when we were going to sneak into his base? Who's the serpent in our midst?

"Who the fuck is selling us out?" I growl, fury bubbling through my blood.

Luna gives me a sad smile. "No one, not in the way you think. I have no idea how he knew we'd try to ambush his base—I don't think anyone does—but as for the rest… Well, we gave Alexander the perfect way to find us," she says, and I recoil from her, horrified. Her hands slide to my wrists, cuffing them. "Remember my tracker?" I give a slow nod. "On the Blessed Road, Alexander didn't fight me because that wasn't what he went there to do. It was all just one big distraction so the Lights he had with him could slip trackers in some of the students' heads. That's how he knew where we are."

"How do you know that for sure?" I demand, shaken.

"Because he left a message in blood, thanking us for the inspiration."

"You mean he sent Ishtar to do his dirty work? She's the

only one he'd trust with this big of a job, and she'd enjoy the slaughter." Guilt swamps me, drowning my rage. "Oh, fuck, this is *my* fault. If I hadn't taken you to Alexander…" If I hadn't brought her to my grandfather to remove that tracker, he wouldn't have Pied Piper'd our asses.

Luna releases one of my wrists and places a finger over my lips. "It's not your fault, and trust me, I've been blaming myself, too, but you did the right thing by taking me there. We had no other option. But now…the problem is that we don't know Alexander well enough to stay one step ahead of him."

She's right. I know she's right, and I'd do it all over again despite what just happened. Because if I hadn't, there's a good chance she'd be back in a cage somewhere, and I'd rather die than let that happen. I had to bring her to Alexander. This isn't my fault, but it sure as hell feels like it is. But anger sprouts in me again. Luna and I are the kids in this scenario. Why in hell aren't the adults behind the damn eight ball? Alexander almost conquered the world before. The Council—hell, even Lucifer and Gabriel—need to start thinking like him. Either they've gotten arrogant in their old age or they still can't wrap their heads around such a young angel running laps around them.

"You're right," I tell Luna. "This isn't our fault. We just made the best possible choice in a shitty scenario, but I really hope this is the thing that finally makes the Council—the Lights and Darks—remove their heads from their asses and start acting like a team. We won't win if they don't."

Luna shifts her hands and braids her fingers through mine. "I know. I hope with my mother and father together again, and with us, obviously, that the others will see that unification *is* possible."

I give her a bitter smile. "They have to for our survival. But hey, if that old dinosaur, Hammurabi, can come around to liking a Gray, then I have to hope that others can change, too. Little flower," I tease and she blushes. Then I sober. "And I think you and I have to stop playing Follow the Leader."

"What do you mean?" Goldilocks asks, brows knitting together in confusion.

I swallow, my mouth suddenly sand-paper dry. "Hammurabi, your dad, they both want me to take a seat at the table, and I thought that's what I was doing. I listen, I do as I'm told, but I gotta do more. You and me, we're not bogged down by ancient history and bullshit. We've spent a lot of time with my grandfather lately. More time than the Council, that's for damn sure. We have to start thinking like him. He has no limits, and we need to start really believing that." Gripping her hands tightly, I say, "You've just proven how powerful you are. And I don't want to say it, and I know you don't want to hear it, but you *are* the fucking Savior, baby. But that doesn't mean some prophecy controls you. Free will exists, so you can guide your own destiny here. You started back at the citadel, telling your parents to back off, and you need to keep doing that. We both do."

Her luscious mouth presses into a flat line, and her lids

lower, shielding me from her thoughts. I tense, hoping I didn't press too hard. I've never outright called her the Savior before because I hate this prophecy with my entire being, and I don't believe fate is fixed. I don't want to spook her, but her power has blossomed, and it is glorious.

"I am the Savior, aren't I?" she whispers, and I lean down, giving her a chaste kiss.

"I'm afraid so," I say, "and that really sucks, but I believe in you, Goldilocks. With every fiber of my being, I believe in you, in my gut and in my balls. I'll be with you to the end, whatever end that is."

Our stares lock and tears glisten again in her luminous eyes. "I love you," she says, "and you're right. We have to start taking control of our own destiny."

I draw her flush against me. "There's my girl." I kiss her again, and this time, there's nothing chaste about it. This time, I throw away the chains of my self-restraint and strip her to her bare skin, wanting to celebrate being alive and desperate to be close to her in a time of such great fear and uncertainty.

twenty-one

LUNA

I SIT HUNCHED ON the edge of the mattress, staring down at the leathery patch of skin Caleb found in Kandahār as I turn it over in my hands. Behind me, Caleb snores softly, his breaths light and soothing in the silence. I long for sleep, but it evades me, and since I no longer need it to survive or function, I'm wide awake, plagued by the buzzing relentlessness of my thoughts.

We're still in Derinkuyu despite the city being compromised by the enemy, but the Council have erected extra protection wards for the time being, and we'll be leaving soon enough once they establish a new refuge for us. *Before* Alexander can return, I hope. The Council doesn't seem as worried about that possibility as I am—as far as they're concerned, he has no reason to come back. I hope they're right, and I'm overestimating his interest in his grandchildren, and he'll leave Aya alone.

And Caleb. Though, the time for bringing him into the fold has passed.

My stomach turns. If Alexander finds Caleb now, he'll kill him. He already nearly succeeded twice—first, just before we escaped the citadel when my parents came to rescue us, then again with the trap I set off. The memory of the pain Caleb suffered stokes the fires of guilt burning inside me, and the dark and terrible feeling stirring in my gut tells me Alexander will succeed if given another chance. Third time's the charm, as they say.

I frown, my fingers clenching tightly around the skin. I wish this could all be over. I wish we knew where Alexander is hiding so we can finally end this madness.

I wish I knew for sure if Alaric is alive.

Dragging in a deep, shaking breath, I shutter my eyes and scrub a hand over my face as the same four words circle through my head on a loop.

Where are you, Alaric?

I don't know what I expect. Some kind of answer from the universe, I suppose, but the universe frustrates me with its silence.

With a disheartened sigh, I force open my eyes, then pause, glancing around the dark space, my pulse an erratic rhythm reflecting my panic as my disorientation builds to a crescendo. My surroundings are different than they were only seconds before, and my breath immediately catches when I register the similarities to what happened to me back at the citadel. I glance behind me to be sure, and not only am I not in my room in Derinkuyu with Caleb anymore, but like then—when I somehow left my body to free the others from the spider web of Alexander's insidious magic—I'm standing when a moment ago, I was sitting. And, just like then, I can see through my hand as I raise it in front of me, my fingers still clutching the patch of skin, which now possesses the same translucent quality.

Unlike then, however, my physical body is nowhere in sight. This time, I am completely detached from my corporeal form, and I can barely contain the hysteria bubbling inside me at the thought of being separated from my body for good. What if I can't get back to it? What if I'm stuck like this forever?

Calm down, Luna. Take a breath.

My lips tremble around my slow exhalation, and swallowing, I feel for that tie to my body like how I felt for that thread connecting Caleb to the others when we walked into Alexander's trap. It takes me a moment, but that link is there in the back of my head, and as I wrap the threads of my power around it, I know that if I just follow it, I'll find my way back to my body. Back to Caleb.

But not yet.

I narrow my eyes, trying to work out where I am and why my mind—or soul, or whatever I am at this moment—has drifted here, wherever here is. But just as I take a step forward, I freeze. A bed seems to rise out of the darkness in front of me, and there, with one leg thrown over the blanket, I glimpse the defined outline of a body. Of a man—wearing a T-shirt and boxers—sitting up in the bed, his face, cast in shadow, tilted up toward the ceiling. I could be looking at anyone on the planet right now—friend, foe, or stranger—and yet, I recognize something in the reserved way the man holds himself. Just as I sense something deeply familiar about his aura.

"Alaric?" I whisper, breathless.

There's a brief moment—in the space of time between me saying his name and his amber eyes snapping to mine—when I'm convinced this is a trick. When I fear I'm still trapped in the Council's glass egg where everything I want and love is nothing more than a memory, out of reach. But then the moment passes and our eyes lock, and I see him as clearly as I can see the sun on a cloudless day. I *know* there's no way this isn't real because life can't possibly be that cruel. It's him. Alaric's really here. He's really alive.

I can't bring myself to believe anything else.

I swallow the lump in my throat, suddenly glad I had the sense to put my clothes back on after my latest tumble with Caleb or else Alaric would be seeing a whole lot more of me than either of us would ever be comfortable with.

Scrubbing that thought from my mind, I smile—my lips peeled so wide it almost hurts—but Alaric just stares at me, those warm, comforting eyes pinned wide in disbelief.

Luna? he mouths. He doesn't say my name aloud, and when I take a step toward him, he thrusts out a hand, warning me not to come any closer.

I'm about to ask him what's wrong—to ask him why he won't speak to me—when he casts a nervous look over his shoulder. Unease ripples through me as I follow his gaze...

And that's when I notice the other body in the bed.

The sleeping figure stirs, letting out a soft moan, but, to my immense relief, doesn't wake. Alaric shifts slightly, revealing the blond hair cascading across the pillow beside him, but seeing it doesn't spark any feelings of horror or anger or disturbed recognition like it might for anyone else were they to find themselves in my position. Because I already know who it is. I know it as irrevocably as I know that I'm in love with Caleb.

Alaric's focus drifts away from Alexander and settles back on me, then holding up a finger to his lips, he nods toward the door. I nod back, clamping my mouth shut, watching as the Nephilim carefully untangles himself from the bed sheets and slides from the mattress with the grace and finesse of a prima ballerina. In the time we've spent apart, I almost forgot how tall and lithe he is, and yet, instead of awe, I watch his every movement with terror and unease as he pads across the floor toward where I wait by the door. Terror because I'm anxious I could be ripped back into my body at any moment without finding out where he is. Without getting the chance to speak with him and find out if he really stayed away because he had no other choice or if something else was keeping him here. Something like his feelings for Alexander. And then, behind the terror, there's that sense of unease because he's always seemed so normal to me—or, at least, more so than the other Nephilim and angels I met—but now, with his hair mussed and deep purple bags under his eyes, he looks more vulnerable and human than I've ever seen him.

There's a strange intimacy to seeing him like this. Not romantic—never romantic—but like seeing someone who always seemed impervious to pain crying over a cut.

I watch him closely, never daring to blink in case it breaks the connection between us. I want to hug him so badly. I want to touch his face, to prove to myself that he's real, but I can't. Not like this. He must feel the same because he reaches for my wrist as soon as he's beside me, but his fingers pass through my arm, touching nothing but air.

Recoiling as if he's been burned, he looks down at his empty palm for a moment before gaping at me, a dozen different questions written into his features. He only mouths one.

How?

I don't know how to answer that question—I'm still not entirely sure how I'm doing this. So, instead, I lift the hand still holding the skin patch as my lips soundlessly shape the words, *We need to talk.*

Alaric stares at my upraised hand for a moment then composes himself, wiping the shock from his face. Nodding again, he creaks the door open—slowly, so slowly—and slips out of the room, beckoning for me to follow. The corridor beyond is equally dark, but I can make out the buttery stone surrounding us easily, every crack and crevice visible to my eyes. Alaric still doesn't dare utter a word, and as several long moments pass with me just following blindly, I wonder where he's taking me. Is there even a safe place here for us to talk?

As we progress through the long hallways, I take stock of my surroundings, hoping they'll provide me with an obvious clue as to where we are, but I'm not a history buff like Caleb and, to my dismay, I recognize nothing. Whatever this place is, though, it's exquisite, with tall pillars and rich colors lining the floors and ceilings and tapestries on the walls depicting an ancient world I can't even begin to imagine.

"What is this place?" I whisper to Alaric, but he just shakes his head and presses a long finger to his lips again.

My building anxiety ratchets higher the longer we spend in silence. While I don't feel any particular strain being this far from my body—aside from a burgeoning anxiety at how freaky this whole thing is—I don't know how long I can hold onto this connection. I need to speak with Alaric now, before this chance is lost to us.

"Alar—" I begin, but his name dies on my tongue when he disappears through a door on my left, and I follow him without hesitation into…a bathroom?

At least, that's what I think the room is. There's a chair made of stone with a hole in the seat that resembles a toilet and a large wash basin on the floor that reminds me a bit of a bird bath, although both look so old I'd be afraid to use them. Like

Kandahār, this place isn't exactly rife with modern amenities.

"I'm sorry," he says in a rush, turning to face me. "It wasn't safe to speak with you so close to Alexander. At least if he wakes and finds me here, it won't rouse any suspicion."

I blink at him, then give a slow nod, but when I open my mouth to speak, I find I'm suddenly at a loss for words.

"How are you here, Luna?" Alaric asks before I can manage my thoughts. "Are you even here?" He reaches out a hand to touch my shoulder, but like before, his fingers pass through me. "Am I dreaming?" he whispers.

"This isn't a dream," I rasp, and as tears puddle in my eyes and his, I consider how bittersweet this reunion must be for both of us. This is the first time we're together again and we can't even hug or touch hands. Hell, we might as well be on different planets. The pain growing inside my heart at that realization— at this unwanted distance between us—could crush me.

"How are you here?" he asks again, his voice thick.

I shrug, wishing I could give him a better answer than the only one I have. "I don't entirely know. I…can leave my body somehow? I only just figured out I can do it. Must be a Gray thing," I mutter as a lame aside, shrugging one shoulder again.

"More like it's a you thing," he murmurs contemplatively, then he gifts me a smile, wiping his wet eyes on his forearm.

"A me thing?" I echo.

He nods. "Whatever you're doing…I have *never* seen that power before. Not even in Alexander. But then, you are the child of two of the most powerful angels to ever exist, not to mention you are a Gray. It is unsurprising you would possess such a unique talent."

I let that sink in for a few seconds then say, "Are you sure? I mean, maybe he just doesn't flaunt it."

Alaric arches a brow at me. "This is Alexander we're talking about. If he had such a power, he would not only flaunt it, he would most certainly use it. It would be perhaps the greatest weapon in his arsenal..." He trails off, shaking his head, then in a softer voice adds, "He cannot do this, I promise you that. I know because...I know everything there is to know about him." Shame kisses every word leaving his lips. Heaving a discontented sigh, he scrubs a hand over his face. "He hasn't changed."

Averting his eyes, Alaric combs back his bedraggled hair as an intolerable hush descends between us. It swallows the cramped space—it swallows me—and I wish I knew what to say to erase it, to ease his remorse and let him know I don't judge him, not for his feelings. Not for anything.

"I'm sorry, Luna," Alaric breathes after a long moment, finally breaking the unbearable silence. "I'm sorry you had to see me like that. I'm...sorry I succumbed to my weakness."

My chest tightens, and I realize he means how I found him together with Alexander. In bed.

"You don't need to apologize for that," I assure him and it's true. If I were in his shoes, and Caleb turned into a psychotic dictator, I still don't think I'd have the strength to stay away from him. I would choose him over everyone and everything, even if it went against every moral fiber in my being.

Besides, I've known about his past with Alexander for a while now, since I was at the Serapeum, and Alaric never lied to me about the extent of his feelings for the Gray. I knew he was in love with him, just as I know how painful it was for him to see Alexander again after so many years apart, especially after millennia of carrying the guilt of having helped the Council entomb him.

Does Alexander know Alaric betrayed him? I quickly push that thought aside. If he does, then the Gray is far more forgiving than I gave him credit for. And if he doesn't…

Then all the more reason to find out where Alaric is and get him to safety as soon as possible.

"I don't?" Alaric says, his tone doubtful. "But I'm literally sleeping with the enemy. How can you ever forgive me for that?"

"Have you switched sides?" I ask.

He balks. "I…what?"

"Have. You. Switched. Sides?" I say again, more slowly this time. "Are you helping Alexander of your own free will or would you rather come back to Team Savior?"

A smile quirks the edges of his lips. "I see Caleb is rubbing off on you."

Heat creeps up the back of my neck. Caleb is definitely rubbing off on me every chance he gets, just not always in the way Alaric is thinking.

I cross my arms and give him an impatient look. "Answer the question, Alaric."

The smile slips from his face, and he sighs. "Of course, I'm on your side, Luna. I love Alexander, and part of me always will, but this—" He gestures vaguely toward the door, his expression defeated. "I can't condone what he's doing."

"Then tell me where you are," I plead, reaching for his hand before remembering I won't be able to touch him.

He stares at me for a few seconds, uncertain. "It isn't safe for you to come here. Besides, I can't leave."

"Why?" I counter. "Why can't you leave?" And then, all the questions I've been holding in tumble out of me, one after another. "If you're on my side, why didn't you come back? Why leave me *this* if you didn't want me to find you?" I hold up the skin patch, wagging it in his face. "You did leave this for me, didn't you?"

His mouth drops open then gradually closes again before he says, "Yes. I did. But only to let you know I was alive. I didn't want you to live with the burden of believing me to be dead, or worse, thinking my death was somehow your fault. Especially after Caleb spotted me at Megiddo. I knew he would tell you he saw me, and I hoped, by leaving that, you would know I wasn't helping Alexander because I wanted to. I...I didn't want you to think less of me."

"I could never think less of you!" I practically shout then draw in a breath to control my rising temper. Exhaling through my nose, I continue, "I'm just trying to understand. You already risked your life for me once, and I can't let you do it again. I can't let you stay with him because if you do, you *will* end up dead, and I couldn't bear that."

"Luna…" Alaric whispers, and there's a tremor of misery in his tone.

"Tell me." I stare up at him, feeling the tears on my cheeks now, even though my body is miles away. "Tell me why you didn't come back."

A dejected expression crosses his face. "The same reason he found out about Derinkuyu."

"I—" I wrinkle my nose, confused. Then it hits me. "You have a tracker, too, don't you?"

He nods, and although darkness swathes us, I see his jaw clench. "Despite how it might look, despite what he's having me do, I'm a prisoner here. Alexander doesn't trust me not to abandon him, so he's taken that option away, treating me like a possession instead of a person. And I…I hate myself for still loving him after he's done this to me." As he says this, his eyes lose their usual luster, their depths haunted. Exhaling, he presses the tips of his fingers into his eyes. "We both know the Council won't come for me, even if you beg them to. There's too much history there to question, and I'm just one Nephilim—"

"They will if it will hurt Alexander."

Alaric just looks at me, his brow deeply furrowed, as if he's not following what I'm suggesting. "What?"

Ignoring him, I glance over my shoulder, looking around the small room, as if by doing so I'll be able to assess the full interior of this place. "Where are the children and weapons he stole? Are they here with you?"

Comprehension softens his features. "Yes, but—"

"Then that's what we tell them," I say, interrupting him again, more forcefully this time. "We tell them we know how to blindside Alexander and take back what he took from us. If he no longer holds their students, the Council will have nothing to fear from him. Together, we can level the playing field."

A flicker of…*something* crosses Alaric's face. Something, I realize, that looks almost like hope. But it fades before it can fully take hold, and once again, he stares at me with that crestfallen expression.

"And what about my tracker?" he presses. "Alexander created his own. It's a Gray device. The Council won't be able to remove it."

This version of Alaric, downtrodden and despairing…I don't recognize him, and it hurts my heart to see him this way. To see what Alexander has reduced him to. Well, I refuse to abandon him like this.

I refuse to let Alexander win.

"Then *I'll* remove it. Along with any others that might be planted in the students he kidnapped." Every word has weight to it, like a sworn vow. I just have to hope Alaric believes me.

But the resignation in his eyes tells me he doesn't. "Luna…"

he begins, my name unfurling slowly on his tongue. I just shake my head.

"I can do it, Alaric. I *know* I can." I'm not sure who I'm trying to convince—me or him. Either way, I can't stop the words from coming, and with every last one that transitions from thought into sound, I feel more certain of myself. And of what I can do. "Really, I should thank Alexander. Because of that trap he left for us in Kandahār, I've finally figured out how to control my power. He doesn't even realize he almost single-handedly turned me into the Savior. But I'm going to make sure he finds out."

I've been fighting the notion of me being the Savior since Lilith first put the idea in my head, but after saving lives instead of being responsible for taking them for once, I can finally feel my perspective changing. I felt the beginnings of acceptance on the Shadow Road after I unweaved Alexander's spell then more firmly when Caleb and I spoke of it just a few hours ago. And now, I know my role in this war for certain.

I am the Savior. And I will overcome the Destroyer, no matter what it takes.

Alaric looks at me, those amber eyes wide, but not in disbelief—not this time. Now, he looks at me in astonishment, as if he's seeing me for the first time. Really seeing me.

"We're in Persepolis," he blurts out. "In one of the palaces here—the Tachara. It looks like ruins to the mortal eye, but its true form is hidden by a glamor."

Rolling my teeth along the curve of my lower lip, I nod. "Okay. I'll tell the others."

"You should wait," Alaric says, and when I give him a bewildered look, he shakes his head as if to clear it of some wayward thought. "To strike when Alexander isn't here, I mean," he clarifies. "To defeat him, you first need to beat him at his own game. Don't just level the playing field, tip the scales." Those words hang in the air between us, and when I nod again, Alaric adds, "I need a little time to come up with a plan. Come back tomorrow night. Same time. I'll be right here, waiting for you."

"In the bathroom," I deadpan, cocking an amused brow.

He grins. "It's the safest place. I can always blame my absence from Alexander's bed on indigestion."

I stifle a laugh at that, turning to leave before remembering I'm not really here. Unlike Alaric, who is in danger every passing moment he remains in this place.

"Alaric?" I whisper, facing him again and holding up the patch of flesh. "I need to know... Did Alexander do this to you? Is that why you didn't contact my father?"

A shadow crosses his face, and he lowers his eyes, staring at the skin in my hand. "I was unconscious for a while after he stabbed me, and when I awoke again, the sigil was gone. I was already healed at that point, so I didn't notice he'd cut it off at first, but then...I found *that* in a drawer in his chambers and put two and two together." He swallows, the sound gunshot loud in the cramped silence of the minuscule room. "Creator knows why he was holding onto it. Perhaps he knew I'd find some way to escape him, and he wanted something of me to keep. Whatever his reasoning, I took it and hid it in Caleb's room just before we left the citadel. I knew, if the two of you came, you would find it."

And we did.

I smile, feeling truly optimistic for the first time in months, but the sensation is fleeting. My lips immediately pull down at the corners as a dark thought crosses my mind.

"Wait, if Alexander was holding onto this like some kind of trophy"—I wag the skin patch in my hand again—"then does that mean he knows it's gone?" My heart rate skyrockets and I let out a tiny gasp. "Do you think he suspects anything?"

Like the Nephilim leaving it behind at the citadel to lead us to them…not that Alexander, or even Alaric, could have ever predicted I'd be able to find him.

"Oh, he knows. In fact, I made sure of it. Just as I made sure to let him know how repulsed I was that he'd kept it," Alaric says through clenched teeth. At my startled expression, he clears his throat. "*But* we don't need to worry," he assures me. "As far as Alexander is concerned, I destroyed it."

I arch a dubious brow. "And you're sure he believed you?"

A wry smile curls Alaric's lips and he lifts one hand, his golden fire erupting across his palm. "I was very convincing. After all, nothing I said was a lie. Other than the part about burning his little trophy, of course." He waves a hand then, extinguishing the flames. "At any rate, you should be going now. I don't want to risk him noticing my absence."

I nod, albeit reluctantly. "Tomorrow," I murmur. It comes out more like a question.

"Tomorrow," he says.

There's a promise behind that one word, and yet, I can't suppress the sudden fear rising within me. Fear that I've found him now only to never see him again, promises to each other be damned.

Driven by that fear, my hand shoots out, reaching for his, as if he is the cliff edge that will keep me from plunging to my death. Although my fingers pass through his, there's a fleeting moment of resistance when I swear I can feel the warmth of Alaric's skin—when I sensed some tangible proof of his hand instead of air. And as the room around me begins to fade, I can tell by the widening of his eyes that he felt me, too.

Returning to my body feels strangely like waking up from a dream. One minute, I'm standing with Alaric in that small closet of a room in Persepolis. The next, I'm opening my eyes to find myself firmly back in Derinkuyu. Except, unlike before, when Caleb was asleep in the bed beside me, now he's kneeling in front of me, hands on my face, his dark eyes wide in panic.

"Luna!" He takes me into his arms, all but collapsing when I mutter his name in confusion. "Thank the Creator," he breathes in my ear, his relief almost tangible in the way he holds me against him. Placing his hands on my shoulders, he pulls back to look at me. "Are you okay, Goldilocks? I've been trying to wake you up for the last five minutes. I was literally about to go grab Auntie Lilith and your parents and have someone call a damn priest. What the hell happened?"

A priest?

I jerk my head, glancing around the unlit room, feeling somewhat drained from the effort of leaving my body. Can Caleb see that on my face? It never occurred to me to wonder what I must look like when I do…whatever it is I can do now. Do I look possessed? Did I look like a zombie? Curiosity scratches at every inch of my brain, and I consider asking Caleb to take a picture next time.

With a startled laugh, I mumble, "I left my body again."

Caleb gapes at me like I've lost my mind. "What? W-Where did you go?" Rising from his knees, he settles himself on the bed beside me, taking my hands in his. "Listen, Goldilocks, until we know more about this newfound talent of yours, I don't know if you should be—"

I free one hand from his and press my fingertip to his lips. "Caleb, it's okay," I assure him.

His narrowing gaze is skeptical, but I shake my head when he tries to speak. Drawing in a breath, I lower my hand.

"I know where Alaric is."

twenty-two

CALEB

AFTER I MEET WITH Aya, Rafe, and Shalina to reassure them I'm okay and back in the land of the living, we crowd in Gabriel's and Lucifer's room—me and Luna, Lilith, and Hammurabi with Asmodeus, completing our secret circle. Despite them being the Messenger and the Morningstar, they only scored a slightly bigger room than Luna and me, and it's positively claustrophobic in here. Luna's parents hover on one side of her, Lilith and I on the other, and Asmodeus and the grumpy Babylonian king both lean against the opposite wall. The power enclosed in this one tiny room staggers me.

After Luna's out-of-body experience gave me premature gray hair, we decided to tell her parents and our most-trusted allies about her ability to project her soul from her body and go on walkabout. The image of her sitting there, open eyes resembling milky marbles, is tattooed onto my brain. On the scale of freaky, it was at *Exorcist* level. Even though the sight of her like that terrified me, pride buoys my chest that my Goldilocks has unlocked this badass ability. That she's gained so much control in such a short period of time. She practically glows with the new confidence and determination she has. She finally believes she's the Savior and it shows.

And of course, Gramps is at Persepolis. That city is a mark of pride for him, where he burned the structures Xerxes helped build, taking revenge for the Persian king destroying the temples of Athens. Ending the Achaemenid Empire. Well, he burned most of the city, but the ruins of Tachara—the Palace of Darius I—still stand. We only *believed* they were ruins. That's a classic Alexander move, and I'm not surprised by it. It was clever of him to glamor a palace everyone thought was the beautiful remains of a faded empire so he had a refuge to escape to. And if we weren't going to war with him—and he wasn't such a murderous asshole—I'd beg him to let me play tourist.

Lucifer clears his throat, drawing me from my musings. His blue eyes focus on Luna, worry written there. "We're all here now, Starlight. Why did you call this meeting? What's happened?"

Gabriel interjects, "Has anyone on the Council threatened you because of what you did in Kandahār? You saved them, those thankless monsters."

"If they did, let's devise a way to put them all in their own personal prisons for a few months after we win the war so they can suffer as we did in our cages," Asmodeus says to Luna, venom dripping from her every word. Hammurabi snorts his agreement.

Luna shakes her head so fast her hair catches on her lips. Brushing the golden strands away, she says, "No, nothing like that, but something did happen last night. Something similar to what happened at the citadel."

Her eyes turn to me, and I nod, encouraging her to go on. Yes, she's confident about her new ability, but that doesn't mean she's not still frightened of how other people will react to it—especially those she loves. And we still haven't dropped the Alaric bomb.

Her fingers braid together, twisting, and I watch as she deliberately relaxes them. Her gaze is steady as she looks around the room. "Certain…recent events have led Caleb and I to suspect that Alaric is still alive," she begins, and I hear a startled grunt escape Hammurabi. "And we found a piece of his skin with your sigil, the one Asmodeus gave him"— she inclines her head toward Lucifer then Asmodeus—"at the citadel in Caleb's old room."

Gabriel's voice is uncharacteristically gentle as she says, "Luna, that doesn't mean he's—"

"I saw him at Megiddo," I interrupt, startling them all once again. "It was from a distance, and I wasn't quite sure, but Aya—my sister—mentioned that a Light Nephilim showed up in the chaos and told her to run. So, when we went to Kandahār, Luna and I decided to see if Alaric left something behind for us to find, something to let us know he was alive."

Luna reaches into her pocket and pulls out the withered piece of skin. My first instinct is to shrink back from it, but the older players in the room don't even flinch. I guess when you've witnessed—and participated in—bloody wars, a little piece of hacked-off flesh doesn't bother you. I hope to the Creator it always bothers me.

"I contacted Alaric last night using this," Luna explains.

"How?" Lilith demands.

"And what do you mean it was similar to what you did at the citadel?" Lucifer presses, taking a step forward as if to snatch the skin from her.

Luna lowers her hand, making a fist over the one piece of Alaric she has within her reach. "I was holding this last night, trying to figure out where Alaric is and why he hasn't contacted me, because I know if he were able to, he would have." Damn straight he would've. Alaric loves my girl. "And just like before, I...stepped out of my body somehow. Suddenly, I was with Alaric, just by focusing on *this*." She shakes her clenched fist.

"You were able to travel to Alaric?" Gabriel asks, shock rippling over her face. She, too, focuses on the dried skin, hidden within the confines of Luna's hand, as if it's a poisonous snake, waiting to strike.

"I've never heard of this kind of power before," Hammurabi rumbles, his black eyes darting between the angels and Fallen present.

Lilith gives a slow shake of her head, regarding Luna with awe. "Neither have I," she murmurs. "I have never heard of an angel being able to loosen their soul from their body, using their shell as a tether."

Asmodeus's liquid green gaze roves over Luna. "Nor I. What a power to have."

Focusing on Lilith, I ask, "So, Gramps can't do this?" I mean, Alaric told Luna he can't, but if anyone has knowledge of what Alexander can do, it's the ex-Archdemon, Alexander's former teacher and fan girl.

Her glossy curls bounce with the force of her denial. "No, he does not possess this gift. If he did, he certainly would have employed it by now."

"Yes, he wouldn't have need to attack us on the Road, planting trackers into the children," Gabriel says. "If he had a power like Luna's, based on what she's told us about finding Alaric, he could've used anything the two of you left behind at the citadel to find you. Or just his blood connection with you, Caleb."

Well, isn't that thought enough to give me nightmares for days. "So, this is definitely a special Goldilocks power then," I say.

Luna's gaze darts between her parents. "Mine and not just a Gray thing, right?"

Lucifer inclines his head. "It appears so, but in all my long years, I've never witnessed anything like it. I don't even know what to name it."

I raise my hand. "Ugh, I'm not being a smartass here, but it sounds like astral projection to me."

Hammurabi scoffs. "Ridiculous," he mutters.

"You've been reading too much mortal fiction," Lilith says to me, and Luna scowls at her.

"Astral projection?" Gabriel repeats, raising an eyebrow at Lucifer, who shrugs, a bewildered expression on his face.

Luna looks at me and nods. "It does, doesn't it?" She shoots Lilith major shade. "And don't all angel powers sound like mortal fiction?"

A loud burst of laughter escapes me. "She's got a solid point," I tell the ex-Archdemon, who glowers at me before a grin curves her full lips.

"I suppose she does. So until we find a better name, shall we refer to your new talent as astral projection?" Lilith says.

Asmodeus's laugh cuts like glass. "Although you know when the rest of the Council gets wind of this, they'll insist they have the right to name it."

"The flower shall tell them politely where to stick their suggestions," Hammurabi rumbles. He smiles at Luna. "Isn't that right, flower?"

His kindness always makes her blush. "If they don't try to lock me up again, I promise I will." She sobers. "Do you think my being able to…astral project will make them suspicious of me again? More than they already are after what happened."

Lucifer and Gabriel exchange a look laced with a thousand meanings before the Morningstar says, "You were able to enter their minds when they were under duress, which is more than enough to frighten them, and now that you can find someone just by focusing on an object that belongs to them, they'll fear their secrets aren't safe." A deep sigh puffs past his lips. "But if we present this to them as an opportunity, as a way to win the war against Alexander, they'll be less likely to revert to their base instincts, which is to imprison first, ask questions later."

"Yes, we must present your new ability as an asset—one we can't win without," Asmodeus chimes in.

"But how do we get them to that conclusion? Unless Luna can use Caleb's blood tie to locate Alexander," Gabriel says.

"We don't need to use Caleb for anything. I found Alaric, remember?" Luna says, her voice tart. Gabriel has the grace to look a little embarrassed about volunteering me without my permission. "Alaric can tell us where Alexander is. In fact, he already has."

Once again, she's managed to stun these old fossils who have seen it all.

"Perhaps you should have led with that," Lilith grumbles, crossing her arms over her chest. "What is it mortals say? Way to bury the lead."

Lucifer stares at his daughter. "So, you didn't just see him, you were able to make contact? Communicate with him?"

"He could see you?" Gabriel questions. "When I felt you in

my mind, I knew it was your presence, but I didn't see you."

"Yes, he could see me. I startled him pretty badly," Luna admits. "He wasn't…alone." I blink at that bit of information, and she holds a hand up to stave off my and her parents' frantic questions. "Don't worry, no one else saw me. He led me away somewhere private. It was just like Caleb and I suspected— he's being held against his will. Being used to track down Alexander's bloodline. He told me they're in Persepolis."

"In Darius I's palace," I clarify.

"Clever bastard," Hammurabi says, begrudging admiration in his voice. "Even *we* believed that palace was ruins."

"It's fitting he chose Persepolis," Lucifer muses, taking his chin between forefinger and thumb. "Considering there are so many places he left his mark on, it would have been difficult to search them all. This certainly is information we—and the Council—need if we're to win the war."

"Who was he with?" Hammurabi inquires, and despite the curiosity in his tone, the fine hairs on my neck stand on end. I'm suddenly afraid of the answer.

"I'm curious to know that as well," Lilith croons, an unfriendly smirk hitching up one side of her mouth.

Dread fills me. I'm surprised Luna didn't mention Alaric's companion to me. She's gotten better at opening up, at sharing her fears and secrets, but I know she still struggles with being forthcoming. But why keep this specific bit of info from me?

Luna tenses, her eyes darting around the space but somehow

managing to avoid looking at anyone. "Um, he was with Alexander…in bed," she admits, her voice barely more than a whisper.

My head jerks back, but no one else in the room looks surprised. Gabriel and Lilith look resigned, Asmodeus sighs, Lucifer just nods to himself, and Hammurabi frowns in disapproval. Once again, I'm the odd man out.

"It's not what you think," Luna rushes on. "I mean, it is. I'm guessing from the looks on your faces you all know they used to be involved, but it isn't like that now. Alaric isn't staying with Alexander of his own free will, I swear it."

I stare at her. "How long have *you* known they were involved? This can't be a recent development." It suddenly all makes sense—the weird tension I sensed between the Nephilim and Alexander. The current between them that I could never quite define.

Giving me a pleading look, Goldilocks says, "They were together before Alexander tried to conquer the world the first time. I've known for a while, but I never said anything because it felt…wrong. This wasn't like the vision Alexander showed me of the academies. I *know* I should've said something about that. But this? It wasn't my secret to share. The only person getting hurt by Alaric's feelings was himself. But now that he's trapped with Alexander again…"

"Proximity took over," I mutter. "I get it, kind of. I mean, I guess he still loves Gramps?" That seems impossible, as Alaric is such a kind, gentle soul, but then again, he knew Alexander before he was the Conqueror, so maybe that's the man he's still in love with. Maybe this Alexander still pretends to be that man for him.

"If he does, can he be trusted?" Hammurabi asks, focusing on Luna. "I like Alaric. I always have despite him being a Light. But now that he's with Alexander again, it does call his loyalties into question, does it not? Love blinds even the most far-seeing people."

"Yes, he still loves Alexander, but he hasn't switched to Team Conqueror," Luna retorts. I can't help but grin at her phrasing. She's been hanging out with me too much. "This is another reason why I never said anything, not even to you." Her eyes flick to mine, apologetic, but I'm not angry with her. Outing someone is never cool, and Alaric's feelings really weren't anyone's business until now. "I didn't want anyone questioning his allegiance. You didn't see him. He looks awful. And lingering feelings aside, he *wants* to leave. The only reason he hasn't is because he has a tracker inside him. Even Alexander knows Alaric doesn't want to stay," she says and I blink, horrified. Gramps sure knows how to treat the people he loves. She whirls on Gabriel. "And he's turned on Alexander before. Right, Mom?"

Gabriel tilts her head. "Yes, he has. He was instrumental in bringing Alexander to heel the first time. He fed the Council information, and we were able to imprison the Conqueror. I convinced the Council to let Alaric retain his memories and work for me because of his loyalty. It wasn't easy for Alaric to betray Alexander. Although I always wondered about the true depth of his feelings, it was well-known to many that they were dear friends, and I know he suffered greatly for turning on him. But he didn't believe Earth needed an emperor. He knew it was wrong." Weariness weighs on the Archangel's face. Her gaze falls on Lucifer. "I have great empathy for Alaric. To betray the person you love most leaves a gaping wound that never manages to scar over."

Lucifer takes one of her hands, entwining their fingers. These little displays of affection between them have grown bolder since we returned from Megiddo. It's nice to see. It gives me hope.

"I hadn't realized it was Alaric who betrayed Alexander," Lilith says softly. "I suppose that changes things."

"As does the tracker," Hammurabi adds.

Asmodeus tosses garnet hair over her shoulder. "I've always been fond of Alaric. My trust in him has never been misplaced. I prefer to give him the benefit of the doubt."

"Let us keep this information about Alaric's glorious return to ourselves right now until he gives Luna something useful we can bring to the Council," Lucifer says, tucking Gabriel into his side.

"Indeed. As Luna said, we don't want anyone questioning his allegiance," Lilith agrees. Her heeled boot taps a steady rhythm on the floor. "And Creator knows we're all guilty of jumping to conclusions."

Hammurabi snorts as I say, "Wait? You guys? No way."

Gabriel's eyes meet Luna's before turning to me. "For now, this goes no further than this room."

I roll my eyes. "Who are we going to run and tell? We avoid the Council like they have the plague or a rampant venereal disease."

A shocked giggle escapes Luna, then she composes herself. "We may have more information to present to the Council sooner than you think. Alaric wants me to meet with him tonight."

"Tonight?" Lucifer echoes. "Are you sure that's safe?"

"Safe as in Alexander might be with him again?" I ask, confused.

"She's just begun to learn to use this talent. Is it safe for her to…astral project so soon?" the Morningstar clarifies. His eyes scan his daughter as if searching for invisible damage. His love for her is obvious, but he has to watch that he doesn't smother Luna with it.

"As long as you keep her physical form safe, she should be fine, in theory. Little birds must learn to fly eventually," Lilith says to Lucifer, a sharp edge to her smile. He frowns at her.

In our cramped space, Luna just has to reach out to clasp her father's free hand. "I'll be fine. I have control over this, I promise you, Dad. Besides, you'll be with me when I do it again, so you can watch over me."

Luna offers these words of comfort as a kindness to her father, but I know she has no idea what will happen if shit goes south when she astral projects again. No one does, and as much as I want to keep her safe, she and I both know our current situation only grows more desperate. Whether I like it or not, Luna has to contact Alaric again. This could be our ace in the hole.

Luna reclines on some pillows on our bed, clasped hands holding Alaric's skin. It's the best seat in the house. Only her parents are with us now, as Lilith, Asmodeus, and Hammurabi decided to give her some space in case Goldilocks gets stage fright. I think she'll be just fine, but I do appreciate having more leg room. Plus, all that power in one room feels loud, like a drum solo that never stops.

I sit on the chair next to the bed and smooth back a golden thread of her hair. My eyes snag on Luna's, and she smiles at me, soft and reassuring. I didn't expect to be more nervous than she is. Although, that could be due to the hovering forms of the Messenger and the Morningstar standing above me.

"Are you ready?" I ask her, doing my best to douse the urge to elbow the two scary angels behind me so they give us some breathing room.

She nods. "Yes, I'm ready to see Alaric again." There's a

fragile hope in her voice, and I know how much she wants him back with her, safe and sound.

"Tell him hi from me and thank him for finding Aya," I say.

"I will. Let's do this." Her eyes close, and she tips her head back, settling into the pillow.

For a few moments, all I observe is her beautiful face, serene and peaceful. Then, just like when I woke up the night before, her eyes pop open wide, milky white covering the entire surface, as if the sclera has swallowed the iris and pupil whole. Her body turns rigid, tension rippling through her muscle, despite the fact that she remains lying on the bed, signaling her soul has left her body. It's scary as fuck to look at my Goldilocks and know she's not really in there anymore. I'm staring at an exquisite shell. My heartbeat explodes in my chest, and I reach out, placing a hand over her clasped ones. I trust her. I do. I know she's got this, but I can't help my rush of fear.

I hear a gasp behind me, then Gabriel is leaning over my left shoulder. "Is that what she looked like before?" she demands.

I see the edge of Lucifer's jaw over my right shoulder. "Is she all right?" he barks, voice guttural, and I shiver at the suppressed violence there. He wants to smite someone if she's not, and I'm uncomfortably aware I'm the only target in the room.

These two are doing nothing to help my nerves, and I want to snap at them both to back the fuck off. But I don't have a death wish, no matter how tolerant they are of me. "Yes, this is exactly like before. It looks scarier than it is. She's in complete control," I say, proud of the confidence ringing in my voice. They don't need to know I'm scared. The calmer I am, the calmer I hope they'll be. "She'll be back soon."

The Morningstar grunts and Gabriel says nothing. A few minutes pass and the tension steadily ratchets up in the room. Sweat beads on the back of my neck and slicks my palms.

"How do we get her to return if she's in danger?" Gabriel asks Lucifer.

"I do not know. How does one call a soul home?" he replies, not bothering to hide his worry.

"She's fine," I grit out. "Have faith in your kid. She's strong—you two should know that."

I feel both their eyes on my back like twin lasers ready to burn through my skin when the cloudiness dissipates from Luna's eyes, and she blinks up at me. Relief is like a flood, rushing to fill all the corners of my body.

"Baby, I'm so glad to have you back," I say, squeezing her hands.

She sits up, staring at me, then her gaze jumps to her parents. "Alaric says he knows how we can draw Alexander out to rescue the children."

twenty-three

LUNA

IF I WASN'T IMMORTAL, I might fear a one-way ticket to Hell for what we're about to do. Then again, even immortals can die by the right blade, so maybe eternal damnation is still a possibility, depending on how this all pans out.

A shiver ripples over my skin as I follow the straight path of the Blessed Road beside my mother, mentally recounting the events of the last twenty-four hours. As promised, Alaric had a strategy for how we could turn the tide of this war against Alexander. A questionable, borderline morally-reprehensible strategy, but a strategy that he swears will work.

Despite the losses we've suffered, the one upper hand we still have is that Alexander isn't aware we know where he is. Although that gives us the element of surprise, Alaric was right—we need to tip the scales before we can beat him, and storming the gates when the Gray and his army are there in Persepolis would only result in needless casualties and a potential, unfavorable early end to this conflict. We need to weaken the snake before we can cut off its head, and to do that, we need to hit him where it will actually hurt.

Alexander might be a narcissist, but even he has a weakness, and from what Alaric told me, that weakness is his mortal parents. They might both be long dead, little more than particles of dust and bone now, but Alexander is apparently sentimental about them—a strange thought given how quick he was to turn on Caleb, his actual flesh and blood. According to Alaric, the Gray even went so far as to place protection wards on his parents' tombs in Greece. Whether that's because Alexander anticipated us attacking the sites or because he does actually intend to eventually raise them from the dead as he offhandedly proclaimed when we were captive at the citadel, one thing is certain: if we ransack one of the tombs, he will come, leaving his new base unguarded for us to then slip in and rescue Alaric and the children.

Between his parents, Alexander holds a greater fondness for his deceased mother, and so, at Alaric's suggestion, that's where I head now with Gabriel, Raphael, and Uriel—to the queen of Macedonia's resting place in the town of Korinos where a handful of the Archdemons, including my father, will meet us. The plan is for us to break into the tomb, then split up, with half of us making our way to Persepolis once we're certain Alexander has abandoned the city while the other half leads him on a wild goose chase on the Roads. The remaining

Council members, along with Caleb, Lilith, Hammurabi, and the other Fallen and Nephilim at our disposal, are on standby in the mountains above the ancient Persian city, keeping an eye on any movement below and ready to act once we give the order. Lilith wanted to accompany me and my mother to Korinos, but I begged her to stay with Caleb—to protect him, should the need arise, even if he wasn't happy about it. The ex-Archdemon makes him uncomfortable, not that he would ever admit it. Still, while I knew Asmodeus would watch over him, as would Hammurabi, I felt better knowing Lilith would be there with him, too.

Getting the Council to agree to this plan was actually far easier than I anticipated it would be—especially considering it was coming from me. Then again, they want to humble the Conqueror and make him realize he's not as invincible as he thinks. Immortals can hold a grudge better than humans, and they want to pay Alexander back for all the trouble he's caused them, both in the past and now. If what Alaric said about him still rings true, there's only one way to do that—by exhuming his mother's remains. The thought makes me queasy, but there's no telling how many wards the Gray put on the tomb, and he might not come at all unless he truly believes his mother's resting place is in jeopardy. Plus, we need something to lead him away from our true aim, which is to raid his base.

"What will we do with it?" I whisper to my mother. "The queen's remains, I mean."

Gabriel's mouth hardens into a line. "Alexander might be a brilliant strategist, but even he is not immune to anger…or slight. Heightened emotions make even the best of us careless, and I am certain he will view our actions in Korinos as a grave personal insult. His reaction today will be his downfall."

My brow furrows, and I turn my head, looking at her more closely. "You didn't answer my question."

Raphael sidles up on my right before Gabriel can answer, interjecting, "We will be respectful, don't you worry your pretty little head. Something of such great import to the Conqueror may come in handy as a bargaining chip, should we need it."

My mother scoffs. "Bait is the more likely alternative. The time for bargaining is long past."

We step out of the Blessed Road at one of the markers in Greece into the dying light of a setting sun. When my feet touch asphalt, I glance around, thrown by the modernity of our surroundings. We're on an empty road in the middle of what I think might be farmland, the mostly flat earth interrupted only by a highway visible to my left through some trees and a gas station and rest stop not far off straight ahead. I'm not sure what I expected to find here, but nothing about this place screams ancient burial site.

A short distance away, there's a large mound covered in trees, under which I notice three Archdemons emerging from a cluster of shadows. Situated between Mammon and Beelzebub, I spot my father, but instead of coming over to meet us, they head for a small structure to the left of the hill, which looks like little more than a wooden roof propped up by a handful of steel beams for cover. The Archangels cross the field to the building without hesitation, but despite my mother nodding at me to follow, I find myself frozen in place, my fingers curling into tight, trembling fists. So much depends on this part of the plan going right. Since Alexander was the one who put the ward on the tomb, it stands to reason only another Gray will be able to break it—assuming Gray wards work anything like Light and Dark ones. But what if I can't? Or worse, what if he's laid another trap in wait for us? One I won't be able to overcome?

Don't think like that, I chide myself. *This has to work.*

This is the only way to rescue Alaric.

Holding onto that thought like a lifeline, I draw in a breath and launch into a run, only stopping once I've joined the others, and we're all gathered together just outside the lean-to, my father and Beelzebub silently assessing the dark opening ahead. Surprisingly, there's no fence surrounding the site, or any sort of deterrent to stop us—or mortal grave robbers— from entering the premises, assuming there's anything left inside to steal. The building doesn't even have a door. It's open to the elements, with the entrance to the tomb on full display.

"I do not sense a ward here," Uriel grumbles, crossing the stretch of wooden planks that form a footpath from the edge of the structure to the tomb opening.

"Some may yet lie ahead," my mother warns, her dark eyes shifting to mine. "Alaric said there is at least one, and he would not lead us astray."

"Perhaps," Uriel retorts, noncommittal, before stepping into the passage beyond.

I scowl at the Archangel's back. He was the last person I wanted to accompany us on this mission—even more so than Mammon, who I'm actually glad is with us rather than in Persepolis with the others, waiting for our signal to begin the rescue. At least while he's here, I know he can't hurt Caleb. But Uriel on the other hand…his presence is a constant thorn in my side, and I know he came with us to keep a watchful eye on me as much as he did for the chance to spurn Alexander.

"How do the wards work when it comes to humans?" I ask, glancing between my parents, who stick close to my sides as we make our way along the unlit stone path, the floor underfoot sloping in a steady decline. The ceiling above us is low and rounded, and we pass two large marble slabs propped against the walls, which I can only assume were once doors used to close off the approaching end of this passage. "I mean, this is an excavation site, right?"

"Different wards serve different purposes," my mother answers vaguely as we reach the end of the corridor and step through the open doorway ahead into a small antechamber. Unlike the plain earthy whites and beiges of the stone blocks in the passage behind us, the top half of the wall intersecting the path directly before us is red. While I'm sure the color was probably vibrant once, now it's the same hue as rust, aged by many long years and decay, though there's a certain grandness to the partition that remains despite the passage of time. It rises in a pointed triangle at the top where the peak meets with the barrel-vaulted roof, seeming to serve as some sort of grand arch.

The official entry to the tomb.

As I take in the details, I think of Caleb, not only because he would be fascinated by the architecture, but because the tomb was erected for a woman who is essentially his great-grandmother. The history-lover side of him would be elated.

"Some wards block entrance entirely while others merely… deter," Gabriel continues after a moment, dragging my attention away from the engraved markings at the top of the facade.

"Think of it like bug spray for humans," Beelzebub grumbles, rolling his eyes, which are bright, like polished sapphires, even in the darkness.

"That would explain why this place isn't locked up or guarded," my father says, crossing the space and stopping abruptly in front of the doorway leading into the next chamber. "Something about this edifice is keeping the mortals away."

"And now us," Raphael adds, sidestepping my father. Raising a hand to the opening, she flattens her palm against what I can only assume is an invisible wall, not unlike the wards I encountered with Caleb and Ishtar under the Serapeum what feels like a lifetime ago.

"Is something there?" I glance between the faces of the angels and Fallen around me, but whatever they're sensing here, I don't feel it. Then again, I didn't feel the wards back in Alexandria, either.

My mother's brow wrinkles in consternation. "A ward, just like we expected. It's blocking our way deeper into the tomb, but…it's unlike any I've ever encountered."

"Of course, it is." Mammon sneers at her. "This ward was created by a Gray, remember? Did you believe it would resemble anything we can create?"

"It matters not," Uriel chides, gesturing to me with an indifferent wave of his hand. "We have another Gray here who can break it. After what occurred at the citadel, the Morningstar's daughter will make quick work of it, I'm sure."

I don't miss the skepticism and distrust in his tone—or the obvious exclusion of my mother from his comment, as if he still can't believe the Messenger could have committed the blasphemous act of helping to bring a Gray into the world. He arches a thick black brow, and my jaw tenses as I suppress the violent urge to break something other than the ward. Like his teeth.

"Come, Starlight," my father murmurs. "Ignore these old cynics and tell me what you sense."

I nod, but the trouble is, I sense nothing.

Exhaling, I position myself before the unobstructed doorway then take a step forward into the next chamber, testing the ward to see if it's anything like the ones I encountered in Alexandria. Like then, I proceed without issue. Nothing stops me and I don't feel myself passing through anything, but then, my exposure to wards—and our world in general—has been limited. Maybe I just don't know what to look for.

Focus, Luna, the voice in my head snaps. *Focus and you'll feel it. You have to.*

Turning to face the others, I draw in a shaking breath, and when I raise my hands—mimicking what Raphael did, pressing them flat to the ward—I close my eyes and force my thoughts outward, searching for any sign of Alexander's magic, just like I searched for the threads linking their minds at the citadel. It takes me a moment but I find it, much to my relief, and exhaling again, I open my eyes, holding the picture of it close in my consciousness. Now, aware of what I'm looking for, I can see it—the wall separating me from the others. But this time, it doesn't take the shape of threads at all or anything I can snap or cut.

It's glass and I just need to shatter it.

Summoning a strength I wasn't even aware I possessed, I throw everything I feel toward Alexander at the barrier. Anger for all the hurt and pain he's caused Caleb. Rage for what he's doing to Alaric. And an irrepressible contempt for how he's forced me into a role that threatens to crush me at every turn. But I won't let it crush me. I can't.

Because I am the Savior and I'm destined to stop him.

A strange energy I've never felt or seen before suddenly explodes out of my palms in a blinding light, cracking the wall beneath my touch and illuminating the tomb and passage behind the angels in white. It heats every inch of me down to my marrow until I'm burning as bright as the hottest fire. No, not like fire. Like a star.

A Morningstar. I smile at the thought.

The light fades after a few seconds, and I blink, my eyes quickly adjusting to the returning darkness of the tomb. I curl my fingers, feeling for the ward before me, but I don't sense anything there. The glasslike barrier hasn't only been broken, it's been obliterated—wiped from existence, with no indication it was ever there at all to begin with. I don't know why that surprises me. I guess I supposed that kind of magic would leave a permanent mark, like a stain that I would still see or sense. Or maybe I just wasn't entirely convinced I had what it takes to break it.

But I did. I overcame yet another obstacle Alexander threw in my path. And now, with the ward destroyed, we're one step closer to turning the tables against him.

We move quickly. We don't have time to waste, and if the Gray ward is anything like the wards the Council placed at the Serapeum to guard his prison, Alexander will already know we're here. He'll know what we've done—what *I've* done, which is exactly what we're banking on.

The middle chamber in the tomb is empty, but the last

room, the burial chamber, has what we came for. Two white funerary beds sit positioned in an L-shaped arrangement. Uriel pushes past everyone, making a beeline for the smaller of the two, which has a snake relief on the front of the stone.

"Is that it?" I ask.

"See, the child *is* useful," Raphael practically purrs, planting herself on the untouched coffin and picking at her nails.

Uriel flashes her a scornful look over his shoulder but stays silent as he lifts the marble box from the floor as if it weighs nothing. Although I've experienced my own angel strength many times now, it's still so strange to witness just how different we are from humans. We really are a separate species, and the more aware I become of that fact, the less I know how to feel about it. Maybe because it reminds me that half of Caleb is human—that he's mortal, and every moment this war carries on is another potential moment the fire of his life could be snuffed out.

"Luna?" my father prompts and I jolt, scrubbing all thoughts of Caleb from my mind.

Blinking up at Lucifer, I nod. "I'm ready."

"Make haste," my mother says, her tone brusque. "We don't have long."

I swallow, distressed by the thought of projecting with several members of the Council watching—of leaving my body vulnerable to their whims—but I know we don't have time for nerves, so I try to take comfort in knowing my parents are with me. That they'll watch over me. Steeling myself, I nod again, then pulling the leathery patch of flesh from my pocket, I think of Alaric. Projecting my soul is even easier now than it was the last two times I did it, and before I know it, I'm back at the Tachara, standing in the cramped bathroom again. Alaric isn't here, but I didn't expect him to be, nor do I expect him to come. Because as much as I can't wait to see him again, my friend isn't what I need right now.

What I need is a sign.

I spot it within seconds. There, on the wall above the doorway, is the sigil Asmodeus gifted Alaric scrawled on the stone near the ceiling in chalk—the signal we agreed upon for him to use to let me know our plan is working. My heart buckles, smashing into my ribcage with enough force to thrust me back into my body, and wrenching my eyes open, I gasp out the words the Archangels and Archdemons are waiting for.

"He's coming."

With a curt nod, my mother rolls up the sleeve of her blouse—my lips twitch at the realization that she still dresses like the headmistress of the Serapeum, even when we're robbing a dusty, old tomb. Once her wrist is exposed, she presses her fingertip to the sigil I share with her and Lilith, and I feel the burn of her call, my eyes dropping to the glowing white lines in my skin as my pulse gallops at the thought of the others in Persepolis.

This is it—the signal they're waiting for.

"Let's move," my mother growls. Grabbing my hand, she yanks me through the chambers, retracing our steps toward the path that will lead us back to the light. Raphael and Uriel follow our lead, the latter still tightly clutching the marble box. I look over my shoulder, glancing past them at the Archdemons, who remain in the shadows, preparing for the role in this heist they still have to play.

"One word of this to anyone, and I swear—" Mammon threatens, but my father waves him off with a smile.

"My lips are sealed," Lucifer promises. Beside him, Beelzebub snorts.

The youthful Archdemon's sudden laughter follows our steps up the incline. "I think I prefer you this way, Mammon," he says through hysterics.

This time, when I look back again, I swear I see two Fallen in the shadows of the tomb instead of the three we left behind. And between them on the floor is the same box Uriel carries, except this one emits a low growl of contempt.

Seeing the Tachara in person is strange, like visiting a place I've only ever seen in my dreams. At first glance, it looks like little more than well-preserved ruins, but upon further inspection—beyond the ripple of the glamor encasing it—I see the truth of the palace's real form. The vibrant exterior colors—the reds, greens, and yellows—along with the intricate carvings into nearly every pillar and available surface, mimic the beauty I briefly saw within the first time I astral projected my soul here. Before, the details were dulled somewhat by the monochromatic darkness of night, but now, in the sunlight, I glimpse every mark left behind by the artists who built this place, and I'm mesmerized by the otherworldliness of it all, of how it makes me feel like I'm stepping out of time and into a once-distant past.

My mother, Raphael, and I skirt around a handful of dead Nephilim as we climb the steps up to the palace. We don't bother to sneak in through a back or side entrance. We don't have to. The skeleton crew Alexander left here has already been overwhelmed by our forces, leaving a clear path for us into the Tachara. Just as Gabriel predicted he would, Alexander reacted rashly to our assault on his mother's tomb, and just as Alaric predicted, he took most of his army with him to hunt us down, leaving this place vulnerable and exposed. Just like when he invited my father to the citadel, expecting him to bend the knee, Alexander has let his overconfidence get the better of his judgment. He was wrong to assume we wouldn't ever find out about his base here in Persepolis.

He was wrong to underestimate me. And Alaric.

Inside the dwelling, the Archangels, Archdemons, and Nephilim who were waiting for our signal are already hard at work, gathering the students who were abducted and the weapons from the Fall that were stolen, herding them all into the main foyer. To buy us time, my father, Beelzebub, and Mammon are leading Alexander astray in the opposite direction from the Persian city, making him believe they have his mother's remains when, in reality, the real funerary box is with Uriel at our new hideout in Cambodia, where we'll meet him once we finish here. At the time we discussed this plan with the Council, the Archangels and Archdemons didn't go into specific detail as to how they would trick Alexander—just that they would use a believable decoy to distract him. Looking back, I suppose I should've paid more attention to the amused looks everyone kept flashing at Mammon.

I bite back a chuckle at the memory of Beelzebub's laughter and my growing comprehension of what I saw just before I left Korinos. Once, Mammon was the star in almost all of my nightmares, his shape-shifting ability tormenting me even in sleep. But now, picturing him in my father's arms, taking the form of a harmless stone box, leaches away some of the terror I feel when I think of him. If only Caleb had been there to see it, then maybe he wouldn't be so scared of him, either.

Thinking of Caleb pulls me back to reality, and my eyes snap between the surrounding faces, looking for him in the crowd. Worry spreads through me, coating my skin like sweat—not only because I don't see him here, but because I can't stop thinking of my father on the Shadow Road, pursued by Alexander and his army. The thought gives me flashbacks to his fight with the Gray at the citadel, when Alexander pierced his body with feathers of silver light, shot through his limbs like arrows. Although I know Lucifer can hold his own in a fight, I'm glad Beelzebub is with him to back him up if needed. If anyone can help my father stave off Alexander, it's the feisty Archdemon.

Pushing my apprehension aside, I tell myself to calm down—that my father will be fine and that Caleb is here somewhere, and we'll be together again soon. But as always, my attempts at self-soothing are fruitless, and I breathe out a shaky breath as I trail my mother's steps through the large, crowded hall—the grand black-tiled floor lined with tall pillars—my stomach clenching at the sight of the frightened children filling the space.

Much like with the evacuations at Sinai and the Serapeum, the angels and Fallen have organized the students, except the lines they form here serve a different purpose to the ones they were separated into at the academies. Now, every student is checked for a tracker—not just the Lights who were ambushed on the Blessed Road but everyone, in case Alexander decided to mark his new property. Then, once they're cleared, the students are ushered into two growing groups by the doors—one for Darks and one for Lights—where they then wait to be escorted into their respective Roads and spirited away to safety. Again.

The progression moves quickly and efficiently, with an undercurrent of urgency I can physically feel in the air. It clings to my hair and clothes like static electricity, and the longer I watch the Lights and Darks work, the more I recognize the sick feeling inside me and why I can't seem to shake my discomfort. The angels and Fallen seem to be having no issue removing the trackers in the students, which means Alexander wasn't the one who planted them—he left that job to his lackeys. But Alaric… he told me himself the tracker inside his head is a Gray one, and I want to vomit at the thought of Alexander violating him that way. Clearly, that was one tether Alexander wasn't going to risk letting the Council remove. Or maybe Alexander is sending me a message. That Alaric belongs to him and not me.

As the Nephilim's tortured face fills my head, my eyes catch on an amber-haired head in the crowd.

"Alaric!"

His name bursts from my lungs in a shriek, and as he turns at the sound of my voice, I lunge forward, crossing the space between us as fast as my legs will carry me.

"Lu—" he begins, grunting when I slam into his chest before he can get the full word out. My arms wrap around his back, and I hug him so tightly he would break if he were fully human, but I can't bring myself to let him go or ease my hold on him even a little. Despite speaking to him previously, despite seeing him with my own two eyes and knowing he was alive, getting this glimpse of him here in the flesh gives me a sense of confirmation and consolation I desperately needed. It's as if part of me didn't truly believe he was actually alive until this moment. As if I needed tangible evidence I could touch to convince my senses of what my heart kept wishing to be true.

Alaric lets out a breathy chuckle and curls his arms around me as well. A contented sigh parts my lips, and pulling away, I grin up at him. "It worked."

"Yes," he murmurs, but the tentative smile he offers me wavers. "For now. But we don't have much time. We don't know when Alexander will return."

I nod, stepping free of his embrace. He's right. There's so much to do here, and we need to ensure we're all miles away before Alexander suspects what we're up to. My father will contact my mother through their shared sigil to give us a heads up if Alexander backs off his trail, but we don't want to take any chances. The sooner we finish here, the better for everyone, especially Alaric.

My smile slips when I think of the tracker still in his head, and more than ever, I'm determined to release him from Alexander's sadistic hold. Alaric doesn't deserve this—to be treated this way by someone who claims to love him. He, more than anyone, deserves to be free.

My mouth sets in a scowl as that returning rush of guilt weighs on my chest. Alexander got this idea because of me… which means I'm partly to blame for any suffering Alaric endured since he stepped in front of Alexander's dagger and took the killing blow meant for me. Hell, even before that, since I let Alexander loose from his cage. But I'm also the only one who can relieve Alaric of this burden, even if that means mimicking the person who did this to him in the first place.

Swallowing, I raise my hand to his ear just like Alexander did to me. "First thing's first—"

"That can wait," he protests, his voice hoarse. I blink up at him, my gaze shifting between his stony expression and the way his fingers clamp around my wrist, holding my hand away from his ear. Clearing his throat, he relaxes his grasp on me, adding, "We have more important problems to deal with right now."

My heart drops into my stomach at the mention of "problems," but before I can organize my thoughts enough to ask what he means, another voice joins the conversation.

"What kind of problems?"

I turn, finding Gabriel standing behind me with one delicate obsidian brow raised at Alaric.

"Gabriel," he mutters, inclining his head at her.

She steps forward, placing a hand on his shoulder, and there's a tender kindness in her gaze when she looks at the Nephilim that's so at odds with the last interaction I witnessed between them. But then, their argument that I eavesdropped on back at the Serapeum was about Alexander. About *me*. In the mountains above Kandahār—before everything went to hell— Alaric told me about Alexander's first conquest for power… and the aftermath. Considering Gabriel was the one who spoke up for him, who fought against the Council to ensure the Nephilim would retain his memories, I can't help wondering if her hostility toward him that day in Alexandria was merely her way of trying to protect him again. That time, from himself.

"I'm glad to see you again, old friend." Although there's a careful distance in the Archangel's voice that I've grown to expect from her, there's also a sincerity to her words that tells me she's as relieved to see him again as I am. In typical Gabriel fashion, however, her tone shifts back to its usual collective coolness almost immediately. "Now, tell me—and be quick— what problems do you speak of?"

"Is it Caleb and the others?" I cut in before he can answer. "Have you seen them? Where are—"

"They're fine," he promises, holding up both hands, palms out, to placate me. "They're here. But"—his honey gaze swings to my mother—"there have been some…complications."

"What *kind* of complications?" There's a razor-sharp edge to my mother's voice now, but all I feel in this moment is panic. What else could possibly go wrong?

Why can't we just catch a damn break already?

Alaric lowers his own voice to a whisper. "Some of the children are choosing to stay. They won't leave."

"Wait…*what*?" I sputter, choking on the words. Alaric can't be serious, can he? I've lived under the same roof as Alexander, and it was the most stressful week of my life, which is saying *a lot,* considering I spent the four months before that trapped in a literal glass egg. Even Caleb, who lived with his grandfather for far longer than I did, got the hell out of dodge, and that was *after* Alexander offered him a seat ruling at his side. But Caleb is his grandson, and these Nephilim are nothing to the Gray—just more numbers for his army. So, what could he be offering them that would make them want to stay?

The same impossible lie he's offered to all the others who have chosen his side in this war, I suppose.

As if reading my mind, Alaric says, "They believe Alexander will protect them. That they're safer with him than with the Council."

"I wonder what lies he fed them to make them believe that," my mother hisses, crossing her arms.

A tired sigh parts the Nephilim's lips, and again, I notice how... *off* he looks. I can only imagine what Alexander has put him through, both emotional and otherwise.

"They're frightened, Gabriel," Alaric reminds her. "They were abducted under the Council's watch and then thrust into a world of perceived safety and riches. And...Alexander has been preaching about the prophecy, proclaiming himself as their Savior. You all don't know Alexander like I do. You don't know how charismatic and convincing he can be. Can we really blame them for wanting to stay?"

My mouth pops open at that, but no sound comes out. I can't seem to find my voice.

I didn't even think about the fact that Alexander might be using the prophecy to sway followers to his cause, and while I doubt that's been his only tactic of recruitment, I can't help wondering if that was how he got those Lights we encountered on the Blessed Road to join him. I've heard the prophecy and often doubted its vague words myself, and while I can say which role I think I fall into, the only being who knows our roles for certain is the Creator. If anyone were to question the prophecy's meaning, it would come down to Alexander's word against mine and which of the two of us they're inclined to believe. Thinking about it that way, I'd be willing to bet those who follow Alexander are convinced I'm the Destroyer just as much as those who stand by me think I'm the Savior.

My stomach ties in knots at that notion. The prophecy doesn't say who will prevail in this war, just that the fate of the world will be decided by the outcome. So, even if we win, we still fail because how can we ever unite our people without proof? Without some way to *show* them I'm the Savior—that I'm meant to heal the rift between our kind and not tear us further apart?

"The fools," Gabriel growls, but she's wrong. These terrified children aren't fools—they're just misguided. And the Council only has themselves to blame. For fanning the fires of division for so long and for allowing the divide to grow so vast that the kids now caught in the crossfire can't believe we'd ever want to mend it.

Assuming that's what anyone following Alexander actually wants. I'm sure there are many who don't care about the divide at all and have only joined the Gray because they're tired of hiding. Because they want to be free to be who they are without fear…or because they just want to lord their superiority and power over humans. In which case, if we do win this war, we have our work cut out for us. Because freedom for us isn't the same as freedom for humans, and to co-exist, we need a middle ground. A way for us to live life how we want without impeding on the safety and liberty of others.

But that's a problem for another day. For now, we need to think about the students whom the Council has a sworn responsibility to protect.

"What about your Calm?" I ask, focusing on Alaric. "Could you do anything to…persuade them?"

The words taste sour in my mouth as I say them. Not that long ago, I resented Alaric using his power on me, and here I am, now suggesting he do the same to others. But I don't know what else we can do. I don't know what other option there is available to us.

As I feared he would, he shakes his head. "I'm only one Nephilim, Luna. To hold that many under at once would require a strength even I do not possess, and the second I let go, even a little—"

"They might run back to him," Gabriel finishes, her mouth pinched at the corners.

"What about the Council?" I propose, looking between them. "Maybe they could do something?" Like take away the memory of the students' time here and any inclination they might have to side with Alexander. It wouldn't be the first time the Archangels and Archdemons intervened in such a way.

Alaric gives me a hard stare. "What you're suggesting…" A grimace crosses his face and he shakes his head again. "Taking them by force would make us no better than Alexander. I think you both know this, and I think I know you both well enough to be certain that's not what you want."

A shudder rolls over my skin at his words. I do know that and it isn't what I want. But hearing the disapproval in his voice only makes it that much harder to admit.

Instead, my eyes dip to the floor in shame, and my hands curl into clenched fists in frustration. Even now, even finding a way to one-up him, Alexander still found a way to defeat us. It isn't right. It isn't fair. If I'm truly the Savior, it shouldn't be this freaking hard to save everyone.

"Then let any who wish to stay remain."

My eyes snap up, and I gape at my mother, wondering if I heard her correctly. Her gaze is blistering when it meets mine.

"Will the Council agree to that?" I ask. Azrael and Belphegor already made it perfectly clear they're both willing to harm any who side with Alexander, even if that means their own students. And there are others on the Council who are probably of a similar opinion. Like Mammon. I'm sure even Uriel would stoop to that level.

"They won't like it," Gabriel answers, her voice almost a hiss when she adds, "but I will make them agree. I will not stand by and watch as frightened, unarmed children are slaughtered, nor will I partake in such sacrilege."

"And how exactly do you plan to convince them?" Alaric presses. "We do not have time to make the Council see reason. They may decide to cut their losses and run."

Gabriel's gaze darkens like the sky before a storm. "We cannot coerce the resistant students and we do not have the time to convince them, so this is our only option to avoid any further, immediate bloodshed. Besides, those who choose to stay may yet change their minds. We need to allow them that chance, otherwise, we really are no better than Alexander. And if they don't...if they *do* choose to fight beside the Conqueror and for all he stands for..." She doesn't finish that sentence but her unspoken words ring loudly in the silence that follows.

Then we'll meet them on the battlefield, and their fates will be decided there.

"That might be harder for some to hear than others," Alaric interjects. "Caleb—"

Panic lances through me as my focus shifts to the Nephilim's face. "What about Caleb? Where is he?" The words come out in a half-strangled shout.

Alaric is silent, his expression dejected, and it takes all my self-restraint to not grab him by the shoulders and shake him until he answers.

"Alaric?" I press, my tone bordering on hysterical.

"With his brother," a familiar voice says behind him.

My eyes drift over Alaric's shoulder to Lilith, who stands

with her arms crossed and dark brow creased in annoyance. She offers me and my mother each a cursory nod. "I've been *trying* to convince him the effort is futile but, of course, no one ever listens to me."

"His...brother?" I repeat, dragging out the word.

I can practically feel all the color drain from my skin as I recall our meeting with the Council before we went back to Kandahār. The Archangels and Archdemons talked then about Alexander's grandchildren, and Beelzebub mentioned a child at Ashkelon—a boy. A boy who was missing...or dead.

A worse realization takes hold of me then. What Alaric said about students refusing to leave and the way Lilith mentioned Caleb's brother...

He's one of those children.

My agonized thoughts must be written all over my face because Gabriel gently squeezes my fingers. "Go. Find him," she encourages. "Caleb will listen to you. But don't dally," she immediately adds in a stern but not unkind tone. "The sooner we can leave this place, the better."

My eyes burn as I return the comforting grip on her hand. Not that long ago, Gabriel wouldn't have cared one bit about Caleb or dared to let me out of her sight in enemy territory. But now, since that moment on the Blessed Road when I grabbed her sword, there's a level of trust building between us that wasn't there before. I'm thankful for it, just as I'm thankful she seems to be coming around to my relationship with Caleb.

"What about you?"

She waves a hand in the direction of the Archangels nearby. "I will aid with removing the trackers. Those afflicted won't be going anywhere with us so long as they remain intact. And"— she lowers her voice to a whisper—"I still have a Council to persuade."

That's true, and us standing here talking about all these bleak things certainly won't move things along.

"Lilith?" my mother prompts and the ex-Archdemon nods, trailing her steps as Gabriel throws one last curt "Be quick" over her shoulder before hastily strutting away.

"Come." Alaric's warm palm grazes my shoulder. "I'll take you to Caleb."

Alaric leads me through the elaborately decorated corridors of the palace, my senses assaulted by broad sweeps of red and yellow, past a communal sleeping area where I glimpse a few dozen students sitting on unfurled mats on the floor—the ones refusing to leave, I'd wager—to a bedroom a short distance farther down the hallway that reminds me of Caleb's room back at his grandfather's original base. It's much grander than the large chamber where the other students are gathered but, like the rest of this building, marked by the time period in which this city flourished. There isn't a single modern detail to be seen aside from the clothes worn by the pair of arguing teens in the room.

It's immediately evident the two take after their father.

Despite having different mothers, they look so similar, there's a moment when I almost mistake the younger Nephilim for Caleb. It's the eyes that stop me in my tracks and make me realize my mistake. Eyes—one brown and one a pale, haunting blue—that are identical to Alexander's.

I stand frozen in the doorway—Alaric hovering closely behind my right shoulder—my gaze fixed on the sulking boy sitting on the ornately carved wooden bed with his arms crossed, his Dark aura a bramble-like tangle of fury and resentment as he glares up at his older brother, who keeps his back to us. It's eerie, like someone took Caleb's face and his grandfather's and mashed their features together, creating this new person who is so familiar in looks and yet, at the same time, a stranger.

"Listen to me," Caleb pleads, his attention firmly set on his brother. I'm certain the boys must've heard us arrive, but if they did, neither one of them spares us a glance or shows it in any noticeable way. Or maybe they're too caught up in their disagreement to care about having an audience. "You *can't* stay here," Caleb continues, his voice tight. "I know better than anyone what he—"

"You know nothing!" the other Nephilim roars, anger turning his bronzed cheeks ruddy. His English is clear but his accent is thick—Spanish, I think. Or Portuguese, maybe. "And you do not know me. We might share blood but we are not family."

"And Alexander is?" Caleb counters.

I glance between them, suddenly feeling a bit like a voyeur—like I shouldn't be watching this—but I can't bring myself to move, transfixed by the scene unfolding before me. It doesn't feel like my place to intervene, but I will if I have to if it means saving Caleb from what I fear is a losing battle. The time we have left to evacuate the Tachara is dwindling, and I refuse to let him risk capture and death at the hands of Alexander or one of his followers trying to persuade someone who obviously doesn't want to be persuaded.

A hostile expression crosses the younger boy's face. "Alexander is our grandfather and a legend. He is the only family I need."

A shiver runs over my skin at his words. Words that sound very much like something Ishtar would say. My jaw clenches, and I can't help wondering if she was the one who put these dangerous thoughts in his head.

Caleb's entire body goes rigid. I can only imagine what he must be feeling—the sense of responsibility that must be eating at him, telling him to rescue his younger sibling and save him from repeating his own past mistakes. "I thought that way once, too," he says. "But the second you fall out of line, he'll disown you. He'll kill you if you cross him, Marcos."

"Why would I cross him?" his brother—Marcos—asks, rising from the bed. When standing, he's almost as tall as Caleb despite being a few years younger. "He is offering me everything I have ever wanted. Obedience is a small price to pay."

I step forward when Caleb grabs his brother roughly by the

shirt, but Alaric stills me with a hand on my shoulder. "This is between them," he whispers in my ear at the same time Caleb shouts, "It's not that simple! Can't you see what he's doing is wrong? I'm trying to save your life, man."

"I never asked you to," Marcos growls. His cheeks are an even deeper red now, his ire rising to the surface like a flush of heat.

"No," Caleb agrees, relaxing his grip a little but not fully releasing his hold on the fabric, "but that's what family does. And I am your family, whether you like it or not."

Marcos bats Caleb's hand away, then shoves him back, unswayed. "You are not family," he retorts, then to my horror, he spits on the floor at Caleb's feet. "You are a stranger. And I do not trust you. I do *not* choose you."

Enough.

For a split second, I think I must have said this aloud because Marcos's eyes—which are so like Alexander's—dart to mine and lock on me like a missile homes in on its target. I stiffen at the derisive look he gives me. I don't know if he recognizes me—if Alexander or Ishtar told him about me, though I wouldn't put it past either of them to tell this boy all about the disappointment of a grandson and the angel who betrayed them—but I don't care enough to ask. I have more important things to deal with, and I need to get Caleb out of here before it's too late. He might feel some sense of responsibility toward his brother, but *my* responsibility—and my loyalty—will always be to him.

"Caleb," I breathe, fixing my eyes on his back.

The tension in his shoulders eases at the sound of my voice, and turning, he flashes a heartbreaking smile before crossing the room and pulling me into his arms.

He hugs me for a long moment before stepping back and gently cupping my face in his hands. "You have no idea how glad I am to see you. Did everything go okay?"

I nod. "Yeah, but..." My gaze drifts over his shoulder, landing on Marcos again. "We don't have much time..." I fall silent because the rest is far too hard to say. It's too hard to tell him we need to leave his brother behind if he won't willingly come with us.

"I hear you, Goldilocks," Caleb murmurs, angling his face to glance over his shoulder, as if he's afraid his brother might run off if he dares to look away for too long. "But I can't leave. Not until I've convinced my dumbass brother to come back from the Dark side."

But he won't. I can see it in the boy's mismatched eyes that nothing Caleb or anyone has to say on the matter will convince him to leave—to abandon the foolishness of siding with Alexander. He'll make the same mistakes Caleb made or worse in his naivety. And he will suffer for them.

"We have no choice," Alaric says from the doorway, echoing my thoughts. Caleb's gaze slides from my face to Alaric's as the Nephilim steps forward until we're standing shoulder to shoulder. "If we take him against his will, think of the danger he may pose," he continues, keeping his voice just shy of a whisper. "Your location was already compromised once. Can you be certain he wouldn't betray us?" Then, even softer, he adds, "And is it a risk you're willing to take?"

"Think of Aya," I plead, grabbing Caleb's hand and desperately interlacing our fingers. "If we force him to come with us, it could backfire on her." A lump rises in my throat, which I struggle to swallow. It distorts my next words with the threat of tears. "I...I don't want to lose anyone else."

Especially you.

And I fear that will happen the longer we linger in this place.

Something in Caleb seems to deflate at my words, and for a long moment, he doesn't say anything, his dark eyes staring blankly at the floor. Finally, after what feels like an eternity, he walks over to his younger brother, grabbing him once more by the front of his shirt.

"Listen to me, you little punk. If you stay here, he *will* make you fight. And if I meet you on the battlefield, I won't go easy on you. I don't want to have to kill you, dude."

The responding smile that stretches across Marcos's face raises goosebumps on my skin.

"The Savior will prevail," he says with adamant certainty, though I definitely don't think he's referring to me. Pushing Caleb away again, he grinds out, "See you on the battlefield, Caleb."

Caleb doesn't spare his brother another glance as he storms out of the room...or me, his eyes dodging mine as he shoves between me and Alaric to reach the doorway. Unease grips my gut as I follow him out into the hallway.

A frown twists my lips as I consider that he might be mad at me, but my worries are eased by a familiar rush of Calm abruptly flooding my senses. I turn my head, glancing up at Alaric, who offers me a consoling smile.

"He isn't upset with you," he says under his breath so only I can hear.

I nod once. I know he's right—that Caleb's just mad he couldn't convince his brother to leave with us. Still, I change the subject. "Your tracker," I prompt, raising a hand to his ear just like I attempted to earlier. "We should remove it now—"

But he grabs my wrist again, stopping me before I can even get the full thought out.

I go still at his almost crushing touch, gaping at his expressionless face in equal parts horror and bemusement. "Why?" I ask, clearing my throat when the words come out raspy. "Why are you so reluctant for me to remove it?"

Alaric's face crumples as his fingers relax their grip. "Because…" Shame paints his face red, and with a sigh, he retracts his hand and scrubs it over his face. "Because, once the tracker is gone, there will be nothing left holding me to Alexander. It will be finished…and knowing that makes me more sad than relieved, as twisted as it is."

Sorrow and pain emanate from him like heat, his aura wavering under the weight of both. I can't even begin to comprehend what this must be like for him—what it must be like to see someone he loves so much corrupted and blinded by power. I wish I could take this pain from him, but I don't know how to do that. I can only give him a choice—the same one we're giving the students. To let him choose which side he fights on moving forward, the way I would want that choice for myself. Or he could decide to sit out of this conflict altogether…not that I truly believe Alexander would give him that option.

"You can choose to stay, too, you know." Out of the corner of my eye, I notice Caleb waiting for us just down the hall, and I ignore the searing look he gives me as I carefully pull Alaric's hand away from his face. The Nephilim stares at me with wide, startled eyes. "If you want," I amend, giving him the same comforting smile he offered me just moments ago. "It's your choice. I won't take that from you."

"No," he says, a little too quickly, then bowing his head, he takes my hand between both of his. "Thank you, Luna, for always understanding. But no. I have to end this toxic thing between us. It's time." He says this last part with a conviction that threatens to steal my breath.

Blinking up at him, I whisper, "If you're sure."

When he nods, I raise my hand to his ear, and this time, he doesn't push me away.

It's easy to remove the tracker—easier than I expected it would be—but then, a lot has changed recently, and I have a firm grasp on my powers now that I didn't possess when I first went to the citadel, seeking out Alexander's help. Just like when he removed the tracker Nzingha implanted in my head on behalf of the Council, it takes only seconds for me to locate Alaric's. Like the pull of a magnet, I sense its presence, and using that same pull, I beckon it to me, watching in wonder as it slides free from his ear canal at my silent call. I clench the silver beetle-like device between my fingertips, but Alaric doesn't ask to see it or react with revulsion like I did with mine. Instead, he keeps his gaze averted the whole time, even once the tracker is removed.

Without saying a word, I crush the device in my fist.

"Ready to go—" I begin to ask, but Alaric cuts me off.

"I want him to know it was me," he chokes out.

I'm about to drop the broken shell of the tracker when the Nephilim's words stall my movements, my fingers outstretched and hand half-tilted toward the floor, as if frozen mid-motion.

"What?"

His amber eyes burn with resolve, and though his voice is a growl, I can sense the tears behind it when he says, "I might love Alexander, and I know I'm probably giving you whiplash"—he shoots me an apologetic look—"but I can't condone what he's doing. I never have. I know I helped imprison him before, but he never knew of my involvement, and I...I don't want to hide behind the Council any longer. I can't. Not this time." He draws in a deep, steadying breath then blows it out slowly before finally adding, "His mother's tomb…the children…the weapons…I want him to know I orchestrated it all. I need him to if I'm going to end this for good."

"One last grandiose fuck you." Caleb grunts in approval, crossing his arms as he ambles back in our direction, his eyes momentarily shifting to the doorway to Marco's room behind us before settling on Alaric's face. "It's as much as the asshole deserves."

I peer between them—between these two people I love so dearly who have been hurt by Alexander. Who wouldn't have been hurt at all if I had never opened that tomb at the Serapeum in the first place.

But I can't take back what's been done. All I can do now is try to help them move forward.

Reaching into my pocket, I pull out the patch of skin Alaric left for us and lay it beside the tracker on my other hand. Extending both to the older Nephilim, I give a firm nod.

"Then let's make sure he knows."

I walk beside Caleb on the Shadow Road a short while later, trailing Hammurabi and Asmodeus as we lead the rescued Dark students away from Persepolis. Thankfully, the majority of those who were abducted chose to leave; only a small percentage opted to stay in the end, and they were left unharmed as my mother managed to persuade the Council to leave them to fight another day. I don't know what she said to convince them, and I didn't ask—I can only assume enough of the Council shared my mother's distaste for murdering their own students. And since the children aren't *technically* helping Alexander at present—unless you count cowering in fear in his palace as aid—they can't be treated as disloyal. Still, I fear for those children. The Council will not show them mercy if they go to war.

As we walk, I mourn Alaric's absence at my side. I hated separating so soon after getting him back, but I was torn between accompanying him or Caleb, and I got the impression Alaric wanted to be alone with his thoughts. After everything he's been through and sacrificed, I owed him that privacy.

Just before leaving the Tachara, we stopped by the bedroom Alaric shared with Alexander, where he placed the broken tracker and the dried patch of skin deliberately on his pillow for the Gray to find when he returns. It was a stronger message than any he could've penned in words, but that doesn't mean it came without great personal cost. I could see the heartache on his face as clearly as I sense the uncomfortable tension radiating from Caleb, his aura an ebbing wave of agitation, the shadows lashing across his skin like small whips committing self-flagellation.

I glance at him, my fingers flexing and curling again with the urge to reach out and grab his hand. He hasn't said a word to me since his argument with Marcos, and while I know it isn't really me he's upset with, that voice of doubt always living in the back of my brain has a way of reminding me that the things I love most can still be torn away. That he can still leave, even if my heart tells me he wouldn't. All my many years of abandonment issues rise to the surface at once, and I shudder, unable to stand the thought that he might be angry because I told him we should leave, or worse, that his failure with Marcos might make him push me away. It's a ridiculous fear—deep down I know he wouldn't—but still, that fear persists. It's happened to me too many times before for it not to.

"Are you mad at me?" I ask in a clumsy rush, unable to keep the thought at bay any longer. "Because I said we should leave your brother behind?"

Caleb exhales a long-suffering sigh. "No," he answers without hesitation, and relief slams into my chest like a wrecking ball. "I know you're right, Goldilocks. It just sucks. I guess I had hoped..."

"That he'd be more like Aya?" I finish when he trails off.

He shrugs, staring off into the distance ahead.

"Well, if it makes you feel any better"—I knot my hands behind my back, trying to keep my tone airy—"I saw Mammon shape-shift into the stone coffin holding your kind-of-great-grandmother's ashes."

That stops him in his tracks. "I'm sorry, *what*?"

Now a few steps ahead, I glance back at him, giggling. "It was weird hearing Beelzebub laugh."

Caleb lets out a long, whooshing breath. "Damn. I wish I could've seen that."

Crossing the space between us, Caleb leans in for a kiss, taking my hand and knitting our fingers together as we continue our forward march. As we approach the marker that will take us to our new hideout in Cambodia, he barks out a sudden laugh.

"What?" I reel back to look up at him, but he just shakes his head, laughing again behind his hand.

"Nothing," he assures me. "It just dawned on me that little B finally has a box."

twenty-four

CALEB

AYA SITS NEXT TO me, her eyes round with wonder as her gaze skitters around our luscious surroundings. We're in the middle of the jungle in Cambodia, and the ancient, abandoned city of Angkor Wat stretches out before us, the largest religious complex in the world, and our new base. Four times as big as Vatican City, this former capital of the Khemer Empire stands as a testament of faith to Hinduism and its gods, Shiva, Brahma, and Vishnu—especially Vishnu. Though later taken over and still maintained by Buddhist monks, the five towers of the central temples were built to represent the dwelling place of the Hindu gods. The architecture is like a rich feast for the senses, each course more delicious than the last.

The conical towers are carved with precision and intricate detail to resemble lotus buds. Unlike what tourists—or even the monks see when they look at the temple—a riot of color greets my eyes. Splashes of gold, scarlet, and blue decorate the building, just as it did when the edifice was created. Bas-reliefs fill the walls of the sandstone temple, illustrating tales of the most famous Hindi epics. The pathways of Buddhist sculptures are a delight. Even the large trees that have meshed with the structure until they are now one with the stone add charm and beauty to this stunning display of human creativity. I can't help but think of how much my grandfather would love this place. How he would covet it for his own. But he never touched this part of the world, and he's not modern enough to Google it.

"I have to head back in," I tell my little sis, standing. Sweat beads at my hairline and rolls down my cheek. The humidity is oppressive, and it's been raining hard on and off since we arrived a few days ago. Birds and insects play a constant symphony that fills the silence, as tourists avoid Angkor Wat in the summer because of the overbearing heat and rain.

Aya and I observe the complex from the wall of the moat, enjoying the break in the weather. After my baby brother chose to stay with Team Conqueror, I decided to spend a little time with her before I have to inevitably leave again to fight Alexander. I don't tell her she has another brother, though. Aya doesn't need that burden, too. She's young and shaken and it's not fair. "We're having a big meeting inside." I ruffle her hair, and she grips my hand. My brow raises in question.

"Can you tell me anything? Are you leaving again?" she asks, fear threaded through her voice.

My large hand enfolds her smaller, delicate one. "No, I can't because I don't know anything concrete. But now that we have the kids back, we have to plan our next move. We can't let Gramps get the upper hand again." I squeeze her fingers and say as gently as I can, "Yeah, I'll probably be going away again. I'm too useful not to be used. And I won't let Luna go anywhere without me."

Her large eyes blink at me. "You mean to fight Alexander?" She shivers when I nod.

And to fight our brother. My gut clenches. Can I kill him? I don't know. I don't want to. "Yeah, to fight Grandfather. I'm not looking forward to it, believe me, but he has to be stopped." I lightly pull her to her feet. "I'll do my best to come back to you, kid. I have a promise to keep."

Her eyes narrow for a moment in thought, then she says, "To meet your mom, you mean?"

"To meet *our* mom," I tell her. "I told her all about you on our weekly call. She's already adopted you. Be prepared to be bossed around." I wink.

Aya punches me in the arm. "You better come back then," she says fiercely.

Rubbing my upper bicep in mock pain, I say, "Ouch, brat. Is that any way to treat family?"

She wraps her arms around me, burying her nose in my chest. Surprised, I hug her back tightly. I know we've only just met, but I've become an anchor for her in this chaotic world she's been thrust into, all the order in her life banished into uncertainty and fear.

"Let's go," I murmur into her hair. "You can walk back with me."

We're silent as we enter the city. I decide to take the eastern entrance of the temple so we can pass by the scene of the Churning Sea. This is one of my favorite bas-reliefs in the entire construction, and I want to sit here and nerd out, but the Council waits for no one. I spot Rafe and Shalina ahead, studying the wall with awe written on their faces. Of course, they'd be nerding out, too. They don't have the weight of the world on their shoulders. Yet.

Before I can call out to them, Aya says, "Let me guess? You're giving them babysitting duty again?" Bitterness edges her voice.

I cross my arms over my chest. "As you keep pointing out, you're not a baby. I just thought you'd like company. If you don't want to hang with them, just say so. Go find your friends from Megiddo. Besides, I thought you like Rafe and Lina."

She shrugs. "I do, but I hate being the third wheel. I don't want them to feel like they have to be my friends just because you're my brother."

Spare me from teenage dramatics. "You're basically just the female version of me, okay? I'm sure they appreciate you for your wit and sarcasm. Look, I don't really like you being alone. Not after…" I shut up when I see alarm flood her eyes.

"You don't think he can find us here, do you?" She can't hide the tremor in her voice, and I curse myself for opening my big mouth.

I shake my head and loop an arm around her shoulders. "No, he can't. I'm just being paranoid as fuck. You're safe here, I swear." Sighing, I add, "Just do your big bro a favor and ease my mind. Go with Rafe and Shalina, okay?"

Aya nods. "Fine, I will. Unless they give each other 'fuck me' eyes, then I'm outta there."

Chuckling, I say, "That's fair."

Shalina spots us and gives a little wave, and we make our way over to the duo.

"Hey, I gotta meet with the Council, and Aya desperately needs some lessons in art history. Can you two fill the gaps in her poor education?" I ask.

Rafe offers a fist bump. "Sure thing, man. And you will tell us what's going on at some point, right?" Ever since Alexander's people attacked us in Turkey, Rafe has been on edge. Not that I blame him.

"Yeah, Caleb, don't leave us out here blind," Shalina says, tapping a foot on the stone.

"I'll do what I can," I promise. "Now if you'll excuse me, I've left Goldilocks alone too long." It's ridiculous that I miss Luna when we've only been apart for a few hours, but we are all fools when it comes to love, and I am one big damn fool for that girl. And I wouldn't have it any other way.

Rafe rolls his eyes. "I never thought I'd see you so whipped," he teases, and I grin at him, unperturbed by his words.

"I don't mind being saddled," I shoot back, and Shalina giggles while Aya makes a face like she's just sucked on a whole basket of lemons.

"Ugh, any reference to my brother's sex life will *not* be tolerated," she says.

"Back at you, kiddo," I call over my shoulder as I walk away. I climb the steps and enter the temple proper. The air is immediately cooler as I move deeper into the interior. The rooms begin as grandiose and grow smaller and more intimate the higher you climb.

Vishnu stands outside the entryway to the top level of the temple. Built like a warrior born to swing a sword, his nose is a blade and his cheekbones knife points. Teal-green eyes gleam against the polished teak of his skin. I'm not fooled by his bored expression. We invaded his territory, and he desperately wants to be in the inner circle. Having mortals think of you as a god lends ancient Nephilim a staggering sense of arrogance and entitlement. Ishtar, anyone? I wonder if he was pissed when the Buddhists moved in.

His eyes narrow on me as I push past the silk curtain.

"Where are you going, young one?" he drawls. "This isn't a place for children."

My smile has teeth. I'm so over these inflated egos. "Vish, you're looking a little blue. Haven't you gotten the memo? I'm more important than you. Maybe if you really had four arms, the Council would find you useful." By the rage in his eyes, I think I just heard a big pop.

He takes an aggressive step toward me, the promise of violence in his eyes, when a tall figure built like a prize fighter steps between us.

"The boy is under my protection," Hammurabi rumbles. "And while I can certainly appreciate your desire for retribution, as the child's mouth tends to run away with him, I cannot allow that."

I take a step back, barely managing not to jump like a spooked cat. Where the hell did he come from? A dude that big should not be able to move so silently. This Christmas, I'm getting everyone silver bells. Still, his words lift me up. Ain't no one better to have on my side than Uncle Hammurabi.

Vishnu's sneer drips with derision. "You cannot allow it? Who are you to allow me anything, Dark?"

Oh, for fuck's sake. Hammurabi's shoulders tense, and I brace myself for a brawl—one that I'm responsible for and feel shitty about—when a slender ivory hand curls over my shoulder, and I nearly leap out of my skin. Bells, goddamn bells for everyone.

Asmodeus's husky voice croons, "While I have utter faith that my Babylonian king can hold his own against you, Light, *I* won't allow you to attack the child. He's *mine* as well, and I always protect my students."

Vishnu goes rigid, wary eyes latched onto the Archdemon. I know he resents her for intervening, for having to obey her.

But she's the great white shark here and he's just a barracuda, waiting to get snapped up.

Asmodeus stuns me by ruffling my hair. "Even when they behave badly, but the poor lamb has had a terrible few months, so you'll have to excuse him, Vishnu. Being the grandson of the Great carries heavy burdens. And you know the rules—no infighting. We are at war. Don't make me report you to Uriel."

"That won't be necessary," the Hindu god pushes out through clenched teeth.

The Archdemon gives him a feline smile. "Run along now"— she flicks her fingers at him as if he's an annoying fly buzzing around her—"Uriel will call you if you're needed."

The Nephilim's cheeks flush a deep red before he stalks off down the corridor. Hammurabi chuckles before turning and delivering a hard stare at me.

"You need to curb that tongue, boy. I won't always be around to save you."

I rub the back of my neck. "He was a dick first," I protest, guilt trickling through me.

"Caleb." Asmodeus's tone is bland but I flinch.

"I'm sorry and super grateful you saved my ass from a beating—not that I wouldn't have fought back," I say.

Hammurabi actually rolls his eyes at me. "Of course, you would. I trained you. I trust you would have inflicted some damage of your own."

"I'm sorry about your brother's defection," the Archdemon

says, looping an arm through mine and leading me inside where some of the Council await. I guess they heard our little scuffle as I'm met with disapproving looks.

Acid churns in my gut. "Yeah, me too," I bite out, suddenly full of bitterness. I just found him and now we're on opposite sides. At least I'm not attached to him like Aya. That's a small blessing.

My gaze snags on the ossuary vessel in the middle of the room, pulling me out of my depressing thoughts. A shiver ripples over my skin, chasing away the last remnants of heat. Olympia's ashes reside in there. That's my kinda great-grandmother. Robbing graves doesn't exactly sit well with me, but it's not like we had much of a choice. Ever since Ishtar concocted the scheme to release Alexander, my whole life has been a series of pick the least shitty option. The only good choice I got to make was saving Luna. That's one choice I'll never regret.

Speaking of Goldilocks, she enters the small chamber with Alaric. Her eyes sweep the room until they meet mine. She leads Alaric to where I stand, holding up the wall, with Hammurabi and Asmodeus. I grin at her, letting my tension melt away, as she wraps her arms around me. She's worried about me—about what happened with my brother—and I appreciate her support, though the role reversal makes me a little uncomfortable. I'm used to taking care of her. I bury my face in her hair and inhale her sweet scent. The others greet each other with quiet murmurs, and when I surface, I see Alaric watching us with an indulgent smile.

He hasn't been out of Luna's company much since we arrived at Angkor Wat. When he's not with her—or the two of us—he's with Hammurabi and Asmodeus or Gabriel and Lucifer. Hammurabi has been especially kind to the other Nephilim, who still appears fragile. Someone as old and strong as Alaric shouldn't look that vulnerable, and my gut clenches at the haunted expression in his eyes.

He left the love of his life—gave Gramps the big middle finger. And despite the fact that I know he wants to be here— that he doesn't want Alexander to take over the world— that shit has to hurt. Even if Luna had turned out to be the Destroyer, I don't think I would have been strong enough to abandon her. Alaric is pure titanium.

"Hey, man, you look rested," I lie, smiling at him. "Happy to have you at these meetings. You can bring in some much-needed warm and fuzzies."

A chuckle bursts from his lips, and he looks surprised, like he didn't realize he could still laugh. "Never change, Caleb. I missed your roguish charm."

I smirk. "I don't plan to."

Hammurabi sighs. "Don't encourage him," he mutters.

"I like you just the way you are," Luna tells me, hazel eyes sparkling. My lips cling to hers for a moment.

"Oh, the fallacies of young love," Asmodeus says, and I

break away from Luna to grin at her. I appreciate this banter between my family. It feels normal in a time where absolutely nothing is.

Then Gabriel and Lucifer walk in accompanied by Lilith and the rest of the Council with a few higher-ranking Nephilim trailing behind, and the levity is broken.

As always, I track Mammon's movements, and his ruby eyes find mine for a brief moment. The hatred there burns so hot I force myself not to cower and hide. Instead, I avert my gaze as if he's not important enough for me to worry about. I know my dismissal of his threat will piss him off even more. Luna whirls around, her back to my front, and glares at the Archdemon, as if daring him to try anything. Her fierceness no longer surprises me, and I rest a hand on her hip and squeeze, letting her know I'm okay.

The one-winged chicken ignores us both and settles next to Uriel. For two beings who warred with each other, they're surprisingly chummy. But I guess it's all the enemy of my enemy and shit.

Lucifer and Gabriel settle on the other side of me and Luna with Beelzebub slipping in next to them. This chamber isn't very large, and with the ossuary taking up space, it's a bit claustrophobic.

"We have taken something precious from the Conqueror, and now is the time to draw him out," Uriel begins, then he nods to Alaric. "Son of Michael, you have our endless gratitude for not only giving us a means to retrieve our children, but to lure Alexander to a place of our choosing to end his threat once and for all. You're forgiven any and all past transgressions and will be greatly rewarded."

What past transgressions is that dick referring to? Loving Alexander or helping free Luna from her cage? Although the Council now believes she's the Savior, I know they're petty enough to hold Alaric's actions against him, even if they were the ones in the wrong.

Alaric just bows his head and says, "I'm grateful for the Council's generosity. I am here to serve."

I smother a derisive snort, as always ever impressed by his grace, even if the Council doesn't deserve it.

"Do you truly believe Alexander will surrender in exchange for his mother's remains?" Azrael asks from his seat in a corner. His mouth is a moue of distaste. "That's very sentimental for an angel bent on ruling."

I want to punch that guy in the face. Lilith rolls her eyes so hard it's almost audible. For the first time, anger stirs on Alaric's face.

"Of course not, but he will come for her," he hisses at the angel of death. "Did he not leave his palace to pursue her grave robbers? His mother meant more to him than anything in this world. Most of you weren't raised with a parent, so you cannot hope to understand, unless you have a child of your own," Alaric says, his voice a blade of contempt. "He will go to any lengths to retrieve her—and punish us for her theft. No, he won't surrender, but we can draw him out."

I guess Alaric doesn't think the Creator was much of a parent. I can't say that I disagree with him. Azrael stiffens at Alaric's tone, but Raphael steps forward and stares down her fellow angel.

"Alaric is right," she says. "We all know Alexander values humans more than his celestial brethren. He especially held his mother dear. Didn't you say, Lucifer, that he would have raised her if he could?" The Morningstar nods. "So you see, Azrael, you can stop with your bothersome doubts. I'm sure you'll attain much glory in battle, which is what you really want anyway."

I bite my lip at her scathing tone. Even on the eve of battle, the angels still squabble like a bunch of back-stabbing teenagers. It hardly inspires confidence.

"Enough," Uriel barks. "Stop yipping at one another like stray dogs. It's beneath you." Raphael and Azrael glower at Uriel, but he ignores them. "We'll need to send a messenger to Alexander with terms for his surrender. We'll tell him to meet us in the Arabian Desert, far from humans. There, we will end this."

There are nods and murmurs of assent rippling around the room. I just want this over and done with. I'm tired of balancing on a knife's edge, waiting to see if I'll get cut, so I raise a hand, waving my fingers.

Uriel's brows form a vee of surprise as his eyes connect with mine. For a moment, I don't think he'll acknowledge me, then he says, begrudgingly, "Yes, little Dark?"

"I volunteer as tribute," I tell him, lowering my hand, and I hear Luna gasp. Winking at her, I say to Uriel, "I'll text Ishtar with the conditions of returning my kinda great-grandmother, and she can give them to Alexander." As the Archangel's jaw slackens in shock, I chuckle. "What? You thought I was volunteering to meet Gramps's people in person? I'm not that crazy." Slipping my cell phone from my pocket, I hold it up. "I have Ishtar's number. Just tell me what to text, and I'll make sure she gets the memo. Easy peasy lemon squeezy."

Stunned silence meets me for a moment as all these beings who are basically primordial sludge—with the exception of Luna—stare at me in bafflement. Goldilocks wears a huge grin, and I bite my inner cheek hard to keep from laughing. At this point, I fully expect the angels and Fallen to take drummers into battle, announcing our arrival.

Lucifer does laugh. "Yes, that makes sense, Caleb."

"My students always show brilliant initiative," Asmodeus purrs.

Uriel gives a slow nod. "Yes, I suppose that will do. I shall dictate what you need to say after the meeting. Well done," he says, his expression turning sour as those last two words leave his lips.

"No problem," I say, smirking at him. Man, will Ishtar be pissed that I'm the one sending demands for Grandfather's surrender—just another reason she'll want to kill me.

Ignoring me, he continues, "Though we are fighting as one, Darks and Lights know their forces best, and we shall lead our own units. Lucifer, as you led the great rebellion, it's only fitting you lead the Darks in this fight." Mammon's mouth thins at his words, and I smother a grin. "You inspire loyalty, not only with our beloved first generation Nephilim, but with your students—of all Dark academies." Huh, the Archangel got all that out without choking. And he sounded sincere. Miracles do happen.

Lucifer inclines his head. "It would be my honor."

Uriel's eyes suddenly narrow on me, and I resist the urge to flinch at his focus. Luna moves a little in front of me, offering protection from the Archangel. I want to kiss her, but Uriel's dour expression cools the urge.

"Students will have to fight, too," the Archangel says, and my stomach sours. Yes, I know I'll fight, but I hoped the student body would be left out. "The loss of our teachers in Derinkuyu has left a dent in our forces. Final year students are capable and trained. We would be foolish not to use this resource. And as Caleb has proven, young Nephilim can be very resourceful indeed. Only a babe and he managed to wound the Messenger and maim the Shape-shifter."

Mammon almost purples with fury at Uriel's words, and I'd like to sink into the stone behind me as his scarlet gaze locks onto mine. The promise of death lies in those red depths. It must be humiliating for him to be reminded in front of the Council that a lowly second generation Nephilim cut his wing off.

"I agree that our students are well trained," Abaddon says, drawing my attention away from the psychotic Archdemon. His arms are crossed over his broad chest. "But they are untried in a real battle. Are they more of a liability than an asset? Will they fight or run? Young Caleb has demonstrated much fortitude in situations even older Nephilim would struggle with, and he should step out on the battlefield with us. But the rest of them…"

"If they run, Alexander's troops will chase them, drawing them away from the battle, and they'll still be an asset. Even if it is as fodder," Mammon says, gaze still on me, his voice so cold I almost have frostbite.

Asmodeus stiffens beside me. "Our students are not fodder, Brother," she hisses, and the air around me loses its tropical warmth as ice crackles along all the surfaces. Mamma bear is turning this place into the Fortress of Solitude.

"Apparently losing your wing made you lose your mind as well," Beelzebub growls, his darkness lashing around him like whips.

"We're at war. This is a reality we have to face if we want to save the world," Mammon counters. "You put unbloodied soldiers into battle, and some will die. This is reality."

I really think he means he hopes I die, but I swallow that thought. "The fodder comment is some cold shit," I say, drawing the attention of everyone in the room. "But kids dying, yeah, that's true. I get why you want to put us out there, and I'll do my best to help the students get ready for what's coming if you do decide to use us." I direct my gaze at Uriel. "I don't like it, but I understand the necessity. That being said, it should be on a volunteer basis. We shouldn't force anyone who is too scared to fight." That's what Alexander would do and I don't want to be anything like my gramps. Still, I should do my best to rally the troops and give us as much of an advantage as we can get. I know the Dark students will step up and listen to me if I tell them the real deal, but I don't know if the Lights will. Guess I have my work cut out for me.

"I agree. Thank you, Caleb," Asmodeus says. "As I've always said, Babel students are exceptional."

Blushing at her praise, my eyes meet Luna's, and I shrug at her stunned expression. She's stepped up into her Savior role. Now, I have to step up, too.

Uriel's eyes dart around the room. "Shall we vote on it?"

Although there is some reluctance, everyone raises their hand in confirmation, and just like that, kids are going to war. A knot forms in my stomach, tightening like a fist.

Uriel nods, a look of grim determination on his face. "It's decided then. Let us send Alexander our invitation and start moving out the troops."

twenty-five

LUNA

THE ARABIAN DESERT STRETCHES out before me like a barren sea, the large outcroppings of rock marking the horizon like violent waves frozen in time. According to my parents, this part of the desert was a lake thousands of years ago, but now, the earth beneath our feet is cracked and scorched—devoid of human life and, today, all life in general, as the animals residing here hide out of sight, aware a threat has descended on their home. As my eyes scan the flat, dusty ground, I can't escape the thought that this all feels somewhat apocalyptic, like an omen. That thought is sobering and reminds me of how much is at stake should we lose.

I peer at my parents and Lilith, who stand to my left side, then up at Caleb, who stands close on my right, his sweaty palm clamped tight to my own. Although I can hear the thunderous clash of his heart against his ribcage, he appears calm, like a duck, perfectly at ease on the water while its legs kick madly under the surface. He looks determined. No…not exactly determined, I suppose, but resigned. Like he's accepted his role in this battle and the inevitability of it all.

Just as I have.

I breathe out through my nose, squeezing his fingers, my nerves a constant, anxious flutter under my skin. The text he sent Ishtar after our meeting with the Council two days ago read like a ransom letter, and I have no doubt it would've only thrown fuel on the fire of Alexander's rage. While that was the point—a necessary evil to draw the Gray here while those heightened emotions make him vulnerable and put an end to this conflict between us, to fulfill the prophecy, whichever way fate intends it to go—I wish we had more time to prepare. That *I* had more time to prepare.

Once again, my eyes slide to my parents and Lilith, my gaze catching on my mother, who stands tall in her golden armor, her bronze-hilted sword strapped to her back. The other Archangels and Archdemons are all dressed similarly, resembling mighty warriors from Heaven. This is the first time I've ever seen my father in his armor from the Fall, and he looks like a gleaming god, his blond curls reflecting the sunlight. The Fallen wear their armor, too, but the Nephilim and people like me who weren't alive to fight during the Fall don't have such a luxury to rely on, and there wasn't time to figure out an alternative. Not when we were sequestered away, just trying to stay off Alexander's radar until the final battle. It was a risk just sending out small teams to the academies—now emptied of angel-killing steel and children, the schools would no longer be a draw to Alexander in theory—to retrieve the training weapons stored at each to at least arm the Nephilim on our side for the battle. But they weren't stocked with any armor other than what was in the museums from the Fall. As such, with nothing to use for additional protection, we remain in modern clothes—jeans, T-shirts, and even one or two business suits among the crowd of checkered gold and shadowed auras behind us, though nothing too loose to be a hindrance when fighting. It's a strange contrast to the almost majestic appearance of the angels and Fallen, as if the past has collided with the present.

One Fall merging with what may well be another.

Like armor, our supply of weapons from the Fall—weapons that can actually kill angels and Fallen—is scant. Although we managed to reclaim most of what Alexander's forces stole, too many on our side are equipped with ordinary swords and daggers that might be able to kill Nephilim but will be useless against the Fallen we're about to go to arms with. Even I face this battle empty-handed. The weapons of our bloodlines are in limited supply, and the two I *am* capable of wielding will be far more deadly in my parents' hands than they would be in mine. With everything that's been going on, there's only been time for a few—somewhat disastrous—sparring lessons with Lilith, and I'm nowhere near proficient enough with a physical weapon to rely on one to keep me alive. But I can't sit this battle out, and I wouldn't, even if that was an option. Fate has dictated that I need to be here, perhaps more than anyone aside from Alexander.

So, the plan is to stay close to my parents and Lilith and to use the innate talents I have to fight. I just hope that will be enough to keep me alive—at least long enough to end this.

"Don't worry, Goldilocks. Everything will go our way. It has to," Caleb whispers, nudging my shoulder with his. "After all, you're the Savior. We're meant to win."

I grin at him, though the expression is forced.

"Caleb's right," a familiar timbre says in my ear, and I glance over my shoulder to find Alaric behind me standing close to Hammurabi, who looms over Caleb like a helicopter parent keeping a close eye on their toddler. A warm smile curls the corners of the Nephilim's lips as his honey eyes lock on mine. "Plus, I'll be with you the whole time, I promise."

Relief flushes through me like a strong rush of heat, and I nod, comforted by the notion of having Alaric by my side through this. I'm going to need him to ground me, to keep me calm, because once the battle begins, Caleb won't be able to—as much as I hate the idea of separating, especially with Mammon out here on the battlefield with us, we'd be too big of a distraction to each other, and I have enough people protecting me as it is. Besides, Alexander's sights will be set on me, and I want Caleb as far away from his grandfather as possible. It's the only way I can keep him safe—the farther he is from me, the more likely he'll make it out of this alive, even if I don't. And Caleb also has skills that can be put to better use elsewhere, not only as a warrior but as a leader. The Archangels and Archdemons have their own forces to lead, and Caleb is someone the students who volunteered to fight can trust—who even the Lights would be persuaded to follow into battle, knowing he rushed into it first, not wanting to seem like cowards next to a Dark. They might not be so willing with an angel or Fallen, who don't need to fear death the way Nephilim do. And that is the role we both know he needs to play, even if it means we won't be at each other's sides through this fight. Even if it means that, if everything goes very wrong, this moment now is the last one we'll have together.

My stomach curdles at that thought as a building panic rises up through my body and settles in my throat, trying to choke me. Immediately, I feel Calm sweep through my senses, putting me at ease. Without it, I'm not sure I'll stay sane.

Breathing out, I offer Alaric a small smile. "No regrets?" I ask.

I don't mean choosing to fight by my side, but choosing to fight in this war at all. While I have no doubt in my mind that Alaric will go to blows with Alexander if it comes to that, that he'll protect me no matter the cost, I need to make sure the events of today won't break him when it's finally over.

"No regrets," Alaric echoes. Then bowing his head, he reaches over his shoulder, producing a short, copper-hilted sword from a leather sheath on his back. The blade gleams in the sunlight, which highlights the swooping symbols etched cleanly into the steel.

"Is that…?" I trail off, my eyes going wide.

"Enochian," Caleb murmurs beside me. "Yeah. That is definitely a weapon from the Fall. I didn't know you had one, Alaric."

"My father's," Alaric says nonchalantly as he stares down at the sword in his hand. "It was found among Alexander's possessions in Persepolis with the other purloined weapons from the academies."

My lips purse. "Do you think Alexander knew it was there?"

If he did, then he's either incredibly confident in his hold over Alaric, or he just enjoys toying with death. Maybe he even got a thrill from knowing Alaric could've ended his immortal life had he any inclination to.

Alaric nods, his gaze growing distant, though there's a tightness to his jaw that wasn't there a moment ago. "I imagine so."

Caleb sneers. "The bastard probably didn't even try to hide it."

"No," Alaric agrees. "Had I thought to search for it, I would've easily found it with the others."

"Kind of brazen of him," I mutter. "How did he know you wouldn't go looking for it?"

"He didn't," Alaric admits, his teeth gritted. "He likely just assumed I would never dare use it against him."

His fingers clench around the hilt, and I frown at the burning intensity of his aura, which pulsates around him like a beating heart. I can only imagine the complexity of emotions Alaric must be working through right now. He probably never wanted to lay eyes on his father's sword, let alone use it, and now, he's faced with fighting the very person he once protected from his father with the weapon Michael would have likely used to kill Alexander. That's a betrayal Alaric can never come back from. The final nail in the coffin of the love he shared with the Gray.

I open my mouth, hoping to say something reassuring, but I can't find the words, and a sudden shout distracts me from any further attempts.

"Forces sighted!" a Fallen scout who had been hovering a half mile above us bellows as he descends, retaking his place among our army.

"Looks like shit's about to get real," Caleb says, and his hand tightens around mine as I narrow my eyes on the rocky horizon, waiting for whatever the Fallen saw to appear. I don't have to wait long. Within seconds, a dark silhouetted herd emerges from the hazy distance like a mirage in the desert heat. I can sense Caleb's fear in the way his pulse flutters rapidly under the skin in his hand, the movements reflected in his aura, and in the muttered string of curses slipping past his lips. My own heart trips at the size of Alexander's force, my only consolation being that ours is bigger—though not by much from the looks of it. Still, unease grips me because too many on our side are unseasoned in battle. Like me. So much is riding on my shoulders, and I'm about as competent at fighting as I am at flying. Quality over quantity, as they say, and experience will win this battle over numbers.

I turn my head side to side, my gaze drifting over my shoulders, searching for the familiar faces of the Archangels and Archdemons scattered tactically among our forces.

We have the Council, I remind myself. *We have the most powerful angels on our side.*

My eyes stray to the Light and Dark to my left, standing side by side, hands tightly clasped.

We have my parents.

That alone has to count for something.

I swallow, forcing myself to focus on the incoming threat—to have faith that we can and *will* succeed—but apprehension drowns out what little confidence I manage to find among my darkening thoughts when it dawns on me that Alexander is nowhere to be seen. A solitary figure emerges from the enemy force, their face sliding into sharp focus as they draw closer, but that figure is not the Gray I'm destined to battle here.

It's Ishtar.

Caleb tenses beside me, and I cling even tighter to his hand for support, though I don't know if I intend it for me or for him.

I spare him a glance, noting the hard lines of his face, and a scowl hardens my own as my mother calls out, "Goddess of love and war, where is your master?"

Ishtar pauses her advance twenty or so yards away—close

enough to converse with us while keeping a safe distance from the angry flock of angels who would all happily tear her to shreds. She's wearing a black armored vest over her clothes, modern in look, like a human soldier heading to battle—just like the armor Alexander's soldiers donned that first day in Kandahār when we were escorted to the citadel like prisoners of war. It's human-made—nothing that will protect her from a blade from the Fall—but protection enough against our mortal weapons. And more than our own Nephilim have to protect them.

Caleb goes even more rigid as Ishtar approaches, his hand a vise now, strangling mine.

Shrugging, the goddess gives a lazy wave of one hand, fluttering her fingers. "Around," she coos, her tone flippant and taunting. "He's sent me as his emissary to oversee our… negotiations."

"This isn't a negotiation," Uriel snaps. The Archangel steps forward, moving to the front of the crowd to stand near my parents and Lilith, and for once, they appear as a united front instead of as reluctant allies. "If the Conqueror wishes to see his mother's remains returned intact, he *must* surrender. If not, he will die. As will you. Those are our terms."

"Just fucking accept, damn you," Caleb whispers, as if he's trying to will the thought into existence, even if we both know that will never happen. My eyes peruse his face again, and my heart breaks for him in this moment—for how much he mourns the teacher he once loved and looked up to.

But that woman, whoever she was before all this, is gone.

Ishtar crosses her arms and taps a long finger against her chin, her dark eyes skimming the ground as she paces, as if she's genuinely considering the Archangel's offer. But I know better. I can tell by the ease of her steps and by the glint in those eyes, which she turns on Caleb as a wicked smile curls the corners of her lips. He flinches under the heat of her stare when she hisses, "Not if we kill you first."

Then, in a movement that's almost too fast for even my eyes to track, she lifts her hand, and all I see is the concealed blade leaving her fingers before I have the chance to fully register her words. It's not a large dagger, but, like any blade, it's large enough to kill should it hit the right target.

Especially if that target is mortal.

I barely have time to think as the knife sails toward Caleb, and with more force than necessary, I yank on his hand, pulling him down to the ground. I shift then, taking his place in our line-up so no one behind us takes the hit in his stead. I don't hesitate. After all, I'm an angel. This dagger can't hurt me like it can hurt Caleb or any of the other Nephilim—

A surprised grunt escapes my lips as the sharp sting of metal pierces my skin, then terror unlike anything I've ever felt burns through me as fire spreads across my shoulder and the blade sinks deeper, cutting through sinew and bone.

"Luna!" several voices shout, though the one that rings the

loudest is Caleb's. He scrambles to his feet, but I'm barely aware of him or the others swarming me, my thoughts focused solely on the dagger embedded in my right shoulder.

Wincing, I wrap my fingers around the silver handle and pull, and as the blade slides free of my flesh, I glimpse the Enochian symbols etched into the blood-coated metal.

My eyes widen. From a distance, this looked like a normal blade, the symbols masked by Ishtar's grip. But it's not. It's a weapon from the Fall—belonging to one of Ishtar's parents, wherever they may be. I don't understand. When we were in Kandahār, I never once saw Ishtar with one of these blades. Was this why? So she could take us by surprise? But by throwing this dagger at Caleb, she all but tossed it away, like trash to be discarded. There's no way we'll return it to her, so what's her plan for defending herself when the battle begins and my parents go after her? And they *will* go after her for this. They'll be out for her blood.

I find Ishtar through a gap in the worried faces around me, and she smirks as if reading my mind before turning and sprinting away, retreating to rejoin the waiting army in the distance.

"Is that…?" Caleb begins, trailing off when I toss the bloodied dagger to the ground with a sneer.

"Angel-killing steel," my father says grimly, hovering over my injured shoulder.

"Why waste an Enochian blade on a Nephilim?" my mother

asks, giving voice to the same thoughts plaguing me. She glances between my face and Caleb's, her brow creased with the fear of what—for a fleeting moment—she might have thought she lost.

"She didn't," I whisper as the realization hits me. The angels and Nephilim crowded around me—my parents, Lilith, Uriel, Alaric, Hammurabi, and Caleb—all look at me, not comprehending what I just have. I clear my throat, holding in every urge I have to weep at the pain, and press my hand to my shoulder, which bleeds as if I'm human again. Blood, warm and sticky, seeps between my fingers. "He wasn't her target. I was."

Because she knew I wouldn't let Caleb die. That I would make the exact idiotic assumption I made and step in front of any weapon thrown his way. That I would mistake my immortality for invulnerability. Had I been standing a few inches to the right, she could've ended this battle before it even began. And then, the Conqueror—the Destroyer—would've won.

And I would have cost us everything.

For Ishtar, that chance was worth losing such a weapon.

"That bitch is even more sadistic than I am," Lilith seethes, the tendrils of her aura snapping like a tattered cape in the wind.

"And she will die here today," my mother vows. Fury gleams in her orange-ringed eyes as she turns her sights on Alexander's army, drawing her sword.

I nod, biting back the searing pain in my shoulder and pushing it behind my anger. It won't heal quickly—I know from the wound my mother received under the Serapeum—so I just have to hope the distraction of battle and literally fighting for my life will keep me going. "Just like Alexander," I promise.

"He was given a chance," Uriel growls, and exchanging a meaningful look with my father, he spreads his wings, taking his weapon in hand. A shadow darkens Lucifer's gaze as he nods at the Archangel and pulls his own sword free of its sheath. Ebony feathers cut through the air with a whoosh as he extends his wings, and then, with one final, worried glance at me, he raises his hand, giving the signal to attack.

Chaos ensues as angels and Fallen sprint forward at my father's unspoken command, their bodies racing past where I stand in a blur. I follow their movements, my heart a symphony of hurried notes, a needed rush of adrenaline spiking through my blood that helps stave off the pain.

Curling my hands into fists, I once again glance at the army in the distance, only to find Alexander's forces have grown closer and grow nearer yet with every passing second.

This is it, I realize.

The battle is beginning.

My eyes cut to Caleb's when he frantically grabs hold of my uninjured arm. "Luna." His gaze wanders to my wound, his expression conflicted, his lips pinched tight in concern. Concern neither of us have time for now.

"I'll be okay. *Go!*" I urge him.

"Stick to the plan, boy!" Hammurabi shouts, roughly grasping his shoulder. "The flower will be fine."

Caleb hesitates for only a second before taking my face in his hands and pressing his lips to mine in a bruising kiss. "I love you," he says. But behind those three precious words, I hear two others.

Be careful.

"I love you, too," I whisper.

Grimacing, he lowers his hands and runs in the opposite direction of the awaiting fray toward the other Dark and Light students who agreed to fight alongside us. Like me, Hammurabi watches his retreating figure for a moment before he races off to join Asmodeus's forces as planned. They have their own task to deal with today. And I have mine.

My mother's dark eyes dart over her shoulder, locking on mine, and I give her a nod. I'm ready. Or as much as I'll ever be.

Lilith and Alaric flank me on each side while my parents position themselves in front of me, leading the charge as we move forward together, the dirt and sand kicking up around our feet as we shift across the cracked earth. Every impact of my feet against the ground sends a shock wave of pain through my shoulder, but I clench my jaw and keep going, refusing to let this injury slow me down or stop me from what we came here to do. I don't want my parents, Lilith, and Alaric to worry about me anymore than they already are, either.

As we run, closing the distance to what may very well end up being my demise, Alaric says under his breath, "Don't show it."

I risk a questioning glance at him before turning my gaze back to the approaching army, which rolls toward us like a violent wave. We're mere moments from colliding, and I only hope I won't be drowned by the force of it. "What?" I ask him, unable to hide the tremble in my voice.

"Your astral projection," he answers, and I don't miss the warning in his tone. "Don't show it until the last moment. It's one of the only elements of surprise we have."

I choke out a doubtful laugh. "We have others?"

"Just one," he whispers, the words so low I almost don't even hear them.

A frown tugs at my lips. "I'm a little short on other party tricks, Alaric," I retort, feeling more unprepared than ever. "I don't think my fire on its own is enough."

"That's why you have us!" Lilith crows from my right, and I notice she looks almost excited by the prospect of fighting. "Just watch your back and stay close."

"We will protect you, no matter the cost to us," my father vows, almost shouting the words. He runs a few steps ahead of me, his large sword clutched tight in his right hand, which he raises now, lobbing off the head of a Fallen who foolishly believed they could take on the Morningstar.

"And no matter who has to die," my mother growls, sideswiping a duo of Nephilim with lethal precision, spilling their guts onto the desert floor.

There's no more talking after that, only the somewhat maniacal laughter that keeps coming from Lilith. Uriel has vanished among the horde, and I only catch passing glimpses of the other Council members, on missions of their own to downsize Alexander's forces. Around me, I hear battle cries and the clash of metal on metal, but so much of the noise is drowned out by my thundering pulse as a near debilitating terror courses through my veins like a drug. My feet are in a constant shuffle, my brain screaming at me over and over again to turn my back so I don't leave myself exposed. Flames erupt across my palms like lava, but when I'm not busy hurling fire at anyone who comes too close or floundering at the brink of a panic attack, I find myself watching Alaric, his figure as graceful in combat as it is in all other manners of life. He wields his father's sword with deadly accuracy, which surprises me given his kind and gentle demeanor that makes it hard to envision him even hurting a fly, let alone another person.

Like Alaric, Lilith is a force to be reckoned with. She brandishes her own weapon from the Fall—returned to her by the Council after our last meeting to aid us in this fight—a long, curved dagger of devastating consequence that resembles a farming sickle. Her death of choice is the throat slit, which she executes at least a dozen times in the span of only a minute. I'm both in awe of and terrified of her, perhaps because, in a lot of ways, her fighting style reminds me of Nzingha and Ishtar— graceful like Alaric but almost catlike, as if she's playing with her food before eating it.

Maybe that's just the Dark way of fighting, I consider, or maybe Lilith, Nzingha, and Ishtar are just a bit more twisted than the rest of us.

A blood-curdling scream has me whipping around as shadows submerge the battlefield, and from their midst, I glimpse Beelzebub, walking forward without a care in the world, his youthful face murderous with intent as he rips one Nephilim after another apart from within using his terrifying power. Abaddon lurks beside him, cutting down any strays, his vigilance around the other Archdemon reminding me of a sworn knight watching over a child prince.

Beelzebub's eyes find mine in the disarray, and he touches his pointer finger to his right temple, giving me a little salute before concentrating his wrath on his next victim.

My chest heaves as I search for other familiar faces in the throng. I spot a few—Nzingha taking out several Nephilim with her kunai, Uriel slashing at Lights, possibly even the ones who attacked us on the Blessed Road, Asmodeus encasing her victims in ice and then shattering them into frozen pieces with a swipe of her sword—but aside from them, there are too many bodies—both standing and slain—on the battlefield, and after a few moments, I recognize nothing except a deep, crippling sense of danger.

Briefly, I let my harrowed thoughts drift to Caleb, but I push them away as soon as they form. I can't think about him right now or else the worry will eat me alive.

The minutes stretch uncomfortably long, and I do my best to keep up with the others and ignore the ceaseless pain in my shoulder. Around me, my parents, Lilith, and Alaric move in tandem with me always at the center, guarded by them on all sides. But I know this shield of protection can't last. Eventually, I'll have to face Alexander. And when that time comes, I have a feeling fate intends for me to do it alone.

Movement in the corner of my eye grabs my attention, my gaze catching on a Fallen approaching Lilith from behind as she fights off two Dark Nephilim.

"Lilith!" I shout.

She spins, cutting through her two attackers with the curved side of her sickle, then snaps her head toward me as fire blazes across my palms, my shoulder protesting when I raise my hands. With all the force I can muster, I then push my power outward, directing it at the Fallen, who shrieks as the flames lick over her wings.

Lilith whips around, blade raised and ready, but the Fallen writhes on the ground now, trying to put out the hungry inferno, all thought of killing the ex-Archdemon forgotten. Lilith doesn't hesitate. She drops to one knee and brings her arm down with brutal force, dragging her blade across the Dark's throat.

"Cheers, doll," she calls, shooting me a grateful look.

I let out a relieved breath and straighten slightly, shaking out my arm and carefully rotating my injured shoulder. The wound from where Ishtar stabbed me hurts like hell—a burning agony that screams every time my skin stretches and moves. The pain is only made worse when an unseen force knocks me off my feet, slamming my back into the ground. The impact itself doesn't hurt—not like my once mortal mind trained me to expect—but the vibration running through my shoulder is a different kind of pain altogether.

Clenching my jaw, I force myself into a sitting position and clamber to my feet, coughing as I breathe in what feels like a lungful of sand. The air around me is suddenly thick, my vision obscured by a swirling storm of beige, and my teeth are gritty with dust, which hovers over the desert floor like fog. I peer through the haze, apprehensive of the oppressive surge of power crackling through the atmosphere—like lightning on the cusp of striking—trying to pinpoint the source of it, even if my gut already knows that answer.

As I scour my surroundings for Alexander, I note the angels, Fallen, and Nephilim struggling to rise up from the ground. They must've been pushed down to the desert floor, just like I was, and yet, there's something...prohibitive about their movements as they climb to their feet. Worry eats at me as I try and fail to find Alaric and Lilith. I scream their names—I scream Caleb's name—but no one answers me, not even my parents. Desperation is a physical force crushing my chest, my focus shifting between the faces around me so fast it makes me dizzy. When I finally locate Gabriel and Lucifer through the now-blustering winds, my eyes snag on my mother. Even from a distance and through the dust storm still raging around us, I can see her reaching out to me, just like that day under the Serapeum when the Dark ward stood between us. But this time, I can't hear a single word she's saying, although I can read my name on her lips.

My father's face is equally agonized, and it's only when I take a step toward them that I see it—the wall of energy separating us. The glasslike barrier just like the one I destroyed in Olympias's tomb.

A Gray ward, I realize, a surge of bile rushing up my throat.

The relief that chased away my fear at the sight of my parents disappears as quickly as it surfaced. How the hell did Alexander erect a ward around me and separate me from the others so easily? I snap my head side to side, taking in the full scale of the ward, my dread growing in size to match its breadth. It's *big*—significantly larger than the one I destroyed in the tomb in Korinos. I'm not even sure I can break it and I'm nowhere close enough to its boundary to try. Swallowing, I take another step toward my parents, my heart a lead weight in my chest, then falter when the howling winds suddenly die—the dust and sand that was swirling through the air now falling to the ground like rain.

A strange sensation prickles my skin, and I whip around, searching for those mismatched eyes amidst the thousands of others watching me. I can feel him, just as I feel like a sheep that's been corralled exactly where the lion wants me to go, my movements growing increasingly frantic as I search for his face in the surrounding crowd.

I hear his chuckle before I see him, and when I spin on my heel, our gazes finally clash. Alexander walks toward me, his pace leisurely and dagger in hand, dressed like a king in a white tunic and red chlamys that scream of his intention to rule over all, a golden crown of leaves on his head. His aura is a swirl of razor sharp glass that I half expect to lash out and slice me to ribbons.

I glance around again, desperation and terror rocking my core, searching for help I know won't come, and that's when I see it—the bodies twisting on the sand that now climb to their feet like revenants rising from the grave. Horror spreads through me, hot and fast.

He's resurrecting them. A sick feeling twists my stomach in knots. *Just like he said he would.*

I try to swallow the lump lodged in my windpipe, but my mouth and throat are sandpaper dry. Flop sweat beads at my hairline, even as I tell myself to be brave, but how can I be brave when Alexander is resurrecting his soldiers, leaving us with no true way to defeat them unless we kill their master and sever that connection? When the death of said master now hinges solely on me, and I don't have the means to put him down without help? My fire might hurt him for a few moments, but on my own, I'm powerless to kill Alexander, whereas one plunge from his dagger will snuff out my immortal life.

I take a step back, stalling for time. I'm so far out of my depth. I was foolish to think we could ever possibly prevail. I'm completely defenseless, I'm injured, and I'm going to die here on this battlefield, just like everyone else I care about.

My thoughts flip through their faces like the pages of a photo album, but most of all, they linger on Caleb, and my heart aches thinking of everything we won't ever have. I wish I could see him one last time before I die, but I have no clue where he is or where Alaric or Lilith got thrown when Alexander erected the ward.

But I do know where my parents are, and once again, my eyes slide in their direction—to Gabriel, who bangs her fist on the invisible wall, while my father screams at me to run. But run where? There's nowhere to go. I could sprint to the edge of the ward and try to break it before Alexander reaches me, but I know there isn't time to even attempt to, not with him steadily closing the distance between us. There's nothing for me to do now except face the prophecy head on and try to achieve the one thing fate led me here to do.

Even if, in the end, I lose.

Resolve hardens my quivering insides as I narrow my eyes on Alexander, and a menacing smile curls the corners of his lips when I widen my stance and raise my hands, blood-red fire exploding across my palms.

"Are you so eager to fight me, little dove?" he asks, amused. He saunters closer, the inches between us quickly dwindling with those steps, prowling toward me like the predator we both know he is. "So certain are you that you will prevail? The Council must have you quite convinced that you are their Savior."

My upper lip curls back in a sneer. "They didn't have to convince me of anything. I *know* I am."

I might not have always believed it, but as I stand here facing Alexander, I know that anyone willing to plunge the world into the kind of chaos he has planned for it can't possibly be the Savior.

Because he isn't.

My heart trips in my chest at this thought because it isn't coming from me, but from a distant voice outside myself that's somehow foreign and familiar at once, as if I've heard it somewhere before. Long, long ago—perhaps as a baby when some powerful force spirited me away from that tomb on Easter Island. It doesn't even speak in words exactly so much as in a strong, overwhelming conviction that spreads through me like a comforting warmth before settling with certainty in my gut. And as it speaks, I feel a tingling in my shoulder that steals away my pain, the skin knitting itself back together, as well as a sudden weight at my back—an offering of strength when I need it most.

I recognize the tinny echo of angel-killing steel ringing in my ears before I register the strap around my chest connecting the scabbard to my back, hidden from all eyes, even mine. I don't hesitate, reaching my hand over my now healed shoulder with intent as Alexander scoffs at the audacity of my words. As my fingers curl around the hilt, pulling the blade free of its sheath, the calming voice of the Creator speaks again, encouraging my use of this gift. He tells me that I *am* the Savior the prophecy spoke of.

And He tells me I will win.

twenty-six

CALEB

THE LATE AFTERNOON SUN brushes the sky gold and pink in the west of the Arabian Desert, but the heat remains obnoxiously oppressive. Fighting for my life certainly hasn't helped me cool down, either. Not for the first time, I'm jealous of the angels and Fallen because the scorching air doesn't bother them. Sweat isn't making it hard for *them* to hold onto their weapons.

The plan was to attack in waves—angels, Fallen, and first generations upfront, second wave, students and everyone else. But now we are all in the fight, and carnage reigns.

Copper coats my tongue and my skin, and I feel like I'll never rid myself of the taste of blood. Rafe, Shalina, and I fight back-to-back, moving as one unit, ducking, slashing, and parrying. The once hard-packed, rose-colored sand now resembles raw brick, squelching under my feet and threatening to throw me off balance at a time when I can't afford to make any mistakes.

I spot Hammurabi through a gap in the mayhem, whirling like a dervish, a creature of grace, delivering death like it's an art.

The Nephilim I battle smashes a punishing overhead blow against my sword, and I grit my teeth as my muscles scream in protest. My back foot sinks into the now-muddy sand, and Alexander's lackey grins as I stumble backward a step, knocking into Shalina. I hear a startled grunt before I use her body to right myself, snarling at the Mohawked motherfucker in front of me. He's about my height and weight, and we're on the same power level, which sounds good on paper, but he's older than me. Everyone I've fought today is *so* much older than me.

Mohawk presses his blade into mine, throwing his whole weight into it, but I hold steady against him. Something has to give. We can't stay in a clutch forever, and he's better with the sword than me. Fuck it. Jerking to the side, I fall back, taking him with me. I thrust my feet out, catching his hip bones, and use all that forward momentum to toss him over my head. Springing to my feet before he hits the ground, I spin around and watch as he lands on the flat of his back. Two seconds later and I'm above him, my blade thrust into his chest. Bottle-green eyes regard me in shock, and he manages to bring up his sword and push my own away. I slice across the back of his hand, and his sword loosens from his grip, then I slash his throat open, adding to the gore soaking into the ground.

A heavy weight slams into my back, and I'm kissing bloody sand, the air whooshing from my lungs. I blink the grit out of my eyes, my brain momentarily stunned, but my survival instincts claw their way to the surface, screaming at me to get the fuck up. Before it's too late. I manage to get my hands under my chest to push this asshole off me when the crushing load pressing down on me goes limp. I wriggle free of the body and stand, meeting the fearful eyes of Rafe. His sword is out in front of him, wetted with fresh blood. Glancing at the ground, I see the body of a Nephilim with dark blond hair. I roll the corpse over, meeting the lifeless eyes of my father.

My throat tightens as I stare at his face. Gramps sent him to murder me. My own father. Then I snort at that. He was never a father, just a sperm donor. But still, it's not like he had a choice. Alexander resurrected him, so I doubt he had much free will left. I wish I could say I feel sad, but mostly, I'm relieved.

My gaze catches Rafe's, and I give him a grateful nod. Rafe dips his head then turns, jumping right back into the melee. I go to follow when I catch sight of my baby brother, and I still. He's staring at our father, and my heart clenches at the thought that I might have to fight him—kill him. Marcos's eyes lock on mine, and I study his expression, trying to anticipate his next move. Suddenly, he stiffens, his mismatched eyes—our grandfather's eyes—round with fear, and he scurries away like a rabbit in front of a bigger predator.

My body hair stands on end as I catch the sound of a metallic whine careening toward me. I duck and roll, my shoulder hitting the sludgy sand. Popping into a crouch, my eyes dart up, my sword ready. Terror renders me momentarily frozen as I meet Ishtar's pleased gaze, her teeth bared in a feral smile. It's shocking she can look so regal with blood streaked across her face like war paint. She's come to kill me then.

I can't say I haven't been expecting it. In her eyes, I betrayed her—and more importantly, I betrayed Alexander. I guess I did, but she betrayed me first, manipulating my need for family—for a father—to play me. Feeding me bullshit that Luna wouldn't get hurt. It's not like I don't accept my part in freeing Alexander. I do. I'm guilty as shit, but Ishtar, the woman I thought loved me like a son or at least a favorite nephew, twisted my feelings to get what she wanted and then turned her back on me the moment I decided not to be a good little sheep and fall in line. And the sad thing—the thing that pisses me off the most—is that a part of me still loves her. A part of me still wants her to love me like she used to, or like I *thought* she used to. And I hate that. I hate her for disappointing me so badly. I hate her for injuring Luna. Fuck, she could have killed her, and for one horrifying moment when I saw Goldilocks's blood, I thought she had.

Rage fires me up and I straighten, never breaking eye contact as I sheathe my sword. Ishtar's brows arch in surprise. The familiar handles of the knives we used to train at Babel slide over my palms, offering comfort like an old friend as I grip them. I can't best her with a sword, but I have a chance—albeit a slim one—with my daggers. I don't know if I can kill her, but I might be able to damage her enough to escape. Though her body armor is going to pose a bit of a problem, it can be penetrated with enough force, especially if it's not made to defend against blades. The last time we had a mock fight at Alexander's citadel, I was out of practice, but Hammurabi has whipped me into shape since then. For all his bulk, he moves like lightning.

Ishtar's full lips curve as she also sheathes her sword, fingers curling around the hilts of her own daggers. "Good choice, young one. I don't want to kill you too easily. There's no pleasure in that. Now, I can whittle you away one cut at a time."

She lunges at me, steel flashing. I get my blades up, catching her attack. She's like an adder, viciously striking at me again and again. I know only a couple of minutes have passed, but time no longer has any meaning, stretching into infinity. For a while, I keep up with my former teacher, muscle memory kicking in, and I deliver just as many blows as she does. My knife catches her in the bicep, penetrates her side through the Kevlar, and slashes along her forearm. Fresh blood wets her black clothing, causing it to cling to her tall figure.

But slices decorate my torso like stripes, slowing me down. My angelic blood is working overtime to heal me, but I'm not as close to Heaven as she is. She heals faster. She *is* faster. I don't move my arm down quickly enough, and she manages to stab me under the armpit. Lucky for me, the strike is too low and glances off a rib instead of sinking into vulnerable flesh, sparing my life. It still hurts like a bitch, and the terror I've managed to hold off rushes to the forefront of my mind.

I can't beat her. I'm good but she's better. I'm going to die.

Panic seizes my chest, stopping my heart. Immediately, my eyes seek out Luna amongst the brawling celestials, but I can't find her. I want to see her one more time before Ishtar puts me in the ground. My neck tingles, and I slide out of the way as metal kisses the air where my throat just was, but I'm off balance. I fall to one knee, and the goddess of love and war looms over me, a triumphant smile turning the corners of her mouth.

"You shouldn't have betrayed Alexander," she spits at me. "You never turn your back on blood."

I know this is the end, and all I can think about is Luna and how I'm leaving her. How she'll have to face Alexander without me. How I'll never get to tell her I love her one more time. How life is so un-fucking-fair.

I meet Ishtar's black, pitiless gaze, and suddenly, my heart stutters back to life, clinging to hope. Ice crystals form lacy patterns over her brown skin like frost hardening grass. Her ruby lips fade to blue, and fear creeps into her gaze. Maybe I'm an asshole, but it's gratifying to see that fear. She has no problem dishing out terror.

And in the middle of the clamoring chaos, I spot Asmodeus, striding over to us as if she doesn't have a care in the world. Hammurabi trails behind her, alert and tense, gaze sweeping the area for any threats that get too close to his mistress. I rise to my feet, mouth agape. The Archdemon stops behind Ishtar, slipping one arm around the Nephilim's waist and the other around her neck, like a lover. She's shorter than Ishtar, but far more terrifying. Everywhere she touches, the ice blooms, crystals growing into solid sheets of bluish white. I'm cold just looking at my ex-teacher.

Asmodeus slides her fingers into Ishtar's braided locks and tilts her former friend's head down so she can whisper in her ear. Her garnet hair shimmers like a beacon in the desert.

"Young Caleb isn't the one who chose wrongly, dear friend," she croons, her voice honeyed venom. "He's not the one with dreams and ambitions that far exceed his station. He was wise enough to recognize Alexander for what he really is. A wisdom that you sorely lack, though your years are much more advanced. *You* betrayed *me* after I spared your life. Because I loved you. Because you were my friend."

Ishtar's skin loses its warm color, turning pale as the crystals thicken. Her eyes round with horror, and I know she realizes this is the end. There are no do overs and Gramps ain't around to save her.

"Know this, traitor, that Alexander will die, and the world you envisioned—the world where you had your own little kingdom to rule with the King of Uruk beside you, lording over mortals the way you believe you deserve—will die along with him. There are no second chances this time, and I won't mourn for you."

Ishtar is frozen solid except for her eyes, darting back and forth rapidly in their sockets, as if seeking help. It's disturbing as hell. Asmodeus moves both hands to rest under the Nephilim's jaw. My stomach clenches and I glance away as the Archdemon says, "Goodbye, dear one."

I hear a sickening crack followed by a thud and shudder as something hits my foot. Against my will, my gaze pulls down, and I see Ishtar's head resting against my boot. I really wish people would stop rolling heads at my feet. You'd think with as much blood and death that I've witnessed today, that nothing would bother me, but this makes my stomach churn and bile creep up my throat. I step away from the decapitated head, my eyes finding Asmodeus's.

"Thank you," I say, my voice hoarse. Clearing my throat, I repeat, "Thank you for saving my life." For giving me a chance to see Luna again.

She inclines her head. "You're welcome, child. Judgment had to be passed upon her, and it was my responsibility to dole out punishment."

A roar cuts across the fray, somehow drowning out the sounds of battle, of screams, of the dying. I whip around to see Gilgamesh charge toward us, anguish and rage twisting his features into a mask of pure fury. I scramble out of his way, but he doesn't even see me. His whole focus is on the Archdemon who just slayed his lover. I grimace at his suicidal actions, knowing Asmodeus will end him as surely as she did Ishtar, but when he brings the weapon down, I see bright scarlet swell on the Archdemon's shoulder. Her shock mirrors my own.

Gasping, I pivot toward Hammurabi, screaming, "He's got a weapon from the Fall!"

But Hammurabi is already on the move. He slams into Gilgamesh like an enraged rhino hitting a tourist jeep. He lands on the King of Uruk's chest, holding guard position, and wrenches the angel-killing weapon from his hand before smashing his head into the Light Nephilim's. Bones crunch. Gilgamesh screams. He manages to get an arm free and punches Hammurabi in the face, rocking him back. But the Babylonian king is in a frenzy of his own, steadying himself and delivering a matching staggering blow. He then hits Gilgamesh over and over and over again. I glance away from the other Nephilim's mangled face.

My eyes land on Asmodeus, whose bleeding has slowed, as G only managed a shallow cut. She meets my gaze, and I don't bother to hide my horror.

"That's enough, King," she calls. "Finish him."

Her eyes remain locked on mine as I hear a strangled cry then a gurgle. Then nothing. Grief seizes me. No matter that they were my enemies, Ishtar and Gilgamesh were two bright flames that just got guttered. They can never be replaced. It's so goddamn tragic. This whole fucking situation is tragic. Asmodeus's smile holds sorrow and sympathy.

Then her face is swallowed by dust as a sandstorm rushes

toward me, whipping around me, rendering me momentarily blind. What the fuck is happening? I know in my bones this storm isn't from Mother Nature. Magic saturates the air, causing me to shiver despite the heat. I recognize that magic. It's left scars on my mind.

Alexander.

I feel a ripple of energy, a mere warning, before I'm blasted off my feet, eating sand for the second time. Shaking my head, I struggle to stand, as if my feet are encased in drying cement, blinking as the haze clears. My mouth slackens as shock punches through me. Bodies rise, including Gilgamesh and a headless Ishtar. For a moment, the sight is too gruesome for me to process. Fuck me. Gramps actually did it—he resurrected the dead. As I stare at the King of Uruk, his eyes eerily empty, I hear someone screaming my name.

"Caleb, where are you?" Rafe's panicked voice pops the little balloon of silence surrounding me, and I wince. I forgot all about him and Shalina as soon as my former teacher decided to kill me, and I left them vulnerable to attack. What a shit friend I am. And with Alexander raising his own zombie army, we're even more fucked.

Pivoting, I search for him, as we got separated when I squared off with Ishtar. I spot him and Lina, and they're bloody but alive, thank the Creator. Rafe is waving his arms frantically and pointing. Fear reflects on his face, and dread seeps into me. I follow the direction of his finger, and my fucking heart nearly stops in my chest.

Luna—my precious Goldilocks—faces my grandfather, with a sword drawn. Where the hell did she get a sword? And her shoulder's not mended yet. I know she's powerful now in her own right—she's the *Savior*—but she can't beat Alexander the Great with a blade, especially wounded. She's all alone, too, and my eyes search for her parents. I spot Gabriel screaming and pounding on air. It takes a few precious seconds for my brain to catch up. The Conqueror has erected a ward around them.

I'm sprinting before I'm aware my brain has given my legs the command to run. My eyes remain trained on the two combatants, and I shove bodies out of my way, ducking blows as I clamor to reach Luna. I'm not going to make it in time—I can't even help if I do. I don't have the power to break a ward, but I have to get to Goldilocks. She needs to know I'm there for her. My mind urges me on once more, and I race over the sand.

I dodge and weave until I reach the barrier, my fists banging on the now-solid air, hardened like resin. My throat scrapes raw as I scream over and over again for what feels like hours, but I know is only seconds. Unsheathing my sword, I hack at the ward, even though I know it's useless. Even though I know I'm wasting precious energy. Luna doesn't hear me, the entirety of her attention focused on her enemy.

My breath stutters in my chest when I see Gramps lunge for her, dagger arcing in a precise strike. But then Luna's wings unfurl in a snap, and she takes flight for the first time, soaring over Alexander's head. My steps falter as she climbs higher as if reaching for the clouds, wings booming in a steady beat, sword raised like an avenging angel in a Renaissance painting. Determination slides over what I can see of her face like a battle mask, the breadth of her wings bolstering her slender form, the silver feathers a symbol of hope in all this death. Despite my terror, I can't help but admire the glow radiating from her being. In this moment, she manages to outshine the Morningstar. Then Alexander rises in the air after her, his own metallic feathers glinting in the sun.

Luna must sense him because she turns, raising her blade in defense, and my own sword sags as it finally dawns on me that *her* sword has Enochian etched into the steel. That sword doesn't belong to either of her parents, which means… Fuck me, which means the *Creator* gave her that sword. That's the only explanation.

Though my chest aches with fear and the thought of watching, helpless, as my grandfather cuts down the love of my life, hope manages to break through my crippling panic. If the Creator gave her that sword, that means He is present right now. He intends for her to win.

I hold onto that thought like a lifeline in a tempestuous sea. She's the Savior. I have to believe she will prevail because I can't live with the alternative.

I can't live if she dies.

twenty-seven

LUNA

WHEN I WAS TRAPPED in the Council's glass egg, there were many times when I would just sit there and wonder what it would feel like to fly. I would stretch my wings out as much as the cramped space of my prison allowed and try to imagine the feel of the wind in my feathers—of a weightlessness I found myself desperate for after so many years crushed by the burden of my trauma and guilt.

Now, I realize even my most detailed daydreams didn't come close. The breeze runs over my wingtips in a gentle caress that only comes second to the feel of Caleb's fingers brushing against my skin, sending a thrum of exhilaration through my system. Or maybe that's just the adrenaline in my blood—the fight or flight reflex that launched me off the ground when Alexander swung his dagger. I didn't even mean to fly—didn't even think I *could* yet—but in that moment, it was a natural impulse, as if my wings knew what they needed to do, taking the thought process away.

Now, as they carry me high above the ground, my eyes drawn away from the desert below to the blazing sun overhead, I'm reminded of the story of Icarus—of what happened when he dared to drift too close to that light. For the first time, I fathom the true extent of temptation. Of grasping for something just out of our reach. And suddenly, I understand why my father fell—not only for the right to love without restraint, but for this exhilarating sense of uninhibited freedom.

For the chance for each of us to live how we choose.

A choice. That's all I ever wanted. And as I consider what losing that would mean to angels like my father—to the Fallen who fell for the right to choose—I realize just how much Alexander threatens not only the liberation of those who stand against him, but also those who fight at his side. Promising to bring our kind out of obscurity isn't the same thing as freedom, and if he succeeds here, he will inevitably shackle us all just like the Darks once felt shackled by the Creator.

Well, I won't be shackled. Not again. Not by humans, not by the Council, and sure as hell not by some megalomaniac on a power trip. Or even by fear. I've wasted too many years terrified of what I am and what I'm capable of, and I'm *done* being afraid. I might not be as skilled or as smart as Alexander, but I am far from weak, and I will use what strength I have to fight for the same choice my father once did. For the chance at a life not confined to a cage. For a life, however brief, with Caleb.

Savior or not, victorious or not, what I do now is for me.

My fingers tighten around the hilt of my sword, reaffirming my grip, as a loud gust drags my gaze down just in time to glimpse Alexander taking off from the ground, his body rocketing toward me faster than I can dodge him.

I raise my blade, and sparks fly as metal strikes metal, Alexander's dagger meeting my sword with enough force to push me back several feet, my legs flailing in my panic, searching for purchase where there is none to catch me. My stomach flips, and for a heart-racing moment, I think I'm going to fall. But I don't. I remain airborne, my wings holding me aloft and steady, once again doing exactly what I need them to do, even if I'm not entirely sure how they're doing it.

Invisible hands seem to push at my back then, and I wonder if it's the Creator, offering me support, or if I really am somehow doing this on my own. Either way, my wings flap with fervor, launching me toward Alexander, who sneers, batting my sword away with ease. I swing it again, probably a bit more overzealous in my attempt than is wise, and he cackles, stoking the flames of the fury rising inside me. I'm no match for him and he knows it, but I can't afford to go on the defensive because as soon as I give him the opening to turn the tables and he comes at me full strength, I know what the outcome will be.

Alexander's victory here will only come at the cost of my death, and though I was willing to fight to that point if that was the required price for defeating him, I can't afford to die. I have too much to live for. Caleb's face flashes through my head, and fueled by my desperation to see him again—to live out his mortal days together—I grit my teeth and lunge forward, aiming the blade tip for Alexander's heart. Like the Nephilim below who weren't alive during the Fall, he isn't donning armor—not even the modern variety his own soldiers are wearing. Maybe he doesn't want to tarnish his appearance as an ancient king of legend, though I'd wager the lack of protection is down to his pride and the misguided belief that he'll triumph here today. That he doesn't need armor if it's his destiny to win. Even if he's right—even if I'm not meant to survive this—I take advantage of the opening his overconfidence has given me, allowing myself the small and dangerous hope that I might not only make it through this, but come out as the victor.

To my bemusement, instead of trying to block me, Alexander sheathes his dagger as I close the distance between us, as if he has no intention to fight me. Alarm bells ring through my skull because I know he isn't willing to die, but everything happens too quickly. When he makes his move—shooting out an arm and grabbing me by the throat—that hope inside me burns out like the last embers in a hearth.

"You fool," he hisses, his fingertips squeezing my windpipe as his other hand grabs my wrist, stopping my advance before my blade even comes close to piercing his flesh. I let out a cry as he twists my arm back, but I clench my fingers tighter despite this new, excruciating pain in my arm, doing everything in my power to keep my grip on the pommel.

A deranged chuckle parts the Gray's lips as he sneers at me—our faces so close I can smell honey and wine on his breath—and horror floods my body as it dawns on me that he gave me that opening, luring me in with the intention of catching me like a fly drawn to sugar. I could've struck out at him a hundred times, and it wouldn't have mattered.

I never would've gotten close to landing the blow needed to stop him.

"You should have joined me when you had the chance," he seethes, his eyes creeping over my face with contempt. His gaze then dips to the sword still clenched in my hand. "Your strength of will is admirable, little dove, I will give you that. But *I* am the one who shall prevail here. It is my birthright to be great—to save this planet from its constant chaos and strife." His lips peel back into a smile that sends a chill through my bloodstream, and pulling me closer until his breath touches my ear, he says, "There is only room in this world for one Savior, and though you all fight it, it is *I* who will cleanse the Earth of its savagery, not you."

The blood rushes to my head as his fingers grip tighter, and although I know he can't suffocate me, my life flashes before my eyes as if I'm standing at the brink of death, facing down my final moments. Maybe because I am. Any second now, he'll reach for his dagger and run me through and that will be it.

I'll have failed and the Destroyer will have won.

"You're wrong." The words spring from my throat in a gasp, though I'm not entirely sure if I'm talking to Alexander or myself. All I know for certain is there's a fire inside me—that hope I thought extinguished now a raging inferno, refusing to accept that this is the end.

"Don't show it until the end."

Alaric's voice echoes in my memory as I play the only card I have left in my hand and focus all my power outside of myself—one final attempt to outmaneuver death before it comes to claim me. As my eyes slide shut in acceptance of whatever comes next, my fingers loosen their grip on my sword. Time seems to slow as the pommel slips from my grasp, and as it drops, my mind slips fully free of my body and I reach out— not with my physical form, but with my astral one. I channel every thought and hope I possess, willing my intangible fingers to catch the hilt…

And when I feel the metal graze my palm, I seize it.

Taking the sword in both hands, I thrust my arms upward, only catching the barest glimpse of my face—of Alexander's fingers still taut around my throat—as the blade sweeps up behind the Gray, slicing through the flesh and bone of his wings. The roar that expels from his lungs is inhuman, rippling through the air around us like a shockwave, and as he tumbles to the ground far below like a giant bird whose wings have been clipped, I watch my immobilized body plummet alongside him, as if we're experiencing a Fall of our own.

Darkness washes over my vision, blotting out the sky and the desert beneath me, as I will my current form back into my physical one. As the two slam together, rejoining, I open my eyes with a strangled cry. They water from the air whipping at my face as I free fall, my body a tangle of thrashing limbs. My wings flap wildly, attempting to slow me, but the desert floor is rushing upward too quickly to stop the impact I know is coming. I've fallen too far already and the speed of my descent is too great.

I hit the ground only moments after Alexander. He crashes into the earth, now sludgy with blood, like a meteor, leaving a small crater in his wake—as destructive even when bested as he's been in his conquests. I don't see where my sword or his dagger fall, but I do hear his wings as they flop, one after the other, against the dirt with grotesque *thuds* that would turn my stomach if the world wasn't blurring and spinning out of control. The force of my collision rattles my bones and punches the air from my lungs, robbing me of breath, as I skid and roll across the ground, tricking my once-mortal mind into believing I might actually be dead. Thankfully, it doesn't take long to regain my senses—to remember I'm immortal—and realize I'm not actually injured, even if, for a moment, my mind thinks I've broken every bone in my body. The pain of the impact is fleeting, but the phantom touch of Alexander's fingers around my throat remains, and coughing, I raise my head, searching for something to ground me—to assure me I didn't just imagine all this, and he isn't still strangling me up in the clouds.

Blinking away the bleariness of tears, my eyes immediately lock on Alaric, who stands only inches away from me, pounding on the glass-like barrier between us. Behind him, the battle rages again, more furiously than before, as if everyone can sense that this moment is the apex, and that what happens now will dictate what happens to us all moving forward.

My movements are sluggish, my arms shaking as the adrenaline coursing through me wears off. Like how I felt after my first soul journey to Persepolis, my body is drained of energy—this time, completely, likely from the power I exerted to force my projection to interact with the physical plane. Exhaustion cripples my senses and limbs, but I push myself upright enough to thrust out a hand toward the ward, my fingertips brushing the surface, willing it to break—or, at least, to crack enough to let Alaric through.

Alexander doesn't try to stop me. My eyes trawl over my shoulder toward the last place I saw him, where he kneels in the center of the crater, his hands limp in his lap, blood oozing from the wounds in his back as he stares down at the sand, his eyes unfocused. His hair is askew and the crown that previously adorned his head is gone, lost during the fall back to Earth. He doesn't look up even when a funnel of sound comes rushing back to our isolated pocket of the battlefield.

A hand brushes my shoulder and I snap my head up, only catching the side profile of Alaric's face as he slips through the narrow hole I created in the ward and walks past me, his stride slow and steady. Determined. A soothing wave of Calm funnels through me, almost disorienting in strength, as if he's trying to smother me, but it's not enough to tamp down the building ache in my chest or the knowledge of what he's going to do—of what he's sparing *me* from doing.

The prophecy might have foretold this battle, but it never explicitly stated that one Gray had to die by the other's hand to fulfill it. Only that the Savior had to draw on their strength to defeat the Destroyer, and I have. The people willing to fight by my side have been my greatest strength. Even now, I feel them here with me, especially Alaric. And as I watch him walk toward Alexander, all I can think is that maybe things were always meant to play out this way, with the Gray's story coming full circle, beginning and concluding with the one person who was there through it all.

The crunch of sand beneath Alaric's feet is almost deafening, his proximity pushing all other sounds into the background, like I'm hearing them from underwater. Alexander, shaken from his stupor, lifts his gaze, finally noticing the Nephilim's presence, and when their eyes meet, he utters Alaric's name with a gentleness I didn't think him capable of.

"Alaric…"

Shushing him, Alaric steps into the crater and slowly drops to one knee, close enough now to Alexander he could lean in and kiss him. "I wish this time could have ended differently."

Although his back is toward me and I can't see his face, the pain in Alaric's voice rings like a death knell above the chorus of war leaking in through the hole in the ward.

Alexander's mismatched eyes spring wide, just visible over Alaric's shoulder, as if whatever daze consumed him in his pain is now fading in response to the Nephilim's words, jerking him back to this moment. But the realization gripping him comes too late. Alaric curls one hand around the back of the Gray's head and pulls it close to his chest, while his other reaches for his sword. And as the blade slides free of its sheath on the Nephilim's back, Alexander chokes out his lover's name once more, that single word escaping his lips like a plea. Alaric doesn't give him the chance to finish.

Around us, the bodies that were resurrected collapse to the ground, the strings holding them to their puppeteer snapped as their connection is severed by death. For a long moment after, Alexander and Alaric remain frozen in their final embrace—Alaric with his head bowed, his forehead resting against Alexander's golden hair, while the Gray stays on his knees, slumped over the long blade impaling his torso.

I don't know whether Alaric killed Alexander so I wouldn't have to or because he felt it was his duty to put an end to the monster he helped unleash on this world. Maybe it was a combination of both. Either way, my fated role in all this is complete. The Destroyer is dead.

And this madness can finally be over.

Familiar voices shout my name, and I glance up to see my parents and Lilith calling to me through the barrier, searching for the invisible hole where Alaric came through. It's only when I feel the heavy blanket of Calm lift off my senses and I find the strength to climb to my feet that I notice the rest of the desert is eerily silent on the other side of the ward. The fighting has come to a standstill, as if Alexander's death has broken a spell that's been cast over us all, freeing everyone here from the desire to spill anymore of each other's blood.

I glance away from all of them, my attention focused solely on Alaric, who stands now, his movements languid. Carefully removing the sword from Alexander's chest, he lays him back against the flat earth, lingering for a moment in a squat beside the Gray's unmoving body before leaning forward and brushing his lips gently against his forehead.

"I will remember you…as you used to be," I hear him murmur, then he straightens and takes a step back, abandoning his sword on the ground beside Alexander.

"Is it over?" I ask when Alaric looks over at me, and he hesitates for only a moment to scan the sea of faces around us before nodding.

"Yes," he says. Closing his eyes, he lets out a sigh as if to shed the heavy weight that's been tormenting him for millennia. "I believe it is."

But there's a melancholic note to his tone, and as I trail my gaze across the ominous stillness of the battlefield, noting how many have fallen today, it dawns on me that we might have won this battle, but there was never any winning this war. Not truly. This really is like the Fall all over again, with too many deaths on both sides to see this whole ordeal as anything other than tragic. Our victory here was always going to be hollow at best.

But tragic or not, it's still a victory we need to grasp, and I can only hope, now that it's over, we'll finally find it in us to overcome our division. That this time will be different. That the prophecy, now that it's come to fruition, will ensure that war among our kind can finally be put to rest and that we no longer need to endure such pointless devastation moving forward.

That we *can* heal the rift, the way fate and the Creator intended.

Heaving a sigh of my own, I scour the herd of angels, Fallen, and Nephilim on the other side of the ward again, this time searching for Caleb. With Alexander gone, we can do what we wish. No more running. No more fearing imprisonment. Hell, the Council will have no choice but to acknowledge me as the Savior and dismiss their whole anti-Gray agenda now that the real threat is eradicated, which means we'll be free to be together without any obstacles or the divide standing between us.

Buoyed by that thought, I continue my search, and to my immense elation, I find Caleb within seconds, as if some unseen magnetic force is drawing us to each other. Relief slams into me like a brick wall at the sight of him standing at the opposite side of the circular stretch of desert still encased by the barrier, his mouth shaping one word, silently shouting my name.

A smile tugs at my cheeks, and as I feel the shock of this battle wear off and my energy return to full strength, I begin to walk toward him, drawing on my power and readying myself mentally to demolish the rest of the ward, which had begun to dissipate with Alexander's death, the magical connection destroyed, though not enough for anyone to step through yet.

But I don't get anywhere near it before I find myself stopping abruptly, my heart jumping into my throat when I spot the red eyes gleaming behind Caleb's shoulder. Mammon's movements are lightning quick, and the words to warn Caleb die on my lips before I even get the chance to say them.

Caleb's expression contorts, and although I can't hear him, I can imagine the sound he makes from the look of surprise flitting across his face. He looks down, his eyes locking on the Archdemon's hand as it punches through his chest. And then he's gone, collapsing in a lifeless heap to the ground, taking my sanity with him.

twenty-eight

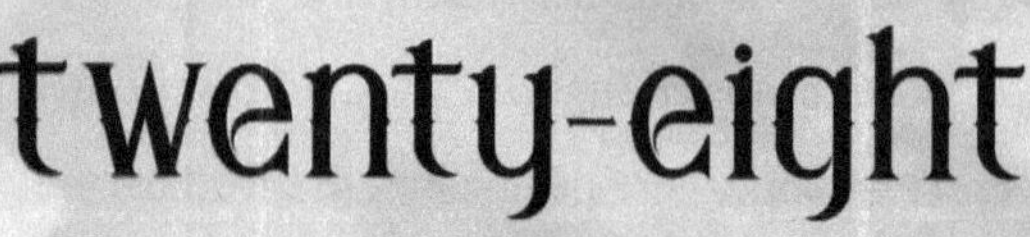

CALEB

I CLUTCH MY CHEST where my heart used to be, but to my utter astonishment, there's no longer a ragged hole there. My agony vanishes, my pain disappearing in an instant. All that remains now is warmth spreading through my body… But I don't think I *have* a body. Not in the physical sense anymore. I hold my hands up before my eyes, but they seem translucent, as if I'm only a spirit now, no longer tied to earthly things.

Grief gutters out that warmth for a brief moment—an icy douse on a hot summer day. A keening ache arrows through me. I know I'm leaving someone I love behind. Someone who means more to me than anything. Then the heat wraps around me again with comforting arms, and whispers surround me, assuring me that everyone I love is okay. That I'm complete.

That I can let go.

But I don't want to let go. She—Luna, Goldilocks—needs me, but drowsiness overwhelms me, and the whispers urge me to rest. That I've earned it. That I've been brave and true. That I deserve this reward.

I want to laugh. I'm a Dark, and the Creator doesn't reward Darks. But the voice tells me I'm more than just a Dark, and the Creator rewards those He sees fit. Languidness overwhelms me and I give into the voice, slipping away into the vast velvet pool of darkness.

twenty-nine

LUNA

MY BREATHS ARE DEAFENING in my ears, blocking out all sound aside from the rapid burst of my pulse. It pounds through the entire length of my body with furious denial, from my feet—rooted to the earth in shock—to my trembling fingertips, which now raise, reaching out, although I don't really know to what. My eyes burn, locked on the bloody lump in Mammon's hand…

On the still beating heart in his fist, which might as well be my own.

"Ca…" I begin to say, stumbling forward an uneasy step, but his name catches in my throat. This can't be happening. We can't have made it this far—through all the pain we've both experienced and separation and near-death encounters—for our story to come to a grinding halt here. This isn't how this was supposed to go. Alexander is dead. We *won*. This was supposed to be over. And we were supposed to live and spend however many long years together Caleb's mortality was willing to give us. His fire wasn't supposed to extinguish. Not yet. It was supposed to burn fiercely, the way I've burned for him since the very first moment we met. Our love was supposed to keep us together. Not forever—I'd already accepted we didn't have that long—but we were at least supposed to have longer than this.

I inch forward another step, the lump in my throat growing as my gaze drops to the unmoving body at Mammon's feet. The shell *looks* like Caleb, but that's all it is now. A shell. I give a jerky shake of my head, and the sob building in my chest transforms into a deranged scream that tears through the air with rage and abandon.

After so long fearing I was a monster…after so long wishing and praying I wasn't…for the first time, I actually wish I *was* the Destroyer because if this is the price of being the Savior, I don't want it. This wasn't his burden. Alexander might have been his grandfather but this battle was mine.

If anyone was going to die here, it should have been me.

Please, take me instead. Just let him live, I silently pray, but if the Creator is listening, He does nothing to show it.

The grief rising to drown me is short-lived, overwhelmed by an anger so visceral and all-consuming that it makes me want to destroy the world, not save it. I can't hold it in—the energy and loathing and pain lancing through me that all climb to the surface at once—and it dawns on me I don't want to.

Not until I make Mammon pay.

Voices shout at me from the other side of the ward, but I don't listen. I don't spare them a glance. My focus is only on Mammon. Hands clenching into fists, I latch my eyes onto the Archdemon, my hatred for him boiling the blood in my veins until every single inch of my insides are on fire. The inferno spreads outward, blasting through what remains of the barrier— throwing the Nephilim and angels surrounding me back. Only Mammon is untouched by my outburst of power, left isolated without potential allies so I can kill him. Flames the same ruby as the Archdemon's eyes ignite along the skin on my arms as I begin to walk toward him, burning the fabric of my short sleeves away. My wings fan out, spreading the flames farther.

Mammon's lips twitch with amusement. "Haven't you learned anything, little girl? You can burn me all you like, but just like the last time, I will heal. I will *always* heal." He waves an indifferent hand. "Be glad it was his life I took and not yours," he adds with an indignant sneer at Caleb's body. "Now, we can consider the debt of my lost wing repaid."

A life for a wing. It's not a fair trade.

None of this is fair.

What am I supposed to tell Aya? When we said our goodbyes before leaving Cambodia, I promised her Caleb would be okay. That her brother would come back to her in one piece.

What am I supposed to tell his mother?

These thoughts only stoke the fire of my fury as I draw in a shaking breath through flared nostrils, ignoring the overwhelming wash of Calm suddenly crashing into me, once again attempting to penetrate my senses and bring me back to sanity—the only thing managing to reach me in my blind rage. In my peripheral vision, I glimpse Alaric's familiar outline, his eyes watching me with a terror and worry I can practically taste. Other eyes watch me, too, yet I don't turn to look at any of them, though in the crowd of faces tracking my movements, I'm aware of my parents and Lilith. But they don't attempt to interrupt my advance. No one does, not even Alaric despite how hard he's working to subdue me—even harder than he was when he first stepped through the crack in the ward, though I cast it off with ease this time as a strange new power thrums under my skin. Maybe because they're all horrified by what Mammon has done—by this horrific betrayal of our truce with the Council. Or maybe because my power is holding them back, keeping them out of the way of my wrath—a sort of ward of its own.

A darkness I've never felt before—not even in my worst moments when I was so close to tumbling over the edge—swamps my entire being alongside the inferno until every negative feeling eating at me begins to ooze out of my pores, taking the form of shadows pouring out of my fingertips and palms like sentient tendrils of ink. The humor and conceit drains from Mammon's expression, and all the Nephilim and angels around us—already pushed back by my power—retreat even farther when I raise my arms, the fire and the shadows fusing into tangible whips of wrath, which lash out with intent at my silent command. They wrap around his wrists and throat like hands determined to suffocate him, dragging him down with a force that reverberates through the earth as his knees strike the now clay-like sand. He grunts from the impact, and as I hold him down like prey pinned in a trap, he stares up at me with an emotion flickering in his gaze that I sincerely hope is terror.

Exhaling loud, quick breaths through his nose, the Archdemon strains against the pulsating darkness, which squeezes around his windpipe. I might not be able to suffocate him or kill him like this, but I can still make every second hurt. The flames lick across his skin, hungry in their outrage, charring his nose and cheeks a deep black. "This won't kill me," he wheezes, the stench of his burning flesh pungent.

"No," I agree, somewhat surprised I'm able to find the word in my fury.

I stand before Mammon now, only separated by the body lying prostrate on the ground between us, using every last ounce of control I possess to stop my eyes from once again dipping to that broken shell of the person I love the most. Grinding my teeth, I focus on the Archdemon's right hand, outstretched before him as if he's offering the organ clamped in his fist to me, his arm held aloft by the tendril, which constricts until his fingers go slack on reflex. My own hand shoots out, and I catch the heart when it drops from his grip as my other hand curls in beckoning, using the darkness pouring out of me to find my sword. A thick blackness pools over the sand, flooding the area, as if returning this patch of desert to some semblance of the lake it used to be.

"But this will," I promise as the searching tendrils retract back into my body, and the hilt of my sword collides with my palm. Grasping it, I thrust the weapon forward, the gleaming tip piercing the center of the Archdemon's face, cutting through the cartilage of his nose. A discomforting gurgle escapes him as the blade slides through his skull like butter, and for a moment, I just stand like this, staring at the point where the steel meets his skin, my hand trembling around the golden hilt of this gift from the Creator.

My lower lip wobbles, and finally, I can't hold the growing pain in my chest at bay any longer. It fills my lungs like water, drowning me from within, and as a primal scream tears free of my lips once more—that part of me that remembers what it's like to be human gasping for air, for relief from this agony—the shadows and flames pouring out of me seem to explode, pulling the Archdemon's head and limbs in different directions. Hot specks of blood splash my face and arms, and gasps ripple around me from the watching crowd, but I barely notice any of it. I feel like I'm trapped in a soundproof box, or worse…like I'm back in that egg where everything I can see is just there to torment me. To remind me of what I can no longer have and can never have again.

Like his shell.

I tilt my head, and slowly, my eyes drop to my feet. Up close like this, with Caleb's face turned to the side, one cheek pressed into the dirt, I can count every lash lining his closed eyes and glimpse every year in his features—eighteen years, which is so much less than what I hoped for and yet so long compared to the less than one we shared. I try to stop myself from looking away from his beautiful face, but I can't help it. My gaze inevitably strays to the gaping hole in his back, to this horrific proof of his mortality. To the wound that not even his angelic blood can heal.

Tears scald my cheeks, burning thick lines into my skin and pooling at the corners of my lips, assaulting my mouth with the tang of salt and a grief I know I will never overcome. Not in this lifetime or any.

"I can't," I gasp, dropping to my knees, my wings going limp around me as I fight for air through the pain. The power surrounding me fades to a fizzle as the sword pommel slips from my fingers, the blade falling flat to the ground as my hands clumsily flip Caleb over and paw mindlessly at his face, his features blurring through my tears. "I can't do this without you," I breathe. "I can't. I *won't*."

Then don't, a voice says in the back of my head. *My* voice.

The voice of what used to be my conscience, now as warped by this loss as I am.

"Then don't," I echo, the words a whisper, my eyes widening as understanding sinks in. I reel back, my attention shifting to his mangled chest then to the heart still in my hand—to the missing piece of the broken puzzle he's become.

A puzzle I can fix.

I only considered this once—the first time I was forced to acknowledge Caleb's mortality, and at the time, I vowed I would never do it. I would never resurrect him. But now that I'm faced with actually living without him, I see no other option. I nearly lost him once when that bomb went off at the citadel. I can't lose him again.

Without thinking of the consequences—without thinking of anything other than my desperation to have him here with me, alive—I shove his heart back in the hole in his torso and clamp my hands over the open wound. Blood seeps through my fingers as I think of the moth back at the Serapeum, of that fateful day when I first heard Alexander's voice in my head, and I sink into myself, picturing those fluttering wings and how they represented a return to life, not that unlike a pulse. *I* did that. I brought that moth back from whatever lies beyond mortality. *I* did it…and I can do it again. I don't care if it goes against nature. I don't care if it's a power meant only for the Creator. I don't even care if Caleb comes back different.

I just need him to come back.

"Wake up," I plead, my breathing ragged.

Warmth flashes through me as I push every thought and all the power I know I'm capable of into the picture forming in my head and the silent words encircling it like a prayer. I imagine

Caleb's body stitching itself back together and his heart, still beating in my hands, reattaching itself to the places it needs to in order to bring him back to me. More than anything, I imagine him waking up. Of this all being nothing more than a nightmare.

"*Please*, Caleb, come back to me."

My fingers curl, attempting to push the cavity closed, but if the damage, inside or out, is healing, I can't see any sign of it.

"Please!" I say again, screaming this time.

Fingers wrap around my forearms and tug as something familiar and powerful invades my senses like a sudden blast of heat from a furnace.

Calm, I realize somewhere in the back of my mind, but the thought is hazy and fleeting.

"Luna, stop," Alaric pleads, his soothing baritone so close and yet so far away. He's next to me now, the barrier of my power no longer keeping him and the others at bay. His grasp on me tightens, but I shrug him off, shutting out his voice and his gift as he tries, yet again, to restrain me.

"Starlight, please," another voice begs. My father's voice.

I shake my head, muttering the same word over and over, all logic and reason gone. "No, no, no, no, no..." *Wake up!*

"Luna."

My mother kneels beside me and sliding one hand across my back, she rests the other on top of mine where it lingers over Caleb's exposed heart. At first, I think she's going to stop me, but she doesn't even try to pry my fingers away. She just leans in, whispering soft words in my ear.

Words that wrench my own heart in two.

"Caleb wouldn't want this."

My anger and grief collide then, forming a cyclone of agony that rips me to shreds from within.

"You don't know what he would want!" Using my wings to shove her and Alaric away, I glare at them and then at my father and Lilith, who stand a short distance from us, their gazes shiny with pity and unspoken remorse. "*None* of you know!" I shriek.

Because no one, human or otherwise, knew Caleb like I did. To the world, he was cocky and confident but I got to see the hidden sweetness inside. I got to see his vulnerability, even in the moments when he tried so hard to hide it. I shake my head again, firm in my certainty. No one else saw those sides to him. No one except maybe…

I turn my head, searching the crowd for Hammurabi. As if sensing my need for him, the Babylonian king emerges from the sea of bodies with Asmodeus beside him, pushing through the barricade of Nephilim and Fallen, snarling at those in their way to move. He stumbles to a standstill at the sight of Caleb, his pupils blowing wide, his large chest catching on a breath. He stays that way for a moment, shock written into his features, then he looks at me with those dark, silvered eyes, and I'm suddenly not sure what he mourns more. The dead boy on the ground I'm certain he loved or me, the broken girl he gave the rare gift of his kindness who we both know will never recover from this.

"He wouldn't want to leave me. He wouldn't," I mutter, speaking only to the ancient Nephilim. The one person here who might actually be on my side and want Caleb back as much as I do. "*Please*, Hammurabi, you know him. Tell them he wouldn't want to leave me."

Everyone—my parents, Alaric, Lilith, Asmodeus, and the thousands of others around me—all watch as Hammurabi closes the distance between us. No one dares to utter a word in the silence.

Crouching beside me, the Babylonian king plants his large hand on my head. "He loved you, flower," he begins, then clears his throat, his fingers sliding over my hair. As his arm drops and he stands again, a tear slides down his cheek, disappearing into the thick hair of his beard. "But your mother is right. Caleb wouldn't want this."

"No," I breathe, the pain in my chest like a festering wound turning septic. "No, I won't let him go." My hands move away from the hole now, gripping frantically at the collar of Caleb's shirt. "Caleb, wake up," I bark, shaking him roughly. His head lolls lifelessly against the ground, which only makes me shake him harder. "Wake up, damn you!"

I reach for his heart again, silently pleading to the Creator or fate or whatever or whoever is dictating our roles in this world to listen to me, to bring him back. But again, if anyone is listening, they don't respond, and gradually, the beats pulsating against my hands slow to a standstill.

"No, no, no." Unsure what else to do, I push against his heart with my flattened palms, repeating the movement and praying that if I can't save him as an angel, then maybe human methods can do it. But no matter how hard I push, no matter how much I wish for it, no matter how hard I search for the power inside me to reverse this—to turn back the clock and save him—I can't. Time is immovable, a barrier I can't seem to cross.

Even the Savior doesn't have that kind of power.

A choked breath catches in my throat. "Why?" I breathe, glancing at my mother, who's standing now, her face a smear of cream framed by black through my tears. I blink, and her features sharpen for a moment. "Why isn't it working?"

It worked for Alexander. He raised his soldiers, even ones who had been cut limb from limb, so why can't I raise Caleb? Why can't I fix him? This is a repeat of what happened in Kandahār all over again but with the worst possible outcome.

Gabriel frowns, her hands balled into trembling fists at her sides, as if she's fighting back the urge to reach for me. To console me. She says nothing, but then, I don't think I really expected her to have the answer.

I think I knew from the moment I saw his heart leave his body that I wouldn't be able to bring him back. He's too broken, his shell too damaged, and I don't have the experience or power Alexander possessed. Or maybe that's just an excuse

I tell myself now to assuage the guilt of my failure. To shift the burden of Caleb's death off my shoulders because I already carry too many others. There isn't space. And my own heart can't take it.

Or maybe it's none of that, and my mother was right. Maybe Caleb doesn't want this and that's why he's not coming back.

The tears come more quickly with that thought, my breaths panicked and harrowed as I try to breathe through the hysteria clawing at me from the inside. I grab at the dirt to ground myself, to find an anchor in the darkness, but the world suddenly feels too big, and I am hopelessly lost in it. Like I've drifted from the marked path in a dense forest, and I'll never find my way back again.

Caleb was always that anchor for me, the one who managed to make me feel safe and like I belonged in a world that was determined to make me feel neither…and now, he's gone. I might have Alaric again and my parents, but the hole of Caleb's loss is too great. I can already feel it beginning to swallow me.

Drawn to him even in the cold stillness of death, I reach for his face—to touch him for what might be the final time—but something stops me, and lured by the vibrating hum in the air, I glance down at my sword where it lies abandoned in the dirt. As if in a trance, I wrap my fingers around the pommel, testing the weight, the gleaming blade sharp enough to pierce even rock. It's angel-killing steel, which means it could end this pain. It could end everything so long as I'm the one to wield it.

No, Luna.

I shutter my eyes, and a shaky breath escapes me as I relax my grip, letting the sword fall to the ground. If I could carve this pain from my heart, I would. I'd bear the scars so long as it meant no longer feeling like this. But not wanting to live without Caleb isn't the same as wanting to die. And I don't. I *want* to live. I *want* to experience life and everything this vast world has to offer. I want another taste of that freedom I felt up in the sky. After so long trapped in one cage after another, I deserve that much.

But Caleb deserved it, too. *We* deserved the acceptance we fought for. We deserved our chance at a life together, free from the opinions and prejudices of others. Hell, we never should have had to fight for it in the first place.

"Are you all happy now?" I rasp, prying my eyes open and trailing my heated gaze across the drawn faces around me. Lights and Darks with me in the middle, the sole Gray in a world that should be vibrant with our shared existence, not divided by such pointless disdain. My eyes narrow, taking them all in— the angels, Fallen, and Nephilim—and somewhere inside me where I can still feel something other than this terrible agony, I'm pleased to find they all look ashamed. "Are you *satisfied* with what your hate has accomplished?"

I slap a hand over my mouth as a wracking cry grips my lungs, and buckling, I bend forward, pressing my forehead to Caleb's chest. What a cruel twist of fate that we would fight to heal the divide only to be separated in such a permanent way before that could happen. I just wanted the freedom to love him, but I never would have let myself love him at all if I knew this was where the road would end.

"Come back…" I whisper this again and again until the words become lost on my tongue, and the only sounds escaping me are sobs.

Come back.

A hand grazes my back, offering comfort, but I shy away from it, sitting up slightly. The only touch I want is Caleb's and if I can't have his, I don't want anyone's. Undeterred by my rebuff, fingers creep along my spine, and a warm palm flattens against my lower back, applying just enough pressure to push me back down a little. It feels like an embrace, but that can't be right. Because the only person this is bringing me closer to is Caleb, and I know there's no one left inside the empty vessel beneath me.

"Stop," I beg, my eyes clamped shut as if to escape this nightmare, but the word has barely passed my lips when a low, husky voice whispers, "I hate it when you cry, Goldilocks."

I lurch back, snapping open my eyes again, a tremor that's part horror and part disbelief racing through me. The feel of that hand slips away, making me all the more certain I must've imagined it. No, I know I did. It was just a hallucination—a desperate wish manifested in my mind, nothing more. I've clearly reached my breaking point and maybe I've finally taken that long-awaited step off the cliff edge into insanity. But even if that's the case, there's a part of me that doesn't care—that would take even a figment of him over nothing. And deeper than that, there's a part of me that still hopes.

That knows a love like ours can overcome anything, even something like death.

"C-Ca...?" I stammer, my mouth and brain at odds with each other, unable to form his name in my shock.

I stare down at his face, hastily blinking the tears from my vision. His eyes remain closed, his features as unmoving as they were moments ago when I last looked upon them, his stillness destroying the flicker of hope igniting in my broken heart. But then I see it—a subtle twitch to the lips.

"Caleb?" I force out in a strangled breath, certain I didn't imagine that movement. My fingertips shift, my nails digging into the torn fabric of his T-shirt.

At the sound of his name, he opens his eyes. "Didn't think you'd be rid of me that easily, did you?"

His mouth tilts with a crooked smile that steals the breath from my lungs, and as he raises a hand to my cheek, his thumb brushing the tears from my lips, a million thoughts and feelings race through me at once. Elation. Confusion. A deep-seated doubt.

Because as much as I want this, I don't trust it.

"But you were dead," I manage to say after a moment. "And I tried..." I trail off as my gaze returns to his chest, and it takes a full minute for my brain to comprehend what I'm seeing. Although his shirt remains torn, the exposed torso underneath it is healed, his bronzed skin gleaming in the afternoon sun. There are no marks or scars to be seen. No proof at all that Mammon ever laid a finger on him, let alone ripped his heart from his body.

Speechless, I stare at his chest in a daze. With a grunt, Caleb sits upright, and looping his arms around my back, he pulls me close without a word, hugging me tightly as if I'm the one who just departed this world and not him.

Stunned whispers erupt from the onlookers around us, and above it all, I hear my father's voice saying, "So, it worked? She resurrected him?"

I don't turn to look at him, so I'm not entirely sure who he's asking or if he's merely thinking aloud, as gobsmacked by this turn of events as the rest of us.

"This shouldn't have been possible," Hammurabi says, dropping to his knees and yanking Caleb away from me enough to take him by the shoulders, his dark eyes scanning him up and down for injuries that no longer exist. "Your heart was *outside* of your chest, boy."

I wince at the thought, but Caleb just shrugs, that lazy smile unwavering. "And now it's back *inside* my chest where it belongs. All's well that ends well and all that, Uncle H."

I glance at Hammurabi, tears still streaming down my cheeks, and he looks nearly as bemused as I feel. His eyes shift to mine as he stands, and as he inches back—presumably to give us space—I don't miss the weighted look he shoots at Asmodeus, who watches Caleb with a concerned yet observant expression, her head cocked to the side like the doctors at the hospital used to look at me. One long finger taps her chin.

Caleb inhales a deep breath, pulling the warm air into his lungs as if for the very first time. The sound draws my gaze, and as I watch him, I can't stop one single thought from escaping.

"Are you still you?" I ask, my voice trembling.

"I don't know if when you resurrect someone…they come back right."

The words he spoke in Kandahār after Alexander resurrected his father still haunt me, and although I didn't care when he was lying here dead and the alternative was not having him at all, now I grapple with the very real fear that this isn't really my Caleb but a mere shadow of him. A fabrication that's just saying the things I want to hear because the magic I used to bring him back is forcing him to say them.

But I don't want the lie. Unlike Alexander, who was willing to use resurrection as another means of control, I don't want to pull Caleb's strings. I would rather not have him at all than have a poor imitation of the real thing.

He blinks a few times then runs a hand through his hair, pushing the thick strands back off his forehead as his face melts into an even deeper smile. His gaze isn't void like his father's was after Alexander resurrected him. If anything, it shines with a newfound light, and I don't think I've ever seen him look so happy or content, which only makes the feelings building inside me that much more conflicted. Tears glisten in the corners of his eyes as he lets out a small laugh. "I'm sorry if I'm scaring you, Goldilocks, I'm just processing. But yeah, I'm still me in here, I promise. Plus a little more…thanks to the Creator."

I blink, unable to mask my surprise.

The Creator?

Before I can ask Caleb what he means, large appendages unfurl from his shoulder blades covered in sleek black feathers. They're massive, at least double the span of mine, but there's no mistaking what they are.

"Wings," Lilith gasps, stealing the word right out of my mouth.

It can't really be possible, can it? For all the Lights' preaching about Ascension, no one has actually achieved it before. Besides, Caleb is a Dark. Darks don't Ascend because to Ascend is to be selfless and to love the Creator more than anything or anyone on Earth. Caleb might be able to tick the selfless box but as for the rest of it…

Unless that's not how it works.

My eyes widen. Perhaps Ascension *is* a reward, just not in the way the Lights have always believed. Ascension isn't something you can earn through piety and certainly not through the continued enforcement of the divide. Hell, if the prophecy has made me realize anything, it's that the Creator *wants* us to be united again, and that unification is something Caleb literally gave his life for.

My own wings shudder as I reach out a hand and graze my fingertips through his smooth ebony feathers. Caleb shivers as a sound that's half laugh and half sob escapes me. "You've Ascended. You're—"

"Like you now, yeah." Clearing his throat, he threads his fingers through mine and tugs me forward until our foreheads are touching. "I guess the big guy upstairs felt I deserved a bit more time here on Earth."

"I didn't bring you back. The Creator did." I let out a shaky breath, feeling somewhat foolish for believing I had and at the same time so incredibly relieved I didn't. That the Caleb I see before me is completely, entirely him and not some warped recreation I created in my grief.

Caleb nods. "And He sent me back with a message."

His tone is mirrored in the look in his eye as he pulls away to meet my gaze, both somehow reassuring and unnerving at once.

"What kind of message?" my mother asks, beating me to it.

Using his wings for balance, Caleb stands, dragging me to my feet alongside him. He's only been an angel for all of five minutes, but his movements are incredibly graceful—as if he was born into the world like this. I guess, in a way, he was. Because he wasn't just resurrected. He was reborn.

My knees wobble and I feel light-headed, like I might pass

out from shock. Or maybe it's happiness that threatens to plunge me into the depths of oblivion.

As if sensing my need for support, Caleb wraps an arm around my waist, holding me close.

"It was more of an edict," he clarifies, raising his voice loud enough for everyone on the battlefield to hear. "One final command for his children." His gaze strays to my parents as he says this part, and I watch as my father's hands tighten around my mother's shoulders where he now stands behind her, his mouth contorting into a deep frown as he bristles at the word "command." As for my mother, she wrings her own hands nervously in front of her waist, her expression far more dismayed than my father's. Before today, she was the only celestial being the Creator ever tasked with imparting His words, and yet, Caleb stands before us all now with who-knows-what kind of message from the Heavens.

He clears his throat. "The Creator says the fighting ends here. That it's time for a blank slate…for all of us." He turns his head then, sweeping his eyes across the desert, taking in the carnage, the corpses interspersed among the living. There's something strange about his expression—as if he's aware of something the rest of us aren't yet or as if he's not entirely himself. As if, perhaps, the Creator is in there somewhere, looking out through his eyes just for this moment.

Suddenly, the sunlight seems to grow brighter, and as one, all the angels, Fallen, and Nephilim lift their heads, looking up at the sky. Caleb taps my waist, drawing my gaze, and when our eyes meet, he jerks his chin toward the ground—toward the bodies and the blood soaked into the sand, which now illuminate with the same blinding intensity as the sun, glowing a vibrant gold. Startled gasps echo around us like a ripple effect as all evidence of the death that occurred here gradually dissolves into particles of light before floating away, wiping the desert clean.

A clean slate, I realize.

Just like the Creator wanted.

Even Mammon's scattered remains disappear, though the last victim of this war to fade is Alexander. Alaric stumbles forward an uncertain step toward his body as it's engulfed by that warm golden light—as it's lifted high into the sky where it breaks apart into what looks like a cluster of stars before blinking into nonexistence, never to do us harm again. I frown at the Nephilim's stiffening back and the way he raises a hand and then lowers it, as if he's had to forcefully hold himself back. Even now, he's so conflicted in his feelings—torn between his love for the Gray and the ever-present need to put it behind him. I wish I could take those feelings away, to cleanse him of his pain the way the Creator cleansed this battlefield of our blood.

When the last of the glowing light has vanished, everyone turns to look at Caleb, their expressions equally eager and wary, waiting to hear what he has to say next. I look up at him as well, my heart racing with anticipation, every beat sitting too close to the surface, making my entire body vibrate. Sensing my gaze, he glances down at me, gifting me another crooked smile. Whatever I saw in his eyes before is gone now. This person standing beside me is entirely Caleb but with an added weight to his existence that seems to elevate him above us all in this moment. And as he lifts his chin, his voice cuts through the silence not like a knife, but like a bolt cutter through chains, setting us free.

"From now on, the past must stay in the past. Set aside your differences and go live your best lives, however, wherever…and *with* whomever you wish." He grins at my mother as if this last part is intended specifically for her, and who knows, maybe it is. Maybe the Creator was listening that day we met with the Council in India when my father said almost these exact words, and this is His way of honoring that desire. After everything they both sacrificed—Gabriel especially—the Creator owes them that much.

A tentative elation bubbles in my chest, but I can't find the words to express it. My parents gape at Caleb, but neither one of them says anything, either. In fact, everyone in the vicinity—immediate or otherwise—seems just as tongue-tied, each expression as visibly taken aback as the last. Everyone is quiet except for Asmodeus, who chuckles under her breath.

"I'd say a Dark being the first known Nephilim to Ascend would have been message enough, but I think we can all appreciate the clarity these past moments have afforded us.

This gives us much to consider, I'd say. Wouldn't you all agree?" She arches an imperious brow at the other Council members, who have found their way toward us and stand dotted in a loose circle around me and Caleb. They all nod in agreement, including Uriel, who stares at Caleb, his dark eyes unblinking.

As if shaken from a daze, he murmurs, "Yes, this certainly changes things. For all of us." His gaze strays to my face, and in the split-second our eyes lock, I know I don't have to worry about the Council locking me away again. His attention then shifts to my parents, and he watches Gabriel and Lucifer for a long, thoughtful moment. "We might have our differences, but the Creator's intentions could not be any clearer. We would be unwise to ignore His wishes for us."

In an oddly unified motion, everyone relaxes their grip on their weapons, dropping their swords and daggers to the dirt—not sheathing them for a later time but discarding them altogether. A promise to end the fighting for good.

"Thank the Creator," Beelzebub says, rolling his neck on his shoulders as he tosses his own blade to the ground. "This whole ordeal was beginning to bore me." Beside him, Abaddon hums his agreement, a satisfied grin playing at the edge of his lips.

"Indeed," Asmodeus trills, bobbing her head. "Though, now the true test of our mettle begins." With a satisfied sigh, she shutters her eyes for a moment before glancing back at Hammurabi. "There is much work to be done. Let us be gone from this place, King."

Hammurabi bows his head then steps toward us again, placing one hand on my shoulder and the other on Caleb's, his face scrunching as if he's searching for the right words to say something sentimental or endearing to sum up everything we've been through together and what we mean to each other.

To my surprise, he ends up saying nothing, instead tugging us both into a tight hug that threatens to squeeze the air from my lungs. I don't expect it—Uncle Hammurabi never struck me as the physically affectionate type—and it soothes me in a way I don't expect, either. My free arm winds around his back, returning his embrace, and in this moment, I know that if my heart could break from happiness, it would.

When we part, he spares us each a fond glance then grunts out, "Boy. Flower," before tailing his mistress, who flashes a smirk at Caleb over her shoulder as they strut away, her emerald eyes beaming with pride.

"I've always said Babel students are extraordinary," she murmurs, and the mischievous twinkle in her gaze tells me she can't wait to go around bragging about how one of her own students was the first Nephilim to Ascend. It certainly seems like the type of thing she would do. And I have zero doubt Hammurabi will boast about it as well. Except his pride comes from a deeper place. Not just as a teacher, but as Caleb's family.

Beelzebub and Abaddon mimic Asmodeus's lead, and one by one, the remaining Council members follow suit, which encourages the angels, Fallen, and Nephilim alike, who all leave this place and their hatred behind. The Lights step through pockets of light, disappearing into the depths of the Blessed Road, while the Darks shuffle off to search for the nearest patch of shadow. Everyone is eager to return to their lives, whatever that may look like moving forward, and within moments, the only ones left on the battlefield aside from me and Caleb are my parents, Lilith, and Alaric.

The latter heaves a trembling breath. "Finally," he murmurs.

Relief paints his face, and though I'm eager to bask in it—to experience such contentment for myself—I can't ignore the niggling unease poking at the back of my mind. It's strange—and almost hard to believe—that Alexander's reign of terror is over and that, by working together to overcome the chaos he wrought on our kind, we've begun the process of demolishing the divide. We might actually be experiencing the first taste of real, lasting peace, and yet, I can't escape the thought of how that peace was hard won. And how, for some, healing from this conflict will take a lot longer than it will for others.

"Will you…" I hesitate, rolling my teeth over my bottom lip. "Will you be okay?" I ask.

Alaric's eyes flutter shut then open again, and he gives a tentative nod. "With time."

He moves toward me then, and I meet him halfway, stepping into the warmth of his arms. "Thank you," I whisper, pressing my face into his shoulder. There are a thousand things I could say to follow these words.

Thank you for finding me.

Thank you for getting me out of that hospital.

Thank you for bringing me into this world where I belong. For being a friend when I had no one else.

Thank you for helping Caleb break me out of the Council's prison. For always choosing to rise above the divide.

Above all, thank you for doing what you knew was right, even though I know it caused you immeasurable pain.

Thank you…for everything.

His swallow is audible, and as he hugs me tighter, he whispers back, "You deserve all the happiness in the world."

A long moment passes before we part, and when I finally pull away, I wipe a tear from my cheek. "What will you do now?"

He shrugs. "Back to work, I imagine. As Asmodeus said, there is much to do now. Though, a brief respite is needed, I think." His gaze strays to my mother, as if seeking her permission, and she nods, offering the Nephilim a small, consoling smile of understanding.

"Seconded," Lilith drawls, flicking at some dried blood on her sleeve. "I would *kill* for a bath right about now." Looking up, she struts toward me, planting herself in the space that's been created in front of me now that I'm no longer hugging Alaric, and takes my chin between her fingers. "You take care of yourself, sweetling. I expect to see you very soon. Don't think you can just abandon Auntie Lilith now that no one is trying to kill you."

Beside me, Caleb snorts and I bite back a grin. "I wouldn't dream of it," I assure her.

Pursing her lips, she glances between us with a haughty brow raised, then blows me a kiss and turns, throwing her arms around my mother.

"Take care of my Gabriel, Lucy," Lilith commands when the two friends break their embrace. Her voice is lilting and friendly enough, though her eyes shoot daggers at my father. "I might have found it in the goodness of my heart to forgive you for taking my wings, but I won't be so benevolent if you hurt my friend."

Lucifer holds up his hands in surrender then drapes one arm around my mother, pulling her close to his side. "Duly noted," he says, and Gabriel's cheeks burn as they share a swift glance. "But I don't think that will be a problem for either of us. Not this time."

A smirk shapes the ex-Archdemon's lips. "Good." She lets out an airy sigh and puts her hands on her hips. "Well, I'm off. I have a date with a bathtub and a bottle of red. Be seeing you, darlings."

I can't help the surprised laugh that escapes me when she walks away, sauntering toward the mountains in the distance. It's crazy to think the terrifying woman I encountered in Kandahār would end up becoming my family. Just goes to show first impressions aren't everything.

I suddenly find myself reminiscing about another first

meeting—the day I met Caleb. What would my life look like now if he had let his initial impression of me and his past distrust of Lights keep us apart?

I immediately shove that thought away when I feel the familiar warmth of his hand on mine, meeting his gaze when he takes his place by my side. Because a life without Caleb is a life I don't want. And now that he's immortal, I don't even need to consider it.

A throat clears, and my cheeks flush as I look away, meeting Alaric's gaze. He winks.

"I shall take this as my cue," the Nephilim says with a respectful bow of his head toward my parents. "I'm sure you all have much you wish to say to each other without any spectators present." He looks at me then, and panic twists my insides when it dawns on me he's leaving.

Don't go, I want to say, but those words sit heavy and thick in my throat. I don't want him to leave me, not yet. I only just got him back. But I also know demanding he stay for my own selfish needs would be no different than what Alexander did to him, and he deserves better than that. He deserves a true friend, someone who cares about his feelings more than their own, not a leash.

"I'll still see you…right?" I ask instead, my voice wavering.

"Of course," he answers, his tone a low, calming croon that soothes the jagged edges of my nerves. "With the Roads, no one is ever really as far as we think. And in the meantime, I'm only a phone call away."

A smile as radiant as his aura lights up his face, and then, before I can say another word, he's gone, swallowed by the blinding glow of the Blessed Road.

For a long moment after Alaric departs, Caleb, my parents, and I stand in awkward silence, uncertain what to do or say next—the lone presence in the now eerily quiet desert. I don't think any of us allowed ourselves to really think about what would come after the battle. A sort of self-preservation in case things didn't go our way. I know that, for as much as I wished for the future—for real freedom—I never let myself dream about it in detail. The thought of it was always hazy, as if I was looking at it through clouded glass and all I had to do was step around it to see that future clearly. Even now, I struggle to see it—not because I don't want to, but because there's a lingering fear under my skin that I can't seem to shake telling me this is all too good to be true.

"W-What now?" I stammer, glancing between the three faces staring back at me, hoping one of them will have an answer that will quiet that deep-seated sense of foreboding.

"Well," my father begins, a faint smile tugging at his cheeks. He looks at Caleb and holds out his hand. "I suppose we should officially welcome you to the family. Especially now that you aren't going anywhere anytime soon."

A chisel seems to chip away at some of my residual fear as I peer at Caleb, watching the surprise flit across his face. A grin quickly rises in its place as he eagerly shakes my father's hand. "I hope you don't mind me sticking around for a while."

Gabriel lifts her chin at his words, giving a delicate sniff. "Just don't keep Luna away from us for too long. Remind her she has parents who will miss her if we don't see her often enough."

My brows raise as she risks a glance at me, looking more vulnerable than I've ever seen her—even more so than when she was bleeding out under the Serapeum after Caleb stabbed her. I didn't expect her to let go of me so easily after everything that's happened—to do anything other than smother me with attention and love to make up for lost time…in whatever form that would take coming from someone as emotionally distant as the Archangel.

She offers me a tender smile, and fresh tears prick my eyes as comprehension sinks in. Now that we're safe, she would sacrifice seeing me—not forever since we have all the time in the world, but she would give up the foreseeable future together so I can experience real freedom in a form I choose for myself. It's selfless in a way I didn't know she could be, and more than that, it shows her acceptance of Caleb, even if she won't dare say it aloud.

Steered by emotions I didn't think I was ready to feel, I step forward and wrap my mother in my arms, crushing her to me as that blood song rages between us, escalating into a beautiful sympathy. Gabriel lets out a surprised huff, but then I feel her hands on my back, and I clutch her tighter.

"I love you, Mom." The words slip out unintended, but in this moment, I realize I mean them. I *do* love her, and that love guides me around that clouded glass wall in my head, allowing me a peek at the other side. At the never-ending future awaiting us all.

She doesn't say it back, but she doesn't need to. I can see it in her eyes and in the glistening streaks of moisture decorating her cheeks when she pulls away. I see an eternity of love in those tears.

"Come," my father says after a moment, taking my mother's hand. When she looks up at him, he brushes the tears from her cheeks. "Let's leave the children alone to process, shall we?"

Gabriel beams at him, and with one more glance at me, she nods.

Leaning in, my father kisses me on the top of my head, and then, with my mother's hand in his, they amble away like two people who don't have a single care in the world, their auras a tangle of shadow and golden wisps in the late afternoon light.

As I watch them walk away, Caleb slings his arm around my shoulders. "It's crazy to think back to how all of this started, and now look," he says, jerking his chin toward my parents. "Didn't I tell you we might start a trend?"

He nudges me and I muster a smile, hoping he's right. Hoping beyond all hope that the angels and Fallen will really put aside their differences—not just long enough to face a common enemy, but for good.

"By the way," Caleb says, his airy tone a balm to my inescapable worries, "I'm starting to think your mom might actually like me."

I narrow my eyes, feigning deep thought, and then shrug. "Maybe. She at least seems to have moved past wanting to murder you."

A thoughtful expression crosses his face. "While it's definitely an improvement, we should probably make sure her sword is out of reach during family dinners. Just in case." He winks at me, and though I know he's joking—that my mother's sword lies abandoned in the sand just like the other weapons from the Fall, a gesture of peace and promise to end the fighting between us—his comment raises a curious question.

"Speaking of…what do you think will happen to them?" I ask, trailing my gaze across the barren desert, the ground spotted with blades of all shapes and sizes like a patterned blanket beneath the sun.

"I don't know," Caleb admits. "But I imagine the Creator has a plan for them."

"Just like He does for everything else," I say softly.

The Creator set this war into motion by delivering the prophecy to my mother. And in doing so, he brought me and Caleb together. But despite Caleb swearing he doesn't care about free will when it comes to loving me, I can't silence the voice of doubt in the back of my head. It grows stronger in the presence of that gnawing fear.

"Hey, what is it?" Caleb cups my face in his hands, brushing his thumb across my lower lip. It trembles beneath his touch.

"Is this what you want?" I manage past the threat of fresh tears, that terror inside me like a hand choking me.

Caleb's brow furrows and he pulls back a little. "What do you mean?"

I shake my head. "You...like *this*..." I wave one hand, gesturing to the still staggering sight of his wings. "We never talked about you being immortal because neither of us thought it was a possibility." I hesitate, hating how self-conscious I sound. I don't want to doubt this, but the part of me that's so used to disappointment can't help it. "I know what you said back in India about taking whatever time with me you could get, but now you have all the time in the world, and it wasn't exactly your choice, and I just—"

"You're wrong."

His tone is firm, his mouth set in a serious line. I balk under the intensity of his gaze, his molten eyes piercing, as if they can see every thought and feeling writhing inside me.

I blink, unable to mask my surprise. "What?"

He readjusts his grip on my face, pulling me closer. "About this not being my choice," he says, his breath hot on my cheeks. His brow creases as he licks his lips, and for a moment, it looks as if he might cry. "When I had my 'come into the light' moment, all I wanted was to be back here with you. To *never* leave you. And the Creator gave me exactly what I wished for." With a breathy laugh, he leans forward, once again touching his forehead to mine. "Honestly, Goldilocks, I wouldn't have cared how He brought me back. Shit, he could've brought me back as a human. A few decades, several thousands years, an eternity, I'd take any of them so long as I get to spend them with you."

The last of my fear withers and dies at these words, that terrible voice of doubt silenced as a happiness unlike anything I ever dared let myself believe I could have fills me up until I am bursting to the seams with it. It makes me feel weightless, and suddenly, I'm not just looking around that clouded glass wall but over it. And up here, I can see everything. The future, beautiful and vast before us.

Flinging my arms around Caleb's neck, I bury my face in the space where his chin meets his shoulder. He hugs me back, his wings folding around mine, and we stay like this for what feels like an eternity until he's touching my face again, pulling me away enough to kiss me.

A shiver tears through me and I sigh. I might be an angel, but I don't need Heaven.

Not when I have this.

"I love you. More than anything," I breathe against his lips, repeating the exact words he said to me the first time we made love.

Smirking, Caleb tilts his head back to appraise me. "Good.

Because I meant what I said to your parents. I fully intend on sticking around for a while." He scrunches his face in consideration then adds, "How does forever sound?"

A soft laugh escapes me, and for the first time in my life, I feel truly happy—unburdened by fear or dread of what might come after this blissful moment.

Now, for the first time, I truly feel free.

Smiling, I rise onto my toes and press another kiss to his lips. "Forever sounds perfect."

epilogue

ONE YEAR LATER

ALARIC STANDS AT THE base of the Sacré-Coeur in Montmartre. The interior of the church isn't all that impressive, but that's not why tourists flock here in droves. It's not even its majestic white domes reaching for the heavens, offering a testament of faith. As stunning as this architectural display is, it doesn't compare to the panoramic view of Paris seen from the church's steps. The wonders of the city to be discovered on both sides of the river greet him, painted with a bold brush of color and curving lines. That special blend of art and culture and food found only in Paris.

His eyes rove over the narrow, winding streets below him paved with cobblestones, crowded with shops, patisseries, restaurants, and cafes. Alaric can still taste the bold espresso he had minutes earlier at a tiny cafe bar, the scruffy interior still charming with its classic chairs and tables and vintage rock posters. The heavy scent of good butter and dark chocolate caresses his nose, and he yearns for a pain au chocolat. Yes, he's in Paris on business, but one can't visit the city without indulging in its pleasures as well.

Alaric pauses in his casual perusal, breath trapped in his chest as he spots a familiar golden head. Luna. She leans over a tiny cafe table, a sable-haired handsome young man beside her, his body bent to meet hers. Caleb. The two are scarcely apart, and where one is, the other will surely be. Their fingers are braided together, their foreheads almost touching. A spark of pure joy shoots through Alaric as he observes their utter happiness. The intimacy and freedom they're enjoying just being two young people reveling in that special magic Montmartre brings to the world.

A shadow dims his elation as images of the final battle assail him. Even though a year has passed, as much as Alaric would wish it, he can't banish the vivid image of him slipping the sword into Alexander's heart. The stunned expression on the angel's face. The betrayal. He can't banish his love for the Conqueror, either, only that love is now wrapped in nostalgia. Of his dreams for what could have been had there not been the divide. Had Alexander not been obsessed with power. When he was younger, he clung to the naive hope that one day he and Alexander would be like Luna and Caleb. Free of cares and in love. He mourns the loss of that dream, lets the last embers flicker and die until nothing but ashes remain.

His dream never came to fruition, but Luna—the daughter

of his heart—is building her dreams on those ashes, like a phoenix reborn. When Caleb Ascended and received his wings—his immortality—the divide was well and truly destroyed. Or maybe mended is the right word. The fact that the Creator gifted Caleb, a Dark, with angelic status finally proved once and for all that the hurts and betrayals Darks and Lights harbored for each other could be placed firmly in the past. The Creator no longer holds onto his grudge from the Fall. There is no room now for grudges and petty grievances. There is no more Light and Dark, just Nephilim. Just angels. Just a beautiful girl and boy loving one another so deeply they defied death to be together.

Some angels have even descended from Heaven to help integrate the academies. Free from their rigid allegiance, they can walk among mortals and take pleasure within this world if they so choose. A soft smile curves Alaric's lips. Peace is a wondrous thing.

Gazing at Luna, he slides his phone from his pocket, his thumbs swiftly typing out a message.

How are you enjoying Paris? Is it everything you hoped it would be? -A

He watches as Luna's head jerks away from Caleb, and she reaches into her jacket pocket, bringing out her phone. He sees her delighted grin, and his heart swells with love. She shows

Caleb the message and he smiles. Alaric loves the boy, too. He treats Luna like the treasure that she is, and one can't help but like Caleb and his roguish charm.

His phone pings and he looks down at the screen.

It's better than I imagined and everything you said it would be. I'm in awe. I can't stop eating! I never want to leave. Where are you?

Alaric considers that for a moment. He wants to see Luna, but he doesn't want to interrupt this moment she's having with Caleb. He wants to give them a little time just to breathe. They earned it.

Out scouting for Nephilim children with Hammurabi. Despite being a rather terrifying presence, children adore him. -A

He watches Luna and Caleb exchange words and grin, then his phone pings again.

Caleb wants to know how Hammurabi is doing. Actually, what he really said is, "How's that old dinosaur? Still a grumpy asshole?"

Alaric chokes back a laugh. Caleb has such a way with words.

Hammurabi took Alaric by surprise when he decided to leave Babel to help him find and shepherd Nephilim children. Alaric knows just how attached Hammurabi is to Babel. And its mistress. Though the Babylonian king would never admit to his feelings for Asmodeus, even under the threat of death.

He's well. He's actually shopping, believe it or not. -A

LOL. Caleb says he's not that surprised. He uses shopping as a way to pick up women.

Alaric's brow raises at that because he knows Hammurabi is buying Asmodeus a gift. Apparently, the ex-Archdemon loves ridiculous tourist trinkets. He can't imagine a creature as terrifying as Asmodeus being amused by human knick-knacks. That knowledge somehow humanizes her.

Hammurabi materializes next to him then, a delicate cotton-candy pink paper bag clenched in his large first. Alaric suppresses a grin at the image.

"Did you find something worthy of her?" he teases the stoic king, unable to resist a bit of ribbing.

"Nothing is ever worthy of her, but I found something that will amuse her." Hammurabi scowls, growling, "I should have never revealed her indulgence to you."

"It makes me admire her more," Alaric says, earning a genuine smile from the other Nephilim.

"How are the children?" he asks, nodding toward Alaric's phone where Luna's name glows. "Freedom has made the little flower bloom."

"They send their regards," Alaric says, warmed by the affection in the king's voice. He watches Luna take a sip from her coffee cup, her eyes clinging to Caleb's face as he speaks to her. Yes, freedom has indeed made her blossom into the strong, capable woman he always knew she was meant to be. Freedom and love.

Hammurabi releases a skeptical snort. "I doubt the boy was that restrained. He's become even worse since gaining his wings. There will be no living with him now."

Alaric grins, not fooled by Hammurabi's gruff words. He knows just how much the Babylonian king loves Caleb, knows how relieved he was when Caleb cheated death and Ascended. And Alaric knows, that like him, Hammurabi is especially proud of the example Caleb sets for others in overcoming all boundaries between Darks and Lights, going so far as to embrace the younger brother who fought against him. The last Alaric heard, Caleb even introduced the boy to his mother.

Alaric's phone chimes and he glances at it.

Will I see you soon? I miss you.

Tenderness envelops him at Luna's words. His thumbs quickly move over the keyboard.

Sooner than you think. -A

He slips the phone back into his pocket and focuses on Hammurabi. "Shall we go meet the child we've come to find?"

Hammurabi nods, still clenching his ridiculously frilly bag. "Yes, it's time."

As they turn to walk away, Alaric gazes over his shoulder. Luna and Caleb share a kiss in the warm Parisian sun, their beauty so stunning his breath catches—not just their physical beauty, but the beauty of their love. A love that was strong enough to heal an ancient divide and give the world hope. A love that gave him a world he's grateful to be alive in.

He blinks back tears as he faces forward again and follows Hammurabi. Now, endless possibilities await him—and all their kind—as they step into this new world together, released from the shackles of their past. Truly…finally…free.

THE END

ABOUT THE AUTHORS

M. A. PHIPPS and **REBECCA JAYCOX** met while working together at a small publishing house in the United Kingdom as a cover designer and editor respectively. Having forged a strong friendship, and sharing similar interests, they decided to co-author.

THE ORIGIN PROPHECY is their first series together, but it will not be their last.

Find them online at:

WWW.BOOKISHDEN.COM